An Innocent Fashion

An Innocent Fashion

a novel

R.J. HERNÁNDEZ

HARPER PERENNIAL

NEW YORK • LONDON • TORONTO • SYDNEY • NEW DELHI • AUCKLAND

With special thanks to HarperCollins and Trident Media Group, especially my editor, Hannah Wood, and my agent, Erica Spellman-Silverman; also to my parents, without whom this book would not be possible.

HARPER PERENNIAL

FIRST EDITION

Designed by Jamie Lynn Kerner

Library of Congress Cataloging-in-Publication Data

Names: Hernández, R. J., 1989– author.
Title: An innocent fashion : a novel / R. J. Hernández.– Description: First edition. | New York : Harper Perennial, [2016] Identifiers: LCCN 2015037268| ISBN 9780062429544 (paperback) | ISBN 9780062429612 (ebook) Subjects: LCSH: Young men—Fiction. | Fashion—Fiction. | Periodicals—Publishing—Fiction. | New York (N.Y.)—Fiction. | BISAC: FICTION / Coming of Age. | FICTION / Satire. | FICTION / Literary. Classification: LCC PS3608.E7676 I56 2016 | DDC 813/.6--dc23 LC record available at http://lccn.loc.gov/2015037268

16 17 18 19 20 OV/RRD 10 9 8 7 6 5 4 3 2 1

For Justine

"Why do we call all our generous ideas illusions,
and the mean ones truths?"

—EDITH WHARTON, *The House of Mirth*

chapter one

With all the tall buildings everywhere, you'd think it would be easier to kill yourself in New York City. The trouble was, to get to the top of one of them you'd have to live in it, or know someone who did. This seemed to be the trouble more generally: to get to the top of anything was just so difficult, and my biggest fear in growing up was that it would only become more difficult until it became impossible.

Everywhere all those horrible, record-breaking high-rises; I could zigzag all around them and blink at them from below and even chat up their friendly doormen, but at the end of the day, when all I wanted was to jump off some gratuitous altitude, it was, "Hey, kid, who you here to see?"

I finally understood why rich people paid a premium to live on a penthouse floor, adding another unfair advantage to the list that in my mind grew longer every day: if you could afford it, you got to kill yourself without a fuss. It made more sense to me than paying to see "the view" of New York City every day; I mean, if I was rich I'd pay *not* to see the view, with all those skyscrapers jutting up like a bed of nails.

At the magazine people talked about suicide all the time, but usually they were referring to fashion suicide, which was like social suicide but much more serious. Fashion suicide was when somebody in the fashion world committed an error so egregious that they would never be welcome there again—a slipup caused by burnout or a temporary lapse of sanity. Depending on how you looked at things, the latter could alternatively be considered a restoration of sanity; either way, it was usually summed up as, "I can't fucking stand this anymore."

A textbook example was that committed by the former fashion assistant—a doe-eyed trust-fund doll who one day last spring just stood up from her chair with a glazed look, and left. She didn't even bother to take her bag with her, a $10,000 cast-off that came into her possession when the senior fashion editor pleaded, "Get this vile thing away from me—it keeps appearing on my desk." To be fair, the bag was pretty vile—it was covered in distressed python scales and golden buckles the size of prison padlocks—but it was also a $10,000, yet-unreleased Versace runway sample, so she kept it. She kept it right until the end when, flaccid and shedding its horrible rotting skin, it wound up where the editor had dumped it in the first place. From there the assistant joined a convent, or a nonprofit—I'm not sure, but something with a redemptive ring to it.

Other perpetrators of fashion suicide included another former assistant who quit her job to write a tell-all roman à clef about her famously diabolical boss, and a gay intern who charged a $15,000 Bergdorf shopping spree to the managing editor's corporate card after he was made to work through his Christmas vacation. Neither of them would ever step foot in the office of a high-profile fashion magazine again, although the former did end up with a *New York Times* bestseller and the latter with a two-month vacation in a county jail in Westchester.

It's not as hard as you might think to actually walk out on *Régine*. After you've been there long enough, it feels like you're just going across the street to grab a pastrami sandwich for lunch, even though you know you're never coming back. Getting beyond the double doors is the hardest part. Once you're past them, with the colossal video screen playing fashion shows on a loop behind you, with girl after leviathan girl on your heels, a nightmarish, never-ending procession of the chosen ones you'll never be like, you finally do become like them. Rigid and unfeeling, you just walk, and you're in the foyer, where two cream parlor chairs and a cream sofa border a cream coffee table with a single potted orchid—just a bright green calligraphic stroke, with its blossoms like snow-white moths who landed there and got stuck.

I suppose if I'd wanted to, I could have just pressed Up at the elevators, popped out on the top floor and found a fire escape to the roof, but even disillusioned dreamers have their dignity. To jump off the Hoffman-Lynch building, that horrible behemoth of New York City architectural innovation, with its unprecedented vaults and soaring, hope-flooded windows, a staggering display of "harmony between old and modern" (according to the plaque in the foyer)—all to disguise the depressing white offices inside—well, no thank you. Who wanted to nose-dive into midtown traffic, anyway?

Then again, access to the convenient heights of the Hoffman-

Lynch rooftop was almost certainly a privilege denied by my limited-access ID, which read INTERN and didn't include a photograph of my face or even my name.

One way or the other, I knew I needed to get out.

I would have jumped off the roof of my own walk-up apartment, but the building was only four stories tall, and I'd heard once you had to do it from a minimum of six stories if you hoped to actually die. This wasn't so much a mental note I had made for this occasion as one of those tidbits that stuck inexplicably in a person's head for years, like the fact that tongue prints were as unique as finger prints, or that Napoleon had been five and a half feet tall. It made logical sense, too, that you'd want to jump from somewhere high; if you jumped out of any old window, you could just end up with a broken leg, or else, maimed for life—either way, worse off than you'd been in the first place.

That's why I went to my boss's house, because he was rich and living The Dream in a fifteen-story Fifth Avenue co-op with a gym and classical molding throughout.

WHEN I ARRIVED AT EDMUND'S APARTMENT BUILDING, I SAID "Hello, Horace" to the doorman, because even though I was about to kill myself, it wasn't his fault, and I'd always liked him.

"Welcome, Mr. St. James!" Horace wore a gold-trimmed hat like a ship's captain, and round glasses like mine. Unlike me, Horace was as portly as a fully suited watermelon and stood there all day with his hands resting on the top of his stomach. It was a shame I'd never live to be that old; all my life I'd been slender, and it would have interested me to know what it felt like to swell up like a balloon in my old age. "You're all wet," he informed me.

I almost didn't believe him, and glanced sharply up behind

me. The whole sky was swirling like the mist in a crystal ball. Gray clouds moaned like a chorus of captured souls, while the thunder laughed, and all around, the deluge tried to drown them out with a dull roar.

You know you're concentrating very hard on the matter of killing yourself when you don't even notice it's the end of the world outside. With a sudden shiver, I wrapped my arms around myself and noticed the puddle I was spreading over the marble floor. The mosaic that read 25 FIFTH AVE sparkled under my feet, while all around me tinkered raindrops like diamonds off a broken necklace.

"Need a towel?" Horace offered.

I said no, thank you, and he handed me a square brown box, the size of a pastry container. "Here's a package for Edmund." He pushed PH on the elevator for me. "Come see me on your way out. I'll lend you an umbrella."

I smiled sadly at him, knowing it would be the last time, and for a moment, I closed my eyes and thought, *Wouldn't it be better to just tell Horace everything?* Surely he would understand. He would lay my head on his stomach, pet my wet mop of hair with his gloved hand, and tell me, *"There were times I thought I wouldn't make it either, plodding around in this wool suit in the middle of a sweltering summer, but in life you just have to keep fighting."*

It'd be a nice alternative to dying, I thought, opening my eyes—just as the elevator doors concluded otherwise, and closed.

EDMUND'S MAID HAD HER BACK TO ME WHEN I STEPPED INTO the foyer of his apartment.

"*Hola, Rosita*," I said as she dusted a coffee table tome on

Linda Evangelista, to which my boss Edmund had written the foreword. I gently set down Edmund's package on the table beside Linda's apathetic visage, and Rosita hefted herself around to greet me.

"You wet, E-tan!" she gasped, despite my frequent insistence that she not trouble herself over the pronunciation of my name. Like a brown-skinned Lady Liberty leading the revolutionaries, she swirled her feather duster in the air and waggled over. "Lay me get you towel."

I raised a hand to stop her. I was soaked through, but to inconvenience Edmund's underpaid maid was the last of my dying wishes. My own mother cleaned houses for a living, and on top of that, what good was a towel to me now when awaiting my momentary arrival was Edmund's roof and my long, wet plummet down? For that matter, what good was any more effort at all spent in the service of my ill-fated body? In the course of my foolhardy life, enough energy had already been wasted providing for my lowly human needs—warmth, comfort, and all the pointless rest of it.

She couldn't have known this, of course, as she hurried away toward Edmund's linen closet and its supply of gold-trimmed sheets. If she had known what I was about to do, Rosita would have considered me luxuriously spoiled. When she looked at me, she saw someone like Edmund, "*un americano rico*." How self-indulgent for someone like me to want to kill myself—shining with the glimmer of privilege and youth, yet unable to bear my insignificant troubles—while everywhere people like her toiled for a tiny measure of the advantages I had inherited at birth.

The truth was that I was a lot more like Rosita than she would ever have guessed. If, like a piece of jewelry, I had been inspected through a microscope—my surface scratched for some telling signifier of my value—my appraiser would have shaken his head, pursed his lips, and silently grouped me with the cubic zirconia. Fortune had spared me all telltale signs of my inherited otherness, but my mother was the child of an unlikely military marriage in New Mexico—white-skinned with dark brown hair, fathered by a buffalo soldier—while my father was Mexican. His face was brown and leathery, stubble crawling across it like an army of black ants. By some fortuitous celestial oversight, my own face betrayed neither my heritage nor, incidentally, my age—except for my chin, which was punctuated by a prickly row of elliptical black hairs. I had dark, wavy hair and a childish face; an obligatory outburst of teenage hormones had manifested itself as a fashionable growth spurt, leaving me tall and lean, but otherwise the halfhearted advances of a reluctant puberty had left me with a perennially boyish appearance.

In exchange for these considerable courtesies, I was marked by one single visible exception to ensure I would never forget I was the progeny of disharmony: mismatched eyes, each pupil encircled by different-colored orbs, one blue, one brown. They were existential eyes, large and searching, a pair of happy and sad theater masks—both sides of humanity, whose only common behavior was to blink open and closed. My heterochromatic eyes were a harmless irregularity that nature had installed in me as reminder of my bastard status, but nothing I couldn't hide behind a pair of horn-rimmed glasses—another testament to the power of fashion. In the end though, what did fashion matter? I stood there now in a designer suit gifted to me at *Régine* while Rosita wore an apron, yet I was the one who wanted to die.

The first time I met Rosita I had been delivering lilac and

periwinkle hydrangeas to Edmund's apartment. "*Hola*," she had said. My instinctive reply was like a rumble from a volcanic crater that for many years had remained dormant, "*Hola, señora, ¿cómo está?*"

"*Ay, qué bien hablas*," she had replied in surprise over the waft of her duster. I paused, and remembered myself. "I learned Spanish in grade school," I lied through an American accent. Unlike my Spanish-speaking forebears, who had relished in the dramatic confluences of their romantic mother tongue, I had for years forced my words into the unromantic security of American pronunciation. To certain ears it was dull and un-sensual, but to mine it covered up the secret of my inferior heritage.

Now Rosita draped a towel fringed with gold over my wet back like a cape, and smiled. She reminded me of Walita, my grandmother on my father's side—with the same crinkled black eyes embedded like warts in a weathered vegetable, and wiry white hair sprouting from a brown scalp.

"*¿De dónde eres, Rosita?*" I had never sought to learn much about Rosita before. Now that she was the last person I'd ever talk to, she seemed suddenly to occupy an important role in my life, and it seemed fit that I should at least know something about her.

"*Soy mexicana*," she replied. I smiled, and a nervous laugh escaped me. Like an unfaithful Catholic who doubts for a lifetime before pleading on his deathbed, "*God! Forgive me!*" I fell upon Rosita with a sigh, and a hug as warm and close as if I had known her my entire life. Rosita accepted my embrace without an inquiry or a moment's hesitation, as though to her it was the most natural reaction in the world. She rubbed my wet back as I took a deep, comforting breath of her cheap perfume.

Then, with a sad smile, I stepped away and proceeded to the roof.

OUR HOUSE IN CORPUS CHRISTI, TEXAS, WAS A GRAY ONE-story rectangle with a flat, faintly caving roof. The front lawn resembled a piece of bread: brown, with patches of pale green mold, bordered by strips of crumbling concrete like a gray crust. The chain-link fence sagged in the middle, from when Tío Domingo crashed his Jeep on the Cuatro de Julio. Every day after school, when the bus dropped me off at home, my mother would greet me and then press her shoulder against the metal to make it stand again. For a few seconds, the fence obeyed; then my mother turned around and it slumped right back, like a child awaiting a moment of parental distraction to stick his tongue out.

My mother, Alicia, was never ashamed of what we had. On the contrary, she was proud of our unremarkable home and, as a cleaning lady by trade, determined to lavish it with the best of her domestic expertise. Three times a week she scattered fertilizer over the dead lawn with the hopefulness of someone pushing vitamins down the throat of a corpse. Inside, she dusted and scrubbed and polished. Yet the dignity of my childhood home was precluded by its very makeup: shag carpets, faux-silk curtains, vinyl tiles, and a racket of rightfully marked-down beige-toned wallpaper. We had stripes in the hall and fish in the bathroom, then in the living room, woefully misprinted flowers—a hundred daisies with their middles missing, each empty ring of petals gazing at the grainy television like a floating, unblinking pupil.

Around dinnertime every day, a pair of white lights would beam through the curtains in my bedroom.

"Elián!" my mother would call to me. Her collection of trinkets and figurines, shored up from dollar stores, garage sales, and the Salvation Army, rattled on shelves throughout the house—miniature cuckoo clocks paired with angel-shaped candles, ceramic kittens with polyresin replicas of the Crucifixion.

The truck door would slam and, with a manly declaration of his appetite, in barreled my father Reynaldo, who owned a flailing family construction company and an ever-proliferate number of sweat glands. He would always kiss my mother, who giggled as his mustache tickled her, then peel off his shirt and drape it around his neck like a sweat-drenched horseshoe.

"*¡Cerveza, corazón!*" He collapsed mightily at the head of the kitchen counter, and at the sight of me, bellowed "*¡Oye, cabrón!*" The next moment I would be swept up in his rancid embrace, helplessly tumbled into a thicket of curly black chest hairs.

My mother would swing open the refrigerator door for a Corona, flypaper ribbons whooshing overhead. Suspended, crisscrossed, across the ceiling like party streamers, they ensured an untimely end for any festivity-seeking trespassers, who got stuck like raisins on a sticky bun and suffered slowly among my mother's rooster-themed placemats, dishtowels, and refrigerator magnets.

"*Dame un beso, cabrón,*" my father would say, patting his damp, stubbly cheek for a kiss. For many years I thought "*cabrón*" meant "son," or some other term of endearment, until I found out it meant "motherfucker"—alternatively, "male goat"—the knowledge of which I could hardly bear. To be fair, I knew my father meant it with affection—although I could never fathom why, in relation to me, his affection should be best encapsulated by the invocation of a farm animal.

When my mother plodded out with dinner—a normal day meant chicken or pork with rice, chili, and tortillas—my father would put me down and slap my behind. Then, if my mother was near enough, he'd slap hers too. I always shuddered at this. The gesture wasn't cruel, or even unloving—it was just like *cabrón*, my father's rudimentary way of showing affection—and my mother seemed to enjoy it. Usually, she pretended to be offended: "*¡Ay, Reynaldo!*" she would scold, before teasing him with a wink.

My father *loved* my mother—he never cheated or raised a fist. By anybody's standards in Corpus Christi, that should have been enough, as even in my youngest years I knew about divorce, and that in other families love was scarce. Yet I was always struck—as I was by the jagged outward contour of my entire life—by the inelegance of my parents' love, by its crudeness, its vulgarity.

I had no reason to think it should be any different. After all, nothing in Corpus Christi was very beautiful or interesting. The local high school resembled a fortress, with the brown, corrugated walls of a high-security penitentiary; the mall, situated over a cavernous concrete parking lot, was anchored by a beef jerky outlet. The most popular hangout was a bottomless BBQ pit, complete with a drive-through, its windows filled with neon signs and sun-faded photographs of coleslaw and sloppy joe.

It wasn't all *bad*, necessarily. Good and bad was a different spectrum altogether, at least as far as God was concerned, and everything I learned at church. But if it wasn't bad, it was boring, and it was ugly—and those were the two things in life that made my blood run cold.

Nobody else seemed to mind, or even notice, that Corpus

Christi was a famine of beauty, and that nothing ever seemed to happen there. From this I gathered early on that other people were born with ashtrays for eyes. They could shore up all the rot and ash just fine, and tap out the muck every once in a while, but for some inexplicable reason, my eyes were more sensitive than that. *I* was more sensitive than that, and ultimately I think that's why I was ill-suited to work in the fashion industry: Fashion is an ornate mirror held up to the world, and the world is all rot and ash.

CORNERED BY THE CREEPING SUFFOCATION OF A LIFE WITHout beauty or stimulation, my only defense when I was younger was to read picture books. Every day I stuffed my backpack at the elementary school library with six, the maximum number, enough to keep me occupied all evening as I read to my dog Lola. Lola was a mutt, like me—a cross between a Labrador and some unknown breed—but beautiful and lithe, with a luminescent black coat. During dinner, Lola would lie under my father's barstool, knowing that some pork or shredded chicken might fall in her vicinity during the ferocious transference of food between the plate and his mouth; then, when I was finished with my plate, she would sniff a moon-shaped crescent around my father's stool and follow me to my bedroom, where she was familiar with my nightly routine. I flipped pages for hours, mumbling the words out loud, with increasing proficiency, to her upraised ears. Books of fairy tales were my first favorites, because in them the kind-hearted beggar children always ended up ruling some huge kingdom or, in a worst-case scenario, were transformed into birds or squirrels. They also had the best illustrations, and when

I wanted to pretend I was inside of them, I stared at the wall, which was blank except for a laminated poster of Jesus Christ with a thoughtful palm upraised and his thorn-wreathed heart bursting through his chest. It was like this every night, Lola by my side as I willed myself through sheer force into another place, another life.

Outside my window I could always hear the neighborhood boys as they bounced around lumpy balls, or yelled over to who got to control a battery-operated car. There were six or seven of them around my age, all led by Cesar Montana, who was one grade older and resembled a boulder in a T-shirt, with a pebble balanced on top for a head.

"Oh, come on, *amorsito*—you and Lola must be tired of all these books," my mother said the first time she dragged me by the hand onto the sidewalk. She was only trying to help me. The other boys played outside, therefore so should I—but what she didn't know was that the other boys wanted nothing to do with me. I was too quiet, too gawky, and clearly I was afraid of them, so why should they accept me? Not an hour after this initiation of our playdate, I was crumpled on the asphalt, sobbing, with a bruise swelling on my knee while Cesar Montana laughed and the other boys said nothing, because they knew that if he wanted to, Cesar Montana could probably just sit on them and they would never live to operate a remote-controlled car again.

I hid the injury from my mother, and thereafter she appeared regularly at my bedroom door, imploring me to join my "friends." She always had such a hopeful look—all she wanted was for me to be normal—so I would put down my book and leave the house, with Lola by my side. We wandered around the neighborhood as the shouts of the neighborhood boys faded away and the sky steeped, like tea, into a melancholic lavender twilight. As the dust of another day settled all around us, I pulled up flowers from the neighbors' yards—smelled them, stroked their velvety petals, peered inside of them, and twisted their stems together to make bouquets. If I heard a noise, I would ring my arms around Lola's neck, pressing our faces together. "Do you hear that?" I would whisper, imagining someone had finally arrived to take me away, to the kingdom that was my birthright. Surely it would be my fairy godmother, or at least the angel Gabriel who, according to Padre José at Sunday Mass, had chosen an ordinary day to tell the Virgin Mary that she was pregnant with Jesus—which meant *any* day could be the day an angel popped out of nowhere to change your whole life. Of course, the sound always turned out to be just a cat slithering past a rattling chain-link fence, or a ball bouncing in a powdery yard.

I must have made a thousand bouquets, and read as many books, when the day came that Lola didn't follow me after dinner—didn't even look up, or budge.

"Lola is old now, she's going blind," my mother said, and it was true. I had noticed for some time that Lola's luxurious black coat had begun to shed, but I had no concept of aging, no understanding that she was getting older, as was I, along with my parents and teachers and the neighborhood kids, all of us moving helplessly toward a bleak, common end. I cried over her as her hair faded and the pus pooled up in the corners of her milky eyes. When I touched her, she tucked her nose under a paw as the tears dribbled down her face, and I realized she was ashamed. My only friend, once so beautiful, had betrayed me—she'd become another sad, ugly thing in the sad, ugly world I lived in.

Months later, Lola was dead. The veterinarian's name was Dr. Ramos, and his certificate was from a university in Guadalajara, a Mexican city near the town where my father had grown up. Dr. Ramos laid out Lola on a cold aluminum table—whimpering kennels all around us—and waited for my mother and me to say good-bye. Then he held up a large black trash bag and unceremoniously pushed her inside. She was stiff, legs out, like a pig on a spit.

Having only just entered middle school, I had never seen death before, but I didn't cry. My mother, on the other hand, was choking on her own fluids, a wad of crumpled tissue pressed to her face as tears escaped her chipped red fingernails. Later I learned that she'd suffered a miscarriage before my birth, and in the months afterward my father had given Lola to her as a small comfort while they tried again.

She peered into the black bag and buckled, the fat flapping beneath her arm as she groped blindly for my shoulder. Her watery eyes must have mistaken wetness on my own face, because she pulled me close against her and shakily assumed responsibility for my consolation. "It's okay, *hijo*," she choked. "Lola was safe and happy for many years. She had food and a place to sleep—" she swallowed a placental wad of phlegm "—*una buena vida*." A good life.

And after that I did cry—not for Lola, it was too late for her—but for myself, because somehow from the depths of my mother I had emerged wailing and alive, and now in that black trash bag I saw my own future foretold: I would be trapped in Corpus Christi my whole life, where I would have food and a place to sleep, and eventually die. *Una buena vida*.

That night I left the library books in my bag and crawled into bed alone while elsewhere in the house the usual sounds were muffled. No Coronas snapping open, the television turned down, then just the mournful howl of the vacuum cleaner eliminating the last of the dog hairs. Alone for the first time without Lola, I twisted into a fetal position under my paper-thin sheets. Eyes squeezed shut, I clasped my hands together and begged with all my might for Jesus to come out of the picture on the wall, lay his body over mine, and hold me.

"Lord, please save me from this place." I dug my palms against my eyes. "*Dios mío, ayúdame.*"

WHEN I ARRIVED AT THE HOFFMAN-LYNCH BUILDING FOR MY interview, I handed the security guard my Texas ID and received in return a printed pass. Four years ago, my name had been Elián San Jamar. Now my ID read ETHAN ST. JAMES, a name born of my own willful determination that, despite the conspiracy of my birthright, I should have a second chance in the world. Through these letters I upheld myself to the solemn promise of a new identity that defied the bleakness of my former existence. I thought briefly of my own ghost as I reached out to claim that pass and my rightful destiny. Like a victorious soldier on his passage home, I clutched it and watched the future soar as the battlefield shrunk far behind. This was the long-awaited homecoming.

"When you get to the twelfth floor, you can wait in the lobby," the guard instructed me. "Somebody will come get you."

I pressed my thin frame against the turnstile, half-expecting that it would press back, then, easily—*click!*—the metal bar rotated and I was on the other side, one step closer. Black marble underfoot, I stood with a row of elevators on either side of me. Digital panels flashed scarlet numbers as beautiful people were transported to and from the twelfth floor, the floor that housed *Régine*—the only floor of the Hoffman-Lynch building that mattered. I held my breath, trembling hands at my side, trying hopelessly to be discreet as I swiveled around. Peering back toward the lobby, I saw a few women engaged in boring chatter—ordinary-looking, like a bunch of office supplies on a desk. One of them badly needed to re-dye her roots, which looked like the revolving fringe inside a car wash. They had nothing to do with *Régine*.

An elevator pinged. The chrome gates parted. Raised to an immortal height on Corinthian stilettos, two long all-black pillars towered before me adorned with cell phones and structured handbags, and topped off by white faces like Narcissus flowers.

Now, *these*—these women had come from *Régine*.

"—spattered red paint *all* over her!" exclaimed one, her lips the color of Gorgon's blood. "Afterward she moaned to the cameras, 'It's not even fur—it's only pony-hair!'" They both laughed as they circled around me, trotting fast. Together, sliding their sunglasses over their eyes, they hit the turnstiles—*bam!*—and reconvened into a canter, clip-clopping toward the glass revolving door. In a daze, I stepped into the elevator and pushed the button, hardly believing that in a moment I would be rocketed skyward to the heavens from which these beauties had descended.

The only other noteworthy floor of the Hoffman-Lynch building housed *Régine*'s teenage sister, who sagely reassured high schoolers that they would fit in by pairing their Converse sneakers with five-hundred-dollar dresses. Every other floor existed merely to make the building taller. There were several men's fashion magazines—widely known ones, I guess—but their intended readership skewed toward hopelessly unfashionable "guy's guys," the adult approximation of the neighborhood boys I had grown up with, who had graduated from bouncing around their own basketballs to watching other people do it on TV, and needed to be taught every month how to tie a Windsor knot.

Having long ago mastered the fundamentals of men's fashion, I was dressed that day in a wine-red suit—one of my favorites—and was trying to decide whether to undo the last jacket button when a woman joined me in the elevator. She was older, with gray hairs drawn into her businesslike bun and a mouth crowded by severe wrinkles. The twelfth floor button already radiated, but she pressed it once more for several seconds, as if she believed she could force it to move faster. I never understood why anybody did that, as if without the influential push of their own finger the world would get lazy and forget to rotate.

My excitement rose with the elevator as I gazed at the woman's impeccable outfit. She wore a black dress shirt and matching pencil skirt, with no frills or fun of any kind, yet unlike my clothes—which, despite being tailored to fit, still gave away their outmoded Salvation Army origins—hers gave that special impression of being very expensive, somehow sewn more precisely with a finer thread on a sharper needle, then selected right off the back of a runway model months in anticipation of the general trend. Her three-inch heels were black patent leather, shiny enough to have been unwrapped from their box that same morning.

"Your shoes," I gestured, unable to help myself. "Divine."

She didn't reply. From the mashing of her thumbs on the keyboard of her cell phone, she could have been playing a game with a timer, but more likely she was preoccupied by something a hundred times more thrilling; an e-mail about ostrich-leather handbags or candidates for the cover of the September issue. I figured then she must not have heard me, so I repeated myself, more clearly, "I like your shoes!," the words as bright and crisp as a soap bubble.

The elevator pinged at our destination. She turned her face toward the parting doors and said simply, not to me, but to the air before her, "Christian Dior."

My little bubble spun around, stunned, and quietly burst as she disappeared through a set of glass double doors. On one side of me now loomed a floor-to-ceiling television—showing runway models walking on a loop—and on the other side, a huge red logo: *RÉGINE*.

I WAS TEN YEARS OLD THE FIRST TIME MY MOTHER DRAGGED me along to her nail appointment at a local salon called Angelina's—the one regular indulgence of her otherwise unglamorous existence. There, beneath an unfading waft of acetone, against the dramatic soundtrack of the afternoon soap opera, I stumbled upon *Régine*. Around our house, the only magazines were the tabloids my mother piled up by the bathroom toilet, with features titled, "Your favorite stars look just like you without makeup!" Headlines always involved the latest cheating scandals and speculation over surgical procedures, while inside one was sure to find several pages dedicated to which rich and famous women had worn which unflattering dress to some party or award show: on the whole, every kind of stomach-turning, and printed on bad paper.

But *Régine* reminded me of the illustrated fairy tales I used to check out from the school library. Like all fairy tales, with their stock characters and predictable endings, the magazine had its fair share of faults, not least of which were the celebrity profiles it proudly touted on the front cover. What did it matter to me if the star of some forgettable summer blockbuster had birthed yet another child with her second husband, or that it took her just four months to work off the pregnancy fat? It didn't matter to me, either, that anybody had attended this or that party, or that they had worn Gucci for the first half, then—surprise!—changed into Dior. And my one enduring question was never answered: What was an anti-wrinkle serum, and why were so many pages dedicated to them?

Once I got past these minor irritations, however, I flipped through one breathtaking picture after another, fingers trembling, my heart throbbing with longing. *Régine*'s power wasn't merely in the beauty of its models, with their long endless legs and little noses that hit the light just right; it was in the whole *world* they lived in. They could be fanning themselves beneath an arch in a Moorish palace, or frolicking on the beach of some private Caribbean island, yet they were always part of a picture that was perfect and complete—color-coordinated by somebody, with nothing ugly or wrong to mess it up.

Later, as an art history major at Yale, this was what I would love about all my favorite paintings, whether by Renoir or Van Gogh or Pollock. In the space of a canvas, they could create a whole world that was beautiful, and made *sense*. The best fashion spreads were just like that, only better because they were photographs, taken from actual life; and even though I knew they were staged and airbrushed, they still seemed *real*, as if I could set out looking for the perfect world they showed and find it. I had inexplicably imagined the *Régine* office as one of these worlds—

women majestically lounging about in magnificent long gowns, lacing up each other's embroidered corsets, their swanlike necks dripping with the world's finest jewels.

When at last someone entered the foyer through the glass double doors, she wasn't wearing a ball gown, but rather an ash-gray sheath and matching sling-back stilettos, and holding a copy of the current *Vogue* issue while she bit into a green apple.

"Ms. Walker!" I exclaimed.

She looked up at me for one second (that was one second longer than Ms. Christian Dior, from the elevator) and uttered, simply, "No," before calling the elevator and returning to her magazine.

"I'm sorry." I recoiled like a gustless paper party horn. "I'm just waiting for Ms. Walker."

Evidently she had been looking forward to her apple all morning; a series of crunching noises was her response. When she disappeared a second later into the elevator, the fruit was no more than a fragile stem. She tucked it like a bookmark into her magazine, and the doors closed.

A second woman appeared after five minutes (black secretary blouse, black pencil skirt, black kitten heels—not Ms. Walker), and a third another five minutes after her (gray silk jumpsuit, black stilettos—also not Ms. Walker). As I waited, I mentally sifted through all the answers I had practiced the night before, like index cards before a midterm: my accomplishments and my strengths and my career goals, all of which I would share in a humble yet confident tone while also reminding them I went to *Yale, Yale, Yale* at every opportunity. The only other interviews I'd had were for library posts in high school and college, and both times I'd just entered with a big smile and the fresh-faced ease of a person who has just returned from a summer holiday. But this wasn't just any interview—it was the most important interview of my life. When Ms. Sabrina Walker asked me about my strengths I was prepared to bubble up, like champagne from a just-uncorked bottle, about my imagination and my great eye for beauty—then, before I came across as too frothy, I would bow my head with a sober crinkle of my brows and add that I also knew how to "get things done," that I was smart, and resourceful, and had received high marks from all of my professors at *Yale*.

In my mind, Ms. Walker would nod her head agreeably at this, and smile. Even after observing several of her colleagues in dark monochrome, I inexplicably maintained my belief that, like an angel, she would shine very bright—the hallowed gatekeeper who would admit me to my fashionable destiny. When, after a series of my well-pitched responses, she asked me why I wanted to work at *Régine*, I would reply, "Because my life's purpose is to make the world more beautiful," and she would open her arms to me, with a pearl-like tear in her eye, and say, "Come, child: you belong here," and the cream-colored lobby would glow like blond hair in a shampoo commercial, and a wreath of laurel would descend from the air onto my head, while around the world everybody laid down their guns and cancelled the bombings and all the hungry children got an organic fruit basket with my name on the calligraphed gift tag.

I TOOK A MOMENT TO REARRANGE MY PINK TIE, WHICH WAS held by a tortoiseshell pin to a crisp white shirt curtained by the velvet lapels of my suit. My younger self would have been amazed. Years of devotion to the crowning principles of *Régine* had inspired an insatiable pining for beautiful new clothes; growing up, I wanted a suit most of all—the standard, it seemed, for any man who wished to love a *Régine*-caliber woman. I didn't dare ask for such a frivolity, however, at least not within earshot of my father, whose only aesthetic indulgence was "extra-soft" toilet paper and whose single biggest complaint about America was the insufferable flamboyance of its men. He possessed extremely traditional Hispanic views of masculinity, believing that a man's worth was determined by his strength and earning power, and a woman's by her merit in the domestic sphere. Consequently, any man who defied these conventions (his tirades against pretty-boy actors and limp-wristed television hosts were particularly pointed) must be a menace and a bad Catholic and probably a "*mariposa*"—a butterfly, a faggot.

Although she expressed only a passive tolerance of his perspective, my coupon-clipping mother shared his view of new clothes as unnecessary, at least in light of more pressing expenditures on unglamorous things like gas and weekly groceries, the importance of which I hoped she might one day overlook so that I could have a dress shirt, or a necktie, or even just a pair of colorful socks. My wardrobe was sourced entirely from the clearance bin at the local discount mart, from which the most common takeaways were elastic shorts and plastic-wrapped packs of "assorted" three-for-one T-shirts.

A lucky break came toward the end of seventh grade, when Tío Domingo announced he would be marrying (pregnant) Cecilia Maria in June—next month!—and that he hoped my parents would be his Best Man and Matron of Honor, and would they mind having the reception at our house? The imposition sent my mother scrambling all over town, squawking about flowers and bridesmaids' dresses and a tent for the backyard, all the while complaining that her brother-in-law never did anything right and he was going to ruin Cecilia Maria's credit like he did to his first wife's. Not to mention the inconsiderate suddenness of hosting a shotgun wedding, the cost of which she had hardly budgeted for. She had to buy shoes! a dress! a necklace! and—a suit for me.

Boasting a markdown of 75 percent, my first suit was unearthed from a bargain-basement sale by my mother, who then yanked a button off the sleeve and haggled for a greater discount. It was dust-bunny gray, considerably out of fashion with four buttons on the jacket and deep pleats down the length of the pants, yet I wore it to the wedding with a hundred times more dignity than that possessed by the groom himself, who during the cramped backyard reception was offered one too many Coronas by my father and knocked the three-layer cake off the folding table. My mother and my grandmother Walita, all my *tías* and my *primas* and other female relatives, could barely contain themselves: "*¡Qué guapo! ¡Qué lindo*! What a smart and handsome gentleman!" I just sat there and smiled, because I already *knew*. I knew that in my suit, with my hands folded elegantly on my lap, I looked like more of a gentleman than any of their lumpy, unchivalrous husbands did. Not because my suit *made* me a gentleman, but because it made known to others those qualities which all along I had seen in myself.

The Monday after the wedding was the first day of my summer vacation, and while my parents were at work and all the other kids slept in and then watched reruns on TV, I put on my new suit and walked the familiar path to the district library. I had spent my last two summer vacations the same way, loafing around the library as casually as if it were my own living room, reading books until they kicked me out. Having long since graduated from fairy tales to "chapter books" like *Peter Pan* and *Treasure Island,* the district library had become my favorite place in Corpus Christi. It had two floors, and ten times as many books as my library in grade school; flooded with stories and sunlight, it was an oasis in the arid wasteland of my life and I preferred to be there all day than to ever borrow a book to read at home.

The crowning achievement of my reading list that summer was *The Age of Innocence*. I had already fallen in love with the Brontës, and Jane Austen, but Edith Wharton's sentences were easily the most elaborate I had ever encountered. The library closed at six, and on many evenings I was awakened by the librarian, who had found me snoring with the open book aflutter on the table and a dictionary on my lap, as every paragraph had me looking up the meaning of words like "perfunctory" and "parvenu."

It was the dead of summer in Texas, a dry, bristling heat, but I wore that suit every day. All I could think about was what a man I finally was; what the other kids would say on the first day of school. A growth spurt during those months ensured that by the time the school year actually arrived, my suit was no longer as dignified as it was laughably ill-fitted. But my conviction to wear it, despite the prominent nakedness of my wrists and ankles, was unshakeable.

Two weeks into eighth grade I was perched alone on top of a wooden table in the middle of the dusty, sun-baked lunchtime courtyard, beneath the shade of a rustling oak tree. Chatter all around attested to the preoccupations of my peers—restless recapitulation of last night's TV shows and hushed rumors about

Corpus Christi High kids who were "doing it" in the bathroom stalls—while I sipped from a grape soda, reading to myself from *The House of Mirth*, my second crack at Edith Wharton: "'*I really think, Mother,' she said reproachfully, 'we might afford a few fresh flowers for luncheon. Just some jonquils or lilies-of-the-valley—*'"

"Ey, Elián!"

I looked up to find Cesar Montana running laps around my table. Cesar hadn't changed much since our failed playdates—he'd only grown bigger and acquired the valuable skill of imitating the noise made by race car engines.

Now he came toward me and shouted, "Why you such a *mariposa*?"

A ball of terror rose in my throat. "*Mariposa*" literally meant "butterfly," but I knew Cesar meant it "the other way," the way my father often did. To me it was preposterous that any man or woman should seek to be *unlike* a butterfly—one of the loveliest creatures in the world—yet I always paled when I heard it spoken at the kitchen counter. "*To think a married man could prefer pink socks over gray!*" my father would rant, breaking into another beer while I silently prayed he would never apply his favorite insult to me.

A small crowd was forming around me and Cesar—mostly boys, gaggling with open mouths while my tormenter flapped his arms, presumably like a butterfly.

"You heard me, *mariposa*? Why you wear dis fuckeen suit? Readin dis stoopit book?" He stopped in front of me to jab his finger at the spine of *The House of Mirth*.

I gulped at his formless face, my eyes locked on a mole on his cheek from which a hair stuck out like an antenna, when suddenly, having gained extra gall from the attention of the growing audience, Cesar reached out and struck the bottom of my drink. The aluminum can hit me square in the nose, grape soda bursting over my suited chest. Fizzling purple liquid trickled onto my white shirt, while the can tinkled to the dusty ground at Cesar's feet.

Eyes widened. Lower lips dropped. Then a dozen arms were flailing, and in a haphazard stampede of hooves the herd scrambled in the opposite direction. They all knew what was next—they must have seen it in my face—and so did Cesar, a bully who had taunted a caged animal, only to see the bars suddenly vanish.

In my head, the cacophony siphoned into a single buzz of ambient noise. I propelled myself into the air, book in hand . . . in slow motion observed a shifting of the ground below me . . . then I crashed onto Cesar's back. He went tumbling beneath my body onto a tangle of upraised oak roots. The collision raised a cloud of ashy dust around us, and the din in my ears exploded once more into high-pitched wails: "Look! Look! *¡Elián va a matar a Cesar!*"

I raised *The House of Mirth* and delivered a backhanded *crack!* across Cesar's face.

I had never felt more hatred than I did in that moment. I hated Cesar, I hated the way he looked and the way he spoke and the way he moved. I hated him so much that when I looked down I didn't see a person at all, but everything that was ugly and wrong with life. Everyone who might hate *me*, just for being different. The fact that in Corpus Christi, and the whole world, there were thousands of people like him, and that ultimately, if they wanted to look down on me from the dumpster pedestal of their own mediocrity, there was nothing I could do about it.

His flesh yielded like dough as I hit him once more, on the

side with the antennaed mole, and then, as he covered his face and voices screeched like out-of-tune violins, I struck him again! and again! and again!

From somewhere far away, a hand tried to pull me up.

I was suspended from school, but it didn't matter. For once, my father was proud of me, and I spent the following two weeks at the district library, where I obviously preferred to be.

That such a perfect word as *mariposa* could be regarded as an insult in my hometown was confirmation enough for me: I would find a way to escape Corpus Christi, and in the meantime I would wear never less than a full suit, not to the grocery store, or the dentist, or to my grandparents' house. I got my first job at the district library checkout counter, and with my limited funds I graduated to ownership of many suits—thrift-store acquisitions in different styles and colors—all tailored by my indulgent mother to fit the dimensions of my lanky frame, while my father, perhaps in denial, looked the other way.

It was the only act of rebellion I knew—to be worthy of such an insult as "butterfly."

YALE WAS EVERYTHING I'D EVER WANTED, BUT COLLEGE doesn't last forever. After four years spent in exultation of a realized dream, I knew of only one other destination with the same promise of beauty and success, a name that echoed in my head, the sound of my life's calling: *Régine*. When the e-mail came, it was as though all the tectonic plates of my life met right beneath my feet. The subject line was *RÉGINE*, in all caps, with the accent and everything.

Dear Ethan St. James,

We have received your résumé and believe you could be qualified to work as an intern in the office of Edmund Benneton. Please respond promptly if you are available for an interview tomorrow at 2 p.m.

Sabrina Walker
Fashion Assistant
RÉGINE

I fired an e-mail back to Sabrina Walker so quickly that I charred my fingertips. To see Edmund Benneton's name in my inbox, together with the implication that he might want *me*, that it was *me* who could soon be at his side—well, I won't get too carried away, but let's just say it meant the whole wide world was all right, spinning around as it should, and that if I dreamed of anything hard enough, it would happen.

Edmund Benneton was the fashion director of *Régine*, and after Ava Burgess, *Régine*'s editor-in-chief, he was the single most important person in the world of fashion. With his work appearing every month on newsstands and front porches and little side tables in salons, Edmund reached an audience of millions, therefore possessing the power to affect the whole world—or at least, the *look* of the whole world. His was the life I envisioned for myself—basking in endless beauty, cavorting with artists and models and designers—

"Ethan. . . ."

My Elysian dream was interrupted by a faraway voice. "Oh!" I exclaimed, accidentally uncorking the bottle of enthusiasm I had planned to reserve until the right moment. I turned and rose to my feet, stretching out my hand, bursting, "You must be Ms. Walker!"

I'd correctly guessed only one thing about Ms. Walker: She was, by virtue of a stilettoed boot, extraordinarily tall. Other than that, well, she was clearly my age, around twenty-one, and hardly a "Ms. Walker" at all. She had the fresh, collegiate face of someone I could have been friends with at Yale—blushing cheeks, blue eyes incandescent with ambition. But the rest of Sabrina Walker distinguished her sharply from any friend I'd known.

Her white-gold hair was pulled up into a high ponytail; baby hairs shellacked into seamless oblivion, a long, infallible tress swishing uniformly over her nape like a silk tassel. She wore black from head to toe; a crepe secretary blouse, bow-tied with military stiffness around her throat, and a gabardine skirt, its razor-sharp pleats encircling her waist in a synchronized regimental march. Her glossy thigh-high boots were made of reptilian skin, with heels like bayonet blades. Her footsteps on the marble floor sounded *click, click, click*, like the clacking platinum balls in a Newton's cradle—a perfect balance of ease and exactitude.

My heart spiked instinctively as her hand glided into mine. With frosted delicacy, she permitted the briefest physical contact—a gesture which escaped the crudeness of an undignified joggle and the intimacy of a presumptuous clench—then, like eager Orpheus, I felt a Hadean chill claim her back, her fingers slipping away.

Sabrina smiled, her teeth glacier-white. "Burgundy suit—how bold." Her voice was surprisingly husky. It was easy to imagine her, a few years earlier, in a plaid version of her short pleated skirt, smoking smuggled Parliament Lights out of a dormitory window at some mist-wreathed New England boarding school. She sat down, while in a daze of cryogenic uncertainty my outstretched hand remained suspended behind her. "Résumé?"

I hastily conducted an inventory of my disobedient limbs. The folder containing my résumé appeared miraculously in her hands, and my body in the parlor chair before her.

"You're the Yale boy, right?" She opened the folder and barely skimmed the page. She was chewing gum, and smiling again—a conspiratorial smile, as if we were part of the same club—and said, "I have friends that went to Yale."

Against her amicable tone, I perceived the loud, self-destructive irrationality of my own nerves. *Why* was I so uncomfortable? Not only was Sabrina smiling, but she was going out of her way to be friendly. *Don't ruin this!* I took a deep breath, prepared to redeem myself with a masterful round of the name-game ("Oh, of course I know so-and so!" followed by anecdotal evidence of her friend's and my closeness—"We were classmates! Neighbors! Practically best friends!")—anything to calm my terror and seal the deal with Sabrina Walker.

"Do you know Cecilie Harris?" she asked, as I unconvincingly attempted to place my hands in a casual arrangement on my lap.

I felt my pent-up shoulders relax. Cecilie Harris was actually a good friend, and the invocation of her name was like a trickle of relief through my petrified veins.

Sabrina caught the flash of recognition on my face. "An expensive mess, isn't she?" she said. Her eyebrow rose with cruel relish. "Our fathers both work at Sotheby's, so we've summered together. She acts like some kind of hippie, when her parents own a château in Saint-Rémy." Leaning forward, her voice thrilling with scorn, "She wore a *caftan* to a Commodore's Ball at the Nantucket Yacht Club."

I laughed nervously as my shoulders tensed up even more than before.

"God, I wish I'd gone to Yale," she moaned. "Went to Dartmouth. Have you been there?" She reclined into the damask chair, its cream flourishes forming an elegant backdrop for her mockery. "If you haven't, don't bother, unless you're a fan of sweatshirts and cheap beer. The experience was distressing." She laughed to herself unexpectedly before waving away her transgression. "Anyway, where are you from again? Originally?"

It took me a second to remember. "Corpus Christi," I managed.

She cocked her head.

"It's in Texas," I clarified.

"Oh." Her expression, which a second ago had been so convivial, was suddenly obscured by a dense fog. "I had assumed . . . from your last name . . . St. James, you know, like Georgina St. James. I thought you were her brother or something . . ."

Unsure of what to say, I searched for a clue on her disobliging face, then admitted, "No, I . . . I've never heard of her."

The fog was penetrated by a ray of complete bewilderment. "Never heard of Georgina St. James?" Her voice spiked. "Not to be rude, but how do you *not* know her? She's a major 'It Girl' right now. She attends *everything*."

I tried desperately to conjure up some appropriate response—but what? The tie that had bound us—Sabrina's mistaken impression that I was a member of a certain club, well-bred, with a sibling on the society circuit and derisory regard for the philistines with whom I was forced to "summer"—was suddenly severed.

Sabrina's eyes steeled upon my résumé as one, two seconds passed, then she pressed the folder shut. She crossed her legs, laid my folder against the top of her leather-sheathed knee, and began to lightly rock her high-heeled boot toward the glass doors. She clasped her hands, and a charm—a pair of interlocking C's, unmistakably Chanel—rattled on her silver bracelet. "So then—tell me about yourself," she said, her enthusiasm replaced by the curtness of someone abandoned by her friends at a cocktail party and therefore obligated to make small talk with an unattractive stranger.

The flowery response that I had planted in my memory for this very occasion—*"I want to make everything more beautiful!"*—had utterly wilted in my head. "I majored in art history," I said, "with a minor in classics. For a short while I had hoped to be an artist, but. . . ." Here I had been prepared to tell an amusing anecdote about the first and only drawing class I had ever taken, wherein my depiction of a bowl of oranges was mistaken for a grassy knoll by my professor (*"A nice landscape, Mr. St. James, but did you mishear the assignment?"*). In this very instance, however—when the only interest Sabrina Walker seemed to have in me involved my relation to an invisible timer in her head—self-deprecating humor seemed decidedly the wrong note. How could I possibly reveal to her now the intimate admission that all I'd ever wanted was to work at *Régine*, the dream-world that for years had made my life bearable?

She was glancing once more into the folder at my résumé—out of boredom, perhaps, or a renewed sense of duty—and chewing her gum with slow deliberation, each bulge of her jawline like the agonizing crank of a medieval torture device.

"I want more than anything to work here," I ventured, suddenly changing my approach. It was now or never; if she wasn't swayed by my background or my résumé, then my only hope was to impress upon Sabrina the sheer intensity of my passion. "Everyone I know from school—they're all off to law school, consulting firms. They think they're going to help the world, and they are, I guess, but to me—beauty is more important than all those things. When people are sad, lonely—they don't look to their lawyers or consultants." I pointed to an issue of *Régine* that was laid out neatly on the cream coffee table. "They look to art, fashion—they escape into pictures. Working here, making the world beautiful, more bearable for those people—it's my dream."

The effect of this appeal was a momentary pause, then the completion of Sabrina's transformation into a smoldering piece of dry ice. "When you refer to beauty," she replied dully at last, "you mean our Beauty section? Like makeup, and skincare?"

I let out a little breath—the gasp of a little part of me, dying. My voice almost cracked, *"Yes, like skincare,"* just to save us both the trouble, but this seemed like an awful offense to the most sacred things in my life. "Not like beauty *products*. . . ." I croaked. "Like—I don't know . . . *beauty*. It's so much bigger than makeup—bigger than fashion."

"*Bigger* than fashion . . . ?" Disapproval decorated every syllable. "Then what are you doing at *Régine*?"

"I—I want to be a fashion editor," I replied, as the desperateness of my situation set in. "I just—I have so many ideas, so many worlds in my head. The only thing I want is to work here—to make them come to life."

"That's ambitious," she replied, with a skeptical arch of her brow.

"I know it won't be easy," I rushed in, trying to predict

her thoughts. "I'm prepared to work my whole life—just for a chance—but that's all I want, to be here."

Revealing in full her assessment of the situation, she looked like she was preparing to step around a puddle that was forming on the floor. "I'll be honest with you, Ethan," she said slowly, "because you seem like a smart boy." She observed me closely, as though she had earlier allowed a preconception to define my outer edges and was now filling me in. Her eyes passed with measured intensity over my suit, my shoes, my shaking hands, and when I thought she had finally met my gaze, I realized she was squinting at my unruly hair. "We hire two kinds of interns here. The first kind is what you'd expect anywhere, really—went to a decent college, usually majored in fashion or communications. We're very fair, and we'll take them from anywhere." As an aside—"Well, no state schools, but anywhere else, as long as they're competent."

She absently folded down the corner of my résumé. "They put in their time—a semester, or a summer—hard work, but in the end, they're grateful. I don't have to tell you that, for a career in fashion, *Régine* is the best name anyone can have on their résumé. They put it on the top in bold letters, and when we send them on their way, they end up in retail management, or public relations. Normal jobs, you know—and for the rest of their lives, they get to tell people—*they were here*."

Sabrina's Chanel bracelet clinked as her hand paused over the page, and a moment was granted for my consideration of this generous scenario. She flapped my folder open and closed. "If what you want is what I just described, then by all means—I'm happy to end this interview, and I'll see you on Monday."

I stared at her. I wasn't here because I wanted a line on my résumé, or a recommendation for a job in retail. I was here because I wanted *everything.* "What is the second type of intern?" I asked.

Sabrina permitted herself to flap open my folder one last time. Then she shut it, the breeze stilled, and she returned to her previous pose: hands clasped in a kind of prim finality. "Well, some interns we intend to bring on staff. But they're a very special case . . ."

As Sabrina trailed off, I felt a blaze of irritation. In exactly what ways was I *not* a "special case"? Hadn't I gotten into an Ivy League school from the middle of nowhere, with zero advantages and almost every obstacle stacked against me? Didn't she realize I was the *definition* of a special case? I glared at her, and in the next second she rather suddenly filled the silence. "Did you know we're the only Hoffman-Lynch publication that doesn't accept applications through Human Resources?"

I shook my head, suspecting that Sabrina had already delivered this conciliatory speech to a number of intern rejects before me.

"It's true," she continued. "We only hire from within. We used to work through HR, up on the seventeenth floor, but they kept sending the wrong types of people—HR handles all the magazines at Hoffman-Lynch, twenty-something titles, but some of the other magazines aren't as . . . discriminating as *Régine.* You understand, I'm sure—the qualities *Régine* seeks in a staff member are very hard to determine from a résumé. We can't just get anyone off the street, who can technically do a 'job.' The perfect candidate has certain *other* qualities—they look *Régine,* they act *Régine*—they know *Régine* because they *are Régine.* When they leave the office after a day at work, people need to be able to say, 'That's a *Régine* girl'—or boy, in your case. They have to be a person we can *groom*. We take them on as interns—special cases, you know—and when a position opens, it belongs to them. Because they belong. . . ."

Sabrina's hand fluttered open, like she was demonstrating for me the way her own delicate fingers *belonged*—or, perhaps, inviting me to appreciate her ring of diamonds encircling a shiny emerald. Draping one forearm over the upholstered arm of her chair, she dangled her hand over the adjacent glass side table. Her wrist was moving lightly in a circle, as if she had picked up a martini glass by its rim and was swirling around an olive inside. "I'd be happy to see you in the first category," she conceded at last. I realized I had been holding my breath. "We'd give you this opportunity, as a minor endorsement of sorts . . . you'd work hard, and then we'd send you on your way. I'm just . . ." She kept toying with the invisible glass. "For some reason, I'm just not so sure . . . that you fall into the second category."

My head raced through alternative interpretations of the words that had just left Sabrina's mouth, but there was nothing to interpret: Sabrina had declared me ultimately unsuitable for *Régine*. It was a judgment overwhelming in its offensiveness, yet she appeared so calm, so lovely reclining there, as though she had merely commented on the weather.

In a kind of stupefied daze, I shook my head. "I'm sorry, but—did I somehow give you the impression that I'm unqualified for this?"

Upon detecting my indignation, Sabrina livened up. "I don't mean to upset you," she equivocated grandly, with an expression so deliberately innocuous as to acquit her of all malign intent. "But with these things, I think it's important to be honest, don't you? If I let you have certain expectations—for instance, that you stand a reasonable chance of becoming a fashion editor at *Régine*—well, that wouldn't be very considerate of me, would it?" The corners of her mouth turned up, with the wistfulness of a weeping willow branch caught in the wind, and in a second, my latent suspicions of her malevolence were confirmed.

"But, I'm *extremely* qualified," I protested. "I—my whole life I—"

Sabrina gestured lightly toward me. "Who makes your suit, Ethan? In that lovely color."

"What?" My disorientation was complete. "I—I don't know," I replied. "It's just . . . thrifted."

She pressed her lips together and nodded. "Thrifted?" she repeated with a feigned ignorance, as though to spare me the dishonor of my own admission. "I've never heard of them." Then she slipped a finger under her Chanel bracelet and rotated it so the charm with the diamond logo was facing up. "I'm guessing your shoes too—'thrifted,' right?"

I suddenly saw us from above, as a fly would see us if it was buzzing in a circle around our heads. I saw Sabrina's bracelet and her ring, the alabaster gleam of her white-blonde hair, her arms arranged gracefully over her lap—her skin polished and smooth, like pale, lacquered wood. Then I saw myself as she must have seen me, as some kind of clown in my outdated suit from the Salvation Army—too colorful, uncouth—with my scuffed-up shoes, and my lop of curly brown hair. An outsider who didn't know the language. She sat coolly back in the chair, as comfortable as if she was in her own home, while I . . . I was leaning forward like a bent antenna, my dignity betrayed by my total desperation.

"What did you say your parents do?"

This wasn't her fault—I knew I had brought it on myself, all of it—but did she have to be so cruel? She somehow must have known. Over one shoulder, perhaps, she saw my mother, rotund and reeking of Clorox; over the other, my father, covered in curly black hair, his brown, sweaty stomach hanging over his belt. "I don't know what that has to do with this," I croaked.

"It has everything to do with this. Let's put it this way . . ." She began to balance her words like wooden blocks. "Have you ever tried to fit a piece of yarn through the eye of a needle?" She shrugged, and the tower teetered, then came crashing down. "It just . . . doesn't work."

Her casual suggestion that, of all things, I should consider myself *a piece of yarn*—a common, homespun twist of unsophisticated fibers, too coarse, too unrefined to ever fit in at *Régine*—swung through me like a wrecking ball. It was an evaluation she had made in less than ten minutes.

Her chewing gum made a sickly sound as she relegated it slowly to a crevice between her back molars and crushed down. "I'm sorry—I can see this isn't going to happen," she said. She pushed my résumé quietly toward me on the coffee table and stood up. Her pleated skirt rippled all around her, like a pond whose surface had been momentarily disturbed, and was now returning to untouched stillness. "We'll be in touch."

"I—what?" No. It couldn't end like this, not after how far I'd already come. My dream was slipping away like life from a dying body, intravenous tubes dripping and a monitor above the bed blinking, TRAGEDY! TRAGEDY!

I fumbled to my feet behind her, knowing that if I didn't stop Sabrina Walker, I was never going to hear from her again.

My entire future hung in the balance of the next moment. We stood two feet away from each other. She smelled like a particular kind of smoker, the kind who tried unsuccessfully to temper the evidence of cigarettes with perfume and ended up smelling like a flower that had tumbled into an ashtray.

"Can I meet with Edmund himself?" I blurted.

She let out an incredulous guffaw. "Don't be absurd! After Ava Burgess, Edmund Benneton is the most sought-after person at *Régine*, which makes him the second-most sought-after person in the fashion industry." Then, in a tone that was, for the first time, not veiled with some calculated affectation: "Do you think he cares about an intern?!" She added offhandedly, with undisguised satisfaction, "I'm sorry, but try *Teen Régine*. I have work to do."

My blood rushed to my head. "Look," I demanded. "I have a great eye for beauty." I took a step closer, with an avowal as futile as all famous last words—"*I belong here.*"

She exhaled toward the marble floor, like she was embarrassed on my behalf. "Ethan St. James, let's keep this dignified, *please*. Do you think I have time to bother with you and your 'great eye'? I'm sure your skills will be appreciated somewhere else."

Striding to the glass doors, she turned around to reveal a row of tiny velvet buttons down her spine. As the heart monitor teetered on silence (*beep . . . beep . . . beep!*) I half-shouted, "I mean, really—*Régine* is a *fashion* magazine—how can it possibly be that hard?"

At this, Sabrina pivoted just her head, so that her chin was pointed over her shoulder. "You think working at *Régine* would be not—that—hard?" The corner of her eyebrow flickered, a crack in her otherwise self-assured countenance. "All right,

Mr. St. James, with the 'great eye,' who went to *Yale*—" I felt the soul of my dying dream approach the final threshold, as Sabrina pressed her ID card against the reader—*beep!*

"Monday. Nine o'clock." Without taking her eyes off me, she pressed her back against the *Régine* door, and with a final combative glare said, "Wear something deserving of your presumptuous sweat."

chapter two

If I had possessed a greater sense of self-awareness, or a lesser sense of self-importance, I might have appreciated the perfect irony of my interview—that Sabrina Walker considered me inferior to the standard at *Régine*, when for the past four years I had entertained a kind of superiority complex toward the world.

I hadn't always been as confident as I was by the time I got to Yale. Despite my obsession with reading, or maybe because of it, I had been a terrible student throughout elementary and middle school; semester after semester spent suffering bossy, simpleminded teachers, who believed the height of knowledge was memorization and never had good answers to the important questions. There was no reason for me to think high school would be any better; based on the rumors, it promised to be much worse. Along with the rest of the incoming students, the course I dreaded most was Freshman English, taught by the infamous and decrepit Ms. Duncan, who was "too hard," assigned too much homework, and failed more students than any other teacher. She ran her classroom like a ballet studio, in which the slightest flail at the barre was cause for ruthless admonition, and unlike the other "mean" teachers who redeemed themselves by selecting favorites, I'd never heard of anyone being spared by Ms. Duncan.

Desperately hoping she wouldn't pick on me, I took a seat in the back row of her class on the first day, as she prattled about her "rigorous standards" and distributed worn-out copies of *The Great Gatsby*. Pausing two desks in front of me, she caught my eye and gestured toward my suit, which admittedly distinguished me from my peers. "Looks like we have ourselves a Mr. Darcy," she commented with a self-amused smirk.

Having read *Pride and Prejudice*, and almost everything else by Jane Austen, I knew exactly who Mr. Darcy was, but lowered my gaze to the desk to discourage further negative attention.

Ms. Duncan mistook my silence for a lack of comprehension. Raising a droopy brow, she sighed, "I should know better than to make literary references to illiterates."

I was one second flabbergasted, the next inwardly erupting like a furnace that had just been stoked. Who did she think she was to make such an assumption about me, when I had probably read more books than she had? My anger bubbled upward as she creaked slowly down the aisle and thrust a book on the student's desk in front of me; I watched her long, woolen dress swing nearer, and before I could control myself Austen's own words escaped through my teeth with the searing precision of a lighter's flame: "'Angry people are not always wise.'"

Her wrinkled jaw dropped, then she recovered. "That's a line you learned from the movie version, surely." Her shadow fell onto my desk. "Let's see how well you do writing ten-page literary essays based on terrible movie adaptions. You won't be the first who tries, and you won't be the first I've failed." She slammed a tattered copy of *Gatsby* onto my desk as a conclusive retort, and if I hadn't been so infuriated, I would have laughed out loud. I had already read it. Twice.

For two weeks, I participated in class through scalding glares. Then our first essay was due, and out of sheer spite, I turned in fifty pages, a whole dissertation about East and West Egg representing states of mental illness. I received the paper back after the weekend, tossed from Ms. Duncan's hand and with a red F on the top. "For not following the word count," she spat. "I'll need a word with you after class."

I fumed silently as she went on to berate the entire class: "With all the vocabulary in our magnificent language, I would have hoped you all could find better words to describe *The Great Gatsby* than—" she pulled out a list of words my classmates had employed in their critical essays "—*cool—awesome—fun—nice—really nice*—and my favorite, *great*, used without ironic relation to the book's title." It seemed obvious to me that she had experienced some kind of bitter failure in her life; she had probably dreamed of being a great writer herself, before getting rejected by all the publishing houses, and being forced to teach dullards at our deadbeat high school.

When class ended, I tried unsuccessfully to slip by her.

"Sit back down, Darcy!"

I rolled my eyes and faced her desk while the other students flooded around me and out of the room. The door slammed shut behind them, and Ms. Duncan pointed at a desk in the front row.

"I'm going to miss my bus," I said, and refused to sit.

Her eyes narrowed. "I requested your records from middle school," she rasped, patting a folder on her desk. "Dismal at best. As I'm sure you are all too aware. The comments are all the same—you miss classes, you don't participate, and you only do the bare minimum to avoid failure."

I shifted my weight and glared above her gray head at a quote from *A Tale of Two Cities* tacked to the wall, loath to give her the satisfaction of my full attention.

"Where did you learn to write?" she continued. "Because the person who wrote this, the person who—"

"Look," I snapped. "I didn't plagiarize that essay if that's what you're getting at. I obviously know what my grades were like in middle school, and if you keep hassling me, I'm going to miss the—"

Ms. Duncan pounded her desk with two fists, her nostrils flaring as veins emerged on her forehead like cracks in an old vase. *"Don't interrupt me, Darcy!"* The pens rattled in the cup on her desk. "I know you didn't plagiarize that essay—that's the first thing I made sure of." Her shoulders lowered. "Yours was the best paper in the class."

She paused for a moment, perhaps expecting that through flattery she would gain my respect, but I continued doggedly to refuse eye contact, preferring to clench my teeth and reread over and over: *It was the best of times, it was the worst of times. It was the best of times, the worst of times, best of times, worst, best worst best worst—*

"It was insightful, and well written. It was, in fact, one of the most provocative analyses that I have read on *The Great Gatsby*, and trust me, I have read a lot of them."

I nearly blurted, *"Then why did you give me an F?,"* but it was true that I didn't want to miss the bus, so I crossed my arms over my chest instead.

"Not interested to hear it, are you? I suppose you don't care what your teacher says?" She tapped the butt of her pen against her desk while I switched to staring at the door. "Now, where are you going to college?"

I responded with a paltry shrug.

"You don't know . . . ? Then I guess you envision yourself in Corpus Christi forever, don't you?"

I finally looked at her. She was sitting there, beadily judging *me*, and repulsion rose in my throat: "Nothing in the *world* could make me stay here." These were words I had never said aloud: words from deep within, which inside of me had always seemed so strong and complete, but suddenly flung into the open air they sounded fragile and thin. In my terror that the words might not be true, more words came flying out, shattering against the wall and tinkling to the floor around Ms. Duncan's desk: "Four more years and I'll be out of here—out of this school, this town—I'll be far, far away, while you and everybody else will just rot here, and if you think I can't do it—" I gulped.

Ms. Duncan silently twirled a pen between her bony fingers. "And how do you plan to make it anywhere with these grades?" She gestured once more to the front row. "Sit down, Darcy, and let's have a chat. If you miss the goddamn bus I will take you home myself."

MS. DUNCAN WAS THE FAIRY GODMOTHER I HAD HOPED FOR. Our long conversation in her classroom that afternoon marked the first time certain synapses in my brain had connected to form an important thought: I might actually be able to reach my destination, if only I followed a map. I swore to follow Ms. Duncan down every turn if it meant I would have a chance in the world, and thereafter my success was her fiercest passion, as I became her one chance at achieving whatever glory had eluded her in her own life.

I read and studied and followed a rigorous schedule of college prep exams; and ironically, after I had dedicated myself wholeheartedly to escape Corpus Christi, I finally started to feel okay there. My suits got more colorful, my attitude more eccentric, and the more comfortable I was with myself, the more comfortable others were around me—girls, at least.

None of them were attracted to me romantically. Evidently it was a truth universally acknowledged that a boy who wears a suit and pink socks "must" be gay, and pretty soon it was not only Cesar Montana but also the rest of the students who had applied that truth to me. It was a fair enough assumption. The prevailing gay stereotype in Corpus Christi centered on criteria abundantly satisfied by my fundamental qualities: my preference for female company, my disinterest in typically masculine activities, and especially my love of fashion and the arts. Even though I'd never had a boyfriend or a girlfriend, and was in fact hilariously ignorant about sex, the boxes were otherwise checked.

I didn't *want* to be gay. At least not at first. Growing up, I knew that being gay was the single least-acceptable thing I could do in life, less so even than becoming a drug addict, or failing school. Yet, outside the context of my own home, being gay actually made it *easier* for me to be accepted. At school, nobody had understood me when the only label they could apply to me was "strange," but when that label was replaced with "gay," I became as predictable as the head cheerleader, or the football quarterback—a character everyone could "understand," even though nothing about me had changed.

Whether or not I was *actually* gay didn't matter. Because everyone else thought it must be true, so did I, and either way it made school bearable. Of course there were the kids, like Cesar Montana, who "hated" gay people, but they weren't going to like me regardless of whether I was gay or straight or anything else.

By the end of sophomore year, not only did I have friends, but I had enough of them to be voted into Student Council. Granted, Ms. Duncan pushed me to run, and within my apathetic class the competition wasn't intense, but it was the start of something—and the year after that I was voted president. I was running the class, working at the library, and taking college prep exams with Ms. Duncan; when I wasn't busy, I was with my best friend, Claudette, who would pick me up in her dad's Jeep and take me shopping at the local strip mall.

My mother thought all the commotion was wonderful. She tailored all my zany suits, exclaiming, "How different the styles are for boys these days!" Not only that, but I finally had friends—"girlfriends!" she giggled in either a brilliant display of denial, or sheer cluelessness. The one dark cloud was my father. For years, the tenets of our family dinnertime routine had remained exactly the same. The sweaty embrace; "Ey, *cabrón*!"; the hug and smack on the bottom. The two differences were my height and his girth, until I began to notice that in the light of my brighter self-image, his own view of me had darkened; soon he was barely speaking to me. By that point, though, I didn't really care what he thought, and he remained tight-lipped until, one day, I suppose I took my differentness too far.

The piercing was Claudette's idea. A black pearl stud in my upper ear—a reckless whim, but then again, I was sixteen, and it was just for fun, and I had paid for it with my own money.

Within minutes of arriving home: "*¡Mariposa!*" my father roared. He grabbed me by the collar and pinned me against the wall, bellowing in Spanish, "*You won't be a faggot! I WON'T LET YOU BE A FAGGOT!*" And as I prepared to defend myself and shout, "*You don't know anything about me!*," I realized he had *tears* in his eyes. My poor, stupid construction-worker father, who had grown up in another country, and had no hope of understanding me, thought that because I had a pearl in my ear there was something *wrong* with me, and furthermore, that it was *his fault*.

A shadow descended on the house after that, and six months later, Ms. Duncan was driving me to a college fair in Austin. There were booths for Columbia and Brown and Stanford—each one promising the best four years of my life—then there was Yale, under a banner which read, *Lux et Veritas*.

"What's it mean?" I asked the boy at the booth.

"It's Latin. It means light and truth."

WHEN, ON MY FIRST DAY AT *RÉGINE*, THE ELEVATOR DOORS parted—my own reflected likeness split in two—Edmund's head intern was standing directly opposite me in the foyer, having somehow foreseen exactly which of the twelve elevators would shuttle me up to that floor. His first words to me were an accurate summary of the relationship we would come to share: "My name is George, and we have a *million* things to do."

George Beckett was as short and as round as a prize-winning pumpkin. Underneath a hardened shell of shiny orange hair—his white side part appeared chopped by a knife—his upturned nose assessed me for barely a second before he barreled away.

"Good to meet you!" I scrambled to catch up to the heels of his black oxfords.

George wore a dress shirt and trousers, all black. Despite this, he was Sabrina's physical opposite—pasty and white, the sole color on his face supplied by a bounty of freckles scattered like toasted nuts over his doughy cheeks. I was struck by the fact that, for a body of such Lilliputian proportions—I think he grazed five feet—his gait was astonishingly accelerated.

"This'll be my first time in the office," I confided, as we approached the glass doors.

He turned slightly. His scrunched-up nose gave him the look of someone permanently in the midst of an objectionable odor. In a voice that was at once nasal and high-pitched, he said, "Great color scheme. You'll fit right in." Then that nose commandeered a pucker of repulsion across his whole face.

I looked down at myself in my head-to-toe raspberry-pink suit, with a white shirt and striped purple necktie. After Sabrina's indictment of my thrifted garb, I had unwisely splurged on a new pair of shoes—plum velvet loafers, each embroidered with a lion's head in gold thread—although when I had dressed that morning, Sabrina hadn't been on my mind. The primary object of my bombastic efforts was my new boss, Edmund Benneton—my idol—who was always traipsing around to parties and fashion shows swathed in shades of ruby, amethyst, and citrine, his fingers glittering like Aladdin's cave of jewels.

I'd had a fever dream the night before about our first encounter. In my dream I had been minding my own business, tending the flowers in some meadow—obviously—when Edmund rolled past me in a golden carriage. "*You there!*" he'd called out across a ripple of long emerald grass. He ordered the carriage to a screeching halt, and leapt out in breeches and leather lace-up boots, like some Don Juan on the cover of a historical romance paperback. "*Don't you look stunning!*" he proclaimed. "*How about I be your mentor, and help you get everything you want out of life!*" Naturally I demurred, and just as I was preparing to accept his invitation—to ride with him in his carriage into the sunset, toward a life full of photo shoots and exclusive events—a giant casserole dish fell from the sky, and we were instantly crushed.

Beep! George now pressed his ID against the electronic reader.

"When we go through this door, you cannot speak," he threatened. It was hard to take him seriously, with his little freckles and bright red hair.

He pushed open the glass door, and I prepared myself to enter the hub that had rocketed so many into the glittering cosmos of fame and beauty. A million years from now, when all the friends who loved me were gathered at a dinner party in my honor, I would recount this very moment. Edith Wharton would be sitting at one end of the table, and Edmund at the other. "Ethan used to see beauty everywhere," my mother would whisper to Edith, reaching into her purse for the disintegrating remains of a flower garland I had made as a child. Ms. Duncan would be telling them the *Gatsby* anecdote, and then Patrick Demarchelier would say, "*He was the best editor in the world, always just—full of ideas!*" There'd be roses on the table—lavender and pastel yellow—and everybody would be drinking out of bone-white teacups with Oriental dragons painted on the sides. "*When I entered Régine for the first time*," I would say, my lips holding the attention of the entire room, "*everything was perfect at last.*"

At *Régine*, there would be none of the ugliness that I had spent my life trying to escape, first by losing myself in the pages of the magazine itself and later, as an art history major, through marble and oil paint. Here, people would all have sensitive eyes like mine. They would appreciate the beauty in life, and share my goal of making the world more beautiful.

I followed George through the glass door.

WHEN WE PULLED UP TO THE FRESHMEN GATE ON MOVE-IN day, Yale was just like I'd imagined, with its turrets and wrought ironwork and stained glass windows and—

"Are you sure this is it?" my mother gaped. "This looks like—I don't know, a castle or something."

"*No, mi amor,*" my father corrected, "is just *el famoso* Jail." He laughed at his own joke and almost swerved into a parking meter.

Since the arrival of my crest-emblazoned acceptance letter in the mail, all interactions with my father had included some variation of this overplayed joke: When he attempted to pronounce Yale, his coarse Spanish accent produced "Jail" instead.

It was, I suppose, better for both of us than the icy curtain that had descended after his outburst against my ill-fated earring. At some point, he seemed to actually realize what that letter meant—I was leaving for college, far away, and those months would be the last time I would live with them. Furthermore, in the time he had been silently condemning me, I had been trying hard to actually accomplish something. He had no true context for the significance of "getting into college," let alone getting into Yale; nobody he knew had ever even *done* that, and Corpus Christi wasn't like any town in the Northeast, where every parent drew their child from the womb and then immediately enrolled them in college-prep exams while prodding them to acquire hobbies and passions and admissions-worthy "special skills." Independent of him, I had done this "great" thing, and—most crushing to the pride he took in being the family breadwinner—he was no longer needed to provide for me. Yale was paying for everything. As a mixed-race boy from a small town, with SAT scores and accomplishments to rival anyone who had attended Hotchkiss or Horace Mann, my application was an easy case for a diversity-craving admissions panel.

"You excited, *cabrón*?" he had started asking me at dinnertime, reeling me into one of his sweaty embraces. "I hear dey have good food over der in Jail!"

Now my father said, "*Mira los* prisoners!" I didn't hear him through the wind coursing around my ears. Like a child, I had unbuckled in the backseat and thrust my head out of the window, an uncontrollable grin spreading over my face. I was dressed in a navy double-breasted suit, with an orchid pinned to my lapel, ready to introduce myself to the next four years of my life. The New Haven air cooled my cheeks, coursed through my hair, sent my silky open collar flapping around my neck.

"*Welcome! Welcome!*" yelled face-painted upperclassmen, herding awestruck tenderfoots to their residential dorms. "*If you're in Calhoun dorm, come with me! Branford, come with me! Davenport! Pierson! Berkeley!*"

I couldn't breathe. I was like an orphan who had been disappointed on every Christmas morning of his life, only to be confronted this year by a mountain of presents grander than he'd ever dreamed of.

All around, there were people just like me—odd ones, outsiders. A black father, photographing Wife and Daughter's first tread through the hallowed gate; an Asian girl, calling for her dad to help unload an armchair. One Indian family consisted of at least twelve well-wishers in tunics and saris, crying and clasping their hands together. The beneficiary of their profuse affection was a ponytailed girl in a Yale cable-knit sweater who beamed visibly with relief, like a crab who had outgrown her shell and was finally clattering toward a roomier arrangement.

There were all the white families too. Mostly New Englanders, all of them cut out of some preppy catalogue, the mothers with their pearls and their headbands and the sleeves of their dainty sweaters tied over polo shirts; the fathers with monogrammed dress shirts tucked neatly into pleated khakis; a coordinated mélange of summertime colors—pink and tangerine and azure blue—like a fete of colorful umbrellas gathered on a beach in Nantucket. These were the "old money" families, from a class I had never known—families with stock portfolios and black cards and sprawling legacies of personal worth, with memberships at golf clubs and an ancestral claim to passage on the *Mayflower*. For their progeny, today was a preordained rite of passage, the culmination of a lifelong debate over whether they would choose Yale like Daddy, or Princeton like Mother, or maybe pull a radical stunt and end up at Harvard in the footsteps of loony, lovable Uncle Charlie.

Once we had parked, my father couldn't get enough of them. "*¡Mira estos locos!*" he exclaimed, drunk with bewilderment, and my mother had to scold him for pointing openly at all the white people. Having never traveled beyond Texas or New Mexico, she seemed frightened by all the banners and turrets. She held on to my father's arm in a daze, while I ran ahead of them into the swarming courtyard.

I could scarcely tell what was happening. From the car to my dorm was a blur of green lawns—I couldn't believe how *green!*—but somehow I knew exactly where to go, and when I arrived at the dorm entryway, the door was vaulted and the stairway was stone and the windows leading up the tower (yes, *tower!*) were stained glass, and I realized this wasn't just a dream, but that every day, from this day forward, I would pass through that vaulted door, and climb that stone stairway, and pass those stained glass windows, and when I got to the top there would be a door—*my* door—and inside would be *my* room, full of *my* things, and *my* beautiful new life.

I was jostled by faces moving up and down the stairs, shouting, "*Hello! Hiya! How's it going! What's your name! Where are you from!*" every voice an affirmation of community, of friendship, of you and me and us together, every moment a handshake and a set of white teeth and a new friend, exclaiming, "*I'm Charlotte! I'm Nick! I'm Fatima! James! Cecilie! Francisco! Jessica!*" like hands raised in the air in a collective declaration: *We're here! We did it! We're together now, and we will never be sad or alone or unhappy again!*

Amid the faces were the things getting dragged, exchanging hands, or going *clonk! clonk! clonk!* on the steps—a lamp and a bookshelf and some pillows and an armchair and another lamp and more pillows and a box full of books and a picnic basket and an ironing board and a cage with a parakeet squawking,

"Mildred! Mildred!"—all of things we brought to make this place belong to us.

The transport of my own belongings to my dorm suite was a process quite unseen by me. One moment I had flung open the door to an empty common room, greeted by the sight of a stone fireplace; the next, my parents had appeared with my suitcases and my rolled-up art posters and my potted calla lily, which was already swaying on the mantle.

"What do you think of this here?" my mom asked, holding up to the mahogany-paneled wall my poster of John Singer Sargent's *Portrait of Madame X.* I didn't look up, but ran to the bathroom and dementedly proceeded to test the faucets—open and close—thinking, *My water! My sink! My bathroom!* as the water guzzled out in abundance.

"Elián . . . ?"

I flew back into the common room, where my mother remained with her flabby arm upraised, defenseless Madame X curling dejectedly onto her brown, ponytailed head. Across from the Gothic triptych of arched windows my father had collapsed into a lump onto the pile of suitcases, and was yawningly picking at a back molar with his finger.

"Looks great!" I shouted with a half-glance at my mother, while I poked my head in and out of closets and made a full pointless revolution around the common room.

I just wanted to go outside and smile and nod and shake more hands and collapse onto the feet of one of the noble bronze men standing prim and poised throughout campus, whose job it was to remind us that if we did it right, one day we too could be immortalized forever on a pedestal.

I rushed to a corner, crossing my arms over my chest, and

tried with a deep breath to collect myself. I paced to one side of the common room, then the other, then back, then glanced out the window and, throwing my hands in the air, I bolted out of the suite door—a whole world to explore!—and crashed straight into a mirror.

"It's about time, Daddy," rang out a voice behind the mirror, as resonant as a tap on a wineglass, followed by a "Hear! Hear!" in a crowded ballroom.

It was an antique standing mirror, a white oval frame fastened by a wrought iron pivot to a dainty pedestal. Aside from my own reflection, the only visible sign of a human presence was a pair of feet below, sheathed in patent nude Ferragamo ballerina slippers, each with a chunky one-inch heel and matching grosgrain bow on the front.

"Why do you always let the Powells trap you?" came the voice. "It's all money talk with them—brokers and blue chips . . . it makes me want to just—" the voice faltered under her reflective burden, "*—scream.*" This last word resounded as the bearer of the mirror teetered like the poor, unpracticed cousin of world-bearing Atlas. My reflection swerved toward me. With a clatter of heels, the patent-sheathed feet staggered dangerously backward near the landing's edge.

"Careful!" Reaching out I caught a slender forearm, and the floating mirror swayed blindly toward safety. "Can I help you with that?"

My voice evidently was not the expected baritone. "Oh!" the mirror exclaimed, "I thought you were . . ." She poked her head out from behind the glass.

My heart, which had just a moment ago been racing, came to a halt, like a galloping horse suddenly digging its hooves into the earth. My grasp on her arm reflexively tightened. The mirror's clawed feet pawed the hallway in a series of scrapes, then gave in at last with the crunching finality of wrought iron on stone tile.

The girl blinked her blue eyes, spread apart across exultant cheekbones. Her jaw was wide, almost square, with a shadowed cleft in her chin. A long, unbrushed tangle of thick blonde hair dangled like raw silk around her face.

My grip on her arm slackened. "I'm sorry." I jerked my hand back toward my own body, where I struggled to find an appropriate place for it, and after patting the length of my suit jacket—I must have appeared to have lost something—I gulped, and jammed it awkwardly into my front pocket.

Her hands were on either side of the mirror. Her grip relaxed, and her palms slid down the length of the oval as she cocked her head and drew her gaze toward the orchid on my lapel. Her shiny lips split open like two halves of a ripe, pink fruit, and she burst into a laugh that filled the air with color.

Her eyes wandered next to the buttons on my suit. "Double-breasted!" she remarked. She had a small gap in her front teeth.

With a sidestep from behind the glass, she revealed herself in a toile-patterned sundress, with a knee-grazing skirt blossoming outward from a black satin bow around her waist. She extended her hand toward me. "I'm Madeline," she said, the syllables falling like raindrops onto a lily pond.

"Elián," I managed with a gulp, slipping my hand into hers. I was overwhelmed by the sensation of her pulse against my fingers.

"Ethan?" In the absence of her supervising grasp, the mirror pivoted absently on its hinge like an hourglass. A sudden flash, as the surface caught a sunbeam through the window.

"Did you say—Ethan?" she repeated. But downstairs the entryway door swung open, and suddenly voices were floating up and down the steps again, all the *hellos* and *how are yous*, inquiries about names and hometowns—then someone was upon us: Daddy, or, as I'd come to learn, Mr. Dupre.

"Darling, you've gone up too far," he informed her. With his tucked-in shirt and tasseled loafers, and his blonde hair swept neatly to the side over one ear, he was one of those "*locos*" who had earlier so amused my father. "This is the fourth floor. Your room is on the third."

Madeline turned to him—her hand was still in mine—and started, almost accusingly, "But the Powells . . . I didn't . . . how was I to know?" Then a silly laugh.

He hoisted the mirror onto his chest. "Good morning," he nodded at me, and faced downstairs.

Attempting a noble gesture, I broke the connection between Madeline's hand and my own. "Can I help you with that?" I asked, stepping toward her father.

But he didn't hear me as he concentrated on his labored descent. With a wordless wave to me, Madeline clattered down the steps behind him. She reached out for the mirror's edge, as though her halfhearted touch might alleviate the weight of it.

"I'll see you around?" I called after her.

She turned toward me and shrugged, before disappearing around the corner of the staircase, her footsteps echoing on and on away from me . . . and when I had come to my senses, my mother was calling, "Eliaaán!" and the whole landing smelled like elderflowers.

PAST THE GLASS DOORS AT *RÉGINE*, EVERYTHING WAS WHITE, and everything was quiet. The air felt heavy—thick with an invisible gas. I could sense the faint movements of human beings, tinkling as if they were insects trapped in jars.

I looked behind me as—*clang!*—the doors sealed me in.

George and I were at the beginning of a long passage, with cubicle walls on either side but no view of the people behind them. He heaved through the white hall as if he were walking on a conveyor belt, compensating for his middling stature with colossal strides, never looking back. I struggled to catch up, to breathe. In a lowered voice, he began reciting first-day fundamentals with the ceremony of a twelve-year-old boy giving a presentation in science class—some explanation of the earth's orbit copied verbatim from the Internet.

"Earth's orbit is the motion of the Earth around Régine, *from an average distance of approximately 150 million kilometers away. A complete orbit of the earth around* Régine *occurs every 365.256363 solar days. On average it takes one month—an editorial cycle—for Earth to complete a full rotation about its axis relative to* Régine *magazine so that* Régine *returns to the meridian. . . .*

Hey!" George snapped. "Are you getting this?"

"What?"

On one side the cubicles were replaced by a wall, displaying magazine covers in staggering, larger-than-life dimensions. Each frame contained a cover girl from my dreams, a modern Aphrodite, yet captivity had stripped away their collective power. They gazed out vacantly, a collection of nymphean specimens flattened out and pinned up behind glass for inspection.

"I *said*, we have to prepare for a run-through this morning."

"What run-through?" My heart beat hard, like a captured butterfly—thrashing, confused. Where were all the glamorous people? The colors, the jewels—the outrageous outfits? All I saw was white walls.

"We'll have to do about thirty check-ins," he said, "then organize everything, then—"

"Check-ins?" I asked hollowly.

A door.

"Welcome to the fashion closet," George said, flinging the door open before him.

"Oh." My hand flew to my mouth.

The so-called closet was larger than my house in Texas, with shelves on one side and garment racks on the other—and almost everything inside as white as snow. Along the long wall to the right, floor-to-ceiling shelves were filled with every kind of white shoe imaginable—white stiletto heels, white chunky heels, white kitten heels, white closed-toe flats, white open-toed flats, white ankle boots, white calf-length boots—all white like the shelves they were resting on, so that if you looked very quickly you might think the shelves were only filled with shadows. In front of the shelves were several white folding tables covered with accessories, grouped in an orderly manner by type: hats and handbags and scarves and belts, with gloves and jewelry laid out in velvet-lined trays.

On the opposite side were rows and rows of garment racks. Hanging from the outermost rack were a hundred white, long-sleeved dresses in every texture—chiffon, lace, silk, leather, wool, even snakeskin—arranged from the shortest to the longest and spaced at even intervals, silver hangers protruding from the vast whiteness like the mechanical parts of a giant machine I was now inside.

Through my astonishment I managed to ask, "Is this just where they keep all the white clothes?"

"No, you idiot," George rolled his eyes. "Edmund is styling an all-white-themed fashion story. Obviously. Haven't you ever been in a closet before?"

Gaping all around, I followed George to the left through a gap between the garment racks, which like a hole in a fence revealed a new space, much smaller than the one before. He stepped over a mountain of garment bags and shopping bags on the floor and said, "We sit back here."

Shaped like an L along the interior of the corner was a long workstation: a slick white desk, two Mac computers with matching *Régine* desktop wallpaper, and two black leather office chairs on silver casters. A stiff black leather tote on the first office chair marked George's work area; an adjacent unclaimed seat marked mine.

Beneath overhead cabinets, the wall that defined our workstation was covered by a canvas bulletin board. A dozen sheets of paper were pinned up with clear tacks, listing the addresses of every fashion showroom in New York City, alongside reminders such as:

Hats and headpieces must be returned in their original boxes.

Manolos must be returned by RUSH messenger.

Embellished shoes must be packed with tissue paper.

Givenchy must be returned in original packaging, including Givenchy-brand hangers and garment bags—NO generic.

"Hey," said George. "We have a lot to do. Put your bag down and come *on*."

I barely heard him. What I did hear was the muted whisper of office life: fingers trickling over keyboards, telephone calls clicked to voicemail.

I became suddenly aware that this was, after all, an *office*, and that offices were where adults went every day, and that now, since I was an adult, this was where I would go every day too. My head, always floating in some cloud or another, whooshed down to earth. I felt my feet connecting solidly with the floor, and I realized that twelve stories of steel and glass separated me from the pockmarked concrete face of Manhattan, and somewhere below that rumbled the earth's core, churning fiery magnetic sludge like the rotating belly of a concrete pump and drawing everything toward it, including me, and there was nothing I could do to stop it.

The clouds were far away now, and drifting farther, taking everyone with them: Edith Wharton, and Ms. Duncan, and my Yale friends, all waving down forlornly from an increasing distance, painted figures on a chapel ceiling that was being ripped up and away from me by a crane in the sky.

"*Hey!*" George urged once more, snapping his fingers in my face.

"Wake up," George snapped. "Edmund will be here in two hours for the run-through."

The mention of Edmund Benneton made me come to my senses. I was going to meet my idol! I looked around and took a deep breath through the heavy air, taking stock: I had my own desk, my own computer, my own chair . . . I worked at *Régine* now. This was my dream, right?

For the first time I noticed Sabrina's workstation adjacent to our own, partially obscured by a cubicle wall. Sabrina wore another all-black outfit and was poised primly before her keyboard, her back erect against her chair.

"Hi, Sabrina," I waved, having pledged my determination to erase the negative impressions of our first meeting.

She ignored me, her telephone handset squeezed between her ear and a black silk-covered shoulder as she typed an e-mail while speaking with pointed irritation into the mouthpiece. "Yes, I've been on hold for five minutes already, isn't there anybody who can help me before I decompose? This is *Régine*. We're calling to schedule a shipment to Paris, pick-up will be tomorrow evening, for overnight delivery by eight o'clock the next morning. No, Pacific time," she scoffed. "Of *course* eight o'clock European time. Fifty trunks total, including hatboxes. How much is one-way? Two hundred dollars a trunk? Yes, I just told you, we have *fifty* trunks." She rapped the butt of her pen against her desk like she was sending an urgent message in Morse code.

George interrupted my eavesdropping with a sharp, "Ethan!" He motioned to a monstrous heap of black garment bags and shopping bags by his feet, kicking the garment bag on top with the pointed toe of his oxford. "All of these bags need to be checked in. You unpack and I'll photograph," he said, holding up a small digital camera.

My wordless blink-blink served as enough of a tip-off.

"For God's sake," George rolled his eyes again. "We borrow pieces from the latest designer collections for every photoshoot," he explained. "We need a record of every piece that enters this room, so we photograph each thing when it comes in, and when it goes out. Open that bag," he commanded.

"Goes out? You're sending this all back?" I pointed at the racks all around us, flanked by the wall of shoes.

"No," he corrected. "Now that you're here, *we'll* send it all back." He gestured impatiently for me to open the garment bag which was on top of the heap on the floor.

I unzipped and had barely exposed a sliver of the dress inside before George identified the contents: "Valentino." He reached into the bottom of the garment bag and pulled out a clear plastic drawstring bag—the kind sold full of water and fish at pet stores—except, instead of somebody's pet, there was a pair of glittering white stilettos swimming at the bottom.

I hadn't seen anything so beautiful worn in real life by anyone, *ever.*

George arranged the white stilettos on the floor to photograph—one shoe standing upright, the other on its side, to capture the shape of the heel—while I lifted up the dress for a closer look: head-to-toe white floral lace, with a charmeuse lining and a crystal-embellished bodice.

"Is Edmund styling a celebrity?" I asked George, running my hand over the scalloped neckline.

"Oh, I don't know, I must have missed that when Edmund and I had drinks at happy hour the other day," he said. "Top fashion editors *always* sit down with their unpaid interns to discuss the confidential details of a cover story." He snatched the Valentino dress out of my hands. "Grow up, and get moving."

I unzipped another garment bag. Ferragamo: A patent leather coat, a silk dress shirt, and a baby calfskin skirt, all white. They were the most stunning garments I'd ever touched—more beautiful even than the Valentino—and my heart almost stopped to think that people actually wore them. "Do we get to help him—you know, pick clothes and all that?"

"Just—get out of the way," George grunted, before shoving me with his elbow. He ripped open a stapled shopping bag, and an avalanche of white Christian Louboutin shoes poured onto the floor, their famously red soles boasting the brightest display of color in the whole room. "Here," he said, and thrust the camera in my hand. "Photograph everything, and *fast.*"

I UNPACKED DRESSES, HANDBAGS, AND GLOVES, ARRANGING the latter onto velvet trays on an accessories table, and about thirty minutes before the run-through, I had my first sight of a fashion editor.

She was as long and as elegant as a pruned stem, with skin so dark it was almost violet—a black-petaled orchid in a black Chanel dress suit. Her platinum-blonde hair, waved like Grace Kelly's, caressed her shoulders in a stunning contrast to her face.

"Sabrina?" she called softly, with a tiny lilt of her head and the slightest whisper of a genteel Southern accent that harkened back to debutantes in pearl collars and A-line dresses.

Sabrina, who moments earlier had spewed, *"Can you please connect me to someone with a comprehensive grasp of the English language?"* to some poor person on the other line, slammed the receiver back into its cradle and swung her blonde head up, attention undivided: "Yes, Clara?"

"Who is that?" I whispered to George.

"That's Clara, senior fashion editor." And of course it was. I should have recognized her immediately, having seen her picture a million times—seated with Edmund and Jane and Ava Burgess in the front row at all the major fashion shows, her gloved hands always draped demurely over her crossed legs.

"She's—amazing," I sighed.

"Sabrina," Clara's tone hovered on song, "where are Edmund's accessories from Alexander McQueen?" In one graceful movement she arrived at Sabrina's desk and grazed the surface with her hand, which was as delicate as a doll's, its fingers fused together. Crossing her ankles, she looked like she belonged in a fashion editorial herself.

"They had to be shipped from Paris," Sabrina explained in a professional tone. Her hair today was down, as sleek as a sateen curtain. "I called to check up an hour ago. They said the package was on its way, but—"

"It's *extreeemely* important," Clara implored in her mint-julepy voice. She interlaced her fingers, her nude-polished nails catching the light. "Can somebody just go get it, wherever it is? Don't even photograph it, just bring it straight to me."

The next millisecond Sabrina was back on the phone while Clara was gliding coolly back to her desk.

"I'm calling to track a package," Sabrina barked, in a very different voice from the one she had just used with Clara. "You said it was on a truck an hour ago when I called—where is it? What do you mean you're not sure? I need it *now* . . . If it's not on a truck, what facility is it at? Do you have an address? Do you have a phone number? . . . Yes, I'm looking at that right now on my screen, but your website doesn't help. I need this information *now*. This—is—your—*job*."

"What happens if they don't get it in time?" I whispered to George.

George sighed deeply. "We *have* to get it on time. If we don't, then—"

"Ethan," Sabrina said.

I never found out from George what would happen.

"Ethan, come now." I hadn't even reached her desk before her hand appeared in my face, holding a credit card with a yellow sticky note on it. "Here is my corporate card, here is the address, here is the tracking number. Get the McQueen package here as fast as possible. It *must* be here before the run-through."

Flowing with girlish loop-de-loops, Sabrina's Post-it reminded me of the fake love notes cheerleaders slipped into the fat kids' lockers in high school. I slipped her note into my pocket with her credit card ("Sabrina Walker, Hoffman-Lynch Publications"), and processed my task, turning back to retrieve my wallet from the desk. "Be right back," I told George.

He waved me away as Sabrina rolled her chair into the farthest corner of her cubicle. I checked around in case I needed anything else, and was grabbing my wallet when Sabrina exploded over the wall with the intensity of a jack-in-the-box. "What are you still doing here?!" she shrieked, her head swinging like it was attached to a metal coil.

"I—?" I scampered out of the closet like a child from a haunted house, tripping over the Louboutins, and when I was just outside the Hoffman-Lynch building, amid the whir of cabs and gray suits, my cell phone vibrated with a message from George:

Are you there yet?

chapter three

The girl with the mirror's full name was Madeline Dupre, and she reappeared on our first day of classes. I had been hoping to see her before then around our residence hall, but in the two hectic days comprising freshmen orientation—a blur of welcome banquets and introductory meetings and mixers put on by the Student Council—I just never ran into her.

Now, my heart jumped as I watched her tuck her white chiffon dress underneath her and take a seat opposite me at a round wooden table. She spotted me and waved; I looked hastily down. With a deep breath, I tried to redeem myself with a glance in her general direction, but she had turned red, and was embarrassedly avoiding me by engrossing herself in the erratic dilly-dallying of our professor, Lloyd Pemberton.

Madeline and I were two of one dozen students gathered for

his Political Systems course, a seminar, which thereafter would meet twice a week on the second floor of a hall called Lindsey-Chittenden. Having never been much attracted to politics, I had been invited to join the course by Pemberton himself, a jovial, tweed-loving Brit who served as a supervising dean of my residential hall and who, during the welcoming luncheons, had sat across from me and declined every dish except for four servings of bread pudding.

We would begin with a quiz, Professor Pemberton now announced, which would place us on a political spectrum, essentially categorizing us based on our liberal, or conservative, persuasions. "It's not a *real* quiz—no right or wrong, that is—although . . ." he added, twirling his gray-haired moustache as he helicoptered around the table ". . . the same can be said for any political matter—there's never a right or wrong, and that of course, is the trouble with politics." He stopped mid-putter and crossed one hand over his wooly suit, the other propping up his chin for one second, two seconds; made a "*hmm*" sound; then, remembering us, perking up with his wrinkled finger in the air.

"Introductions first," he said, and began scratching a long horizontal line on the chalkboard—the *economic* spectrum, buttressed on opposite ends by the words *left wing* and *right wing*, then crossed through the center with a vertical line denoting the *social* spectrum. "Before you take the quiz, I want you to tell the class where *you* believe you fall on the political spectrum."

Madeline's crystalline voice resounded first. "I'm sorry to start us off, Professor, because—well, I disagree with both sides of the spectrum and I *despise* the current state of politics. I despise it so much, actually—I plan to be a senator, and turn the whole thing upside down." She glanced around the table. "That might sound silly but it's true," she shrugged, "so nice to meet you all, and vote for me!" She flashed a consciously exaggerated politician's smile, and the whole class laughed.

Professor Pemberton's hand traveled over the board toward the farthest corner of the left-wing realm, where he chalked down a star with Madeline's name. "We'll put you over here for now. A rotten anarchist," he winked, "but I'll admit, a charming one."

I stared at Madeline. Her loose-fitting white dress had a neck tie and sheer billowing sleeves, and I wondered if, like me, she had once endured a confrontation with her own Cesar Montana, and decided that to dress like a lady elevated her to the last true bastion of humanity. The anticipation mounted as the class cycled through introductions: Katy McCutcheon considered herself a "boring liberal," Anthony Griffith-Jones a "libertarian in a love-hate relationship with Marx," and Anne Harrison a "Tea Party conservative, but please, no teabagging jokes, and no, I don't hate gay people," but to me Madeline Dupre could have been the only other person in the room.

Madeline had no idea what she'd stirred in me when we met on the landing outside my dorm—that moment she misheard my name as "Ethan." After she had left with her father, a chill had run through me as I thought: *Why* couldn't *I be Ethan?* College was supposed to be my new life, my new chance—if I was so committed to leaving behind Corpus Christi, then why not leave behind Elián too? I ran to the bathroom and looked hard in the mirror at my generic features: white skin, dark hair. I could pass for an Ethan. Why not just become him right then, before anybody learned my real name?

There had been a name tag on the door of my new suite, but

I ripped it away and shouted, "Mom, Dad! I'll be back soon!"—and the next thing I knew I was at the registrar's office. "I want this name to appear on my ID," I said, and handed the secretary a scribbled piece of paper. "I'd like it in my school e-mail, my transcripts, everything, and ideally, it would change before my professors got their class rosters."

She lifted a pair of pink cat-eye reading glasses from a chain around her neck, and inspected the paper.

"What?" I asked. "Do my parents need to sign something?"

She lowered the paper from her face, and said, "You're an adult now. I could change your name to Martin Luther King if that's what you wanted."

My parents didn't protest. Through an explanation marked by ambiguity and feigned nonchalance, I misled them to believe the school had required the anglicized name change; less than a year later, I would file a legal petition with the court clerk's office of Corpus Christi, and the transformation would be official.

But by the time my turn to speak had arrived in my Political Systems class, freshman orientation—a two-day period featuring the endless exchange of introductions with new peers and professors—had already offered me innumerable opportunities to practice saying my new name.

"I'm Ethan," I said confidently now to my new class. "Ethan St. James." Nobody questioned me, and I continued, "I guess I'm with Madeline, except I don't want to be a senator. Maybe it's simplistic, but governments rarely seem to do much good, for all the money they spend. If it were possible, I wouldn't mind a governmental do-over."

"I should have guessed," Professor Pemberton said. "With

that ascot, you're a threat to the establishment, or at least, to denim and 100 percent cotton. Hurrah! Another anarchist!" The class laughed as he put my star next to Madeline's, and Madeline blushed across the room.

For the rest of the class period I somehow *knew* she was aware of me, even though after my accidental rebuff of her greeting earlier, her every move now attested to the contrary. This went on for several class meetings, during which my desire to make eye contact was met only by fervent avoidance, so that our faces became like two magnets dancing in dipolar repulsion.

I ALWAYS KEPT AN EYE OUT FOR HER AROUND OUR RESIDENtial hall, but only saw her once, when she practically ran away from me ("Hello!—I'm late!—Good-bye!"). Although it was unclear to me what kind of game we were playing, if any, what became quite clear was the extent to which Madeline was deadly serious about her radical politics. By the end of our second class she had established a habit, both endearing and exasperating, of usurping the round table discussion. It manifested in a galloping tangential rant, always scarcely related to the topic, which our professor indulged only in light of her heartbreaking sincerity. Her tirades began the same way every time: Some harmless comment would irk her, setting a timer in her head. She would start to fidget—one hand over the other on the table, then one hand under her chin, or in her hair, or flapping around on her lap while the other tried to contain it, and all along her weight would shift from side to side in her wooden chair—until finally she burst, as flustered as a wet bird, and with a look of breathless desperation thrust her delicate hand in the air.

Upon professorial permission, Madeline would disappear behind a flutter of animated arguments—a series of haphazard gesticulations, her Tiffany bracelet jangling as she denounced the current political state and made frequent use of the ominously indefinite phrase: *"The Institution."* Coming from her mouth, these truculent, almost mannish, diatribes only accentuated her dazzling femininity; the extraordinary contrast was rendered total when, at the end she always concluded that the *only* solution (it was so obvious to her) could be no less than the obliteration of the current governmental structure. Nobody had the heart to contest her, even though hers was obviously not a view shared by our entire class: Her guileless idealism made her so sympathetic that to oppose it with an appeal to conventional rationality seemed almost malevolent.

Soon I had made a silent sport of predicting what would send her over the edge. In the fifth meeting of our class, we were discussing policies for raising the minimum wage, and I sensed Madeline would get worked up by Katy McCutcheon's assertion that "a few extra cents could mean a new microwave for a struggling family." Madeline's face wrenched in regal horror, ignited the typical squirming, then—

"I don't see how these trifling policies solve anything!" she cried out. "Raising minimum wage can't make a fundamental difference to human happiness, and isn't happiness the true goal?" Whenever she passionately jumped in, the sun always conspired with the window to illuminate her with an aura of brilliance: Her hair would seem brighter, her eyes more piercing, and soon her whole body was glowing with otherworldly endorsement. "If the idea is to actually improve the quality of human lives, then the working class of America doesn't need a few cents more so they can save up for a new . . ." she squirmed, her lips uncomfortable repeating a word so philistine as microwave, ". . . a new appliance," she finished.

Now her pre-Raphaelite hair seemed to grow longer and longer, every second spooling further downward over her shoulders.

"The emphasis needs to be on culture—access to beauty and the arts, with enough time to enjoy them. In fact, more useful would be shorter work hours—no more overtime or corporate rat racing. We need a more natural human existence. What happened to being outside? Governments always underestimate the importance of natural beauty on the human psyche—of public parks and gardens and—"

Unprecedented opposition came in the form of Grant Goodwin. "I'm sorry to interrupt," he began. His was a face of noble contours; an aquiline nose and strong, jutting chin, framed by blond hair, were features that made him a well-matched physical, if not philosophical, equal to Madeline. As such, he was perhaps the only other class member whose displays of political passion received a similar blessing, and the dozen faces around the table slanted toward him.

"I appreciate your romanticism . . . I mean, who doesn't like 'culture'?" he continued. "But what you're suggesting is beyond the scope of government. You're talking about a total upheaval of social norms—a whole cultural shift which would devalue quantifiable measures like national income over abstract ideals like—'happiness.'" At this last word, his face expressed a similar displeasure to that of Madeline's over the crass-sounding "microwave."

Yet Madeline, excited to hear her own radical views translated through another person's voice, failed to grasp that Grant wasn't advocating for her worldview, but aggressively disputing it. "That's *exactly* what I'm saying!" she said, with an eager nod.

A lock of his blond hair swept into his eyes. "Well—that wouldn't make any sense," came his conclusive reply. "Think of Brook Farm, or Octagon City. All attempts at Utopia have failed—you can't make happiness a law."

Madeline could only offer a stupefied cock of her head as the actuality of Grant's position settled in her eyes like mercury in a thermometer.

The faces turned to her.

"Who said anything about laws?" she practically whimpered, too distressed to continue in an even tone. "If people just, I don't know, picked some flowers, or watched a sunset every once in a while"—here there was a collective raising of eyebrows—"you wouldn't have all these miserable people, putting in endless hours at these discouraging jobs all because they think somehow the solution to their unhappiness is more money, when of course it's not. It's just—obvious to me."

Attention turned back to Grant, while Professor Pemberton hovered behind him, loathe to interject.

"But people can't be counted on to do anything themselves, even if it's for their own good," Grant said. "To force them, you need laws. And if not laws, then what? You would kindly *encourage* people to pick flowers every day? Suggest they 'look up' more at the sky?"

"Well, sure, and drink more wine and take more trips and have more great romances! Healthy, life-affirming things! It can't be more difficult than funding all these futile government programs, or spending *years* trying to pass a bill that will only add an extra dollar to people's paychecks. How can you *not* see my point, that the root of every problem is this *system* we're all stuck in, this crass worldview, that all that matters is people's credit score? People die *everywhere* without ever experiencing the breadth of human emotion, because nobody considers there's another way."

Grant now manifested his own handsome version of flabbergastedness. "But . . . what about our capitalist infrastructure?"

"Infra . . . structure?" Madeline was scarcely able to push out the syllables. "How about human worth and meaning? That's what government should be trying to raise. If not to be alive, then people are living for the sake of what exactly? Some imaginary bottom line?" She was on the verge of sputtering deflation, pricked by the disheartening realization that anyone could be so staunchly opposed to the ideas she held as truth. "It's the infrastructure that needs to be knocked out! It's like this concrete building that's getting bigger and bigger—it's blocking out the sun, so the government just keeps shuffling people around, from one room to the other, but of course that can't solve anything. The problem is the *whole building*."

She was so vulnerable—hands flailing, cheeks flush with the heat of philosophical passion—that, before I could help myself, it was my own hand flying in the air, and the words came spilling out. *"She's right, you know."*

The spectators snapped in the unexpected direction of my seat. I hadn't spoken much in class before, still accustoming myself to the expressive intellectual atmosphere of college; it was all so unlike my listless hometown that I spent most of my time just listening to everyone else.

"It's not like she's making this up," I said now. "There's loads of precedent for these ideas—think of everybody from Plato to Kant, and nearly every Renaissance poet—they all held beauty up to the highest order of truth. Every great thinker has agreed—human life is nothing without the aesthetic experience. Arts, culture . . . they're not frivolous at all if without them there's no meaning. And if realizing the aesthetic potential of human life is a basic need, and a government has a responsibility to meet the basic needs of its people, then culture should be at the heart of governmental policy . . . Beauty—"

My voice cracked. Madeline was finally looking straight at me, her eyes shining out of the blur of other faces. Before I had even planned the words, I heard myself share my own conviction aloud: "Beauty moves the whole world."

Professor Pemberton tapped his flat hands on the round table. "Very good, everyone. I think we all know now which two among us will be starting a revolution," he smiled. "But alas, Ethan and Madeline, I'm afraid to inform you—the Romantics have already beaten you to the punch, and you're almost two centuries late to join them."

A light ripple of laughter diffused the tension, which rose upward through the air to the crown molding. The professor took the opportunity to herd us back inside the perimeter of our selected texts, and for the rest of the class, I finally had no doubt that Madeline was looking at me. A few times, I had the courage to look up; I tried to be quick, to catch her gaze, but she was always quicker, and the moment my eyes reached hers they were met with a rustling of golden hair and a sudden devotion to the chalkboard, as if her life depended on the memorization of what was there.

After class: the rattling of pens and notebooks into bags.

Madeline took an especially long time packing up her things, neatly organizing her materials—pens, papers, sticky notes—first into a well-orchestrated square on the table. She kept her face glued to the pile, as though she hoped somebody might tap her shoulder so that she could look up in surprise, and utter a startled, "*Oh!*" through her plump lips and the gap between her white teeth.

I started toward her, building up the courage to restore communication between us, when like a thumb over the lens of a camera, Grant Goodwin invaded my view.

"I hope you're not upset," he said, his voice filled with chivalrous détente. "Here, can I help you?" he offered, and reached toward the pile she had so painstakingly tidied up before her.

Caught staring, I forced my head to swivel downward like I had dropped something on the floor.

"Oh, it's all right," Madeline said to him, with a disappointed drop in her voice. I crossed the threshold of the classroom, my strides as regimented as a soldier's, and her words were drowned out by my harried footsteps against the marble floor.

I SPENT TWENTY MINUTES WAITING IN THE LINE AT FEDEX, stuck behind a balding head that resembled the swirling eye of a hurricane. I spent ten minutes waiting for them to retrieve the package, then another twenty in traffic, and by the time I had returned to the *Régine* office with the Alexander McQueen package, I was ten minutes late for the run-through.

Standing by a table of accessories was Edmund Benneton, *Régine*'s fashion director and my personal idol. In a royal blue cape and a matching turban like some great maharaja, I recognized him even from behind.

Sabrina and Clara were crowding around him, along with a male and female editor I hadn't met yet. Behind a fortress of clipboards, they all slanted over his shoulders in an attentive formation, pens poised like bayonets. Edmund was staring at a hat on the table, arms crossed over his chest, drumming jewel-encrusted fingers over his silk sleeves.

I came up slowly behind them, trying to catch Clara's eye so that I could discreetly hand the box off to her. "*It's extreeeemely important*," she had said. "*Don't even photograph it, just bring it straight to me*"—and that was what I was trying to do.

"We thought we could add a couple of 'new' designers this time," Clara was suggesting, finger-miming quotations on the word "new." "Nothing too wild, just—you know, to give you a slight edge."

"A slight . . . edge?" yawned Edmund. "What for . . . ?" He was distracted by his contemplation of the wall—a pause of several seconds—then roused by the recollection of an important fact, which he repeated with the drowsy half-conviction of a bedtime epiphany. "I don't like new designers."

"No, of course not," Clara gently agreed, but, wooing him into wakeful clearheadedness, continued, "though you know sales at *Bazaar* have been creeping up on us—it's all their new stylists, they're taking everything in new directions."

A cantankerous harrumph. "I don't care about the *new* anything," he grumbled, tightening his arms across his chest as the blue silk gleamed beneath the pressure. "The new designers, the new stylists—they last a year and then they all flunk out." With a superior smirk, he peeked out over his upturned nose; when nobody corroborated his assertion, he let out a petulant sigh and conceded to ask, "Who are they, anyway . . . ?"

Clara's finger flicked into the air, then recoiled.

"Well, who are they?" he repeated, this time with a tinge of suspicion. "Who are these new stylists you think I should be concerned about?"

Still nobody answered, and it felt wrong to be eavesdropping from only two feet behind them so I chose that moment to whisper, "Your McQueen box," and held it out toward Clara.

Everybody turned to me at once, wide-eyed faces pulled back in shock. Sabrina's own expression wavered on outrage, as though I had in fact climbed onto a table and revved a chainsaw in the air. If there was anyone who should have been surprised, though, it was me, because I found myself staring for the first time at the visage of Edmund Benneton.

Of course, I had seen him in countless pictures, always swirling about in a cape or a fur coat, but I had never seen his face so close before. Compared to the others, Edmund seemed the least distressed by my interruption, but only because he appeared too tired to muster any expression at all—so unbearably, painfully, wretchedly *tired.* He wasn't much older than forty, yet he had deep frown lines around his mouth and a perpetually worried crease above his brow. On his forehead, beneath the folds of his turban, glistened a layer of sweat as slick as if he'd just rubbed on an ointment, and all I could do was stare at the incredible bags under his eyes: two swollen gray folds like plastic bags full of septic fluid.

"Who are you?" he asked, although he seemed to lose interest the moment the words left his dry, papery lips. I thought I saw his eyelids fall as they capitalized on a stolen moment of silence, while each pore in his loose skin seemed to gaze down like a prisoner through a barred window.

I opened my mouth to reply, but Clara flicked her hand between us—a sort of delicate distraction. She smiled nervously, like I was her toddler and my cries had just interrupted an important dinner. "Don't mind him," she said, with a laugh so forced it reminded me of a girl with a finger in her throat, trying to vomit. "He's . . ."

"He's nobody," Sabrina filled in. As if trying to inflict an electric shock, she clamped a hand over my shoulder then, not wanting to be associated with me, tore it away.

With a hopeful gesture toward the shoes, Clara invited them all to resume consideration of other matters, and they turned away except for Sabrina, whose head directed me to the back of the closet with a nudge so severe I thought her neck might crack.

I stood there for a second in silence. Even in my most pathetic childhood moments I had never been called "*nobody.*" I wanted to shrivel into a fetal ball like the big baby I evidently was, but instead my feet moved inexplicably toward the back of the closet, one dead weight in front of the other.

The small Alexander McQueen box suddenly weighed a hundred pounds. I let it tumble out of my hands onto the floor by George's feet and fell into my chair.

"You're late," George said cheerfully, popping a mint into his pasty mouth.

I groaned, and propped my forehead in my hands on the desk.

"What?" he asked innocently. "I'm sure they're not mad. I mean, I'd have thought from the way you just went up to them that you were all best friends—you, Edmund, and the rest of the gang." He pointed to my shoes. "Go ahead now, why don't you kick back and make yourself at home while you're at it?"

I turned my head up. For an indeterminate number of minutes, I stared at my screen saver—the *Régine* logo twirling blithely about—and when I regained my senses, George was opening the McQueen package, running the box cutter over the top with his pinky out. I had a twisted vision of George slicing his hand, gushing blood all over the *Régine* closet floor. Would the editors stop to help? Or would the run-through continue while Sabrina exiled George to the bathroom before he could stain any of the white clothes?

"These won't work," Edmund was saying now, "this plastic. Who thought that was a good idea?"

I peered at them through a gap in the garment racks.

"It's Lucite," explained the male editor I hadn't yet met, a blond man in his thirties who I'd soon learn was Will, the associate fashion editor.

Sabrina swiped the offending tray of accessories from Edmund's view and laid it to the side.

"I need quality," Edmund said, ignoring him. "*Not* plastic. Who shoots a beautiful woman in plastic?"

I cringed a little at his directness. If before Edmund had given the impression he might fall asleep at any moment, now he was skimming along fast. He seemed to have remembered that there was an office waiting for him, and that the sooner he finished the sooner he could fall asleep in it.

He stared at a tray full of gloves I had laid out earlier and snapped, "I need gloves. Why aren't there any gloves?"

"These are all the ones in white from the Fall-Winter collections," Sabrina assured him. "If you'd like, I can bring you a bigger selection from our archives."

"Yes, what are they doing there, Susan? Please get them."

"Of course, Edmund."

"*Susan?*" I whispered to George, mystified. "He doesn't know her name?"

Sabrina, otherwise known as Susan, had taken two steps in the direction of where the archival gloves were stored when Edmund's voice punctuated the air. "Susan, *where* are you going? Stay here."

"Of course, Edmund."

"You know better than to just walk off like that in the middle of my run-through."

Sabrina mumbled an apology, while I struggled to decide on a train of thought; obviously I was amused to see Sabrina relegated to such an insignificant realm of Edmund's consciousness, but I was also slightly horrified that he would forget the name of someone who worked so closely with him. I turned it over in my head, and decided that because Edmund was a genius didn't mean I should expect him to be perfect; he was required by his job to remember a million names, so why should I villainize him for forgetting one?

"Can we not get anything better?" remarked Edmund, who was now bent over the shoes like a fishing pole over a pond.

I heard Sabrina emit a faint "Ow!" as he flung a pair of needle-nosed pumps over his shoulder.

He was on his feet again. "Is there anything else they can have on their heads?" He poked through the assortment of hats which had been laid out for his perusal. Suddenly, he was seized with inspiration: "THIS. This is it." He raised up an article from the table with two fingers, for all to see. From my occluded view, it was just a piece of limp fabric—like a soggy piece of cheesecloth. "We need more like this. It's perfect. Just imagine it with Look Fourteen from the Marc Jacobs collection, and the thigh-high Ferragamos in patent leather."

The editors scribbled furious notes, nodding fervently. "You're absolutely right," gushed Christine, the other associate fashion editor, who resembled Clara in every way except for the fact that she was white.

"I do *looooove* that," Clara sang.

I watched Will hastily replicate the formless "hat" on his clipboard with a stream of epiphanic scribbles. "I totally understand your vision now," he said. (After the run-through, my own investigation of the captivating headpiece resulted only in confusion, as I remained convinced it was a piece of cheesecloth which had accidentally ended up there.)

"Ooohh, this one I love too." Edmund held up a plastic see-through hat.

I didn't understand—hadn't he just said, "*no plastic*?" Nobody else seemed much surprised.

"Can we see if something can be done about these wrinkles, though—Susan, why don't you steam this?" Edmund held out the plastic hat to the side and dropped it in Sabrina's general direction. She caught it with one hand while continuing with the other to rub the spot on her shoulder where one of the heels he had aimlessly tossed had just clopped her.

"Will, who is doing transparent this season? We need more transparent pieces. Definitely shoes with transparent heels—how about those ones from Michael Kors, can you get those in by this afternoon maybe?" He was careening fast now. "If only Burberry wasn't doing transparent in those garish shades—it'd be smart to work in a few Burberry pieces. See if they don't have a bag or something in regular-transparent, not purple-transparent or orange-transparent or any of those other obscene variations they did this season. Also anything transparent by Wang—Alexander, not Vera—and how about those clutches by Gucci, with the gold studs? Christine, that's your market, right?"

Later that day I would learn that Christine covered all the designers that held runway shows in Paris or Milan, while Will focused on the ones showing in New York and London.

"How are we on credits this issue?" Edmund asked.

Clara flipped through the pages on her clipboard. "We have to squeeze in a Longchamp credit—if we don't feature some pieces, they've threatened to pull their ads again."

It had never occurred to me that the contents of *Régine*'s pages were determined by anything other than aesthetics—let alone by the politics of pleasing advertisers.

"*Blegh*," he replied. "Let them pull the ads, they're hideous."

"We should really include some Céline, and like you said, some Burberry would be good—they're running a six-page spread to kick off their new perfume. Although like you said," she added, to reassure him she had been listening, "we couldn't possibly feature anything in those garish shades."

Edmund glanced at his watch. "All right, that's enough," he said, swinging a tassel on his cape. "Thank you everyone for your work, and keep me posted—although don't expect a reply—and, oh!" He swiveled back around, serious once more. "None of what happened last week with that Dior shoe—that was very disappointing, and an embarrassment. If I ask for it specifically then I'd better get it, and if PR says no, then one of you must have a good reason for me."

Everybody nodded, and he waved over his shoulder as he swooshed through the door. The editors were huddling together, clucking in hushed voices, when suddenly the door flew open and Edmund poked his turbaned head through the crack. "Does anybody have any contact solution? My eyes are all dried up again."

Sabrina pitter-pattered over to her desk to get some, and he plucked it from her hand—"Thank you, Susan"—and disappeared again.

George was on his feet. "Time to clean up," he said, snapping his unscathed fingers in my face, no blood in sight.

What I hadn't realized while watching the run-through was that a complete upheaval of everything George and I had prepared that morning had occurred just beyond my narrow view in a period of less than fifteen minutes. Velvet-lined accessory trays had been dumped out, carefully lined-up shoes tossed asunder. I half-expected a Jacobin from the French Revolution to pass by with a flaming torch, having lost his way to the Bastille and desecrated the wrong place.

Sabrina shot past our desk, still rubbing her arm. "George, have you grabbed lunch?" she asked, taking a seat at her cubicle.

George shook his head.

"Go. Fifteen minutes."

George rushed out, and Sabrina said, "Ethan, I need to speak to you. Bring my credit card and your cab receipts."

My stomach turned. From the excitement in her razor-like tone, I could tell this was going to be enjoyable for only one of us. I dragged myself over to her desk and pulled out the two cab receipts I had stuffed into my pocket, followed by her credit card, and slid them toward her keyboard.

As though by handling her credit card I had somehow contaminated it, she brushed it exaggeratedly against her black blouse. "I really hate to reprimand you on your first day, Ethan," she said with disingenuous docility, "but perhaps I was unclear." She used the edge of her corporate card to flatten out my crumpled receipts, ironing them out once, twice, three times against her desk to demonstrate to me the unacceptability of wrinkles at

Régine, then looked up. "I hired you as an *intern*." She returned her card to the designated slot in her Céline wallet. "You're nobody's equal here—not even George's."

She bent over to return her wallet to a black Hermès bag at the foot of her chair, while I waited like a carcass hanging from a butcher's rack. The handbag fell into the recesses underneath her desk, where her delicate ankles were crossed beneath her black lamé skirt. She turned back up toward me and folded her hands coolly over her knee.

"That incident ten minutes ago will be the last time in this office you speak before being spoken to. Interns just don't do that here. *You* just don't do that here. Not to mention that at *Régine*, ten past two o'clock is not the same as two o'clock." She put a cold hand on my forearm. "I'm not mad, of course. I mean, I'm sure things were different at Yale," she said, with a crackling veneer of compassion. From the cock of her eyebrows, and the satisfaction in her curled lips, I knew the knife in my stomach was coming next: "Unfortunately, here you'll have to *work* for the right to be treated as an equal." She exaggerated the word "work" as if she were teaching it to me for the first time.

Then she rewrapped her fingers around the handle of the blade and gave it one last twist. "You said it'd be easy, right? Who knows? If you work hard enough, then maybe . . . Didn't you want a job here? . . . Maybe one day you can have this."

She gestured across the six-by-six-foot corkboard cubicle that I was meant to covet—and which, in so many ways, I did—then, catching a glimpse of an unread e-mail, she gasped "Prada!" and her hands were sucked toward her keyboard like magnets.

The e-mail that had swallowed her undivided attention had the subject line *Emergency*. Prada needed reassurance that

Look 7 could be picked up from the set of Edmund's white-themed photo shoot in time for a *W* cover shoot the next day. I knew this because in Sabrina's spacious cubicle there was nowhere else to look but over her shoulder at the computer screen, and I couldn't help but read what was there. I wasn't sure if I had been dismissed, but Sabrina's words had left me flush, and the awkwardness of standing there was merely deepening the discomfort of my debasement.

I turned, and she said, "I left a plastic hat on your desk—can you steam out the wrinkles? You'll find the steamer in the corner by the gloves."

"Of course," I said through a veil of calmness, adding under my breath, "*Susan.*"

Sabrina didn't hear me, which was probably for the best.

I FOUND ON MY DESK THE HAT SHE HAD BEEN REFERRING TO. It was shaped like a floppy transparent bell, and I didn't see any wrinkles in it, but what did I know? I rolled out the steamer from the corner where she had instructed me to look. It looked a little like a snake, attached to a pole with a large mystical glass container on the bottom and a swirly hook on the top, where its head rested.

I had never seen one before, and I wasn't sure what to do with it. George was gone for lunch and I definitely couldn't ask Sabrina, so I searched on the Internet: *How does a steamer work?* The search results instructed me to fill the glass container with water, so I set out carefully with it in my hands, trying to find the bathroom.

Beyond the hallway through which I had entered that morning, *Régine*, I discovered, was more puzzling than a topiary maze—just one sharp corner after another, and a hundred cubicle walls in rows, all white—and it was only after running into several dead ends that I found the women's bathroom. I figured the men's bathroom would be next to it, but all I could see was an unmarked door. When I tried to open it, it was locked, and on the other side there was no door at all—just Kate Moss on the wall, her eyes glazed over with indifference.

I didn't want to take too long, so I glanced down the empty hall, and darted inside the women's bathroom. I opened a tap straightaway, and while the water gurgled into my vessel, I thought I noticed a familiar feminine scent, before realizing—the women's bathroom at *Régine* smelled like Chanel No. 5.

Had the smell lingered from an earlier spritz, or did the women's bathroom at *Régine* always smell this way? As I was contemplating the possibility that the supply of the perfume was provided by *Régine* for the janitor to mix into his mop bucket, the door opened and an older woman stepped inside: tall, white-haired, wearing a loose-fitting button-down shirt and a pair of slim blue jeans. She was looking down, immersed in the task of wiping a stain on her collar, but as she drew closer, I recognized her as easily as I had Edmund. She was Jane Delancey, the creative director of *Régine*.

On replaying Sabrina's caustic overtures in my head ("*You're nobody's equal here*"), I remained rooted like a tree stump, pretending not to exist while I prayed Jane Delancey wouldn't notice me, a boy, in the women's bathroom. Water was spilling loudly over the top and down the sides of the container now, but I didn't dare touch the faucet.

"I haven't seen you before," Jane said, her face still lowered as she strode to the adjacent sink and passed her napkin under a stream of water. She scrubbed at the stain—it looked like tomato sauce—and a teeny diamond earring wiggled in her fleshy lobe. "My mother used to say I was a clumsy little girl," she said to me, or the stain. "Now I'm just a clumsy old lady."

I smiled nervously as our faucets gushed in unison.

In photographs she had looked distinguished enough, her forehead flowing with sage-like wrinkles and her long cloud-white hair swept up in an all-American ponytail. In real life, however, she seemed quite plain in her catalogue-white dress shirt and classic tapered jeans, with not a "statement piece" in sight. Her shoes were her only indulgence: white pumps with a diamond buckle—Roger Vivier, I conjectured—and even those were nowhere near as opulent as what she could get away with in her position. For better or worse, she was as simple as a sheet of laundered linen, subtly trimmed, flapping gently on a clothes-line.

Jane looked up from her tomato stain. "Are you a woman?" she asked.

Like a cool breeze, her gaze sent a light shudder through me. Her eyes were pale blue, almost clear, and gave the impression that she could see better than an average person.

I gulped, couldn't speak.

"Okay," she nodded acceptingly, then turned to go. "The men's bathroom is by the copy room. Either way, that's a wonderful suit."

I tried to say thank you, but choked once more. When her wrinkled hand was pressed against the door, she turned her face calmly back to me. "I'm Jane," she said, and was gone.

I turned off the water and scurried back to the fashion closet, afraid I had taken too long; when I returned, Sabrina had gone to pay a deliveryman in the Hoffman-Lynch lobby for her lunch and the only person there was George.

"*How does a steamer work?*" he mocked, pointing to the computer screen where I had unwisely left my innocent search query on display. "What are you trying to steam?"

I gestured to the flaccid plastic hat on the desk. Approaching the steamer, I realized the container in my hands was only half full; after all that, I had sloshed water all over my pants scampering down the hall.

George laughed right in my face, and I could smell the mint he had just tossed in his mouth. "You can't steam plastic, you idiot."

"Sabrina asked me to."

He rolled his eyes. "Not my problem." The next minute the steamer had seared a pink blister into my palm like a cow-brand, and George was snorting with pleasure.

chapter four

Outside the nightclub, under an ominous cloud of cigarette smoke, a funereal line of black and gray figures cast long, spidery shadows.

"How joyless, these 'grown-ups,'" remarked Madeline, with an accusatory lilt on the last word. Sheathed in a milk-white kitten heel, her foot dangled out of the taxi as she waited for my gentlemanly arm to escort her. When she got hold of me, she hopped onto the curb, offering me a blue-eyed blink that said, "*Well—let's* go *already.*"

An hour before, I had been welcomed into her parents' Upper East Side apartment by her mother, who smiled through a face full of well-placed cosmetic injectables, and commented favorably on my green blazer. I blushed, and thanked her with a sense of great honor; a compliment from Mrs. Dupre seemed as sacred and true as any from a deity who had been mummified.

Sitting with his legs crossed on the damask couch, Mr. Dupre waved at me from behind a copy of the *Times*, while above his head soared a portrait of their family photographed before their mantelpiece a few feet away. I had once tried to wrangle a similarly respectable image out of my parents. Among the rest of my books, I had read a lot of biographies growing up and, from Picasso to Gandhi, it seemed that everyone with the hope of any bright future at all had at least one early family portrait in which they visibly radiated with the promise of greatness, flanked by a dignified-looking mother and father. I certainly didn't consider myself highly enough to anticipate a biography would be penned in my honor, yet—who knew? If I ever managed to get out of that small town, it would be good to have at least one decent photo of my parents and me, on the off-chance someone thought to write a chapter about my humble beginnings.

"What for, *cabrón*?" my father had grumbled, preferring to lounge like a half-naked lump in front of the television than to get dressed up and miss a *fútbol* game. Having gotten the idea in my head—and considering it my parents' duty to oblige me at least a single indulgence in life—I begged for it with an insistence my peers reserved for a puppy or a go-kart, and in the end my parents didn't even sit up straight. We came out looking quite how I should have expected: as dignified as a bunch of kumquats.

But the Dupres appeared to be prepared for a portrait every moment: well-postured, with the slow-moving grace of glaciers.

I turned my head to a rustle of taffeta at the top of the staircase.

"Is that you?" exclaimed Madeline with a hint of surprise, as though she hadn't in fact been expecting me. She had a way of making me feel like every moment was a revelation, as if the whole world teemed with blossom-ready buds that, if I went along with her, would have no choice but to divulge their fragrant secrets.

My eyes filled with the sight of her hovering between the chandelier and a cascade of shimmering marble, framed under a mahogany arch like a goddess in an Alphonse Mucha lithograph. She wore a pleated knee-length cocktail dress, bell-shaped and Oriental blue, with the chain of her quilted Chanel purse over her bare shoulder. Just-washed hair fell around her face, tousled and still damp. She rested her hand on the banister in a Greek contrapposto, then pointed her toe toward me, and descended slowly. When she had tiptoed halfway down, her grace was replaced with characteristic urgency as she beamed at me and ran clattering over the remaining steps.

I caught her at the bottom in a leap of outstretched arms and billowing hair, her taffeta dress crushed under my arms as I swung her in a half-moon swirl. When we were still she collapsed onto my chest and laughed.

"Anyone would think we'd been apart for years," she said.

But really, it had only been a week ago that we'd walked together through a Gothic arch on Old Campus amid a stream of navy-blue caps and gowns, the two of us holding hands in the air—the champions of something—after four years of an unclassifiable kinship.

She separated from me, then spun around to ensure I'd got a good look. "Just look at us!" she exclaimed, as if somehow I too commanded the attention that followed her like a shaft of morning light.

"You look stunning," I said.

Madeline kissed a corner of my eye and pulled me up the steps.

"Just look at us!" she repeated over the railing to her parents.

The whole foyer fell away into gilded bas-relief, and when we were upon her bedroom door she pressed her knowing hand over the bag of marijuana in my blazer pocket, and smiled. The white door gave in, and we tumbled inside.

Golden trophies stood proud on every shelf, boasting eminence in horseback riding, ballet, and Model U.N., while the ivory floral-patterned walls were decorated with newly championed idols: Malcolm X over the nightstand and Che Guevara smoldering with purpose behind the lace bed canopy from Madeline's girlhood.

The canopy rotated slowly as we fell onto the powder-blue sheets, faint lacework shadows playing on a bedside picture of the Dupres in front of the Eiffel Tower.

"Do you think your mother noticed the smell?" I asked, as my elbow sunk into the mattress and I began to pack my glass pipe over her sheets.

"Just spray it with cologne next time," she suggested with a shrug.

The herby stench mingled in the air with the lingering aura of Madeline's elderflower shampoo. I compressed the pillowy green buds into the pipe's bowl with my thumb while she turned onto her side and draped her blonde head upon an extended arm.

"I hope I'll have some brain cells left," Madeline said. "After all those graduation parties, a lot of them just had a laugh and disappeared on vacation." She added, "Woohoo!," which in her head must have been the sound of a brain cell on a road trip.

"Do you not want to smoke?"

"Of course I want to!" she swelled, and the next moment she was coughing into my shoulder. "You haven't told me a thing about *Régine*," she said, waving away a cloud with one hand. "Are all the girls there prettier than me?"

"Please," I rolled my eyes, raising the pipe to my own lips. "Nobody compares."

She seemed dubious and, reminded of other beautiful women, sat back a little straighter. "They're like in all the movies? Glamorous, and tall?"

We passed the pipe between us, and I told her all about *Régine*—about the glass doors and the white clothes and the steamer, with its mystical snakelike head and the glass container like a fishbowl. She laughed over Edmund saying, "*Who shoots a beautiful woman in plastic?*" and gasped with incredible sense of personal offense when I told her that Sabrina had called me "nothing."

"Nothing?! Wait till you take her job, that whore!" She winced at her own word; Madeline considered herself a feminist and, in theory, hated put-downs against other women. "I'll call her what I want," she maintained with an impassioned firmness. "She'll be lucky if I never run into her, or . . . Who cares about her! God, I'm so excited to introduce you now," she changed the subject, "tonight, and every night from now on—I'm going to say, 'This is Ethan St. James, and he works at *Régine*, and he's going to be famous!'" We laughed as smoky ringlets unspooled before our faces like promises of fame and fortune, and for a little while she held my hand before, suddenly, she exclaimed, "I almost forgot! I have news too!"

"Another boyfriend for me?" I drummed my fingers on her bare knee.

"Nooo," she scowled, brushing my hand off. "I'm done with that pointless game. You don't know what a disappointment it is to find you someone, then have you dismiss them outright because they don't know who Renoir is, or they bring you the wrong flowers on the first date."

"Those were both horrible, *plain* boys," I protested. "Car-nations? I don't know how you ever thought— "

"You're pickier than I am!" She shook her head, even though that was a lie. Then, on a note that, in her altered consciousness, seemed like an important segue: "You know, since graduation, I've decided to only eat peas. And drink champagne."

"How unlike you," I said with mild disinterest. It sounded to me like her normal diet.

"Yea, it's an ethical thing. Animals, deforestation . . ." Madeline coughed suddenly, eyes watering, then remembered, "My poor makeup." She dabbed with her pinky finger at the corner of her sparkling eyelid.

"So what's your news?" I asked. "The peas?"

She pushed at me and coughed again. "Oh come on, I can't remember."

I reached out before I could stop myself. "God, your fingers," I breathed in awe. "They're my favorite thing."

She held out her fingers over my hand for inspection, then nodded in agreement. They were fingers made long and slender from a childhood of compulsory piano practice, which—never having had such a luxury as music lessons—I imagined as Madeline pounding *Für Elise* onto the keys and then pleading, "*Daddy, I've got it,* now *can we go to Central Park?*" to which he would reply, "*You missed a note, try again and we'll see*," and she'd give a pouty harrumph, and a rebellious stomp of her pink Mary Janes. Privileged fingers.

I took her hand in mine and felt her pulse through her silky palm.

The next moment had the inevitability of a setting sun. Outside a siren whistled through the night sky like a firecracker—then all was quiet as the bedroom blended like an oil pastel.

Madeline ran her hand up my forearm. She leaned forward. The bed creaked.

Her fragrance washed over me; a cool mist after a summer rain, diffusing the aroma of fallen fruit. My eyes closed. Reverberations left my chest and came pulsing back, as though my heart was submerged in water. Then her lips—her wet, familiar lips—were against mine.

The wave of silence rose up and filled the bedroom, lapping over my ears, and I was swimming.

I felt the immediate stiffening in my pants as my blood swelled in my veins like a pupil in a dark room. My tongue left my mouth, felt her teeth—soft against hard. There was a whisper of taffeta as she shifted slowly onto me.

Then, the searing heat of objection inside my chest. The water level fell around me. Its surface slapped my ears, and I could hear the siren outside.

"I'm sorry—" I said.

But Madeline cupped my face in both hands, pressed her forehead against mine. "It's okay. Just kiss me." A series of pecks, interspersed with: "Just think . . ." kiss ". . . both of us . . ." kiss ". . . together . . ." kiss ". . . at last . . ."

She must have felt the stiffness of my lips. "What's wrong?" she whispered, shaking my shoulder. "Things can be different now . . . now we've graduated, left that all behind . . . I know we should be together," she went on. "And just look at you, you always get so excited—" She reached down between my legs.

I seized her hand before she could confirm my unsubtle arousal. "Madeline, please!"

A snap of fingers!—the end of the hypnosis session, and the room returned instantly to normalcy—everything clear, defined, separate. I felt like a soul sucked back into a body after a lucid dream.

"What? Don't you see—this is what's meant to happen?" Then dejectedly: "You're my best friend. This is what best friends do."

I swallowed a ball of misgiving in my throat, eyes lost in the shiny crumples of her iridescent dress. "Not after Dorian."

Madeline winced and raised her hands to her temples.

"It's true though. I can't replace him."

"For the love of God," she seethed. "I *always* loved you more than Dorian."

This was difficult to believe. She seemed to realize this too, and she gazed out of the window as another siren roved through the city.

"Come on," I urged. Our friend Blake was waiting for us at the club.

Madeline's eyes remained drawn to the dark square.

"Hey," I rested my hand on her knee and she remembered me. "Are we all right?" I adjusted on the bed.

"Oh shut up," she scowled. "Yes, we're all right, I'm just . . ." She turned and slipped her hands into mine. Then she shook her head as though she was casting off a troubling thought—rebuffed herself with a tug on my arm. "Let's go to the club—like *adults*!" Since graduation, she had gotten a vicious pleasure from the notion of our embodying this unlikely role.

I laughed at her. "We're hardly adults."

"Speak for yourself," Madeline said. She collected her hair in one swooping twist, and made a businesslike bun on her head. Back erect, she said, "I've gotten a hundred times more dignified in the past week."

"Oh really?" I snuck my hand under her upraised arm and tickled her. She shrieked with laughter. Her hair cascaded over her shoulders as she lowered her elbows against her chest. "Is that really the word you'd use?" I asked. "Dignified?"

She fell backward into a parachute puff of soft sheets. Squirming, she squeezed her arms against her sides and rolled onto her stomach like a taffeta cocoon. "All right, all right!" she howled, barely a breath left in her lungs. "Let's go to the club like kids!"

After we collected ourselves, we saw that we had scattered gray ashes from my pipe all over her sheets. Madeline tried to stand up, tripping on a pair of mislaid heels, and we spent the next moments laughing and stumbling in a clouded stupor toward the door.

MADELINE REMEMBERED HER "BIG NEWS" WHEN WE WERE IN line outside the nightclub. "Guess who's going to be an actress?" she shook me, practically shouting.

"What?"

"That's the news! I'm going to be an actress!"

The people in front of us were smoking up a heavy cloud over our heads, while beneath our feet the cobblestones flickered from the light of the blinking club marquee.

Madeline had never expressed the slightest interest in acting. As far as I knew, her life plan had been the same since our first class together: Attend Georgetown Law School after Yale and then work toward election to the Senate, where she would wear a dress suit every day and commandeer the world to adopt her anarchistic politics.

Even though half the time her political science classes put her into a blind emotional rage (she had no shortage of biting words with which to castigate the "small-minded politicians" in power), she was convinced that "setting things right" in Washington was the cross-like burden of having sprung from a manger of privilege. She told me once she couldn't remember when her radical ideas had taken hold—just that she had always been a purist, and that since she was a girl she had observed the state of the world from afar and thought, *"This is a disaster, and it needs to be fixed, every ugly last bit of it."* More than anything, she was determined not to be merely "humored," and after a life of being patted on the head, had started wearing heels in an attempt to appear older and more put-together than she really was. When she ran every year for Yale's College Council, she made a concerted effort to wear blazers over her little dresses so that nobody could say she'd had the advantage of being "hot," and once she had won, which she always did, the hours she spent practicing speeches in the mirror numbered in the dozens every year.

"What about Georgetown?" I reminded her.

Now she looked up at me with a sigh and said, "I just can't do Georgetown anymore. Everyone is too serious there—I'd lose all my enthusiasm before I got to the Senate."

"Well—that is news," I admitted.

Ahead of us in line, we overheard someone say, "I'm not here to party, I'm here to get fucked up. I'm like the Martha Stewart of getting fucked up."

Madeline continued, "What I've decided to do—to try and

save the world, you know—is be an actress. Actresses are always saving the world. I'm going to gain millions of fans, and then I'm going to introduce my four-step plan . . . you remember my four-step plan?"

Madeline had a four-step plan for when she got to the Senate. The written record of it made frequent condemnation of "The Institution," and delineated the restoration of human dignity through a rejection of "crass capitalistic infrastructures."

"It'll take much less time than being a politician," she said, "and anyway, no one listens to politicians." She tugged at my arm. "What do you think? I know it sounds a little—" she implied some indeterminate adjective with a flick of her wrist "—but it's the only *surefire* way." Perhaps contemplating the obvious illogic of this, she waited one second before rushing in again, "And before you say I don't know how to act—actors never know how to act anymore. The directors just edit the best parts in."

"I guess I'll dress you for award shows then," I permitted myself at last.

She turned her face up toward me and beamed. "I knew you'd like the idea! You make me so happy." She threw her arms around me, and her small breasts pushed up hopefully against my chest.

"And you make me such a hypocrite," I muttered, my arms encircling her waist. As though the scene in her bedroom had not unfolded only a half an hour prior, I lowered my face onto hers.

Her hand tightened on the back of my head.

When our faces floated apart and her eyes opened, I said, "Just one more," and our lips met one last time before her mouth was hovering over my ear.

"I don't blame you for your . . . reservations," she whispered.

We rocked there, side to side, our feet together and her hands around my neck like we were preparing for a slow dance. Then she held me at arm's length. "But you have to promise me one thing. " I could see the words churning in her head. "If, in a year, things between us are the same . . . if we haven't found anyone else, and we still love each other—which of course we will—then . . . you have to forget the past." She held me by the forearms and with an impassioned shake said, "We'll both forget the past—those things that came between us—and we'll get married. Just one year, and . . ."

"A year . . . ?" was all I could say.

She knocked her little fist against my chest. "Like you'd do better than to marry me."

"No, but give it five years, at least!"

"Oh, come on!" she implored. "We'll be dead in five years! And even if we're not, I won't be beautiful anymore, and you'll . . . No, it has to be a year. Then—I'll be an actress, and you'll be a fashion editor, and you'll see, I know you'll change your mind."

"All right," I agreed with a laugh. "I'll wear a white tuxedo."

She beamed and swelled up to her tippy toes as her phone vibrated in her Chanel handbag. "Let's get reckless tonight—just drunk and free, to celebrate . . . I don't know, adulthood, everything!" Madeline reached into her bag to take a call from our friend Blake, who was meeting us inside. "One second," she told him, and she winked at me. She ducked beneath the velvet rope onto the sidewalk, one finger pressed against her ear to hear better.

A black car pulled up. The driver came out and motioned to the security guard at the door, who nodded as the driver held up three fingers and opened the car door. I saw through the marble-like black window a single glint: an eye, or an earring. Then, as promised, there were three of them, sunglass-shrouded faces bowed, and in the time it took for a murmur of speculation—"*Is that? Who?*"—their long shiny legs had sliced through the velvet rope and they disappeared inside like knives into a kitchen drawer.

It was only another second before two more people skipped the line—sort of came at it from the opposite direction and didn't even say anything to the bouncer, just stood there for a moment and waited for him to notice them. The first one was a model, for sure. She was taller than everyone by at least a head and, in a plain black motorcycle jacket, making no effort to impress. She wasn't a celebrity, but I felt like I had seen her face around, or at least like I *could* have seen her face around—she was just that type.

Behind her unapologetic mass of teased-out hair, a boy's face emerged.

I had to catch my breath. It was a face I knew almost better than my own: those bottomless eyes, those lips which were always parted on the edge of all the pain and pleasure in the world. I saw the rush of Frisbees over the campus lawn and felt the accidental brush of warm skin, heard laughter echoing off the flagstone paths of the Old Campus quad.

The bouncer said something to him and he sort of smiled and shrugged, hands in his pockets. The next minute he vanished, just another shiny thing, into the shadows.

Madeline swooped back under the velvet rope beside me. "I haven't told you, you look so attractive tonight," she said, tracing her hand over the lapel on my green blazer. Then—"What's wrong?"

I could barely bring myself to say it after the events of the past hour. "Dorian," I said, and now the name felt vulgar on my lips. "I think I just saw Dorian."

She stiffened like a board. "Dorian-is-in-*Paris*," Madeline said loudly, pounding each word like a piano key. She glowered meaningfully, then struck a high-pitched key, and she tinkered off, "Don't bring him up again!" She glared at me, then looked away, and didn't move.

I put my arm around her shoulders, remembering the grievous shape of them when Dorian left us. She had been draped like a shroud over my knees—head down, her hands pressed into her face, gobs of saliva and mucus swinging through her fingers and her spine heaving as she tried to suffocate herself in the folds of her dress, moaning, "Dorian's gone . . . Dorian's gone . . ." Her tears had soaked through my pants.

"I'm sorry," I said to her. "I guess I just . . . have him stuck in my brain now."

"Well, unstick him please," she replied, giving my hand a firm squeeze, "before he ruins our night."

In front of us now a girl was yelling, "Are you fucking kidding me? We've been waiting in line for fifteen minutes, and you didn't ask any of those other people for ID or *any*thing." She turned to her three girlfriends, hoping with a look of outrage to gain their solidarity.

None of them moved to her defense, and the bouncer just waited. In a dress the shape and color of mashed potatoes, the girl looked like a helping of Thanksgiving dinner. Her thick fleshy legs were pink like uncooked turkey, and each one disappeared into a high heel without ever turning into an ankle.

I got a sickening feeling, predicting an unsavory end.

"I'm sorry, ma'am," the bouncer said, "I'm going to have to ask you to leave." She had made his job easy. Now he didn't even have to lie to her.

"You have to be kidding," she protested. "You have to be fucking—" She swiveled, unbalanced, toward her three friends. "Come on!" One of them looked like her—too big, tottering around like a drumstick—but the other two were reasonably good-looking and probably knew they could get into the club if they stayed. They looked at each other regrettably as their friends swooped huffily under the velvet rope, and after a brief lingering, followed.

The gaggle of girls in front of us swelled to fill the space.

"Together?" the bouncer asked them. "Do you have a party name?"

Between violent gum-chomping, one of the girls said "Bruno," in a loud Russian accent and flipped over her skinny wrist with a harmony of clinking bangles. The bouncer stamped their over-accessorized wrists while the security guard unclipped the velvet rope and skimmed their foreign IDs.

"Should we just say 'Bruno'?" I whispered harriedly to Madeline.

"Oh, just look at us," Madeline hushed me. "We don't need Bruno."

"He with you?" the bouncer asked Madeline.

Our entry was authorized by a red stamp in the shape of a Gothic cross. I heard a sheepish voice behind us whisper, "Can we still get in? We're not really with them." It was the friends of the Thanksgiving dinner duo, pointing to their blundering friends trying to catch a cab.

Madeline grabbed my wrist and rushed me ahead through a black hallway that throbbed like an artery. Two guards in black suits and bowler hats were posted there by a dark curtain. Tossing her arms up extravagantly, she cried, "Open up, boys!" and the curtains parted with a dance-like swing of black fringe. "Oh, how *diviiiiine*!" Madeline laughed.

On one side of the room, a congregation of plush velvet booths facilitated the clinking of liquor-filled glasses between crossed-legged guests; on the other, an empty cabaret stage rose up from the shadows, awaiting the abuse of some inebriated high-heeled feet. Beautiful women hung drunkenly on the arms of eligible bachelors, and everyone was gulping gossip and champagne, overflowing. As accident and design pressed their bodies together, perspiration pushed the perfume out of their pores and the intertwining notes of fragrance burst up above us like fireworks. The ceiling was a mirror—a distorted, murmured re-telling of the scene below. Through it everything happened not once but a million times, reflected in every bead of sweat and glossy lip.

I thought once more of the fat girls outside, plodding around like somebody's dinner, trying hopelessly to catch a cab, and I felt the strangest pang of guilt for getting inside the club. Everyone everywhere pulsed *Glamour! Heat! Sex!* and it almost didn't seem fair that, on a Monday night, so many bodies could be stolen from the cold corners of the world and rounded up in this sophisticated furnace. I remembered my own face—my own *ordinary* face, with its plain, boyish angles—that, without the tortoiseshell frames and the youthful mop of hair and all of my *style* (which really, was just another word for effort) could not compare to what I saw around me, and thought, *Did I somehow fool the doorman, or am I really in possession of a physical beauty formerly unbeknownst to me?* Was it just the place, the lighting, or did every person in here pulse with the seductive carnality of an animal heart? Suddenly I had the urge to check a mirror just in case, by passing through that black curtain, I had transformed, become a hundred times more handsome.

Madeline had spotted our friend Blake—tall, Herculean, head poking up above the crowd. His prince-like black hair escaped from under a baseball cap, and he wore a gray suit jacket over a white linen shirt. She waved toward the back of his head, advancing toward him with me in tow.

Blake turned, exclaiming, "What the fuck is up!" He couldn't have known to turn around, but Madeline had a way of being detected by other good-looking people in crowded rooms. He hugged me, and his familiar laugh resounded with all the comfort of his jockish self-assuredness.

I'd met Blake during the first weeks of freshman year, before my friendship with Madeline had been properly kindled. I was reclining against a tree trunk reading *Swann's Way* for my Intro to Narrative course, when his wayward football plummeted straight into my spectacled face. I clonked to the grass ("*like a puppet*," he later said) and woke up an hour later at the Yale Hospital, with Blake hulking above me, his guilt-ridden countenance dripping sweat onto my face from above.

Madeline kissed Blake's cheek, and held on to the lapels of his jacket. "Can you believe it, all of us in the *real world* together?"

On my insistence, Madeline and Blake had gone on a single date not long after my broken nose had healed. This was before the complications of my advancing self-awareness, when, still under the assumption that I was gay, I saw nothing wrong with setting up Madeline on a date with someone else. The next day I was treated to two entertaining accounts of an evening deemed unsatisfactory by both parties ("*All she wants to talk about is antiques*," and "*He didn't know who* Wordsworth *was*").

Now Blake enveloped our shoulders in a fraternal embrace. "Come on," he said, pulling us toward a red velvet booth where no one was sitting. Madeline squeezed in so she could be in the middle of us, and we were greeted by a cocktail waitress who wore her hair in a bun, with a little wisp on the side dyed lilac.

As though she didn't always get exactly the same drink, Madeline pretended for the briefest second to consider her choice before eagerly clapping her hands together. "I'll have a martini! Boys, you'll have one too, right?" She gave Blake a little nudge. "Let's all of us have martinis—think how fabulous we'll look!"

"Bring mine on the rocks," Blake said to the waitress. It was never any use resisting Madeline.

"On the rocks?" scoffed Madeline. "Three *real* martini glasses, please!"

The lilac-wisped waitress left, and as I traced her slinking figure through the crowd my eyes were drawn, moth-like, to a glow across the room. Beyond the shadow of a hundred heads bobbing, illuminated by a chandelier over his head, I saw him once again.

He was laughing. His head was tilted back, dashes of light falling over his face, like rain.

Dorian.

A stream of shadows passed in front of him, and he disappeared from view.

"Did you hear me, Ethan?"

I turned.

Blake leaned toward me. "Congrats on *Régine*, I said."

I was startled, disoriented. "Oh . . . thanks."

I was going crazy—I thought I could hear Dorian's laugh, *that* laugh, over the music, over all the voices, over Madeline, and Blake, and even over the sound of my own thoughts.

The waitress had returned. Madeline grabbed my arm. “Look at her, Ethan, how do you think she does it, balance all these glasses in the middle of a crowded room?”

Descending upon us, the waitress took one martini glass at a time from her silver tray and placed them carefully in front of us.

With a skeptical look at his drink in front of him, Blake said to Madeline, “I don’t see why you prefer these to a normal glass. It’s like they’re designed to spill all over the place.”

“They look marvelous though,” mused Madeline. “I bet that waitress feels so chic, carrying them around all night on a silver platter. She’s probably an actress, or a starving artist!”

I held my glass to my lips and gazed at the mirrored ceiling, savoring a sip.

“Not yet,” she chastised, raising her own drink to the light. “First, a toast.” Her eyes passing over me and Blake, she surveyed the room and, with an unexpected slop of her drink onto the table, seized her chest with one hand.

“What?” Blake asked.

A haunted look in her eyes, she bent forward and took a sharp, halted gasp, as though someone had stabbed her from beneath the table. “D-Dorian,” she stammered.

I turned. He was standing in front of us, and this time there was no mistaking him: Dorian Belgraves.

He seemed genuinely delighted. “Babe!” he exclaimed to Madeline.

“IthoughtyouwereinParis,” Madeline squeaked, her glass still in the air. “I’m just—” she choked. Her body quivered softly, as if an anesthetic had entered her veins. A slow clear river flowed over the side of her martini glass, down the length of her white arm.

"I just got back today—this morning!—I was going to call you both, I just—" He turned his face to me, his green eyes shining.

Everything was suddenly quiet, like we were inside a music box and someone had pressed the lid shut. I swallowed so hard I think the whole place heard.

"Ethan!" Dorian smiled and reached his hand to my shoulder. He was dressed as unassumingly as ever, in a plain white T-shirt and slim black jeans, his black shoes unlaced—yet he was the most captivating person in the room.

It was difficult to describe him without sounding grandiose, although anyone who had seen him just once would understand. Dorian could be conjured only in relation to great masterworks of classical sculpture. He didn't evoke any particular one so much as the collective weight of their timelessness, possessing features so perfectly aligned that carving them into stone would be only natural—to remind all future civilizations, once our cities had tumbled away and all that was left were strange, protruding relics and a silkscreen of numerical sequences in a stilted stream of digital consciousness, that something had once existed in the flesh that no digits could enumerate, that among mortals perfection had lived. Dorian was Tadzio while the rest of us were Aschenbachs.

Dorian smiled. "I missed you both so much this year," he said. A lock of dark hair fell from behind his ear as he lovingly reached for Madeline's hand.

My whole body tensed and I clenched my teeth, biting hard. The next thing I knew the front of my body was warm. Dorian seemed to notice first, then Blake. Madeline tore her eyes from Dorian and shouted my name. With horror on her face she flailed instinctively with one hand, caught like Jacqueline Kennedy by the suddenness of the bullet.

I didn't notice anything at all. All I could see was Dorian. He was still touching my shoulder, and holding Madeline's hand, the three of us connected like nothing had ever happened between us. I couldn't move. I stared at him. He stared back, his lips parted in shock, while I tried my best to die right there—to stop breathing, to extinguish myself so that the vision of his face would be my last. I hadn't realized my eyes had craved him so much.

The discomfort of something wet made me break away. I followed a dripping sensation on my leg to a spill on the table, where my glass was toppled over into a shiny martini pool. The glass was broken along the rim, and when I realized there were no shards on the table, I felt them like masticated crystals on my tongue.

I reached my fingers to my lips, and when I pulled them away, they were soaked with blood, and I realized—I had bitten my martini glass.

GEORGE WAS WAITING FOR ME WHEN THE ELEVATOR DOORS opened, in a black dress shirt with gray trousers stretched over his huge thighs.

"Hey, George!" I panted. I had just raced from the subway station at 42nd Street. "How are you?"

He didn't seem to hear me. "Start time around here is nine o'clock," he replied.

"It's nine now."

"Which means if you're not here by eight forty-five—" he continued, swiping his ID card with a fling of the glass door "—you're late."

I shook away the mild feeling of dread shivering across my

skin as I entered *Régine* at George's heels. Despite him, it was going to be a good day—a *great* day. I had made it in one piece to my dream job, and had even managed to match my jacket to my socks. I checked my breath: Before fumbling for my apartment door I had even washed my liquor-saturated mouth. I was already a raving success.

George and I passed through the same hallway as the day before—cubicles buzzing, cover girls smoldering—then the enormous-seeming white door loomed before us and we entered the fashion closet. Even though it was only Day Two, for some strange reason I already felt like I was "back" at *Régine*, as though I'd been coming to work here for years.

"What did you do last night?" I asked George, still hoping to establish a friendly rapport.

He turned to me as Sabrina's head came into view, and replied with undisguised irritation, "Why do you dress this way?"

"What way?" I laughed. My royal blue blazer was covered with small pink polka dots.

"Seriously, your clothes—they give me a headache," George said, shaking his head as we took our seats. "Are you planning to dress this way every day?"

"Are you?" I responded, before I could help myself.

He rolled his eyes and started checking his favorite blog. "Whatever, it's you they're going to talk about. And not in the way that you want."

Still clouded by the haze of alcoholic stupor, I couldn't figure out how George presumed to know what I wanted. In lieu of a response, my eyes absently followed the cursor across his screen as he scrolled around over a series of attractive faces from some party the night before.

A face appeared just long enough for the memory of last night to jab me in the stomach. "Dorian," I blurted with a start, and leaned instinctively toward him.

"Who?" George scrolled back to Dorian's white smile. "Oh, Dorian," he said knowingly. "He's a model—Edie Belgraves's son. He walked a ton of shows last season in Paris, and I hear he'll probably get offered a Burberry campaign."

I almost choked with laughter: that George was telling *me* about Dorian Belgraves. To everyone else he was the Dorian who had just "walked a ton of shows," but to me he was the Dorian who had ruined everything. He had ruined Madeline, and senior year, and the worst part was—it had all been my fault. I slowly fell back into my chair, and let the reality swoop over me like a crumpling funerary shroud: Dorian was back from Paris.

Last night, Blake had helped me stop the bleeding in the bathroom. There had been only one men's bathroom in the nightclub, and even though I was able to spit out most of the glass it took about thirty minutes just to get one piece out from the corner of my lip. By the time we were finished there was a line and the only reason nobody said anything to us was because I was still bleeding, and holding a bunch of paper towels to my face like a pulverized bouquet of white and red flowers.

It was pretty much over after that. When Blake and I returned to the table, I had expected to find Madeline and Dorian intertwined like lovers in a Fragonard painting—as rose-cheeked as ever, without sin or common sense.

It was much worse than that.

Madeline and Dorian were gone, and I knew that could only mean one thing: She had left with him. Stupid, pathetic, lovesick Madeline, who spent all of senior year pining over the loss of Dorian, had—after only thirty minutes in his exulting presence—gone home with *him*, the truest bane of her existence, her one true love, and the greatest tragedy of her young life. Now the priceless thing that was already teetering on a ledge had been shoved over, and the only hope was that it might fall through the air forever, instead of shattering. Blake knew it as well as I did, even though he had never been as close to Dorian as me and Madeline. He offered me a gin and tonic as a consolation, and a second, and soon, well—

This was the bad thing about Madeline, that for all her declarations of rebellion, she was (and this was why we were so compatible) just a girl who had read too much Jane Austen—a dreamer. A romantic. A fool like me. She would easily give everything up for a marriage certificate, for a life with Darcy in a renovated Victorian house, and children with golden hair to brush, and who was I to deny her that? To feel jealousy or despair that she would choose this over me, and in signing her name on the dream document, steal Dorian, my other truest and most cherished love in the world?

"*Boys!*" Sabrina's voice startled me from the other side of her cubicle wall. "They're shooting in-house in the small studio next door today, so we are going to have to move all the trunks we're storing there into the photo closet."

I was vaguely amused at her use of the word *we*, wondering if she aimed to aid the cause by moving an empty hatbox.

She stood up for a brief second to glare at us over the cubicle wall—qualifying her instructions with, "*Now.*" She wore a black headband, and a black pleated dress with silver buttons and a white pointed collar. I met her blue eyes as she lowered herself back into her seat, then popped back up like an ember. She smoldered there, tight-lipped; her eyes narrowed, and she began conspicuously eyeing my outfit up and down, so that I would have no doubt that she was doing it—and even though I barely knew Sabrina Walker, I could hear the rattle of a hundred insults tumbling, like the numbered white balls in a Powerball lottery, in her shiny glass brain.

"How *bright*," she spat at last, and I'd never known such a wonderful word could sound so much like a curse.

Ten minutes later, while I was pushing the trunks around, a similar thing happened with Clara, the senior fashion editor. "*Clooooset!*" she sang, in what I came to learn was her preferred method of greeting us all at once. "I need someone to prepare all of Edmund's inspiration boards for the white-theme shoot." She was daintily kicking a white Roger Vivier pony hair pump with the side of her black Manolo when she noticed me.

She betrayed her own politeness with a sudden cock of her head toward me, twitching like a platinum-blonde bird on a telephone wire. Her erratic movement culminated in a stare, and her eyes seemed to fill up with the polka dots on my suit. She nudged herself back, and visibly swallowing a comment, struggled to disguise her gawk with a justifiable pretense. With an effort, she addressed me, "*Ee*-than? It's Ethan, right? . . . Can you please bring me a hard copy of Edmund's references on eleven-by-seventeen paper, with six images per page, and captions numbered from beginning to end?" She sounded a little winded.

I guess that's when I realized George was right: With all of my bright patterns, I looked a little out of place.

I had very little time to reflect on this, however, as I was rushed onto the next thing following the disappearance of Clara's heel through the closet door.

"Okay, so yesterday was *nothing* compared to what we have to do today. All that stuff we checked in—that was just the half of it," George said.

Squeezing through a barely navigable channel between the tightly crowded garment racks, I wasn't sure where the other "half" of the clothes was supposed to go.

"This morning, we'll get in the rest of the deliveries . . . Then this afternoon we'll pack the clothes into trunks . . . And then *tonight* we'll ship it all out," he finished. "The delivery people will be here to pick up at nine o'clock."

"Nine tonight?" On first thought, it seemed rather late for an unpaid intern.

"No, of course not, silly," he said in a saccharine tone, which served as answer enough. "We *never* stay late. We just leave a few million dollars' worth of luxury merchandise unattended in the lobby downstairs so that we can have a nice dinner and get a good night's sleep and be all smiles and polka dots the next morning, like you!"

Five feet away, Sabrina's voice escalated. "I don't see what's so difficult about this request," she enunciated tersely. "Can't you just track it right now? Isn't there a GPS or something?"

"No, ma'am," a calm voice responded over the speaker, "I'm sorry, I wish we could do more, but—"

"Yes," Sabrina cut in sharply, "I wish you could too," and hung up with a crack of plastic. "*Boys!* Are you finished with the trunks? I just got an e-mail—our September It Girl has crashed her car on methamphetamines," she said. "The new It Girl is only available to shoot this week, so in addition to styling the white shoot, Edmund will be styling this second story too." She stepped out from behind her desk. "Edmund's It Girl story will be an off-white theme. That means the first story is *white*—this other one is *off-white*. They are completely different, so if you mix them up . . ." With a special glance in my direction, she left, presumably to discuss an important matter with the fashion editors.

George and I erected a new garment rack for Edmund's off-white story. Because putting the rack anywhere else would have made it impossible to walk through the closet, we had to place it directly behind our desk so that, as the day went on, the clothes multiplying behind us gave the unsettling impression that a crowd was gathering over our shoulders.

As a proudly visual person, I didn't disparage the distinction between white and off-white, but I did wonder why Edmund couldn't think of a theme that was less similar to the one he was already styling for the same issue. The only justification I had for it was that he was a genius, and I just didn't understand his methods yet.

During the first hour of check-ins, George accidentally hung a faintly cream Dolce & Gabbana slip dress onto the white rack. I said, "Oh, that's not white, it's off-white"—not to make him feel bad, but you know, just so he'd be aware—and re-hung it on the correct rack.

From then on he refused to say a word to me, and after photographing the incoming clothes began to leave them in a beige-ish heap for me to pick through as his retort. This went on until around two, when Sabrina's desk phone began to ring nonstop. Usually she picked up on the first ring, or sooner, but she had gone downstairs to pay a deliveryman for her lunch and couldn't know that, twelve stories above, an incessant trilling demanded her attention. George had bumbled to the kitchenette to make a coffee, and a conservative guess deemed me unauthorized to answer on Sabrina's behalf, so I let it ring on and on, until suddenly it stopped, and a voice rung out from the other side of the closet wall.

"*Sa-briiiinnnaaaaaaa*, *Sa-briiiiinnnnaaaaaaaa*!" The sound resembled a fire alarm, which made me wonder—if a fire broke out at *Régine*, would it be my job to save the clothes?

The closet door burst open, and Clara moaned, "*Sabrina*, I have been calling and calling you."

I started to explain that Sabrina was downstairs, but Clara continued in a wounded tone, "Now look at me—I've had to get up."

The closet now contained so many racks—white and off-white garments lined every available space—that the only part of Clara I could actually see was her high heels, barely visible beneath a wall of hanging fur coats. A flailing hand, followed by a faltering ankle and a progressive ripple through the curtain of fur, suggested her ultimately unsuccessful passage.

"Somebody . . . ?" she called, with a hint of despair.

I managed to announce myself and she exclaimed, "Ethan!" sounding much relieved. "Thank goodness! Please, can you bring us the trunk of off-white gladiator sandals? It's *urgent*!"

I was seized with panic. This would be my first time in Clara's cubicle.

CLARA, WHO WAS THE SENIOR FASHION EDITOR, SHARED A large U-shaped cubicle with Will and Christine, the associate fashion editors. As senior fashion editor, she was the highest-ranking among them and directly below Jane, which meant she oversaw Will and Christine, who oversaw Sabrina, who oversaw George, all of whom oversaw me. Due to this hierarchy, intimate relations between their rank and my own should have been impossible—yet an oversight of office design ultimately made it possible for me to know them extremely well. That is, the wall between my desk and their cubicle outside was so thin, I could hear every last word they said. In a matter of weeks, I would become well-acquainted with them and their daily rundown, which went like this:

Clara and the fashion editors would always take their seats at around 9:45 a.m. There was the booting of computers and the muffled rolling about of office chairs—then one of them always began with, "*Good* mooorrrrning, *darlings, how was your evening?*" They all spoke like they were in a beauty pageant, with much-extended vowels through strained smiles you could almost hear cracking. The initial response was, "*Lovely, how was yooouuurs?,*" followed by abridged retellings of their respective evenings prior, always spent unglamorously at a "*little party with nice people*"; enjoying "*a bit of Riesling in bed with the boyfriend*"; or otherwise engaged in some dull goings-on, which was their sad obligation to reveal to the others.

These unexceptional accounts might have constituted normal office talk were it not for the glaring fact that it was their *job* to be the most glamorous people in the world. Consequently, they all knew the truth about each other's boring lives: The "little party" had led to a toast with Marc Jacobs (Clara), and the "Riesling in bed" to sex with a Fortune 500 fiancé (Christine).

To my innocent eye it appeared that the fashion editors were as humble as they were endowed with social grace, at least until my second week, when Clara described an extravagant dinner with Calvin Klein as "simple and charming." From this gross understatement (images from the supremely un-simple event were posted on every major fashion news site), I finally guessed the reason for their tight-lipped reluctance to divulge: They simply couldn't trust each other. A position in the palace at *Régine* could be taken away by a decree as imperious as the one that had given it to them. Just one slipup—a tip-off revealed to the wrong ears, or a secret to the wrong eyes—or a single move that suggested they didn't meet the standard of gilded perfection that was required, and any one of them could be exiled. Privy more than any outsider to each other's lives, nobody posed as great a threat to them as one another. Furthermore, they all knew that, as far as their careers were concerned, there was nowhere else they could go. They would always be welcomed with grand fanfare at another proverbial court, yet no other was as fantastic and powerful as *Régine*—they could hardly do better than their current positions at the top of the masthead. To ascend at all would mean promotion to Edmund's or Jane's or even Ava's role: Each event was inevitable, but how long would it take? And out of the three of them, which one would be chosen? The editors were trapped in the sphere of one another's ambition—confined in a cubicle every day with their own worst enemies.

And so every day their strained niceties went on and on . . . before they became suddenly silent. An hour later the strangeness would reach new heights when they switched to making meaningful consultations over their shoulders about "*Which Chanel slipper do you think is the best for the new story?*" and "*Do you think this Jil Sander coat is quite right?*" and "*Don't you agree we absolutely* neeeeeed *Look Fourteen from* Ferragaaaaaamo?," everything bloated with an earnest sense of purpose, like they had agreed to a momentary truce in the interest of a greater common cause, which at the end of their handbag-filled day they all upheld with absolute conviction.

This sense of united purpose was somehow reflected in the most curious fact about them; that despite any mistrust they hid from each other, they trusted more than anything in each other's *taste*, so much so that they had come to dress alike, and smell alike, and even keep their hair the exact same shade of platinum blonde. They always got their roots re-dyed around the same time, and oddly enough, the more I eventually got to look at them, the more I recognized in the very contours of their faces an identical strain—as if, no matter what they were doing, in the back of their minds they were constantly concentrating on the exact same set of things, like how to tie a difficult knot while balancing a teacup on their head and going up the stairs.

IT WAS THIS COLLECTIVE EXPRESSION OF CONSTANT MENTAL exertion that I mistook for impatience when I entered their cubicle for the first time, depositing nervously at their feet the trunk that Clara had summoned. I was breathless, having tipped over a garment rack of racy lingerie in my unglamorous attempt to extricate the trunk from the overcrowded closet.

Sniffing me out, they wheeled their chairs around me, circling the trunk like slick, muscular sharks. Inside the trunk floundered forty pairs of colorless gladiator-style sandals, captured fish gasping at the bottom of a boat.

With a preoccupied half-glance in my direction, Clara pointed ambiguously to the trunk. "Can you . . . ?"

I knelt down beside the trunk and tried to guess what she wanted me to do.

"Gucci," she clarified.

I dug through the trunk in search of her selection—a task which was made difficult by my trembling fingers and the fact that the editors had beseeched all the PR firms to borrow every designer's version of the same shoe. Gladiator sandals were trending, evidently, that season—and every sandal was the same shade of off-white. The pair by Gucci, which Clara asked me to pull out, was distinguished only by gold buckles that, unlike the gold buckles on the pairs by Christian Louboutin, Bottega Veneta, and Hermès, were carved out in the shape of a double *G*. I identified and offered up the requested pair like a sommelier displaying a bottle of fine wine for the consideration of his distinguished guests.

I waited for someone to tell me if my interpretation of this task was correct as the trio gathered closer to one another and made furtive remarks behind half-raised hands.

"Ferragamo," said Clara at last. I replaced the Guccis and set out digging for the Ferragamos; pulled them out; observed the exchange of more whispers.

"Louis Vuitton," said Will next.

"Chanel," said Christine.

"Manolo Blahnik," said Clara.

"*That's it*," they said together. I jumped.

"That's the shoe!" exclaimed Clara, pointing. A smile broke out across all their faces. I experienced an uncanny ripple of joy; that in some small way I had facilitated a feeling of satisfaction in them.

"That shoe, with the knee-length Armani skirt!" Will exclaimed.

Christine placed a demure hand over her heart, glowing with

the thrill of endless possibility. "Or the Valentino mini, with the sheer side panel!"

"Yes," said Will, resting his own excited hand on the back of her chair, "and the Balmain military jacket!"

"Edmund will love it," Clara concluded with a vivid clap.

Will took one of the shoes from my hands as Clara glanced up at me and smiled, "Thank you, Ethan—you can take away the trunk now."

"Hold on a second . . ." interjected Will as he inspected the shoe. The others had already begun to roll toward their desks when he flipped it over and tapped on the sole. He squinted. "These are a size forty," he announced. His voice reverberated with the grave reluctance of a soldier required to inform a widow of her husband's misfortune in the line of duty.

Clara turned to him, her desk chair squeaking. "So?"

"It Girl's a thirty-seven, and it's open-toe. Her feet will look so bad."

"Oh *no*," said Christine. The tragic realization descended over her face like a shadow.

I stood by while they deliberated. The shoe had been passed to Clara. She counted with an effort. "That's thirty-seven—thirty-eight—thirty-nine—forty—four sizes too big."

"Actually three sizes," corrected Christine.

Clara didn't seem to hear her. "You're right. Think about how big that will look on her." She stuck out her leg so the others could inspect her own delicate Manolo-clad foot. "My feet are tiny, and when I try to wear sample-size, I look ridiculous . . ."

"Great shoe," Christine noted grimly to Clara's foot. "Are those the ones you wore to Jane's wedding?" As a redress for her humorless tone she smiled a little too hard, like a levy about to burst.

"No," Clara smiled even harder, "those were Dior."

"I'm sorry," smiled Christine, "your style is just so cohesive—I couldn't tell them apart."

Will was in a trance. "What do we do?" he lamented, as he stared hopelessly into the trunk full of shoes. "They're too big, but they're the *only* shoe."

"Surpriiiiiiise!" a voice suddenly called out.

They glanced toward the fashion closet door to see Jane, the creative director, in her white collared shirt and cigarette pants, with her white-haired, ponytailed head topped by a pink birthday cone hat. Balanced precariously on her forearms was a heavy-looking crystal platter brimming with chocolate cupcakes, each decorated with sprinkles and rainbow plastic letters that together spelled out, H-A-P-P-Y B-D-A-Y C-L-A-R-A-!

"My, the fashion closet's full! Should have gone the other way!" exclaimed Jane, kicking away a bra which had fallen onto the pointed toe of her nude heel.

I smiled, and looked back at Clara, who was standing with her brown hands clasped. "Oh, Jane," she melted, with an expression of embarrassment. "You shouldn't have." Her A-line dress gave her the appearance of a housewife whose afternoon of diligent homemaking had been disrupted by an unannounced visit from her mother-in-law.

Clara rushed to clear away her desk and make a place to rest the tray. Her fingers fumbled over papers and pens. "Excuse the mess," she gushed, and got carried away straightening up the stickies on her computer screen. Evidently thinking that Jane might be offended by the presence of writing instruments, she opened her drawer and swept all the pens inside with a clatter.

Seemingly unaware of the distress she had inadvertently

caused, Jane approached with a beaming grin, the crinkles around her eyes making her appear less like the creative director of *Régine* than like a grandmother in an advertisement for cake mix.

The platter passed to Clara, and the transference revealed a row of party hats dangling from Jane's wrist. "Here," she said, and distributed them to Will and Christine.

Christine patted her head and smiled nervously while Jane came up behind Clara's glamorous blonde hair and fastened a party hat there.

"You need one too, Ethan," she said, as she offered up the cone from her own head. I accepted, and was flabbergasted that she remembered my name.

Clara turned. She fingered the elastic band around her jaw, grimacing like a person who had been strapped into a restraint collar as the others blinked at each other, unsure what to do next. "You shouldn't have," Clara said once more to Jane, "you really shouldn't have."

"But I did," Jane said. "Come on, everyone," she instructed, "have a cupcake!"

My mouth watered, as I hoped that "everyone" included me. Sabrina had not yet authorized a lunch break.

Jane plucked a cupcake off the platter and leaned roguishly back against Clara's desk, rocking her foot over her high heel. "Oh, go on," she urged the others, unpeeling the cupcake liner, "eat!" She savored her first bite and waved her hand in a circular motion, which seemed to include me.

I took this in good faith and hastily picked up a cupcake, my mouth pooling up with saliva. The editors followed, with visible reservation. Their hands clashed over the platter.

"Oh—sorry." Christine blushed.

"No, I'm sorry."

"Go ahead."

"No, you go ahead."

Clara finally gave in. She held out her palm like a dish—careful not to drop any sprinkles—and placed the cupcake on top, blinking. Hovering her other hand over the chocolate frosting, she took a breath, like she was about to do a daring thing, then lost courage, and deflated. She turned her head almost imperceptibly to the side and whispered to Christine from the corner of her mouth, "Do you have a knife?"

Christine shook her head. Her cupcake was cupped between two upturned palms like a sacramental wafer.

"I'm going to save it for later," Clara said at last to Jane, smiling like a person who had been hit in the stomach and was trying to disguise their pain. "I hope that's all right?"

"Suit yourself." Jane shrugged amicably, and licked a dollop of frosting off her own finger. "How are you celebrating tonight?"

Clara had carefully returned the cupcake to the platter, and was folding her hands on her lap like a Sunday school girl. "Oh, it'll be a quiet night. Julian is just taking me to dinner—you know . . ."

Down the hall, Edmund's head poked out from his corner office. He came billowing down the passage in a linen chemise and clapped his bony hands together.

"Happy birthday, Clara, do you have any contact solution?" he said, rubbing his eye. "Dry eyes again." He prodded a fallen chocolate sprinkle on the crystal platter, and raised his finger to his nostrils for a suspicious sniff.

Relieved by the temporary distraction the task presented, Clara reached into her drawer, and pulled out a bottle of contact solution. He took it from her and said to Jane, "Do you have a moment to discuss this business with the Asian model?" while he jabbed at his eye and walked away.

Jane nodded, pulling the last chocolaty lump off the cupcake liner. She popped it into her mouth and asked through a mouthful of frosting, "What's wrong? Is it another scheduling thing with Lui Wen?" She folded the liner into a heart shape and tossed it into Clara's trash bin. "If you need her to be Asian, why don't you try out Soo Joo, like I suggested?"

They walked away—Edmund fast ahead, and Jane strolling behind. "Because Choo-Choo is not famous enough," he declared, rubbing his eye again. "I don't want to shoot some nobody." And he closed the door behind them.

A moment passed in silence before I realized the only sound was me licking my fingers. I suddenly stopped, and the moist cupcake paper wilted in my hand as I glanced up at the fashion editors. Christine, who was between the others, looked at Clara, then bit her lip and turned to Will. All of them blinked.

Will and Christine still held their cupcakes intact.

"Do you—?" Will began suddenly.

They turned to him.

"Never mind," he said.

More blinking. Christine raised a finger like she had a thought, then recoiled. I was struck by the strangeness of the void between them. They were three of the fashion world's most exemplary models of taste and social grace, each one embodying the person you wanted most to be—a powerful, perfect person from whom you would take any advice, and on whose suggestion you would invest several thousand dollars in an Hermès bag, or a pair of Ferragamo slippers, and who always knew what expensive thing went just right with another expensive thing, and whose conviction in these matters you would regard more highly than your own—yet they could not figure out what to say to each other over a simple plate of cupcakes.

I waited for them to say *anything*: to share some bit of pointless, silly gossip, or even, maybe, to crack a joke. Surely Will would say, "*It's almost three—let's wrap up, and catch happy hour somewhere!*" Clara would blush, while Christine prodded her playfully, "*Yes, it's your special day—we'll go somewhere tacky and fun, just for laughs!*" It would have been normal, even for them. After all, they sat next to each other *every* day, all day, for at least eight hours. Presumably they knew each other very well—better even, most likely, than their respective lovers—yet none of them stirred or said a word. The lives they had chosen dictated that they simply couldn't.

Clara finally put an end to it. "All right, well that was fun," she said, with an almost prayerful clap of her hands.

"Yes, we'd better get back to work, hadn't we?" agreed Will.

"You can go now, Ethan," Christine allowed. "Leave the trunk."

I savored the last of the chocolate frosting in my mouth, which I had allowed to dissolve slowly on my tongue for a whole minute.

"Can you—take these away?" Clara added, pointing at the cupcakes. She peered over toward Edmund's door, to be sure nobody would witness her ungrateful disposal of Jane's thoughtful gift. "See if anybody else would like them, just please—don't bring them back," she said, urging me with a wave of her hand to hurry.

They all turned simultaneously to work, and the whole space seemed to drift foggily back to a state of normalcy.

GEORGE WAS SITTING THERE WHEN I RETURNED TO OUR DESK.

"What are you getting for lunch today?" I asked, as I laid down the cupcakes between us.

"Probably salad," answered George, not looking up from his article about a reality TV star's infected breast implant. The most I had been able to gather from our stilted exchanges thus far was that George was from New Jersey, and had a relative who worked in *Régine*'s Advertising Department. Ever the optimist, however, I was hoping to conspire with him over the strange scene that had just unfolded.

I said, "I think I'm going to get a salad too," even though what I really wanted was macaroni and cheese, preferably not from the just-add-water packs awaiting me at home, which my shoestring budget had ruled were my only option for affordable dinner in New York City.

But before I could initiate a friendship over salad, he commanded, not even looking at me, "Hey, Polka Dot, I need you to do me a favor. Can you get me this volume from the archives library?" With an intense scribble of great significance—still not looking at me—he wrote *Jan–Mar 1964*.

"Um, sure," I said. "Now?"

"Yes," he replied, bored, staring at his screen while stretching his hand out toward me, the sticky floating off one finger. "Now."

The volume George asked me to retrieve was not exceptional in any way. I couldn't be sure what he would do with it, but I brought it to him.

At the end of the day, the sober, brown-leathered volume was still sitting there, and the most he had done with it was rest his elbow on the cover.

chapter five

My first thought upon waking up the next morning was that I was late for class.

It was the familiar state of panic I'd experienced frequently throughout four years of undergraduate life; the same sputtering and aimless flailing, the same frantic attempts to free myself from a tangle of bedsheets. On those mornings I was greeted by intermittent flashes of assignments yet undone while I fumbled for an alarm clock that got perpetually misplaced at the crucial moment, and some memory of which class I was about to be late for.

Now I sat straight up and conked my head. Sooner than usual, everything came back into sharp focus—graduation and *Régine*, Madeline and Dorian, and how could I forget?, the four-foot apartment that I lived in, with the tin ceiling whose duty it was to smash my dream-filled head into waking life.

A lot of people thought I was joking when I told them my New York "apartment" was only four feet tall, but with my negligible income as a part-time library assistant in the Yale Art History archives—depleted constantly by my acquisition of thrifted wardrobe pieces—I had been lucky to afford even that. It had all happened so fast too: graduation day had been on a Wednesday, my interview with Sabrina that Friday, my first day at *Régine* on the following Monday. With my practical sensibilities limited by a background of willful collegiate indulgence, I didn't know the first thing about starting an adult life in New York, or anywhere. I didn't know about rent, or bills, or groceries, or really a single matter related to the "real world," a phrase which before that point had bothered me immensely for its supposition that life in college, with its room-and-board charges sent to the Latino Scholarship Fund, and free heat/water/Wi-Fi that never went out, and dining halls that promised a buffet any time between eight in the morning and nine in the evening, somehow wasn't how "real" people lived.

Of course, I learned soon enough that if the agreed-upon conception of the "real world" necessitated hardship of any kind—desires unrealized, dreams deferred, both manifested in struggles of a practical nature—then for quite some time I had been living out a most unreal life.

THE FRUIT OF MY COLLEGE MEMORIES HARDLY CONTAINED A bitter seed, yet the sweetest moments I traced to Madeline. Once we transcended the stifling barrier of our own mutual fascination, we entered a relationship resembling the honeymoon phase of two newlywed twelve-year-olds—giggling and preening and finishing each other's sentences, each one of us lavishing the other with a regular abundance of flowers and pet names. At the time, we perceived no sexual dimensions to our mutual attraction, because both of us assumed I must be gay. Even though I'd still never actually had sex, or even kissed anyone, the label had become an important part of my identity. It was a surprisingly convenient label, offering—despite its share of unfavorable prejudices—a crucial array of freedoms. I had learned early that to fit the conventional template of masculinity would require me to make unbearable compromises in life. That is, if I wished to live in the world as a "straight" person, I would have to relinquish my entire personality.

A "straight" man wasn't really allowed to like fashion. He wasn't allowed to be "pretty" or "sensitive," or profess any appreciation for his natural femininity, and unless he was uncommonly confident, or surrounded by uncommonly open-minded people, he was doomed to be scrutinized for any flail that jeopardized his passage along a very narrow tightrope. However, if the same man told people he was *gay*, like I did, suddenly all those feminine qualities became okay, even desirable.

Of course, liking fashion or being "sensitive" actually had nothing to do with preferring one sex over another. None of the stereotypes really did, but I was too young to realize that, and if my intellect was supposedly advanced, in almost every other sense—especially sexually—I was a late bloomer. It wasn't that I lacked a physical inclination toward sex; I had masturbated almost every day in high school, under the covers in a dreamy morning idyll, after being half-awakened by my own erection.

I had tried to watch porn too; "straight" porn at first. The first time I did it my parents had been asleep. It was the dead of night, and I was on the shared desktop computer in the living room, with my zipper undone and my hand hiding a bulge as I typed the search query *s-e-x* with the other. My heartbeat accelerated as, gaining confidence in the dark room, I deleted the letters and inserted *p-o-r-n* instead. I clicked on the first thing—something about "creampies"—my eyes widened, and my erection softened in my hands.

After that I tried again, and again, every time with similar wilting effects—based on which anyone would simply conclude that I was definitely gay, and would probably enjoy gay porn instead. But watching two men have sex didn't change anything, as my interest was constantly undermined by the same essential issue—*who were these people, and why should I care about them having sex?* Without a personal context, the sight of a naked body aroused me as much as a Roman nude in a museum—actually less, because at least toward Adonis or Aphrodite I could imagine some kinship.

Of course, I didn't *know* what this all meant—just that I must be gay, and therefore that my relationships with women, including Madeline, were naturally defined by platonic boundaries.

Lacking the insight to consider a more nuanced understanding of ourselves and our own attraction, Madeline and I faced little trouble assuming our logical roles—we were destined to be best friends, what else?—both of us unaware that the buds of attraction between human beings could blossom beyond the crudely fenced-in constructs of conventional categorization.

By October of our Fall-Winter semester as freshmen, we were content to enjoy the breadth of intimacy afforded to us by our conveniently sexless arrangement. We were in love, in our unique way, and although it glowed with a childlike aura, years of quiet disaffection for our respectively un-Romantic peers had given us each the maturity to perceive the rarity of our intense bond.

Inwardly, Madeline and I were like twins who had been separated at birth. The main difference, of course, was that Madeline had been raised over a grand piano by parents who attended benefits and wore expensive *parfums*, while I—well, I simply didn't talk about my upbringing. It was regarding this subject alone that I withheld my true self from her, and the fault of *Madama Butterfly* that Madeline uncovered the reason.

In the early months of our friendship, Madeline heard the new season of the Metropolitan Opera in New York would include a modern adaptation of her favorite Italian tragedy. As opera was one of her greatest pleasures, and I had yet to see one, it was clear enough that we should go together; however, Madeline wanted us to buy orchestra seats, the most expensive, maintaining that I would never be able to relive my first opera, and "*you just won't* feel *the music from a cheaper seat.*" I might have afforded a discount ticket on a balcony, behind some giant column, but never the seats which she insisted on, and neither could my dignity afford to tell her. "*I have an exam that week,*" I said. "*We'll go the next,*" she said. "*I get sick on trains.*" "*We'll take the bus.*" And so on, just a series of excuses, increasing in ridiculousness, until at last Madeline's baffled face lit up with realization: "It's not the money, is it?"

It was the first and last time she ever directly posed such a question to me. My flushed cheeks and hollow intake of breath were answer enough for her, and the next day she said to me, "We're going next Saturday. My treat."

From then on, it was always this from Madeline—"*My treat,*" or "*You can pay next time*"—followed by a masterful demonstration of her unsurpassable social grace: a giddy laugh, then a harmless diversion (commentary on classwork, or the weather). In this way she ensured that there would never be a pause, that I would never have the opportunity to suggest a repayment, or express my gratitude, or demonstrate in any way that her gesture was a cover-up for some inherent inequality about which only I was distressed.

More so than the money itself, these gestures of consideration for my dignity distinguished Madeline as possessing the truest generosity I had ever known. Hers was a special kind of thoughtfulness that was rare in the twenty-first century—attesting her commitment to the manners of more chivalrous times. Therein, ironically through her unselfish view of money, the institutional upholder that she often derided, was her nonconformist spirit most pointed.

Madeline willingly took on the role of my benefactress—my governess and ward in one—who despite my halfhearted protests went to great lengths so I could share with her the fine life which was so clearly our mutual destiny, never knowing the full extent to which her charities fulfilled my lifelong yearnings. Every weekend it was tickets for the opera, and the ballet, and the Philharmonic—experiences denied by my life in provincial Corpus Christi, which she knew I would honor with my hands gripping the armrest and my body leaning toward the stage in wide-eyed appreciation. Following *Tosca*, or Verdi's *Requiem*, would be surprise reservations to dimly sconced West Village restaurants for aged cabernet and croque monsieurs, and miniature cheesecakes topped off with sea salt, syrup, and twisted lemon slivers.

Pledging to include me in every aspect of her rarified life, Madeline even had her parents upgrade their donor's package at the Metropolitan Museum so that I could accompany them to events, and when, on the opening night of the Baroque Legacies exhibit, she discovered a small hole in my thrifted tuxedo trousers, her reaction was tiered as such: a wounded expression, a string of choked-up words *("But why wouldn't you feel comfortable just* telling *me?")*, and a compulsory shopping trip to Bergdorf Goodman. There she had me try on a dozen black tuxedos—Dolce & Gabbana, Calvin Klein, Dior Homme, each more exquisite than the last—until finally she conceded that the three-piece from Giorgio Armani was good enough for me.

Our first "fight" unfolded shortly before Christmas, when I promptly declined her invitation to join her extended family on a holiday in the Swiss Alps.

She had already done too much for me. As much as I wished to share every moment with her, to accept from Madeline's satin-lined pocket a fully paid vacation seemed an abuse of our love. Furthermore, if there was a single lesson my proletariat parents had successfully passed on to me, it was to never indenture oneself; for all of the grief conferred on me by its beige walls, my parents had often remarked with pride that they had accepted no loans in the purchase of their house. As a result the back of my head had already been spinning for weeks with insurmountable calculations as I tried, despite Madeline's fiscal nonchalance, to tally the dizzying debt I felt would be my duty to somehow repay.

When I voiced my initial protestations, we were lunching under vaulted ceilings in Berkeley Hall as sunshine from arched windows filled every mahogany corner. Madeline put down her spoon, her silver tray bearing her typical lunch fare: a bowl of organic Greek yogurt and a cup of strawberries, with an abundantly annotated photocopy of a Noam Chomsky essay at her elbow.

"How presumptuous of me—of course you should spend Christmas with your own family," she backtracked, "I didn't mean to be insensitive, it's just you never talk about them, and—if you want to come, we'll just schedule your flight out of Texas on the twenty-sixth," she said. "That way you can have Christmas with them, and stay for New Year's with us. It would be a short holiday—I don't know, ten days, but then we can catch the flight back together. Do you think that would be all right?" She raised a strawberry to her lips, and if I weren't so embarrassed I could have laughed at her sweet, ridiculous assumption that I would oppose her perfect Swiss holiday because I preferred a miserable Noche Buena with pathetic presents and only my rowdy family as a consolation, with everyone spilling Coronas around a dried-up evergreen.

"It's not the dates . . ." I started. "It's just—" and of course I froze, and turned the same color as the last time we had broached the issue of money—symptoms easily diagnosed by Madeline as an offense to her time-honored benevolence.

Her whole countenance dropped with the weight of a hundred acorns shaken from a tree. "For the love of God," she spat. She tossed the half-bitten strawberry onto a napkin with disgust, and raised her voice: "The *money* again? You're going to make me lose my appetite."

Grant Goodwin passed us with a smile. He was trying to catch Madeline's eye, but had to content himself with my half-hearted grimace on her sour behalf. "Please," I said, reaching over the wooden table, "not so loud, I just—"

"Why are you so *crass* about this?" she hissed, and I had never heard such vitriol in her voice, not even in all her political condemnations of The Institution. "All I want is a vacation with you, and you have to act like a regular philistine about it—I mean, do you want to come with me or not?"

"Of course I do, but—"

"But nothing!" She jabbed her spoon through the jiggly surface of her yogurt bowl. "Jesus, you make it seem like money is *important.* It's nothing you wouldn't do for me, and what else should it get spent on? So what if you can't pay me back? Who cares? One day you'll be rich too, and it will all even out." She let the handle of her spoon clatter with abandon against the side of the bowl—"Really, you've ruined my appetite."

The display of embarrassment on my cheeks moved her to a reformation of her tone. "Listen to me, darling," she said with delicate persuasion, her hand on my forearm and the aroma of her perfume activated by a slight lean toward me, "who ever knows what'll happen to people's money? It's all *made up*—one day we could wake up, and it'll be gone! Don't you think we should spend it while we have the chance? If our society is lucky, everyone will come to their senses soon—" With Chomsky in agreement on the table, she made a grand blossoming gesture with both hands, like she was spreading confetti in the air. "Then we won't even need vacations, or ballets, anything! People will be picnicking around naked, how God intended—like in a Manet painting!"

Coming from Madeline, it made perfect sense, and of course I ended up with her in the Alps, among the cable cars and powder snow and chalet-style towers over bird's-eye panoramas, and on Christmas Day we all exchanged presents and drank too much génépi and Madeline and I waltzed to Mozart around our suite at the Gstaad Palace.

By escaping to Europe, into opera and ballets and the never-ending Arcadia that was our shared dream, we never conceded that we were pantomiming the traditions of a stodgy upper class; rather, we were defending the truest essence of humanity, by thriving in the name of beauty, art, culture—everything crucial in life. We fancied ourselves bohemians. If other people were the herd, we believed we'd escaped the enclosure of their oppressive limits. Of course, at the age of nineteen, we were still cattle—idealistic cattle, but cattle all the same—safe within the protected confines of youth, but lingering at its outskirts and hoping we were actually outside of it.

Given this streak of romanticized rebellion, it was a surprise to no one that sophomore year, we decided to move off campus.

"Our own gypsy enclave," Madeline called it. "I'll pay the rent, and in exchange you can cook me eggs Benedict for breakfast." (Equating a matter of considerable value like rent to a triviality like eggs Benedict had become a new trend, as Madeline had started suggesting these sort of compensatory clauses to offset my discomfort with her emasculating generosity.)

The street was called Lynwood Place, and although frankly it was as central to campus proper as any of the dormitories, rejecting the institutional safety of Yale property by residing in a quaint little house seemed a convenient act of defiance. Built in the Victorian style, the houses on Lynwood Place were painted in shades of white, pink, and powder blue, delivering in excess the charm required by our aesthetic standards. These dainty dwellings became the closest we had to a maternal influence. Amid a landscape dominated by the patriarchal shadows of a hundred Gothic towers, they resembled a cheerful parade of gingham-aproned housewives, who had marched through the turreted town on a pie-baking crusade only to stop, and stay there, after forming a chatty sisterhood with the oak trees.

Beneath canopying laundry lines of leaves that faithfully turned each year from green to gold, they toted party-hat roofs and sing-along porches, which served as a quaint backdrop for the sharply contrasting indulgences of our lost, but hopeful, generation; night after night of reckless undergraduate blundering, of everyone trying to "find" themselves in creative combinations of sex, sweat, and Sam Adams six-packs. The same echoes could be heard every weekend on Lynwood Place, as everyone yelled, stumbled, busted things up. We were swarms of entitlement embodied, and like all mothers, the houses endured us. They took pity on us, knowing well that while they remained there, semester after semester, trying to catch a breath as they wearily waved their dampened handkerchiefs behind us, we would have it worse when we left their unconditional shelter to enter the real world.

For all our prim and proper proclivities, Madeline and I crashed as thanklessly as any other hell-bent undergraduates through the halls of our splintering house. We were a discerning pair, but young—always so, so young; consequently, our discernment tinged all matters but our own carelessness. We filtered life through the kaleidoscope of a fever dream, determined that through the meaningful affluence of our everyday rituals we should recreate the thrill of some great romantic precedent.

Every morning, amid my racket of pots, pans, and half-scrubbed spatulas, it was the destiny of our kitchen to accumulate a new dimension of filth as my well-intentioned incompetence ensured the spatter of Madeline's eggs Benedict onto some new surface, ushering in the beginning of another day. We fluttered out to class, and upon our return blundered around half-naked in flapping kimonos, blasting Mozart and Tchaikovsky over a thrifted gramophone, spilling Earl Grey from Wedgwood teacups stolen from the unloved recesses of the Dupres' china cabinet.

In the evenings, we played host to our "bohemian" friends, floating constantly in marijuana smoke. We added chamomile or lavender to the joints, and when people brought a six-pack to share, we offered them plastic champagne glasses. Once, we painted gold curlicues on the walls so the poor, falling-apart place would look more like Versailles (willfully ignoring what befell its hedonistic inhabitants), and when, during the renovation of Linsly-Chittenden Hall, Madeline discovered a chandelier by a dumpster, I helped her carry it back and hang it from the dining room ceiling. For an impressive period of one month, we pointed it out to all our friends at dinner parties, and everyone admired it with the excitement of Robespierre confronting Marie Antoinette's head. Reflecting the doomed life span of all beloved totems under our care, the salvaged chandelier fell after an inebriated Mary Poppins tried to dangle from it at our Halloween fete. In that apocalyptic moment, it had toppled into the punch bowl, its brass arms raised like the suntanned legs of a synchronized swim team—just a splash of pink pool water, and the sorrowful *thwack!* of lemon circles falling at people's feet like mislaid swim caps.

I MAINTAINED, UPON GRADUATION, THE NOTION THAT LIFE would continue in this fantastic fashion; that the most difficult parts of it would resemble cramming for midterms and the rest would be the same grand party, where everyone continued to get showered with champagne and swing from light fixtures. Except instead of dorms and off-campus houses, the setting would be a

West Village loft, or a nightclub in the Meatpacking District, or somewhere else bigger and more glamorous.

The first indication to the contrary was my apartment search—a wake-up call. Following my interview with Sabrina, I spent the evening copy-pasting an apartment-hunt template to a hundred friends' e-mails. Somewhere in the beginning of the body text was a "personal touch" (*"I heard you got a job in finance, you must be really excited!!"*); a little later, the revelation of my true purpose (*"I'm looking for a place to live!!!"*). The exclamation points were a bad habit, which I had many years ago gotten into my head as a way to "shine through" the impersonal nature of e-mail, and which George eventually derided upon his receipt of an e-mail concerning the delivery of a garment rack to the Art Department: "Ethan, what are you so goddamn *excited* about?"

The first apartment suggested to me was located near Bergdorf Goodman and the Plaza Hotel, which I had read about in *The Great Gatsby*. "Is that for a year?" I responded, referring to the rent. "I'll take it!" Of course, it was soon revealed that what I thought was a yearly cost was *monthly*, and after that came a sickening chorus of corpse-like thuds as the heavy numbers dropped into my poor, unsuspecting inbox. Others had warned me that Manhattan was "expensive," and I had always rolled my eyes: Any detractors of mythological New York City didn't deserve its golden glories and should take their leave to a sadder, merely mortal, corner of the world.

After two nights of increasingly desperate copy-pasting—and eventually, phone calls—I concluded my entire savings would scarcely cover a month's rent in any of these legendary areas of Manhattan, and the hopeless thought crossed my mind that if *Régine* didn't work out, it would be my own life subjected to sub-

mythical misery, after a plebeian-class flight to Corpus Christi ensured the fading of my limitless potential into dust.

Of course, Madeline had offered to put me up. "You can even choose which guest room," she implored. "My parents would be delighted"—and I knew that she was right. The Dupres had loved me since our Christmas trip to Gstaad, especially the perpetually narcotized Mrs. Dupre, who got an adorable thrill from introducing me at events as "*my daughter's co-conspirator, Mr. St. James.*" But by that point, things with Dorian had already complicated matters, and the lines between Madeline and me had blurred. Were we just friends, or something more? And if the latter, what would it mean if Dorian came back?

That Dorian had dated Madeline muddied the crystal waters of possibility between us; although it had only been *after* Dorian had "ruined" our lives that I learned the truth about myself—that all along, I wasn't gay *or* straight, really. I craved neither male nor female company specifically, but rather a deep, existential bond, which I had found in Dorian and Madeline alike. After that, it was glaringly obvious: I was in love with my two best friends, while they had fallen in love with each other.

When the reality of my financial situation set in, the desperate thought passed through my head that maybe Madeline's guest room wasn't such a bad idea. I would only stay a week—a month, maximum, until, I thought, I got a job at *Régine*, and was drenched in fame and fortune. But then Aaron, from my friend Li's sailing team, got me in touch with his older brother, Michael, who advised me to call his girlfriend, Catrina, whose best friend, Veronica, from Cornell had a "loft bedroom" she was looking to rent in Soho. To explain its supernatural cheapness, Veronica did mention its "unusual proportions" in the optimistic tone of a broker who noted the benefits of fine company and nutritious daily platters while renting out a county prison cell. Veronica said the guy before really liked it—"*found it cozy*," was her exact phrase—and I mean, so did I for about five minutes, until crawling up the ladder to inaugurate the mattress with my own blue-and-white striped bedsheets, I smashed my head against the tin ceiling for the first time.

Now I was rubbing my head, and I was late for class—or *Régine*, or *some*thing . . .

ON FRIDAY OF THAT WEEK, EDMUND STYLED HIS WHITE-themed shoot in Paris. Then on Sunday he styled the off-white iteration in London, and on Monday, when I arrived at *Régine* for the start of my second week, all the clothes were back in New York City while Edmund himself had stayed in London last-minute for a "small holiday."

The one essential caveat, it turned out, of borrowing all those clothes for a photo shoot, was that at the end of it all, after the photos were taken, and the photographer and the model and the hairdresser and makeup artist and all of their assistants had moved on, and the Art Department was blurring off the evidence of nature from the models' faces, the clothes still remained, waiting patiently to be returned. We had two days to vacate the closet, to make room for everything being borrowed for the next photo shoot.

Sabrina greeted me that morning: "I need every garment hung on these racks by designer, and every accessory on these tables by category—shoes, gloves, hats, whatever—then also by designer. If you have a question, ask George," and George stuck up his nose and tried his best to look as unapproachable as possible.

George then ordered me to "go get" the trunks. The first trunk wasn't so heavy, but it must have been full of scarves. The next one was worse, and every one after that a hellish joke. It was the accessories that weighed the most: A trunk full of "dainty" kitten heels didn't *seem* like a lot, but seventy-five pounds of them was a different story, and furthermore, trunk after trunk of kitten heels the least dainty thing in the world.

Of course, any way I tried to describe this I sounded like a spoiled child whose real qualm was having to do any labor at all. Older people always said this about those of us just out of college: We didn't know how to "work," and wanted everything handed to us on a silver platter. Yet I would have spitefully invited them to live out four years in the high-minded steeples of modern academia, elevated in dialogues about God and the origin of human consciousness, only to be ruthlessly dragged back to earth by the very enablers of our self-importance—those faceless gatekeepers of adult life, who had egged us on to superfluous distraction before revealing the punchline of their cruel Sisyphean joke: That in fact, the only aim of our over-education would henceforth be to carry it like a boulder up a hill, and watch it roll back down, over and over forever.

Between Sisyphus and me, the only difference I could see was that my hill was a series of white hallways; my boulder replaced by a never-ending batch of garment trunks. I would have been happy with anything to alleviate the sheer boredom of it—even just an occasional word from Sabrina or George besides "*faster.*" A hundred times before me flashed the image of my Yale degree—glorious serif font on bone-white paper, with my name in italics, and evidently no practical significance whatsoever—along with all the laughter, and the champagne, and the riotous off-campus parties, which on that day at *Régine* I feared might go down in my memory as my bygone "glory years," my last taste of the good life.

After I had moved half of the trunks, my forehead was damp and the collar of my buttoned-up dress shirt steeped with cold sweat. I hovered over my desk for a moment, foggily contemplating the removal of my jacket and tie. I felt the jacket fall involuntarily past my shoulders—a cool, momentary relief washed over me—then I froze with a sudden jolt of conviction. I clenched my teeth, and re-buttoned my suit jacket over my sweating body. If my new role necessitated that I be drenched in sweat, exercising no special skills except my brute ability to emulate the motions of a conveyor belt, then at the very least I would uphold my only claim to dignity.

Back and forth between the elevator and the closet (I memorized the labyrinthine white halls that day), I lost track of everything: the number of trunks, the hours that passed. When after two hours I thought I had unloaded everything—for the first time I breathed a joyous sigh of relief upon joining George in the closet—it turned out the delivery truck downstairs was waiting with a second batch. The hallways were an endless white tunnel, back and forth, forever.

When all of the never-ending trunks were in the fashion closet (the last of the trunks I had to line up along the corridor outside the closet, as George couldn't unpack them as fast as I was bringing them), I began to help George remove their contents—dresses, shirts, pants, coats, shoes, gloves, scarves, belts, sunglasses, garment bag upon garment bag, accessory bag upon accessory bag—all while e-mails from designers and PR firms began flooding in and Sabrina yelled, "Gather up all the Cavalli! All the Versace! All the Ferragamo!" so that George had to start combing through them all to find the right things while I was left to continue unpacking, so panicked by the constant barrage of Sabrina and George's yelling that I abandoned the hope of preserving any order and just began pouring things out of bags, every luxury item losing its individual value and becoming another one of many identical, meaningless objects to slosh through.

Of course, all of it was either white or off-white, and it felt as though the fresh, compact white snow that had fallen last week had been ravaged by rain and sun into a dirty gray muck, with rivulets of melting ice pooling everywhere.

After hours of this—I lost track of how many—Sabrina emerged from her cubicle to ask us what was taking so long. When I looked up at her to respond, she was just staring at me as I drowned in perspiration. "You can't touch these clothes when you're sweating like this. Go wash your face," she ordered, and upon my return, yelled, "We need everything Cavalli—urgently! Four dresses, one scarf, four belts—do you remember which? A messenger will be picking it all up in twenty minutes."

I couldn't remember, and had to consult our reference photos. When I had proudly fished out the correct belt and nothing else, Sabrina glared. "What in the world—?"

"It's just—" I whimpered, up to my calves in a pile of handbags, with a dress on my head that George had thrown at me.

"Cavalli is downstairs waiting!" she seethed through gritted teeth, as though it was Roberto Cavalli himself who was glancing at his watch in the lobby and not some hired messenger playing video games on his phone while he waited. Sabrina tore through the closet and came back inexplicably in a minute with the rest of the Cavalli garments, throwing them into a pile with the belt it had taken me twenty minutes to find. I sat there bewildered for a second, staring at the items whose arrival to the *Régine* closet I only vaguely remembered inventorying one week ago.

"I need a label," she instructed, as she flew through the closet to gather up the pieces from Gucci.

"What's the address?" I asked.

"In front of your face," George said, with a motion toward the address list pinned above our computers. He stapled a Return Manifest to a shopping bag of Balenciaga handbags (everything had to be rephotographed the way it had been when it first entered the closet, with three copies of an important paper called the Return Manifest, one of which went to Sabrina, one to the designer's PR team, and one to the messenger who was transporting the thing between the two), while Sabrina's muffled voice called to me from between the racks, "Cavalli goes to Five Twenty-Five West Twenty-Fifth Street, attention Melissa."

At first I couldn't find the labels, and when I finally did in a drawer Sabrina snatched them out of my hands before I could even take the top of my pen off, and wrote it herself.

"Here's all the Gucci next," she said, and again, without so much as consulting her e-mail or a list on the wall, recited, "Send it to Eight Fifteen Madison Ave, attention Charlie." She did that all afternoon—pulled detailed contact information out of thin air—and it became clear she had memorized the address and contact person of every single designer and PR firm in Manhattan, like a human spreadsheet.

In the late afternoon, Jane swept leisurely into the office, winsome and fresh-faced, pale ponytailed hair bouncing over her lily-white nape.

"Hello, darlings," she greeted. "What a wonderful job you're all doing."

"Thank you," came Sabrina's glorious smile, every trace of malice wiped away from her rosy cheeks. "How was your weekend?"

"Oh, it was divine, thank you!" confided Jane, as she poked through her stack of mail on the corner of Sabrina's desk—invitations to shows and parties, and thank-you notes from designers whose creations she had featured in a recent spread. She wore a variant on her usual ensemble: a white dress shirt, rolled up at the sleeves, with royal blue cigarette pants and a pair of lemon-colored pumps. "Took my grandchildren to the zoo." Her ankle rocked with absentminded whimsy over her high heel. "Came this close to getting kissed by a giraffe, or maybe spit on . . . Oh, isn't that nice!—a thank-you note from Alexander Wang."

"He sent flowers too," said Sabrina. "I left them on your desk, along with some from Chanel and Balenciaga. You can let me know if you'd like them messengered to your apartment later."

Jane turned to all of us and smiled, and my sense of despair was briefly alleviated as I thought: *That could be me one day, breezing through the office to collect my cards and flowers.* She left the office an hour later, while I searched on my hands and knees for an opal which had fallen off an embroidered Balmain belt.

MONDAY TRICKLED LIKE MELTING SLUSH INTO TUESDAY.

In the end we returned two dresses, four bags, and one pair of sunglasses to Céline; four dresses, nine pairs of shoes, three pairs of gloves, one scarf, two belts, and one pair of sunglasses to Chanel; three pairs of shoes, four scarves, seven bags, and six belts to Ferragamo; three shirts, three pants, two coats, and two belts to Etro; four dresses, four shirts, two pants, and six pairs of shoes to Alexander Wang; four dresses, two pairs of shoes, and one pair of gloves to Dolce & Gabbana; three dresses, one coat, two pairs of shoes, and one pair of gloves to Altuzarra; five dresses, one shirt, three shoes, and one pair of sunglasses to Marni; four dresses, one scarf, four belts to Cavalli; three shirts and three pants to Pucci; five dresses, three shirts, four pants, five coats, two shoes, and one belt to Jil Sander; three dresses, one shirt, five pairs of shoes, and seven pairs of sunglasses to Versace; two dresses to Derek Lam; ten bags, four pairs of gloves, five scarves, twelve belts, and six pairs of sunglasses to Louis Vuitton; two shirts, three pants, and two coats to Thom Browne; three pairs of shoes, four bags, three belts, and one pair of sunglasses to Rag & Bone; four pairs of shoes, six pairs of gloves, one scarf, three belts, and one pair of sunglasses to Hermès; three pairs of shoes, four scarves, six bags, and two belts to Bally; six shirts, three pants, two coats, and two belts to Saint Laurent; four dresses, one shirt, two pants, and five pairs of shoes to 3.1 Phillip Lim; four dresses, two pairs of shoes, and one pair of gloves to Alexander McQueen; three dresses, one coat, three pairs of shoes, and one pair of gloves to Chloé; seven dresses, three pairs of shoes, and two pairs of sunglasses to Lanvin; four dresses, one scarf, and four belts to Stella McCartney; two shirts and three pants to Rodarte; eight pairs of shoes to Jimmy Choo; three shirts, four pants, two coats, two shoes, and one belt to Theory; three dresses, one shirt, five pairs of shoes, and two pairs of sunglasses to Proenza Schouler; six bags to Marchesa; two bags, one pair of gloves, one scarf, two belts, and one pair of sunglasses to Nina Ricci; fourteen bags, nine dresses, two shirts, three pants, and six coats to Marc Jacobs; seven pairs of shoes to Manolo Blahnik; and so much more I almost just slapped a label onto myself and fell asleep in a bag to be taken away.

Around six-thirty on Tuesday, people finally stopped e-mailing for all their clothes back. As we were leaving for home, George pointed to the volume he had asked me to get from the library the previous week. "Can you take this back? It's just taking up space here."

My upper lip curled. "Sure," I said. But the thing that bothered me was, I hadn't seen him use it, nor did I think he actually needed it in the first place.

chapter six

"I didn't come here to talk about Dorian," I declared as Madeline and I passed the Prada section on the third floor at Bergdorf Goodman. The store was closing in thirty minutes, and despite my protests that I was exhausted from work, Madeline had pleaded for me to accompany her shopping for a dress. I hadn't seen or heard from her since the incident at the nightclub, yet a series of missed phone calls late that afternoon attested her sudden remembrance of me (Madeline never left messages, only called and called until she finally got through). I should have known it would involve Dorian.

Now in response to my frustrated eye roll, she said, "Oh, please, don't be unreasonable," as though I was her stubborn husband who never yielded to common sense. "Dorian and I talked it all out—and anyway, don't take my word for it—he wants to see you for his birthday party next week." A casual hand through her hair meant she had just cleared up everything.

Knowing Dorian and Madeline equally well, it was very hard to imagine him just reappearing in our lives unplanned, looking once into Madeline's sapphire eyes, and realizing the error of his ways. Easier to imagine, however, was Madeline, her hand locked on his knee, begging as she choked up, "*Please, don't go away*"—never mind any questions that might upset him, those whys and hows that over the past year had tortured her, and me too. For a fool like Madeline (a blind, lovesick fool—the worst kind) the price of her forgiveness was too affordable: her lover's noncommittal glance and his halfhearted utterance of any love-like affirmation.

She hadn't just considered herself Dorian's girlfriend—she had been his "true love," like Cleopatra was Antony's, and Juliet Romeo's, with asps and daggers and all. In the tradition of all great, foolish love stories, her reaction to Dorian's unpardonable offense had therefore been to love him inextinguishably more.

The effect of Dorian's departure on my own feelings for him could not have taken a more contrary composition, as in his absence I had hardened like a salt crystal. His crime weighed less upon me than my own complicity: Without my irrational heart as an accomplice, Madeline would have never involved herself with Dorian. She had once despised him—it was me who fell in love with him, and made her fall in love with him too.

I was tortured by the truth of their "great love." Even if their reunion at the nightclub had culminated in the unlikely idyll that Madeline claimed (the two of them intertwined on a velvet booth like Pierre-Auguste Cot's *Les Printemps*, whispering confessions of love with a luminous glow around their heads), where had their passions led *me*? Through misery and ultimately to the bathroom, coughing up blood and broken glass into a ceramic bowl.

"I didn't come here to talk about Dorian," I repeated. "I came here because you said you needed help finding a dress!" My voice was an octave too high amid the racks of cocktail attire. I held my nose in the air and crossed my arms over my chest. "I won't humor you talking about Dor—" I cleared my throat "—talking about *him*, and no, I won't go to his stupid birthday party."

Through her incorruptible blindness, Madeline searched my face and asked, "But—why not?" Then, with great purpose, while she blinked away any uncertainty: "He says he's still in love with me. And he still loves you. He wants us all to be a trio again. He says—sorry."

"*Sorry?*" I could have laughed at her, but I was too appalled. "You act like all he did was step on your foot." I turned away and began to walk in the other direction, glancing at my watch.

With a hasty scratching of her heels on the carpet, she came up behind me and unbecomingly dangled a delicate arm around my shoulder, like a used-car salesperson trying to get me to see the value in some totaled Aston Martin, a once-beautiful thing whose immobile parts now sagged unrecognizably on the concrete lot. "Just think of it, Ethan," she whispered with a wild look in her eyes. "Just you, and me, and Dorian, all over again—this solves everything between us all. It'll be just like it used to be, *the perfect trio*, just like—"

I cut her off. "Are you going to try on a dress or what?"

A year ago, she had sobbed into my arms, "*He's gone, he's never coming back*," and I had stroked her back and stared vacantly at the wall, filled with unfathomable emptiness. Now she implored, "Why? Why won't you give him a chance?" as I flicked away a price tag on a four-thousand-dollar Ferragamo sheath, which boasted an incredible markdown of one thousand dollars.

"Did he explain himself? Did you even try to make him?" I pressed. "What makes you think now he won't just run off again?"

Lost in a nervous trance—she knew she could lose me over this—Madeline poked through a rack of Lanvin dresses, barely looking, just shuffling her hand in and out, and yanked at one. "What do you think of this?"

It was an overripe summery sensation, a rotting strawberry bush uprooted and trailing along the carpet as she came at me in reckless entreaty. I don't think she even really looked at it; she was too busy with her eyes on me, searching my face for the approval I rarely withheld from her—approval about the dress, about Dorian, anything.

"It's too big for you," I said. She didn't seem to hear, and I lagged behind while she rushed it to the fitting rooms, where a gray-suited salesperson with a pug-like face was preparing a room for another customer. Madeline gestured at me to follow her, and the puggish little man said, "I'm sorry, we only allow one person in a fitting room at a time," coupled with a reprimanding snort, like we really should know better than to try that nonsense at Bergdorf Goodman.

This was one of the reasons I hated to shop with Madeline. In New York City there were loads of these uppity salespeople, whose life's ambition was to deny fitting-room entry to best friends in expensive stores. The same thing happened the last time we came to Bergdorf's, when Madeline had lied and said she'd "be right out," and had me tapping my toe outside the fitting room for a half-hour before innocently pretending she had lost track of time because her phone "just didn't work in there," like she expected me to believe that by closing a curtain she had really gone to another country.

This time she knew better than to leave me—I had been generous enough meeting her in the first place, after she had unapologetically ditched me at the club for Dorian. If I had known she was choosing a dress for Dorian's birthday party, I'd have never come.

"He *has* to come in with me," she snapped at the salesman. "I'm an invalid." She waved her hand in his face, pretending to be missing a finger.

"Now doesn't he feel awful?" Madeline said to me, slushing the velvet curtains shut behind us with a full-fingered jerk. Dropping her Céline purse on the floor, she haphazardly strung her cardigan through the handles before turning her back to me. "Help," she implored, urgently tapping the zipper at the top of her orchid-long spine. I resentfully unsheathed her as she egged me on. "We have to give Dorian another chance. He came back—he says he needs us in his life again."

She stumbled out of her dress and made a full rotation around the fitting room, resembling a blind person as she patted everywhere, feeling around for some unknown thing. She patted my chest before remembering the dress she had entered the fitting room to try. "Don't you think it's a sign?" she went on, shaking the loud, ridiculous dress off the hanger. "That we would end up at the same club? Don't you believe in signs anymore, Ethan? You've always believed in *signs*."

The dress fell into a heap, and when she bent over to retrieve it, I watched her stare at the hanger in her hand. Finally she let it clatter to the floor and rose with the dress pulled taut between her hands like a piece of laundry she was about to hang on a clothesline.

"Won't you please say something?" she begged.

I yanked the dress from her and unzipped the back, holding it open for her to step into. "I don't want anyone getting hurt again," I said.

"Hurt?" Her voice pierced the air. She pulled up at the sleeves, wiggling her body in an infantile way. Her eyes darted everywhere. "Who is hurt? I don't know who you think is—"

"Madeline," I commanded. I grabbed her by the shoulders. "Calm down."

She stopped fidgeting; slipped into a startled trance. She blinked several times at the floor before softening between my hands.

"Just . . . forget Dorian," I said. "Just remember—remember what he did to you—remember what it was like, how much pain you felt when he disappeared, how much pain you're still feeling . . ."

Like a person on the verge of hypnosis, her eyes fluttered. I thought she might peer up and murmur, "Dorian who . . . ?" Then I felt her muscles tense, and she twisted away.

"No, *you* remember!" she burst. Outside the pug-faced salesperson was surely contemplating how to get away with silencing the impudent invalid. "Remember how we loved each other," Madeline said, "him and me, and you and me, and all of us together. Remember all the things we did, picking flowers and feeding ducks and—"

"We never fed any ducks."

"—*singing* and going to parties and doing—" she tossed up her naked arms in a flurry "—I don't know—*things* together!" Whatever *things* she was thinking about, they caused her face to wrinkle into a little pinch, and suddenly she began to cry. The dress flapped open and dropped like a fairy ring around her feet, while she wrapped her arms around herself and fell toward me like a whimpering piece of timber.

After Dorian left, it had been devastating to see the things Madeline got cracked up about. One time she didn't go to class because her face mask dried into a sinister shape in the sink—the plasticky eyes clinging shut over a gaping mouth hole—and she said it reminded her of the way winter made the flowers shrivel, and how nobody could stop getting old even if they used a face mask every day. Other times she would go on a date with Grant Goodwin, and come back sobbing for hours. It was a time of agonizing confusion—despite sexual developments made between Madeline and me during Dorian's tenure, Madeline and I had agreed upon his disappearance to renew our platonic distance. "It'll make things less complicated," I remember saying, in an attempt to convince myself, and two weeks later, Grant was trying to be her boyfriend, and she was going along with it to distract herself. As neither of them had changed their incompatible views since our Political Systems class, her post-Grant breakdown always included some despairing allusion to "capitalist pigs"—yet I was never sure if her tears had been provoked by the distressing effects of Grant's political opinions or the mere fact that he wasn't Dorian, and he wasn't me, and maybe she feared that after everything had splintered between the three of us, she would never be whole enough to love again.

"We did things," Madeline sniffled into my neck.

I breathed into her hair, and sighed. She was shaking beneath my arms, and her naked skin felt as smooth as the first time we had done "things" together.

IT HAD BEEN FEBRUARY OF SOPHOMORE YEAR, AND THE three of us had gotten especially drunk at an Around the World party, due in large part to our inspired first encounter with

Goldschläger. "There's *real* gold in it?" Madeline had exclaimed. Twenty-four karat, we were told, and the next minute Dorian and I were fighting Madeline for the last shot glass: "*What have we been missing our whole lives?*" The rest of the night was like a pulsing light—occasionally vivid, mostly dark. The first flash of memory was the three of us at Dorian's off-campus apartment, stumbling into his shadowy bedroom.

In the platonic sense, we had all already slept together many times. While I was still a virgin, Madeline and Dorian had been dating since November, and had been having sex since Christmas, which for both of them had been an enormous development. Although I initially hesitated to insinuate myself into their relations, my reservations had been suppressed all along by their endorsement of their more salient perspective: They were a couple, yes, but we were also a trio. Thus, every moment of free time they *weren't* having sex was spent triply conjoined with me. We spiraled through parties and ballets and operas—the same cycle of diversions which had always swept up Madeline and me, enhanced now by our ancillary plus one—then we all three wound up in bed together, an innocent pile of snores and tangled limbs.

After our excursion that night into twenty-four-karat liqueur, we entered Dorian's apartment to find out he had left the heater blasting in his daylong absence. We moved through a suffocating cloud of vapor, the windowsills puddled with dripping condensation. I jerked open the bedroom window, while Madeline heaved against the bedpost, gasping, and Dorian began to unburden himself: his Burberry trench in an indiscrete heap, followed by an airborne sweater, dress shirt, T-shirt, a farcical series of flying shadows. He was kicking off his shoes, wriggling out of his pants, and then, somehow—Dorian was naked.

I had never seen Dorian naked before.

Before that night, intervening layers of clothing had allowed our slumbering bodies a sexless distance. Now, my arousal at the sight of his naked body was swift, absolute.

The next thing I remember is falling backward onto Dorian's sheets—*puff!*—like I was preparing to make a snow angel. Madeline swooped onto me, leaving a trail of kisses from the top to the bottom of my chest as though she was planting seeds there with her lips. The natural progression: a tug on my underwear. I must have uttered some futile murmur of embarrassed dissent—the elastic clung momentarily to my erection—then I popped right out.

My unsubtle transgression stood erect with deviant pride, an accidental invitation. A frantic wriggling of bodies followed. Madeline's skirt whooshed onto my foot and got kicked away.

Then, a hole of blackened memory.

Then, a flash of remembrance. The two of them were buttressed like a steeple over my plank-stiff body: Madeline nearest me, with her knees straddled around my legs, and Dorian shadowlike behind her. The moonlight silhouetted their upraised bodies. Dorian cupped her breasts from behind, and leaned his head over her shoulder to kiss her. Their faces merged. Her spine arched as he pressed against her—and then, a small gasp.

He entered her from behind; the bed was rocking below me, and they were rocking above. I observed them with awe. When Madeline remembered my body beneath her, she bowed her head onto me.

Wet lips: I was engulfed in warmth.

Her suspended breasts jiggled over my thighs as Dorian held her against his thrusts. My fingers found Madeline's hair and my head rolled back into the pillow, and the clearest memory of all was the ceiling above us—obsidian black, except for a silver triangle of light from the window, like an Edward Hopper painting.

The next morning, I awoke to find Madeline draped on top of me. Dorian lay peacefully nearby, Adonis in repose, and I remember thinking that, in all the night's flashing stages, Dorian had tried not to touch me, or even look at me.

That was our first winter with Dorian. There was one more after that, then—gone.

Dorian had never meant to hurt us—that was the one thing at least we could be sure of—but you just couldn't expect the most beautiful person in the world to stay in one place, or be loyal. He didn't mean anything by it, or realize he had done something wrong; he was just being himself, flitting throughout the world, and how could we disparage him for that when we had celebrated this kind of transience, challenging each other every day to be more carefree, celebrating new lengths traveled in the name of personal liberation? We idolized the Beats, and the Lost Generation, and the Impressionists, everyone who banded together to achieve a goal that had the outward glow of shunning convention. Fitzgerald and Hemingway were favorites for rejecting the American rat race to write novels by the sparkling Seine—and the restless Kerouac most of all.

Like all of them, Dorian had just gotten up and left, no apologies. He barely reached out when he got to Paris, and when he did for the first time, after several weeks of agonizing silence, it was laughable in its oblivious, impersonal nature: an e-mail with no subject reading simply, *miss u guys!!!*

Madeline didn't even know if they were broken up.

I forbade Madeline to reply, promising never to speak to her again if she did. She obeyed, while bemoaning the unfairness of it: For her the thought of being all alone—no me, no Dorian—she couldn't handle it. Eventually after that single e-mail—no phone calls, or letters, or anything more to suggest that the relationship we had all shared deserved greater effort—he apparently just forgot about us.

MADELINE AND I STOOD THERE HUGGING IN THE FITTING room until, at last, she stiffened up a bit, and said, "You know, when a baby is born without the ability to feel pain, it dies within a year."

She told me this in a voice that was vaguely defiant, and before I could ask her what that meant, she had released me from my embrace and was hastily dressing herself in her own clothes.

I stood there bewildered as she tossed the curtain open.

"Who can blame Dorian, right?" she spouted nonsensically to the air, "when everybody in the world just disappoints each other," and I had no hope of following her polluted stream of consciousness.

Giving the salesperson every reason to believe we had been in a fitting-room tryst, she stormed off as though I had said the wrong thing to her while we were having sex on the bench in there. I took a deep breath as she left with the back of her own dress unzipped, flapping open.

Appearing not the least bit like an invalid, she practically dumped the Lanvin dress on the salesperson's head, deciding, "I'll have it in the next size down," even though she had barely tried it on to begin with. At ten feet away, she turned back to me, terrified I might have left.

I stood there among all the things she had left in my care—

her patent leather Céline bag and classic little Hermès scarf, and the pearl-buttoned Marchesa cardigan on the floor beneath me.

"Won't you please come with me to buy shoes before they close?" she asked, coming toward me. She glanced guiltily at all her things. I began to scoop up the cardigan as she delivered her best approximation of an apology in her stricken state. "I'm—nervous." She gulped, and of course, I knew it was true. In general, Madeline was a little foolish, but not like *this*. Dorian had unhinged her.

I always knew it would be like this, when Dorian came back. A feverish pitch in the air, excitement and fear. It was our destiny—the destiny of people entangled.

With her purse over my shoulder, I took her hand. She squeezed it as we descended on the escalator to the second floor.

DORIAN HAD BEEN TWENTY MINUTES LATE WHEN I INITIALLY laid eyes on him the first day of sophomore year.

I was sitting toward the back of the classroom—a small wood-paneled auditorium, with rows of desks all curved like half-moons toward an amphitheatric stage. It was dark, except for a projector blazing a tunnel of spectral white light from behind, specks of dust swirling in and out with fatalistic indifference.

The class was Introduction to European Art; the professor, young and handsome, impressing upon us with his serious baritone the significance of the ancient Greeks.

The door opened.

Light flooded the room like a deep breath of air into a lung. Dorian stood there as the golden inhalation rose upward; then he slowly pressed his back against the door, and the room returned to darkness with a reluctant sigh. His entrance would have gone less noticed had he simply taken a seat, but on catching sight of the projected image he was drawn to it with a moth-like transfixion. His profile illuminated, Dorian stared at the close-up of a marble Apollo from the fourth century BC—and it was as though he was looking at a picture of himself. My own eyes traveled with hovering fascination between them: Dorian shared with Apollo the essence of every feature. The same curved lips and sublimely cantilevered nose; the same bright, hopeful eyes, gazing blindly into a blazing sun.

The professor leaned against the podium, hands clasped over his dark Italian suit. "Very attentive," he said to Dorian. "Please redirect your attention to a chair."

But Dorian's eyes remained on the picture, engrossed as if he were standing alone before a frame at a museum. The professor rapped on the podium. Dorian snapped out of it, staggered backward upon the first row, and fell into a seat, where the only view of him was the back of his dark brown hair.

"*That's the supermodel's son,*" I heard someone whisper behind me, and I immediately made the connection. Everybody had heard of him: Dorian Belgraves, son of the celebrated Edith Belgraves—just "Edie" in the magazines and the society columns—a model who two decades earlier, had made her fortune as one of the most photographed faces of her generation. Dorian evidently had transferred to Yale as a sophomore, trailed by a stream of rumors. In some bubbling accounts he was violent or addicted to methamphetamines; in others, running away from academic probation and/or a sex tape with a fellow socialite. The reports were dubious—famous mother or not, no Ivy League college could accept a student under such circumstances—yet they persisted in light of Dorian's well-documented flickering through the New York society circuit.

Despite the precedence of this reputation throughout campus, however, for most of September he ambled along by himself. He always looked like he had been abruptly roused out of bed—his Grecian locks in a wavy tangle and his book bag spilling off his shoulder as he tossed around the half-chomped fruit that was his breakfast. He liked to draw, or was studying fine art, or something, because he always carried a large sketchpad under his arm. He sketched in unlikely places—on the roof of Davenport Hall, or the terrace of the Pierson Library with his feet dangling through the railing. I caught him once sitting cross-legged in a fountain with the water sparkling right over his head, fully clothed except for his bag and shoes, which were spared in a tumble nearby.

My interest in him was piqued—although it was not greater than my hesitation to approach him—and a week later, I spotted him once more. I was lingering alone after a lackadaisical brunch in Pierson Dining Hall, absently dipping my fingers into a bowl of cranberry granola while I waited for Madeline to finish her Intro to Public Policy seminar, and semi-purposefully reviewing notes for an exam on human evolution.

Dorian didn't notice me at first, just sat by himself at the adjacent table and began to peel a clementine. He leaned back in his chair with his long legs stretched out, like a shepherd napping against a tree trunk, flicking specks of clementine rind like confetti onto the sketchbook on his lap. When he had finished, he scooped the shreds into a napkin and propped up the sketchbook between his lap and the table's edge, proceeding to draw a subject on the wall behind me.

In a white crew neck shirt and blue jeans, he listened to music through a pair of headphones while I contemplated from afar the contradictory elegance of his slouch. This, I would learn, was one of Dorian's many charms: He could collapse his body anywhere and give the impression that he had been deliberately posed by some great artistic master. His gaze flickered up beyond me, then returned with diligent preoccupation to his upraised pad, back and forth, back and forth, as he occasionally took a bite of a clementine segment, juice trickling down his forearm. After a few minutes, Dorian's attention wandered onto me.

My eyes were drawn straight to Dorian's mouth, full with cupid-like sweetness. He lowered his sketchbook in full recognition of me, and my whole face burned with embarrassment. Swiveling toward my study notes, I pretended to engross myself in primates and bipedalism while, at the edge of my vision, I saw him rise up from his table. I cursed myself, and placed the blame for his departure on my indiscreet stare—but the next moment Dorian was peering over me, book bag dangling on his forearm.

"Can I draw you?" he asked, sketchbook pages fluttering.

I peered up without breathing. A chandelier aligned above his head to form a gold crown, and it was easy to picture him as a prince who had climbed out of one of the stained-glass windows in Sterling Memorial Library and ambled over for a snack.

"I was copying the painting of that guy over there," he pointed to Abraham Pierson over the mantle, "but you're way better-looking."

I felt my blush ripen into a deeper shade as he confirmed his corporeality with another juicy bite of clementine. He turned up his wrist to wipe a trickle from the corner of his lips, then leaned in, his face swooping right in front of mine.

"Wow!" he exclaimed. His green eyes blinked inches away

from my own, and the scintillating smell of citrus washed over me. "Are your eyes . . . ?"

"Yea, they're—different colors."

"That's amazing," he said, with greater fascination than I felt was deserved by any aspect of my humble appearance. "I've never seen that before."

Our intimate proximity brought me within earshot of his headphones. "Are you listening to Puccini?" I asked.

He nodded, and his face withdrew from mine. "You like him?"

I laughed outright. "I love Puccini. *Madama Butterfly* was my first opera."

He pulled his headphones down around his nape, his fingers still wrapped around his half-eaten clementine. "Then how about this?" Resting his knee on the seat opposite me, he fiddled with a volume button in his pocket; "O Soave Fanciulla," Rudolfo and Mimi's duet from Act One of *La Bohème*, crescendoed. "You'll let me draw you, and I'll put Puccini here so we can both listen." He unslung the headphones from his neck and dropped them onto my tray with a grin. "Unless—I don't know, are you studying for something?"

"Not really. I just . . ." I was flattered, but confused by his choice of artistic subject. Between the two of us, wasn't it his face which deserved immortalization?

"Then you'll do it!" he filled in, and swung himself into the chair before me. "You don't have to do anything," he promised, "except be still." He turned to a new page in his sketchbook and remembered, "Oh—! I'm Dorian!"

His outstretched hand was like an anatomical study, his smooth, broad-knuckled fingers sticky with clementine juice.

“We have a class together, you know,” I informed him, as our hands met and he gave mine a vigorous shake. “Intro to European Art, with Pericles Lewis.”

“Oh, I know,” he nodded, and I swelled up to hear that he had recognized me. “I like all your suits. I wish I could wear clothes like that, but I’d just get them dirty.” He smiled, and it was like looking straight into a blinding light. “Do you want this?” he asked. His white wrist caught a flash of sunlight overhead as he offered up the remainder of his clementine.

I laid it on the corner of my tray as he lopped his book bag onto his lap and began to shuffle through it. The bag was expensive-looking—camel-tone leather, with elegant brass trimmings—but unfortunately, it also looked like Dorian had run it through a trash compactor, with its crisscross of deep scratches over the whole front, and a shedding piece of yellow gaffer tape wrapped around one strap. Inside, a piece of shattered charcoal had coated the entire lining with a leaden ash.

A pair of blackened drumsticks rolled to one side. “Do you play the drums?” I asked.

“No.” He gave me a quizzical look, then realized—“Oh! Yes. These.” He rubbed the drumsticks together like he was starting a fire and sent a cloud of charcoal dust into the air. “I thought I would learn music, but it’s too hard. All those symbols—you know what they say about language, once you get old, it’s almost impossible to learn a new one, and . . .” He abandoned the drumsticks into the bag with a clatter as his search intensified, and for a second I was sure he would give up and dump it all onto my silver lunch tray.

“Now where did I put my—” He raised his hand to his chin and smudged it with charcoal. “I have the worst sense of—*oh!*”

An unexplained chorus of pine needles drifted idly to the floor as he emerged victorious with a battered box of oil pastels. "This picture needs to be in color," he said. "With your eyes, I'd be stupid to draw you in black-and-white."

He unhinged the crushed lid. "Now, I don't want you to have any expectations," he warned. "I just started learning to draw people, so—I don't really know what I'm doing. I'm pretty fast though—you'll just have to be still for five minutes." He pulled out a bright orange pastel for consideration, and closing one eye as he held it up to my face, decided promptly that it matched my white skin.

I tidied up my evolution flashcards and clasped my hands over my tray. "Where should I look?"

He pointed with two fingers into his eyes. "Straight at me," he replied, then—"Your glasses."

"What about them?"

"Can you take them off?"

I sat paralyzed by self-consciousness. Dorian couldn't have known, but I had never let anybody see me without my glasses: They were as integral to my sense of self as my colorful suits, armor I wore to protect me against the world. Without them, I would be practically naked, yet how could I fear Dorian, whose face defied all malice—its every contour a testament to enduring virtue?

He sat there with the pastel hovering over the page, and a look of earnest willfulness. All around I became aware of doors flying open and closed, but the silence between us was deafening. Eyes closed, I touched my fingers against my tortoiseshell rims. I felt the glasses slide off my face, almost of their own accord; heard the faint clicks as I pressed the two hinged legs closed, one by one, against my chest. I wrapped my fingers around the flattened frame; let my hand fall upon my lap; looked up. When I opened my eyes at last, everything was clouded: Dorian's silhouette, his outstretched arm, the back of his sketchpad like a blurry white swatch in a Mondrian painting. Yet I could feel his eyes on me—keen and unflinching—and my heart began to beat very fast.

"You're beautiful," he said, without a hint of hesitation.

I felt the blood rise yet again to my cheeks, and tried to laugh off my embarrassment: "Says the model's son."

"It's true—I mean, don't get a big head about it, but . . ." He settled back into his chair with a creak. "You know who you remind me of? Remember that Caravaggio we saw in class last week—the young boy, with the black hair?"

I knew exactly which one he was talking about. "The Borghese boy? Carrying the basket of fruit?"

The abstraction of a nod. "Not your face, exactly," Dorian explained, as he adjusted his sketchpad on what looked like his upraised knee. "Just the expression. He's holding this whole basket of fruit, but still—he looks so hungry."

I felt my lips unstick as I let this settle over me; listened to the whoosh of his hand over the paper. A circle, the basic contour of my face. His own hazy countenance shifted up and down—turned white when he looked up at me, then fell into shadow upon the lowering of his gaze toward the page.

"So where are you from?" he asked.

"Texas," I replied, and before I could carry on with some self-deprecating detail, his face lit up, penetrating the fog of my blurred vision with unmistakable delight.

"No way!" he said, although I could hardly guess the reason for his enthusiasm. "Did you own a horse?"

I laughed. "Is that what you envision, when you hear somebody's from Texas? You should think deserted malls and parking lots instead."

"I love horseback riding," Dorian said. I heard him blow on the surface of the page; brush the back of his hand over it to clear off a pitter-patter of unwanted eraser specks. "That's what I wanted to do at West Point—thought I'd get to gallop around with a bayonet or something."

"You went to West Point?!" I leaned abruptly toward him.

"Don't move!"

"Sorry, I just—" I drew my face back and shook away my surprise. "I had no idea."

"Yeah, I just escaped," he smiled. "Or, well—I transferred out, but when people ask I tell them I freed all the horses and then jumped the fence. Except there wasn't really any horses. Or a fence, really."

"How'd you end up at West Point, though?"

"I told you, I wanted to ride horses. I'm just kidding, sort of. I didn't want to go to college, but my mom was going to make me, so I thought I'd do something different."

"It didn't seem drastic?"

"Not more drastic than jumping from Texas to Connecticut. I mean, my mom thought it was extreme, but she's used to it. She says it's what happens when you don't have a Path." He paused to exchange his pastel for a different color. "Have you heard about Paths?"

I squinted, trying to detect some deeper meaning in the word, the translation of which was perhaps lost through my lack of vision. "You mean, like roads?"

"No, I mean—in life. Like when people say, 'Everyone has a Path, and you just have to follow it.'"

"Of course I've heard of *that,*" I laughed. "You make it sound like some big mystery!"

"Well, because it is! Everyone except for me has a Path. I don't know why. I just think to myself, *How am I supposed to pick one thing to do for the rest of my life?* I want to go everywhere, do everything. My Path looks like this so far," he said, and traced a preposterous trail of loop-de-loops in the air with his finger.

"Isn't art like your Path, though?"

"Art is my latest thing. That's how it always goes: I start these things—hobbies, projects—and then I get bored."

"Like horseback riding."

"No, actually I've always liked horseback riding, but other things haven't stuck that long. Like when we lived in London I was obsessed with water polo. In Milan, it was opera. Then I had a mountain biking phase in Toulouse, and a bird-watching phase, and then a cooking phase when we first moved to Paris. That one was bad. I still can't even do eggs . . ." His voice trailed off as he tilted his hazy head up to the white ceiling, and began enumerating on his fingers. "There was gymnastics and painting—both acrylic and oil—" He seemed to have only gotten started when I felt a hand on my shoulder.

"I almost didn't recognize you without your glasses," remarked Madeline, as she bent over to kiss my cheek.

I stirred, remembering myself, and returned the tortoiseshell glasses to my face. The familiar sight of Madeline came into sharp view—her delicate hands and flowing hair, and a floral pink-and-white sundress nipped at the waist by a Tiffany-blue sash.

Dorian, too, seemed to emerge from a blurred world into clarity, as he stared at Madeline, enraptured. "How . . ."

Madeline's hand trailed off my shoulder as she noticed him.

He pieced together a breathless benediction: "How have I never seen you before?"

She blushed, and glanced at me. Then their eyes connected and a shy smile hovered around her lips before her usual charm flooded her face. "Maybe you have, and you just weren't paying attention."

He shook his head. "No. I'd have paid attention." He stood up.

Madeline glanced at me once more—for approval, perhaps, or an explanation—while I just smiled with dumb fascination.

Dorian looked at me, and then at her, and it was as if a circuit had been completed. And in that moment, I knew that Dorian was a piece of us we had been missing.

He extended his hand; she accepted.

Then—"I'm Dorian."

Immediately the electricity that had been coursing between us flickered, the bulb dying.

"Oh," Madeline managed, her face plummeting into shadow. "Your mother is the model . . . right?" Her voice contained all the enthusiasm of a punctured tire, and I remembered that the subject of Dorian Belgraves had arisen once between us. "Narcissistic brat," she had said, referring to his too-photographed appearances in the shallowest social spheres of New York. "He's what's wrong with this country—everyone cares less about world affairs than they do about these talentless, superficial people."

If Dorian had registered the abrupt change in the air, he seemed to have garnered from it another meaning altogether: "Wait . . . You two aren't . . . dating, are you?"

"No . . ." Madeline admitted, and cast me a sidelong look of discomfort.

"Then—are you free for dinner tonight?" he asked.

Madeline realized her hand was still idle in Dorian's grasp. She winced a little and took it back, then slipped her hand under my arm. "I don't know if that's a good idea," she replied.

My chest dropped. I gasped a little, opened my mouth to intervene, to say, "*Wait! Of course she'll go—she's just . . .*" But Madeline's grasp around my forearm tightened. My loyalty wavered as I questioned her poor judgment—then I felt myself rise with a bewildered sense of obligation. Benumbed, I picked up my tray, and she pulled me away.

"Nice of you to ask, though," she shrugged politely. I could barely stand Dorian's crestfallen expression—although between him and me, it was unclear whose disappointment was greater.

IT WAS ONLY AFTER I BELIEVED I HAD ADJUSTED TO LIFE AT *Régine* that the "usual" state of affairs was redefined by a truly un "usual" morning.

"Good *moooorning*, everyone!" Clara strolled through the fashion closet doorway in a black-and-white houndstooth dress suit, her portrait-ready ebony face framed by a black headband in her blonde hair. She held up a flutter of legal-size pages, and beseeched the air: "Can *sooomebody* please make me four copies of this?" She rounded the corner of the accessories table, stocking-clad thighs cutting through her twice-slit pencil skirt, as her smile passed over Sabrina . . . then George . . . then me.

Her passage came to an undignified halt. She backpedaled with a few unbalanced steps, seemingly to get a clearer view of me, and struck an empty garment rack. Naked hangers rocked side to side, squeaking like a series of unlubricated door hinges, as George and I sat at full attention with our backs erect. Frozen next to us in mid-stride, her head immobile, Sabrina's eyes flickered from Clara to George, and finally to me, as she waited intently.

Clara, however, withheld further verbal exposition and lowered the papers in her hand with a precipitous ripple. She folded them edge to edge and remained undecided on her next step, patting the pages with distracted imprecision against her suit jacket.

"Clara . . . ? Are you all right?" It was Sabrina who broke the silence. The white fluorescent glow illuminated the otherwise imperceptible under-eye folds she was developing from too much smoking outside of fashionable parties.

Clara turned to her and nodded in a kind of default resolution to her consternation.

"Actually . . ." she began slowly, with a sudden chipper edge as her eyes seemed to blossom into waking life. "I came to suggest a walk." She smiled like it was the most natural thing in the world. The frozen strangeness of the previous moment melted in the warmth of her charm. "It's a beautiful day out. I think you and George should take a walk."

Sabrina squinted. "But . . ." She cast a sidelong glance to the telephone on her desk, to whose constant attendance she owed her greatest claim to professional worth. "What about phone calls?" She spoke as if Clara had suggested that she abandon her sobbing newborn.

"I think for twenty minutes it should be fine," Clara replied with a forceful edge, an order this time, though still disguised as a suggestion. "I mean—we all deserve a break sometimes, and you work so hard, don't you?"

When Sabrina didn't immediately agree, Clara took a challenging high-heeled step toward Sabrina's cubicle and cocked her head. "*Don't you?*" she repeated, a little sharply.

"I . . ." Sabrina recovered quickly. "Yes, I do work hard." She gulped and looked at George. "George . . ." she trailed off, and the next moment they were pressed together, springing toward the door. Sabrina murmured, "Thank you," to Clara, and George echoed with a mumble of the same syllables.

The door shut behind them. Silence. I looked left and right, but there was nobody else—I was alone with Clara.

"All right now," Clara said, sitting right down into George's chair. She crossed her legs, and the lace from her thigh-high stockings peeked out from under her pencil skirt with daunting refinement. She leaned forward. If, from a distance, her calligraphic mannerisms had an air of spontaneous grace, close proximity attested to their premeditated precision. Every muscle in her face seemed to move in accordance with a grand design.

"Ethan . . . it's Ethan, *riiight*?" She spoke with honeyed politeness, like a Georgia socialite preparing to resolve a minor catering detail before a charity ball. "I thought that after another week or so, this conversation would not be necessary, but—I think it would actually be better to nip this in the bud."

My stomach plummeted as I wracked my brain for a memory of my incriminating offense. In such a brief time, how had I managed to offend *Régine*'s most congenial editor?

"I have to ask you," she continued, "and please excuse my directness, but have you ever had a real job before?"

I shook my head in terror.

Clara responded, "Well, do you like working at *Régine*?"

"Oh, yes!" I rushed in. "Did I give you the impression

that . . . ?" Distressed to think I had somehow conveyed ungratefulness in my brief tenure, my eyebrows wrenched in overcompensatory earnestness. "It's my dream to be here—I'm learning so much. It's just amazing."

Clara smiled gently. "That is wonderful news." She considered for a moment how best to redirect my enthusiastic reply. "And when you say that you are learning a lot, does that include anything in terms of rules? That is, have you learned any of the *unwritten* rules that constitute our code of conduct here?"

The unbearable strain in her face had me on the verge of hyperventilation. "Whatever it is I've done, Clara—I mean, Ms. Bellamy—ma'am . . . I just—I'm so sorry. I can't tell you how much it means for me to be here, and to jeopardize that in any way . . ."

"Don't be afraid," she soothed me. "You haven't jeopardized anything. As I'm sure you've guessed from my accent, I'm not exactly from here either. I understand what it's like to not know the rules." Her generous circumvention of my embarrassment rendered her powers of graciousness complete. "Let me put it this way," she said. "To be at *Régine* is a privilege and, as with any privilege that may be conferred onto you in life, there are many corresponding rules to ensure that your privilege is balanced with the proportionate share of responsibility." Her palm flowered out toward me. "For example, you wouldn't say hello to someone you didn't know on the elevator, would you?"

I gulped, and my head twitched. Of course I already broke this rule on a regular basis, trying to initiate conversations with eternally uninterested passengers.

"Of course you wouldn't," she filled in on my behalf, saving me again. "For all you know, they could be the CEO of Hoffman-

Lynch Publications, and that wouldn't exactly be appropriate, would it? For an intern to distract the leading executive of our company? Nor would you leave the office for the day with tasks left undone, or let an e-mail go unanswered, or take a bathroom break without notifying your colleagues." I ran a mental scroll of these unwritten tenets, of whose existence I had been woefully ignorant.

"I understand Sabrina has already explained," she continued, "that you should never interrupt a conversation between your superiors, and by the same token you should *never* wear an outfit which is inappropriate for your rank."

I gasped with realization and glanced down at myself. Head-to-toe turquoise suit, with a flower-print shirt and a pink tie: my boldest outfit yet. In merely three weeks at *Régine* my style had flourished to peacock-worthy proportions as, day after day, new levels of demeaning office drudgery increased my need to feel dignified, worthy, and unique. My cheeks burned with self-consciousness, conveying my rush of insight to Clara.

"I don't mean to embarrass you," Clara said, "but you are an intern. You are here to learn, and to serve others, not to draw attention from the work that is being done."

"I'm sorry . . . I never thought—I just—" The words flooded out, then struck a barrier: I now hesitated to state the explanation that to me was so obvious.

"Go on," she said. "Let's discuss this. That's why Sabrina and George have been dismissed—because this conversation is private."

Realizing that Clara had made such a gracious effort to protect my dignity—the dignity of an intern, whose rank was so beneath her own—sent the guilt free-falling through me. Suddenly my histrionic wardrobe seemed hugely presumptuous, and any defense of it a self-indulgent mistake. I slowly opened my mouth; felt my tongue unstick. "I just thought—since this is a fashion magazine . . ." The words were juvenile, and I knew it before they left me. "I thought my style would be appreciated." I was disgusted with myself, but Clara matched my unworthiness with unfailing sympathy.

She crossed her legs on the other side, and placed her hands calmly on her knee. "Yes," she admitted, "but if you haven't noticed, you are also an adult, and this a corporation, and in a corporation we occupy specific roles, with specific ways that we must speak, act, and dress. The magazine, unfortunately, is not real life. *Real life* is the corporate ladder on which this magazine is built, and the billions of dollars which flow in and out of its pages—a system it is our obligatory duty to uphold."

Saliva bobbed in my throat.

"This is simply the world we live in, my dear," Clara stated. "You'll learn that lesson here, you'll learn it anywhere. Do you think the worlds of fashion, music, fine art—however brilliant and alive they might seem—are exempt from the cold laws of business and the bottom line? On the contrary, they are ruled by them. Aesthetic beauty is an industry. Fantasies are produced to be packaged and purchased."

There was no malevolence in her voice, just an acceptance of general truth. She had herself acquired this essential knowledge long ago, and now she was simply passing it on to me, like a patient tutor relating to her pupil that the letter A comes before B comes before C—even though who knew why?

"The bottom line for you is, in these industries there are rules, and rank. One day, if you are successful, you can wear what you want—look at Edmund—but for now, you're are at the bottom of a very long chain of command, and if you keep dressing like some kind of butterfly you will never see the top of it."

A terrible, rosy-fingered realization seized me, my head suddenly filled with the sound I was convinced I'd heard when I stepped into *Régine*'s offices for the first time—the faint tinkling of people trapped in jars . . . And I understood.

Clara pulled me up from the plunging silence. "This doesn't mean you can't dress well," she said. "I would suggest, if you want to wear a suit—I don't know, a gray suit, or navy blue—something *neutral*. But a turquoise suit is much too bold. You may feel like you are simply expressing yourself, but unfortunately it's not your *role* to express yourself."

I struggled for a response. I could have never guessed that, of all the possible misdemeanors at *Régine*, the ultimate cause of my incrimination would be my wardrobe, which I had cultivated for so long thinking it would help me earn admittance to its hallowed halls.

She offered a helpless shrug of consolation; the natural order had been established long before her. "I suppose, if you must wear color, how about a nice tie?" She let her hand flutter open, to show what a great compromise she considered this sartorial suggestion. "Otherwise, how about just a nice neutral sweater . . . or a neutral—anything?" Seemingly recognizing the totalitarian ring in her own words, she made an effort to lighten my sentence. "It just can't be anything that . . ." She put her delicate hand over her chest, long manicured fingers spread, and jolted her wrist as though receiving an electric shock. "Nothing that . . ."

"Stands out," I finished.

"*Exaaaaactly*," she said with a single extended nod. Her chin gravitated upward very slowly, and I was reminded of a slow-motion playback I had once seen in Driver's Ed, of an accident victim's head whipping back upon collision before, *smash!*, the video sped up, and he went flying through the windshield.

"Do you have anything to wear?" she asked. "Anything at home that's not . . . ?" Elaboration was unnecessary; she knew well enough that in my flamboyant wardrobe there could be little which would meet the standard of neutrality that she was proposing. Unperturbed, Clara rose to her feet, patting out the wrinkles on the front of her pencil skirt. "Come with me—quietly, please."

I followed her with mummified stiffness through the white closet door. She swept through the fashion editors' cubicle, dipping her fingers into a ceramic dish—*clink*—and, without a note of acknowledgment to her colleagues there, continued to glide down the hallway, the glint of a key between her fingers. I glanced behind us, but neither Christine nor Will had noticed the subtle pilferage. We passed a dozen wordless cubicles, through a deafening air of dutiful semiconsciousness.

The key fit into the lock on an unmarked door in the farthest corner of the office, and Clara ushered me inside. The door shut behind us. Darkness. Then she flicked on a dim overhead light, and we were standing in a walk-in closet: two garment racks, and a built-in shelf overflowing with bags and shoes, surrounded by towers of plastic crates that contained a hodgepodge of hats, gloves, and sunglasses cases.

"This is where we keep leftovers," Clara explained, "both men's and women's clothes and accessories that, for one reason or another, were never returned to PR. It happens more than you would think, with so many deliveries going in and out for shoots, and sometimes they overlook things. After several seasons we donate them for a tax write-off, or they get put on consignment toward a corporate account."

Shrouded in shadow, she turned and assessed me at an arm's length. "You're a thirty-inch waist, from the looks of it? Excuse my imprecise methods," she said, and placed her hands around my waist. I lifted my arms as she slid her hands up. "You can relax," she instructed, giving me a light squeeze around my chest. "A thirty-eight-inch chest, I'd guess, with a fifteen-inch neck? And your shoes . . ." She required half a glance in the dark to determine—"ten and a half, right?"

I opened my mouth to confirm the accuracy of her estimations, but my input was outweighed by Clara's expertise. Clacking one hanger against the other in quick succession, she shuffled through the selection of men's dress shirts and emerged with a black Armani button-down.

"This will be a good start," she said. "You can never go wrong with black—or Armani." She hung the shirt on the front of the rack. "You'll need a suit, since you like them so much." Another *clack-clack-clack*, and she was holding up a three-piece charcoal-gray suit. "How do you like this?"

I ran my hand over its sculpted shoulder. "It's gorgeous," I said. The luxurious wool felt cool and new, and the stitched pockets had never been cut open. A lustrous black tag on the interior of the jacket's neck read *Dior Homme*.

"Consider this your uniform," she replied. "You can wear it with and without the vest—it's versatile."

My fingers curled longingly around the delicate sleeve. "You mean—I get to wear this?"

"Yes," she said. She placed the suit beside the black shirt.

"You might have to hem the pants for a more perfect fit, but otherwise—it's as good as yours."

A moment of stunned silence passed over me as I was struck by the magnitude of her benevolence. "Clara, I—I don't know how to thank you."

She leaned over into the shelves and selected a pair of chocolate brown Louis Vuitton oxfords. "Try these. Men's sample size for shoes is an eleven, but Vuittons run small. If they're not right, you can take a pair of Ferragamos, and either way you can thank me with your utmost discretion." She straightened up. "Now, listen to me: You'll change in here, please, and if anybody notices that you are wearing something new, you give them a strange look. That Ethan—the Ethan they remember—that Ethan *never existed.*"

A small twinge rang through my chest at the thought of the self-effacement that her proposition required.

"Once you've changed, you'll put the suit that you are wearing in this garment bag"—she pointed—"and before you reenter the fashion closet, you'll hang the bag on the coat rack by my desk. Then when you leave for the night, you'll pick it up and never speak of this again."

"Really, I—" I glanced at my new Dior suit hanging there, and choked on a rush of gratitude. "I don't know what to say."

"Don't say anything—never mention it," she said. "You can thank me when you make it in life. Send me flowers. I'm a Southern girl, so I love a nice bouquet." She smiled, and in the obscure light, I noticed a strange mark above her right eye. It was the closest I'd ever come to her, and now I could clearly see a scar from her hairline to the top of her cheek, slicing right through her eyebrow. The fine highlight of the raised skin was the only evidence of it; blended in by the same brown foundation on the rest of her smooth, poreless face, the gap in her otherwise exquisitely groomed eyebrow filled in with a perfectly matched pencil, yet—there it was when she tilted her head in the shadows, a fine glimmer, like something had slashed her deeply. Whatever it was that had hurt her, it was a wonder it hadn't taken out her eye, and I shuddered, realizing that even perfect Clara was just a person, covered in skin that could be broken by scars she could never fully hide.

Her voice punctuated the silence, in a register I hadn't heard before: obscure, unrehearsed. "You know . . ." she trailed slowly, "like I've said, you're not the only outsider here." She placed her hand on my shoulder. "Some of us have come very far, and take it from me—if your dream is to make it in this world . . . it *is* possible to do it." Like the boughs of an overripe tree, her words were heavy with meaning.

Clara glanced sidelong at the rack, then at the floor. Her mouth opened cautiously, and she seemed to be on the cusp of an important caveat. "The thing you must know is . . ." she unburdened herself at last, with a look bordering on desolation. "Sacrifice is at the heart of every dream." She continued to gaze at the carpet, at the shoes and the crates and the shelves, all shrouded in shadow. "Nothing we want in life comes without sacrifice, and you realize this as you grow up. I did. We all did." She looked up at me now. In the darkness, I had the impression that her densely mascaraed eyelids were two flickering black wings.

"It is a lovely style you have," she lamented. A mournful pang continued to weigh down her buoyant lilt. "I regret that you should have to change it, but—I always tell myself, for every thing I loved which I have given up in life, there was something that I gained." She reached out and touched the knot of my tie. "Sometimes I know that it's a lie, but—it's what I tell myself. And this is what you must tell yourself too."

I felt her delicate fingers tighten around the knot, shift it slightly one way, then back, and remain poised there. "Tell yourself every day. Otherwise, one day you'll turn, and you won't recognize your dream, or yourself, or—" She had choked on her own saliva.

"I'm sorry," she smiled nervously, and swallowed. Even in the dimness, her mouth was perfect lipstick-red; for the first time I saw the resemblance between lipstick and the greasepaint of a clown's smile, both of them a well-plotted deceit. "I've said enough." Clara patted an imaginary spot of lint off my turquoise suit and took her hand back. She straightened up, and the familiar, white smile followed, with a sweet incline of her blonde head. "Now wait here, and come out when you are ready—and please, remember what I've told you."

She slipped out, and it was as though nothing at all had happened between us.

I FOLLOWED CLARA'S INSTRUCTION'S PRECISELY—wordlessly hung the garment bag by her desk, then passed through the fashion closet door in my new designer outfit. I sat down without a rustle, and reached toward the keyboard. The gray sleeves flashed with strange unfamiliarity over my wrists, and for a second I mistook my hands for another's.

In her cubicle, Sabrina was eating cottage cheese for breakfast, one hand on a plastic spoon, the other on her computer mouse.

"Did you just get Anna's e-mail?" George was asking her.

"Anna Swanson?" She chewed absently. "Why does that name sound familiar?"

"She was the PR girl at Saint Laurent last season, remember? She kept nagging you for their velvet hangers back."

Sabrina gulped, and I could hear her scrape her plastic cup for another spoonful. "Ugh, so annoying. Why is she asking for job opportunities?"

"They fired her. She gained a lot of weight."

Sabrina stopped chewing. I heard a reluctant gulp, and a rustling whoosh as she tossed the cottage cheese into her trash bin. "I thought her dad was the president of something," she finally said, and trying to satisfy her hunger, pried open the plastic lid of her iced latte with a click and took a long *gulp-gulp-gulp*.

"He owns Poland Spring," George said.

She must have finished her beverage, as she tossed the cup into the trash with her cottage cheese, ice rattling. "Is that all? I thought it was something luxury."

"No, but do you know how many people drink Poland Spring? That's like all the water coolers in America. Can you imagine owning *water*?"

"We should go out for drinks with Geneva Chapman," Sabrina said, presumably triggered by the subject of water to contemplate less sober libations.

"From Prada PR?" he asked. "Have you ever met her?"

"No, but after enough e-mails, you feel like you do. Her e-mails don't have spelling mistakes, and she gets back to you in five minutes. I feel like she'd be really put-together, and know the best places for a martini."

"How about the Chanel PR girl, your *faaavorite*?"

"Oh please. I bet she'd like, try to roofie herself or something," Sabrina scoffed, "and then she'd wake up the next morning and e-mail me ten times to return the pearl collar we never requested." She paused. "She's probably really pretty, though. Chanel only hires like, really pretty girls."

George asserted that, *like,* Régine *was pretty much the same as Chanel, so like, you're really pretty too, Sabrina*, and then—*Were you wearing that before?*

"I said," George repeated to me, "were you wearing that before?" He eyed me suspiciously. Weren't you wearing, like, purple or something?"

Sabrina looked over at me. "Is that . . . ?" she began.

"Dior," I replied.

THAT EVENING, I HUNG THE GARMENT BAG FROM AN EXPOSED pipe which ran across my four-foot-high tin ceiling. The pipe was a water line, which unintentionally supplied ambient waterfall sounds when my roommates showered; it was also where my clothes hung, the estimation of a closet in my unequipped habitation. I crawled toward the rest of my clothes now—red, pink, sky blue, a rainbow of thrifted hues which for years had supplied the outermost layer of my colorful identity—and pushed them all toward the far side end of the pipe, relegating my past to the shadows with a single shove and one last whimper of squeaking hangers, swinging blithely in unison.

I placed an empty hanger in the middle of the naked pipe, and began to undress. Brown Louis Vuitton shoes, gray Dior suit, black Armani dress shirt. My body relaxed as the air rushed over my skin. At no point in the day had my skin dared to make direct contact with the interior of my new suit; my reluctance to damage its silky lining had yielded seven hours with my elbows raised (consequently, a box of gloves spilled over George's head and also a number of innovative poses).

Kneeling bare, in my underwear and socks, I inhaled deeply, uninhibited at last. I hung up my new outfit: folded the pants, buttoned the shirt, patted the shoulders of my jacket; placed the shoes neatly below.

I thought of the younger me, who read fairy tales in bed and stole flowers from the neighbors' yards, all the time dreaming of another world. If only he could see me now, with these beautiful things, this beautiful life ahead of him.

I shuffled on my knees to unzip the garment bag, which had facilitated the out-of-office smuggling of my turquoise suit. I pulled out my illicit embroidered loafers first, then my flowered shirt and wrinkly necktie, and finally my boldly hued jacket: nondescript, unbranded. I hung it with a sigh beside its gray Dior replacement.

In transit, the turquoise pants had crumpled to the bottom of the black garment bag. "*That Ethan is dead,*" Clara had said, and indeed, it appeared that I was staring at a body bag—my corpse had just crumpled to the bottom and melted right through it, leaving only a splash of color as a form of identification. The next instant I had a vision of myself at Clara's desk, tailored in designer clothes from head to toe, my unruly hair clipped beyond recognition, my back straight like there was a wire holding me up—and all around pictures of shoes and handbags, and sitting right next to me, my two faceless coworkers, whom I sat beside for eight hours a day yet barely even knew. "*Your beeeeaaauutiful dream*," they cooed, their eyes rolling like colossal white pearls.

As I kneeled there in my loft, dizziness overtook me. My stomach turned and my head swayed side to side, and I felt myself falling as if in slow motion. My arms reached out around the turquoise suit, hugging it like a person begging for forgiveness, then the weight of my body pulled the jacket off the hanger—*crack!*—and I fell forward into a lump, face buried in its turquoise folds. I lay there in silence, eyes shut, breath teeming in and out of my nostrils, while the feeling continued to flow through me—the feeling that I was falling, falling . . . falling . . .

It was a feeling I'd had only once before in my life, after the first time I rolled on ecstasy. We'd all done it in East Rock Park, steeped among evergreens and a great lake—me and Madeline and Dorian, also Blake and his then-girlfriend Kim, and a few other consorts from our enchanted circle. On ecstasy the whole world was pregnant with poetry—just one little pill, and then suddenly it was eyes wide open, everybody bursting from their chests, and each little unappreciated thing around us like a perfect word in some transcendental scripture. We danced swaying under the moon, buzzing like fireflies with a single night to live; took off our shirts and rubbed each other's skin all night, while overhead the branches of the trees murmured about all the creatures of the earth silently aching for love. Time was a throbbing heart we were inside, and consciousness a fever dream of skin and sweat and damp kisses and our collective breath leaving our bodies like the sigh at the end of a full, contented life.

Then they all fell asleep, and for me, the plummet came.

It was exactly what Ted Hamilton had cautioned us about

when he sold us the pills in his dorm: "*You'll get high, then you'll come down hard*," he'd said, "*like a depression*."

Only it was more than just depression, more than just the typical sad thoughts that filled my head and then swiftly moved on. If you've never done ecstasy, and you don't know the feeling, well—it's your whole body, a swooping feeling, like you're in an elevator spinning downward, only there's no end, and you realize that for your entire life there's been something holding you together and now it's falling through you, flowing downward, not in a cathartic way but in a hopeless, never-ending way, and the world you loved will never be the same because you see it now through a gray lens and everything is sharp, and you notice the details, the cracks, the whole gray world made up of flaws and ugliness, and you can't breathe and you think, *I'll never have it again*, *I'll never be happy again*, and when you look around nobody is there to comfort you, to save you, and you realize: Nobody cares and you're all alone, and you'll always be alone forever, and it makes you want to walk away, just walk away until you die, but—you can't because your cell phone is in Madeline's purse and if you missed an exam tomorrow you'd be in trouble and anyway the party you've been planning is next week and on top of everything you're hungry, and thinking all these stupid, sad thoughts about your stupid, sad, futile life makes you plummet farther down, down, because you realize you couldn't walk away if you wanted to because you're trapped, you're a human being and you're trapped in the web of your own body and the web you've made for yourself connecting to all the other bodies.

That's kind of what it felt like as I lay there, clinging to my former self, with nowhere to go but forward. The thought flashed through my mind that clearly this felt wrong—this dream felt *wrong*—yet, how could it be, if all my life I had dreamed it? And if it *was* wrong, what else in the world was there for me?

I WOKE UP TO THE SMELL OF BURNING TOAST.

I swallowed hard and sat up, my head grazing the Dior blazer. The fabric was so elegant. Elegant and cold.

"Hey!" I called cloudily in the direction of the ladder. "Is everything okay . . . ?"

My roommate Veronica replied from downstairs, "Sorry! Yeah—I just can't—figure—out . . . " A metallic rattle and a low moan. "My God, this toaster is *complicated*."

Even though we lived together, I didn't see Veronica much. Having just graduated from the same class at Cornell, she and her boyfriend Jonathan were both consultants. Whom they consulted, and on what matters, I had no idea, but they were never home, and spent the entirety of their free time at dinner or drinks or Sunday brunch (otherwise *talking* about dinner or drinks or Sunday brunch).

Evidently giving up, I heard Veronica shut the bedroom door behind her—a sign that she and Jonathan were settling down for the night, after returning from dinner while I had snored in a heap several feet above them.

I felt around for my cell phone. Six mixed calls from Madeline. I remembered at once: Dorian's birthday party.

For a moment, I pressed my fingers against my eyes once more. I stumbled down the ladder and to the medicine cabinet in the bathroom; pulled out the bottle of aspirin; began to brainstorm excuses for why I couldn't go with her to Dorian's party.

I never got headaches, so I didn't even know how many to take.

I turned the bottle over to read the warnings. *Misuse could lead to serious side effects, including stomach pains, and in rare cases—death.* I blinked, and wiped a bead of sweat from my brow. The summer heat was the worst in the bathroom, where it got trapped, making it difficult to know after a hot shower whether my body was wet from water or sweat. Right now I kind of felt like that—unsure of what was stuck to my skin. The bottle suggested two aspirin pills, but it didn't seem that I was having a two-aspirin kind of headache. I gulped down three and called back Madeline.

"But you promised," she replied, sounding on the verge of tears.

We argued for ten minutes until finally I said, "Fine, I'll go, but only for half an hour," and she replied, "Good, because I'm already in a cab to your apartment and will be there in fifteen minutes."

WE MADE ONE REVOLUTION THROUGH THE CROWDED LATE-night lounge before I pulled at her and said, "Well, I guess Dorian's not here."

"Don't be ridiculous," she scowled. "This is his own party."

Bossa-nova notes flowed upward from speakers toward a red ceiling, mirroring the ripple of the aquarium walls. Rectangular slabs of polished wood made low-lying tables between sofas upholstered in flax linen, and everywhere white orchids rose out of modern blown-glass vases. Despite the tight guest list at the door, the room was at capacity—nobody else from Yale, just fashionable shadows from his many other lives, whom Dorian evidently counted as his friends.

His first word to us both, like a rope bridge tossed over a vast precipice, was, "*Babe!*"

A drink in one hand, Dorian was lounging behind a table adorned with tumblers and Belvedere bottles. He was surrounded by silhouettes, illuminated from overhead by a red sconce which caused a shadow on his lips, as if a butterfly was resting there. He swooped to his feet—the butterfly flew away—and as he hopped cheerfully over other people's sandals and high heels and polished oxfords, he gave the impression of a young acrobat trying his luck on the tightrope.

I steeled my will against him; remembered the mental promise I had made to myself. No matter what happened tonight, no matter how charming or beautiful Dorian was, I wouldn't forgive him, wouldn't forget that he had abandoned us, that he was no more my friend than any person whose shoulder I bumped on the subway.

He came closer, in a white T-shirt and tuxedo pants, having never quite learned how to dress up. With every step I became surer of the inevitable next thing: his bright, effortless smile, and the complete annihilation of my feeble defenses. I knew the trap ahead—I knew it by heart—yet I was returning to it, like a ghost haunting the site of his own demise.

I had the urge to turn around, to simply push through the glamorous crowd that had gathered in his honor and escape, panting, into the night. Madeline, however, was holding my hand and practically dragging me toward him.

"Babe!" he said once more, when he was almost close enough to touch us. The word sent a jagged spike through me, like a rumble charted on a seismograph, which plummeted on recollection that Dorian called everyone "babe." He had done it all through college in that playful tone of his, an exclamation over monkey bars and swings—*Babe, babe, babe!* If you didn't know him, you would just assume he really liked you and wanted to play; then, if you were as unlucky as we were to fall in love with him in the sand pit, you later learned that it meant nothing. Sure, maybe he did like you, but in the end your friendship was just one of the many games that preoccupied his roving, amusement-powered life, and you were no more special to him than a daisy he had enjoyed looking at, or a song that made him want to dance—one that he would turn off when he got bored or heard a new one he liked better. Madeline seemed to have forgotten about all this as she closed in on him now.

He kissed her lips while she regarded him with the reverence of a pious Sunday school girl. She was a fool. I knew, and Dorian knew too—anybody who *knew* her knew—that she was just one of those women who would sooner pardon a hundred unpardonable blows before admitting her bruised body to a hospital. He enveloped me next, and I remained as hard as a pillar while he was soft and warm and familiar, like a favorite blanket on a winter night.

"You look great," Dorian whispered, his low, penetrating voice coaxing out the reluctant longing in me. His breath smelled like gin and tonic as he kissed me with unhurried sentimentality on the cheek soft lips, hovering too long, too innocently: I tightened my jaw, and he let me go at last. "It's really great to see you, babe," he whispered with heart-wrenching earnestness as he took my hand and squeezed it. He smiled.

I smiled foggily back. The only thing I could think to do was stay completely still, afraid that my body would betray me, that I would throw my hands around him and moan, "*I missed you so much.*" Madeline saved me from an inevitable collapse by pulling him toward the sofa. She was holding his hand like nothing had ever happened, while I silently resented that, like a coat of paint over a graffiti-desecrated wall, she was willing to simply bury the ugly marks he had made on us both. I had made a terrible mistake. I had known it would happen this way, and yet I had let it happen: I was *letting* it happen.

They approached the sofa, and I followed them like a puppy on an invisible leash.

"Are these your model friends? Hello," Madeline interjected forcibly, making a visible swinging spectacle of Dorian's and her locked hands. "*I'm Madeline*."

It was too loud for anybody to hear. Dorian's friends smiled blithely at us from the couch before returning to hushed conversations with each other. I surveyed their silhouettes, recognizing the frizzy-haired one from outside the club where I first saw Dorian in New York—Penny, who last season had been the face of Givenchy and various other campaigns. Beside her sat the current face of Dolce & Gabbana, then Versace, and then the English girl who had starred with Naomi Campbell in an Alexander McQueen campaign. They all slid to the side to make room for us while we stepped over their shoes, which like the monthly accessories feature in *Régine* seemed to illustrate the latest trends: rhinestones, Western-style fringe, and the dusty pink color that, after appearing in the latest Prada collection, was being emulated everywhere.

I ended up next to Dolce & Gabbana, with Dorian sitting between me and Madeline. The sofa was the enveloping kind—too comfortable—with any illusions of a fast exit dashed, or rather swallowed up, by its plush linen cushions.

"Have a drink," Dorian said as he leaned forward toward the ice bucket. He poured Belvedere into two tumblers, and topped them off with orange juice—a generously inverted ratio, which at our prestigious university we had learned was prerequisite for a distinguished evening.

Madeline winked at me over Dorian's back as he poured, but before I could respond with an expression of discomfort she looked away, unable to tolerate a moment in Dorian's presence when she was not fully absorbed in exultation of him. Dorian handed us each a drink and settled back in the seat.

"Are all your friends from Paris?" Madeline asked in a loud, hollow voice, like a "cool" mother fishing for details about her son's new friends whom she suspected of introducing him to sex, drugs, and other forks off the straight-and-narrow path.

"From shows," he nodded, picking up his own drink, a gin and tonic which had begun to leave a sweaty moon-shaped puddle on the glass table. "I'm done with modeling though—I quit yesterday."

"Done? You only just started," she protested, with a startled clink of her own glass.

"Yeah, but I'm tired of it. I want to be creative again."

I rolled my eyes. It was the one thing that could be counted upon in human nature, that every person should set out to prove their weakest virtue. Beautiful people always wanted to be more talented than they really were, and talented people more beautiful. Despite his constant attempts to be the exception, Dorian would always prove the rule—as would any person who tried to challenge fate.

"Don't get me wrong," Dorian rushed in, "it kept me busy. They call it Fashion Week, but it's more like a whole month—there's one in London, Paris, Milan—each one's a week, plus castings before. I mean, I was barely going to class. I would go to auditions with all my French homework, and practice pronunciation in the makeup chair at shows—everything was crazy—and still the whole time I was so bored."

"Isn't it fun though," gawked Madeline, "meeting people, wearing all the clothes?"

"Sure," he admitted, "the first couple of days it's great, but then you realize it's the same thing every day, and all anybody wants from you is your picture. If I thought nobody took me seriously before—well, over there nobody cares what I have to say about anything. Backstage is always loud and chaotic—hair dryers going, people barking into headsets. Interviewers come around from all the magazines, and yell the same questions at me—'*Dorian Belgraves! Enjoying Fashion Week so far? How do you like following in your mom's footsteps?*' It's like, what am I supposed to say to them? '*Hi, I'm my own person, and can we talk about something else?*'"

He rolled his eyes and went on, "If they think they're being really clever, they'll know about Yale, so they'll say, '*How do you like being a* smart *model!*' and they just laugh like it's the funniest thing they've heard all day. They just—assume we're all stupid, when really, I mean they're the ones that are. Let me put it this way—my best friend through it all—"

I gave myself away with an upward glance, curious to hear about the "best friend" who had replaced me and Madeline in Paris.

"—he has a PhD in microbiology, though nobody ever asks him about it. He has a really 'commercial' look, so he gets a lot of department-store jobs—big billboards and stuff—he told me, '*Don't sweat it. Just nod and smile, pretend they're right about you—at the end of the day, it's a job. You get paid, go home—everybody wins.*'" Dorian swirled around his gin and tonic. "For him, it makes sense, but why do I need the money? If I'm going to do it, it has to be for something else. I have to *want* to, but at this point I'm afraid there's nothing I actually want to do."

He gulped, lifting his drink to his lips. "I'm not like you guys, who always had a Path," he reminded us, and took a deep, ice-clattering swig.

I rolled my eyes once more. Second only to Dorian's own self-amusement—an undertaking that, like a winter fire, required endless fueling—these were Dorian's two all-consuming passions: rejecting the idea of a life "Path," and reminding everyone that he was too special to have one.

I almost made a joke to draw attention to this point, but then Dorian's voice wavered. "Except you know, maybe one day . . ." He trailed off on this hopeful note, his voice getting a little high at the end, and smiled—the familiar, all-comforting smile, which had always confirmed the uprightness of the world but somehow now seemed to shake at the corners—and for once it occurred to me that maybe Dorian actually *wanted* a life Path.

He glanced up to find Madeline just staring at him with a placid smile. She seemed not to have heard anything at all he had said.

"I have been making art again, though," he said. He reached into the back pocket of his pants and pulled out a wallet-sized sketchpad. "I think—I want to be an artist after all." He turned to an ink drawing on the first page, of a long, gaunt face, with sad, all-seeing eyes, and a barbed chin resting on a skeletal hand. "Guess who?"

"I don't know," Madeline shrugged, "but he sure is ugly."

"It's me . . ." Dorian explained, his voice dropping off with a dejected echo. "It's a self-portrait."

"What?!" she balked. "But it's . . ." Madeline gulped. "You always had such a—unique drawing style."

Madeline, of course, hated Dorian's drawings, although she would never bring herself to admit it to him. She thought they were crude while, ironically enough, I had always liked them. They reminded me of the work of Egon Schiele, an Austrian protégé of Gustav Klimt who drew everyone with long, sad faces and atrophied limbs. Coming from Dorian, they seemed unexpectedly flawed and heavyhearted, qualities misaligned with the vision of Dorian that Madeline wished to have, as he was her champion of vitality and unmarred goodness.

Dorian turned the page. A receipt fluttered out like a pale dead leaf. Madeline picked it up off the floor and crumpled it up, tossing it into a tumbler which was pooling with melted ice.

"Wait!" he rushed in, saving the receipt with a scoop of his tapered fingers into the tumbler. "That's not trash." He shook off the drenched receipt and flattened it against his knee. "See, I've been writing poems on the backs of them. Like—art poems. If it's a receipt for cheesecake, I'll write about cheesecake. If it's for soda, then . . ."

"That's clever," Madeline half-consciously mused, her head on his shoulder.

I lost interest and stared at a bead of water that was trembling on the handle of the silver ice bucket, while in the background Dorian unironically recited a poem about Chinese takeout. After five minutes, Dorian had closed his sketchpad and Madeline was asking about Dorian's mother, proving once more how much like a middle-aged woman she could sound.

"She and David got stuck in Milan," Dorian said. "Mom got sick, too many martinis at some Gucci event—said she couldn't get on a flight in time for the party." Dorian's hand fell on my forearm. "They were actually with Jane Delancey—have you met her yet, babe?"

"I'm sorry, what?" I had graduated from my examination of the ice bucket to the ice cubes in my tumbler. There appeared to be frozen raspberries in the middle of them.

"Have you met Jane? The creative director?" he repeated to me. "At *Régine*?"

I told him that yes, I'd met her.

"She's a friend of the family—I'm sure if you ever need anything there—"

"Sorry." I tapped my ear. "It's so loud in here," I said dismissively, motioning all around like it couldn't be helped. I didn't even try to lean toward him.

Now that Madeline was sure none of Dorian's female friends had any interest in competing for Dorian's affections, she sank into the linen cushion and blushed. "Everybody you know is *soooo* beautiful." She surveyed them all with a detached serenity. "It's like . . . 'Fifty Most,' all over again . . ."

I grimaced.

At school, the *Yale Rumpus* had published a special issue every year dedicated to the "Fifty Most Beautiful People" at school, for which—after an unexplained consecration process—portraits of the anointed were taken, and profiles scribed for publication. As more typical subject matter for Yale students concerned race relations or dichotomous cells, descriptive powers for "beautiful people" varied, and the issue touted a smattering reliance on cringe-worthy phrases like "*washboard abs*" and "*cheekbones you could cut diamonds on.*" On the fateful day in February, friendly clusters in Commons dining hall congregated around copies of the issue to see which of their respective crushes had made it.

It was intended as a kind of joke, although nobody ever declined to be included in "Fifty Most," not even the feminists or the politician's sons, and shortly after its publication the selected crop always experienced a spike in dates, love letters, and passive-aggressive glances from the same sex. Unsurprisingly, Madeline and Dorian made the cover in our sophomore year. Our friends Oliver and Helene were in that issue too, and Blake in the subsequent year's, on a page with his fraternity brothers Mike and Marcus; the best-looking jocks were generally herded together for a beefcake center spread, although their answers to the questions were boring. I was the only one who never made it, and I remember thinking it was all right—maybe *someday* I would be as beautiful as my friends, and someone would think to put me on the cover of something.

At the time Madeline had participated begrudgingly in the superficial annual tradition—she hated "*society's pointless obsession with people's least important qualities*," which she felt was a conspiracy of "The Institution" to distract from meaningful original thought. For this reason, she had always maintained a terrible prejudice against actors and the media, yet now Madeline was explaining to us how a budding actress should go about getting the attention of Hollywood producers, and regaling us with the thrilling play-by-play of her first audition, in which evidently she had "dazzled" by virtue of having memorized all her lines.

Dorian caught my eye as I blinked glassily around. He smiled, but I pretended to have something in my glasses, and turned away to wipe them off.

"I mean, I'm perfect for it," Madeline was saying. The role in question was a Weinstein-backed biopic on the "doomed" Mary Queen of Scots, in which she presumed that without acting experience she should play the title role.

A hand fell on my knee. "Drink more," Dorian said. "It's an open bar."

Someone came through with a champagne sparkler. I watched it light up everyone's faces, and yawned.

IT WAS MY OWN ATTRACTION TO DORIAN THAT HAD LED TO his union with Madeline; therefore, blame for our threefold intertwinement (and, of course, our eventual unraveling) fell on my own shoulders—or rather, on my irrepressible heart.

The day after he asked to draw my portrait at brunch, Dorian's excitable voice called to me from the back corner of our European Art class, where he was sitting in a T-shirt and linen pajama pants.

"Rough morning?" I teased him. Next to us, muted jewel tones glowed through a stained-glass mural—the meeting of two angels, representing art and science—as our professor prepared a slide which read, *Mannerism through the Baroque Era*.

"Not at all, babe," Dorian said. It was the first time he had called me "babe"; I feigned nonchalance as I opened to the wrong page of our textbook and offered him a nervous smile. "If anything, it was a great morning," he went on. "I waited up for the sunrise."

An absent flipping of pages as I lost myself in his sculpted hands. "Special occasion?" I managed.

"No. Just Wednesday morning." He flashed one of those ship-launching smiles, which three thousand years ago would have sent a whole fleet of Trojan troops spiraling blithely to the ocean floor, and of course, I was no match for it either.

I was in love with Dorian.

I was in love with him when we sat in class, and he made a

doodle on the corner of my notepad—a billy goat standing on an elephant—and whispered, "Your turn, draw something on mine."

I was in love with him when we studied late-night for midterms and his head dropped onto his flashcards, as he yawned, "Leonardo da Vinci . . . *Lady with an Ermine* . . . 1489 . . . what's . . . an . . . ermine . . . anyway?"

I was in love with him when we took walks, and he pointed out, "My favorite tree, see? Because it's got this knot down here that swirls into a branch up there."

I was in love with him when he implored me, "Won't you talk to Madeline? Please, please? Just one date with her and—"

Of course, I *did* talk to Madeline. If my own love for Dorian was fated to be unrequited, I could perceive no compensation more appealing than his union with my other truest love. In part, my ends were self-motivated: At the time, I was still her "gay" best friend, and if they got together, I would be an honorary adjunct of their coupling. The more glaring motivation, however, I thought was self-evident. Dorian and Madeline would be *perfect* together.

To the contrary, Madeline's mind was already made up about "talentless, superficial" Dorian, and her righteous indignation no trifle to be reckoned with. Perhaps she knew all along that Dorian would ruin us. Until the day I met Dorian in Pierson, Madeline had never met him either; in hindsight, her presumptive reservations were so strong as to suggest extrasensory perception.

Madeline, however, seemed hardly capable of passing judgment on men. Having endured twelve years of private all-girls education, she arrived at Yale stifled by trepidation, cornered by her inexperience into a trap: The longer she waited to enter her first relationship, the warier she became of dating. Consequently, she was obsessed with her first love being "exactly right."

All of freshman year, I tried with frustration to see her coupled, if only to alleviate the sheer pressure of her misguided chastity. She had no shortage of interested prospects, yet she denied me the satisfaction of a single successful match. By year's end, she had—despite all her fiery rhetoric of cultural revolution—exceeded all expectations of romantic conservatism, and began to incorporate into all her objections the laughable mentioning of "marriageability." To Madeline's mind, this dubious quality involved maturity, clearheadedness, and masculine self-assuredness—high-minded qualifications lacking in *any* male twentysomething, but especially lacking in reckless Dorian Belgraves.

Even had he theoretically satisfied her improbable conditions, his gross unsuitability had been established in her mind by his reputation as a dense New York City party boy. It was true that the summer before he transferred to Yale, Dorian's image had been splashed with irritating regularity in every fashionable media outlet with high-society coverage. But as I came to realize during our friendship, the assumptions to be made from Dorian's bad rep were inaccurate; seeking distraction after his brief and disastrous tenure at West Point, helter-skelter Dorian had merely chosen "society" as his latest preoccupation, the way he had blindly selected little papers that read, "horseback riding," "lacrosse," "fine art" from the same magic hat. That he was naturally suited for it was a bonus, although largely irrelevant considering his fundamental disregard for other people's opinions. Parties merely satisfied Dorian's need to feel purposeful. He danced and laughed and drank. People were excited to see him, and at the end of the night, it was almost like he had actually *done* something. By the end of the summer, though, his habit had dwindled, and when he started Yale he seemed to have gotten tired of people completely—for a while, at least—as he wandered the campus in self-reflective solitude, preferring interaction with his charcoal and sketchbook.

Still, this was hardly reason enough for Madeline to renege on her oft-articulated dislike of Dorian—until one weekend in November I was struck with the flu, and unable to join her for the opening of a new exhibit at the Metropolitan.

"For the love of God, just take Dorian," I'd implored, blowing my nose. "It'll give you a chance to get to know him, and I promise," I lied, "if you don't like him, I'll never bring it up again."

We quibbled for twenty minutes, and in the end they went together, and what came next was as predictable as a numerical sequence. According to Madeline's breathless retelling, they talked about Marxism, the origin of consciousness, Ernest Hemingway, North African tribal art, *The Myth of Sisyphus*; blithely wandered eight times around the Egyptian gallery, twelve times around the statue of Aphrodite in the Greek gallery, and fourteen times through the arch with the banner that read "Incan Treasures," leading to the reception party. Between them they had nine glasses of champagne and seven pastries, the start of a habit. It was Dorian who always pointed to the open bar, and Madeline who always suggested "a nibble" at the dessert table—although she only ever took a single bite, and deferred the rest to Dorian's lips.

By the fourth pastry—a bite-size cheesecake, topped with

powdered sugar and an orange twist—the exchange from Madeline's fingers to Dorian's lips involved a lick of her fingers. After the first incidence of this guileless indiscretion, Dorian apologized ("Too eager," he ambiguously stated, through a mouth full of cream and graham cracker crust) while Madeline wiped her hand with halfhearted embarrassment on her cocktail napkin. After the second time, Dorian just stared at her as he licked his tongue deliberately over her French manicured nails, holding her by the waist, while Madeline let her fingers linger there and finally tucked them into the hair on his nape.

Three hours of conversation and pastry-facilitated flirtation led them to the museum steps, where they stood face-to-face in the center under a banner that flapped COMING SOON with a painting by Gauguin. Enveloping her in his arms on the top step, he kissed her—and it was as though their lips had tied a knot between the three of us.

chapter seven

I was counting garment bags in my sleep like sheep when Madeline prodded me awake. "Ethan?"

The last garment bag slumped lumpily over a white picket fence into the fashion closet as I yawned and rubbed my eyes. The lights were on in the club. Dorian's head was on my shoulder, and except for a few lingering clusters, all the people had cleared out. A teenage busboy was leaning over the table, collecting watered-down glasses.

"I have to go." I stirred. "I have *Régine* tomorrow." I pushed off Dorian with a priggish finger and slid away from him and Madeline on the couch.

"You can't just leave us," she said. "What about Dorian?"

At the invocation of his name, Dorian groaned, "I can't *seeee* straight any-*mooore* . . ."

"What about him? He's fine," I assured Madeline. Dorian slumped over. I propped up his head like a mortician presenting a corpse, and said, "See?"

She whimpered and tried to shake him, as he collapsed once more with a snore, his breath reeking of gin and tonic.

"For the love of God!" My nostrils flared at their presumptuousness—that despite Dorian's yearlong estrangement, it should now be *me* saddled with the burden of his drunk body. "Where are all your *model* friends to help you?" I scowled, but the famous faces were all gone, like pages in a magazine that had been torn out. "All right, Madeline, you grab him on that side."

Madeline just sat there limp, like a bouquet of wilted flowers, and blinked. "Don't look at me—" *hiccup!* "—like that. I'm going to play—" *hiccup!* "—the Queen of Scots."

With a scowl, and a flash of self-hatred—Why? *Why* was I doing this?—I tossed Dorian's lazy arm around my neck and excavated him, half-dangling, out of his luxurious burrow. His fingers moved graspingly over the front of my shirt as he moaned again and dragged his feet against the wooden floor. I held him by the waist and guided him past the sweating ice bucket of empty Belvedere bottles.

"Hey, what's the rush?" Madeline whined. "Don't you—" *hiccup!* "—think we should say bye at least?"

We passed two reed-thin girls that had lingered behind. "Happy birthday, Dorian," they said. One of them tipped over like a Chinese bamboo fountain to kiss him on the forehead, and he smiled with the blithe appreciation of a baby being put to sleep.

We stumbled outside into pouring rain. Water rushed down the cobblestone streets in rivulets, and as the ground churned,

I was reminded of something I had heard once about the Meatpacking District—that a hundred years ago, when all the butchers had their shops there, the streets used to puddle with blood.

"Madeline, get that cab!"

Teetering just below the nightclub awning, she pressed her hand against the brick wall and swayed there with her face to the ground.

"Hey," I prodded at her, "can you—"

The cab's lights whirred right past us while Madeline moved away from me a little, staring at her feet.

"Why are you so useless?" I groaned. I ventured out into the street and squinted through the droves. One arm clutching Dorian and the other outstretched for a cab, I was punished for my resentment by a merciless onslaught of wet lashes.

A yellow cab pulled mercifully up to us. I pushed Dorian inside, and tumbled closely behind. "Come on," I shouted to Madeline, holding the door open.

She clopped blindly toward us, eyes closed as the rainfall draped her like a veil. Her billowy sleeves fused like papier-mâché to her outstretched arms, and when her hands collided with the side of the cab, she yelped in surprise. She tilted her head back like she was about to sneeze, then suddenly keeled forward, vomiting all over the car door.

"Dear God, Madeline, we're not at Yale anymore!" I yanked her inside the cab and the driver turned to us.

"She gonna puke in here?" he barked.

"No, she's not," I said, and pulled at her arm, which was dangling in the rain.

"I don't wanner in here if she's gonna puke. She could puke in some other cab."

"I told you, she's not going to vomit in your cab." I finished yanking her errant limbs into the cab before he could protest, and slammed the door. The sound of the rain subdued, and I recited Dorian's address by heart.

Madeline's sopping head started to tailspin toward me. "No," I instructed, as though she was a misbehaving dog, and nudged her upright with a callous jerk of my shoulder. Her hair was plastered to her face with an ambiguous blend of vomit and rain, blonde strands lining the contours of her cheekbones.

She blubbered, and I wiped off her cheeks like a child's with the back of my sleeve. The first time we had gotten drunk together was at a Pi Beta Phi party, where we had our introduction to "jungle juice." "*It's just like Kool-Aid*," she had marveled, having been denied all "sugary drinks" in her youth by her mother, before gulping it down in droves. Back then, it had been funny; now I was tempted to redirect the driver to my own apartment and leave both her and Dorian stranded in the cab when we arrived.

The driver kept giving me sidelong glares while the others dozed away. Despite constant propping, they seemed determined to undermine me: Dorian's head ended up on one shoulder, and Madeline's on the other. We arrived twenty minutes later, and I prodded them awake. "Wake up. It's twenty dollars."

Madeline was cross-eyed, with her chin tilted up like she was trying to balance an invisible spoon on her nose. "No cash," she shrugged.

"Come on, Madeline, I'm not paying for this." I elbowed Dorian—"Hey! *Hey!*" I turned up his thigh to yank out his wallet from his back pocket. Squirming like a cat dangled over a bathtub, he remembered me and let me go ahead.

The rain felt colder the second time. Even though Dorian's building had an awning that extended to the curbside, the two of them took so long to exit the cab that we were soaked anew by the time we reached the front door. It was a familiar door—ornamented wrought iron, in a Gilded Age style—and when it opened to a familiar foyer of mahogany wood bordering peach damask walls, it revealed Harry, the night porter, who was also familiar.

"Mr. St. James!" he exclaimed, fondly patting my wet back with a white-gloved hand. "I'd been wondering when you'd come around again."

During college, excursions into New York City had often led to sleepovers at Dorian's apartment, where compared to Madeline's, parental supervision was appreciably scarce. On the rare nights his jet-setting mother was actually home, we usually found her in the last stages of a "spirit hour" involving Percocet and Veuve Clicquot, sashaying up and down the stairs to help her face mask dry, while Buddha Bar played over the surround-sound speakers, and Nag Champa poured out from a dozen incense burners. "Don't mind me!" Edie would say, twirling a tassel on her charmeuse bathrobe. "I'm just cleansing."

Now I buckled under Dorian's weight while Madeline tried to lean her elbow on my back like a desk.

"Are you all right? Is that Mr. Belgraves?"

Madeline smirked. "*Hiiiii Haaaarrrryyyyyy.*"

"Welcome back, Miss Dupre." He turned to me and asked, "Have you seen Mr. Belgraves's modeling photos from Paris yet?"

I nodded with a sigh. "Can you buzz us up?"

Harry pressed the Up button on the elevator and held the door with a suited arm. "He's looking very handsome these days, isn't he?" He gestured with a proud chin toward Dorian, whose "handsome" knees were almost scraping the hardwood floor. "I always said that boy should be a model. Just like his mother."

"Yes," I agreed. "Yes, you did."

EVERYBODY HAD BEEN SAYING THAT FOR A LONG TIME, THAT Dorian should be a model. That he ended up actually doing it wasn't much of a surprise; the surprising part was how long he held out.

He'd go up to New York City for a ball or a gala or "*some thing with Karl*," and be accosted by a scout or a modeling agent, and every time he came back, his voice would be tainted with a harsher streak of disdain. "*They think with everything I'm capable of, I'd agree to be dressed like a rag doll and propped up for pictures*," he'd scowl. Meanwhile, the "everything" of which he imagined himself capable was known only to him. He loathed to be perceived as just a rich, pretty face, yet had failed to augment this perception with a lasting demonstration of noninherited merit. Madeline had been appeased by his rejection of modeling as a suitable pursuit: She hated the idea of her boyfriend with his shirt off, attracting millions of eyes that didn't belong to her. Once or twice she'd attended events in New York City with him where she had witnessed the attempts. It was a joke between them: "*Three people begged Dorian to sign a contract last night*," she'd laugh while holding onto his arm, proud that it was her who got to have him in the end.

Looking back, perhaps he knew all along, and was merely warming us up to the idea. More likely, though, he had been floating in an infinity pool in Crete when they e-mailed him with an umpteenth invitation to Paris. He probably stirred his gin and tonic with a swizzle stick and looked across the water, then, contemplating his fondness for the Champs-Élysées, thought, *Why not?*—in regard to modeling, and his entire life. It shouldn't have come as a shock. For our trio, it had always been about the next exciting thing. We prided ourselves on intimate relations with the halfhearted cousin of true recklessness—elaborate plans culminating in afternoon naps in each other's arms, talk of road trips and big parties and graduating and going off "*into the world*," occasionally committing to some wild gesture: splashing stone-sober into the fountain at Sterling Library, or roaring down a highway sticking out of the moonroof of Blake's car—the *shape* of change, an aesthetic.

There were plenty of drugs and alcohol to keep us feeling new and exciting, and when all else failed, we just looked around and remembered that we were surrounded by our beautiful friends, our beautiful, young life. Somehow though, it wasn't enough for Dorian—or more likely, it was too much. He thought he had eluded a life Path, that dreaded bulwark of boredom and banality which in his mind equated to a life unjustly compromised, yet maybe . . . the dreaded Path was *us*, and he had unwittingly settled into us as complacently as a gray flannel suit into a seated position from nine to five. We couldn't be sure. All we knew was that—he left. Just didn't say a word to us, and was gone.

After a series of unanswered phone calls, a final call to Dorian's mom's house in Paris confirmed it: Dorian had left. To us, the reason remained a mystery.

Barely able to believe it, Madeline cried and cried. I was upset, too, but at first I refused to take it personally. Like a housewife who convinces herself that her absent beloved must be "working late" or "out to buy milk," I made excuses for Dorian. *He must have had some troubles we didn't know about.* His mother had just remarried for the second time, and I knew his relationship with his father wasn't the best. Money and good looks weren't everything, you know—surely something was bothering him, and he'd be back when he was ready.

Then Paris Fashion Week happened, and the whereabouts of the spectral spouse were finally known. For the first time since his disappearance, Dorian's ghost appeared with a proverbial stumble onto our idyllic, shrub-laced porch, Windsor knot askew over his open shirt-front, and his head swirling like aerated wine. Intermingling with the faded notes of our own disgraced romance was the overpowering stench of the Other Woman's cheap perfume: There is no love whose fragrance lasts forever.

Who knew if between us there had ever been any love at all?

When the splashy headline appeared in the *Yale Daily News* it was the end of September, which had been a month of intimate relations with Madeline's tear-streaked face. "*MODEL STUDENT,*" the paper screamed in block letters, and all was explained with a picture of Dorian on the Jean Paul Gaultier runway. He appeared in pictures on the front page for the rest of the week, walking in a new show every day. Technically he wasn't even a Yale student anymore—he had transferred to la Sorbonne, we later found out—yet his was the only news anybody at school was interested in. At Yale we were used to all the usual newsworthy stories: The pre-med major discovering an elusive cancer cell, or the Rhodes scholar publishing his debut novel. The most insufferable write-ups always happened after summer vacation, when all the do-gooders returned from the corners of

Africa to pen op-ed articles about their acts of compassion in the third world, but Dorian's news-making story was atypical and alluring.

By the third day, the well-worn grooves of campus talk were universally trampled by many *have-you-heard?* pairings of "Dorian Belgraves" and "Paris Fashion Week," the latter term having never invaded undergraduate discussion before. Dorian was like an advancing army of one, whose image steadily laid greater claim to the defenseless pages of our school paper. Over dining-hall trays he had his makeup applied backstage, his foppish long hair clipped up with silver barrettes; on study-room desks, between notes on stem cells and the 1870 Franco-Prussian War, he attended Fashion Week after-parties with all the other gorgeous Impossibles who, we assumed, had run away from their own Yales everywhere. Soon there was not a person or a surface across the Yale campus that didn't know Dorian Belgraves was having the best life of anyone we knew.

It was different for me and Madeline, of course. We were the Kübler-Ross couple, carrying out our grief in the five predictable stages. Denial, because Dorian "could've never"; then anger, because of course he did; then rationalization; depression; until finally, when we should have felt acceptance, just a deep, black lull, as Madeline relied for a few weeks on half-sputtered words and I finally realized that, if once I had loved him, now I *hated* Dorian Belgraves.

Dorian had stolen my own dream. He'd gotten the life full of glamour and excitement, at least ten years sooner than I could even hope for, if it *ever* happened for me at all, because of things he hadn't even worked for—wealth, beauty, and a disposition whose sweetness could attract no enemies—while I prayed every day for a chance at the smallest bit of it. And sure, if you want to know the truth? If I was him maybe I'd have done the same, just left and become fabulous and forgotten everybody. But the difference was that I *knew* that, if I was him, if I was the lucky one and he wasn't, at least I would say *sorry*. I knew I would turn around and say *something*, anything, to acknowledge the unfairness of it; that despite the obstruction of my silver spoon in my hand I would make some self-deprecating gesture toward those I had one-upped, to clear the air of that evil illusion that somehow I had earned it all.

Madeline at least had devoted herself to a higher cause. For every hour we spent together, she spent a dozen in solitude, poring over books that might help her change the world somehow. Even if in the end she never made a real change in the world at all—just chaired a high-profile charity, or funneled money into a leftist nonprofit—at the very least she was conscious of something outside of her immediate self. But Dorian never was. He was never conscious of anything except *living* his enchanted life, and something about knowing that, it just dug into me, as if all along Dorian had been a silver knife that, in my ignorance, I had allowed to pierce me, pushing deeper and deeper, until finally, the only thing to do was just rip it out for good and bandage up the wound with the tattered shreds of my own dignity.

After I realized all that, I was glad I would never see Dorian again.

Dorian is a brat, I told myself. He was too beautiful, too rich; without Dorian it would be one less beautiful person standing between me and the life I believed was my birthright. When I applied for the internship at *Régine*, the thought thrashed viciously across my mind that maybe I should reach out to Edie,

Dorian's mother. To work at *Régine* was my truest dream, and I knew that to guarantee my internship there I only needed to ask for a single phone call from the woman whose face had countless times graced its pages. Edie Belgraves would have happily done me the favor, having on several occasions taken a superior liking to me (apparently I was the spitting image of her first high school boyfriend)—yet to gain any privilege with the utterance of Dorian's family name would be like balancing my life's dream atop a hollow house of cards. I preferred to build a shack from scratch, using my own incomplete deck, than to ever think of him again.

THE ELEVATOR DOOR SLID OPEN TO THE FOYER OF THE BELgraves' private apartment. They owned the entire floor, and the one above. Despite the newly minted origins of their wealth—hundreds of exorbitantly paying fashion campaigns resulting in six-figure checks to Dorian's mother, combined with a fortune made in Silicon Valley by his stepfather—their decor spun an illusion of old money, with all the trappings of anyone with blue-blooded relations. We dripped rainwater onto a Persian carpet as Madeline sniffed at one of the potted palms, watering it with her swinging wet hair.

I fished in Dorian's pockets for the keys while he groaned and pressed his forehead against the toile wallpaper. Captured in a perennial pastoral bliss of fluttering aprons and swinging apple-bearing baskets, the French countrywomen were duplicated every three inches in the same arrangement, their bonneted faces always preferring the peaceful contemplation of produce and pillowing haystacks over us.

"Do you realize where we are?" Madeline whispered wondrously at the houseplant. "Dorian lives here!"

A click, and the door creaked into a grand entrance hall.

I reached for Dorian's waist, tore him away from murmured small talk with his Gallic neighbors. "We're home."

It was quiet in the apartment. Light swirled in from the foyer like cream into black coffee. My eyes adjusted to the phantom before us: Edie, gazing out from a blown-up cover of *Vogue*. All around glowed ghostly eyes that belonged alternately to Dorian or to his mother. I had never realized how similar they both looked; the same timeless almond-eyed countenance, a beauty rooted in the finest sensitivities of both sexes. It made sense that Dorian and his mother had always been extremely close. Most people are, when they remind one another of themselves.

A majestic staircase loomed ahead, shadows from a curlicued wrought iron railing writhing like ivy over the marble steps. Dorian smacked his lips and seemed to regain a bit of his senses. "Do you think you can climb up yourself?" I asked. I gestured to the stairs and his knees crumpled beneath him.

I took a breath, and held my hands around his waist to steady him. The handrail was polished wood, but it felt like ice.

"Darling . . ." called Madeline from behind us, her voice echoing like a penny into an empty wishing well. "Darling, why don't you show Ethan your piano . . . ?"

Having already seen Dorian's piano a dozen times before, I rolled my eyes as she caught up to us at the foot of the stairs. With a tug at my arm, she cooed, "Before I met you, I'd never seen such a marvelous piano." She gazed fawningly at me through crescent-moon lids—evidently, she thought I was Dorian—then let me go, drifting back into the light like a ballerina who had forgotten her steps.

Dorian hung on, wringing his arms around my torso while I began to drag him up after me. His legs twitched in earnest, but his feet always missed the stair—after a few tries he just gave up completely, and it was like carrying a piece of furniture. Halfway up, I took another deep breath and leaned against the rail for relief. His whole body pressed obliviously against me and I wondered, as his heart beat serenely into my ribcage, if this had not been the state of our entire friendship.

"Come on, babe," I urged, not realizing that I had adopted Dorian's habitual pet name.

"Are we—?" Dorian lifted his head up from me with a faded sense of recognition—he loosened his grip around my body and started to slip away. He was coming undone, like a loosely tied towel, and—*flash!*—his head rolled back and his Adam's apple caught the light with a bladelike glint. The stairs below us wavered. My body tensed as Dorian's whole weight rested over my arm, and with a strong heave I jerked him back onto me.

With one hand on the banister, I adjusted him across the front of my chest and tightened my grip around his waist. He buried his face into my neck. He snorted. Snored. We swayed for a moment there and I gazed up into the darkness, which like a black hole in a recurring dream felt both terrifying yet familiar. Then he fastened his arms around my body once more—hugged me, really—and we continued upward into it.

The whole time Madeline lingered behind us, a hand holding onto the banister and the other conducting an invisible orchestra as she swayed from side to side with her eyes closed, a concerto trapped inside her head by her wet blonde hair. "Boys . . ." she called out musically. "Why don't we all go on a double date this weekend?"

"Who'd be my date?" I grunted, as I lugged Dorian over the final step.

"Me," she said.

"What about Dorian?"

She tossed a limp-wristed hand in the air. "Both of you would be my date," she yawned. "That'd be the double part."

Dorian's bedroom was pitch-black, but I still knew it like my own. With a final effort I heaved my charge facedown onto the middle of his four-poster bed. He fell with a cushioned thud, and I crumbled like a demolished building onto his fifteen-hundred-count sheets, just as Madeline's forehead cracked conclusively against the bedpost and she bewilderedly mumbled something about Dorian's piano.

I ANSWERED THE PHONE. "*RÉGINE.*"

"Edmund needs a reservation." I failed to recognize the voice amid a hectic background of New York traffic.

"Er, sure," I replied, reaching for a notepad as a distant car alarm filled in my ear. "I'm sorry, who's calling?"

"It's me," he said, and I realized with horror that I was on the line with Edmund Benneton, who had inexplicably referred to himself in the third person. From my end, a sharp intake of breath; I swelled with embarrassment, back straightening as though Edmund was suddenly right there, ominously slapping a ruler against his palm. "I'm so sorry—" I began, but he ignored me and yawned. "Is this the redhead?"

"No," I replied, "it's Ethan . . . black hair."

He considered this—perhaps trying to remember me—then prodded, "What are you wearing?"

I glanced down at my gray Dior suit, which I had now worn every day for two weeks.

"Not maroon, I hope." He took a long, audible drag off a cigarette, and sighed, "I hate maroon . . . Can you make my reservation?"

"Of course," I gushed, like a tidal wave hitting a city, "yes, yes, I—"

"Good. Somewhere well-reviewed, and new." He puff-puffed once more, and specified: "New in the past six months. Make sure it's below Fourteenth Street—eight o'clock for two people, under Edmund Benneton. You can confirm to my personal e-mail."

The words were still forming on my tongue when he hung up on me. I sat there at the edge of my seat, scribbling furiously while murmuring to myself, "Well-reviewed. New. Eight o'clock. Below Fourteenth."

I brandished the note in the air like Charlie Bucket with his golden ticket as the significance of the moment descended upon me: This was it. This was my big break. A seemingly insignificant task, but I had guzzled enough Horatio Alger Kool-Aid to know that a few favors here and there, and pretty soon I'd have worked my way up the ladder. I would be traveling the whole world with Edmund, going to photo shoots and helping him dress all the top models, and—

"Who was that?" asked George, fat fingers pressed around a carrot stick.

"Er—" I had a vague idea of what would happen if George learned I had intercepted an assignment from Edmund. "Nobody," I lied, "just Jenny from HL Group."

"She's so loud, I could hear her from over here," he crunched.

I stood up with an abrupt scrape of chair casters against the carpet. "I'm going to use the bathroom," I announced in a flat voice.

I enclosed myself in a stall, and began to scroll on my phone through restaurant reviews. Without much time to waste, I settled on the first restaurant I found that fit his description, a Spanish-Japanese fusion restaurant in the West Village that was only three months old, boasting a series of "unclassifiably succulent" squid dishes according to the *Times*. Good enough for me. It certainly sounded extravagant, like one of those places nobody really enjoyed but that sophisticated people raved about while drinking musty wine and making superior remarks: perfect for Edmund.

On my return to the fashion closet I ran into Sabrina, who was strolling to the kitchenette with an unprecedented air of amusement. Like a Homecoming Queen upon recent acquisition of some third-period gossip, she passed me with a spring in her stilettoed step and her eyebrows elevated by malicious pleasure.

"Who's *D*?" she asked.

I didn't know what she was talking about, until a moment later I found my desk nearly swallowed up by a monstrosity of hydrangeas.

"Somebody has an admirer," George remarked dryly, "although I can't imagine who."

Thank you for last night, the card read, in a familiar, near-illegible scrawl. *Love ya, D*.

I gulped, feeling as though Dorian had violated a restraining order I had issued against him. He wasn't allowed to come near here. The fact that Dorian had found a way to invade my life at *Régine*—with his Trojan horse of colossal flowers, the best that money could buy, surely—well, I ripped up the card into tatters over the wastebasket and, before the last shred had fluttered to the bottom, dunked the bouquet upside-down after it. It sunk with a tremendous thud, and the underside of the vase sparkled cheerfully with cellophane.

AT AROUND EIGHT O'CLOCK THAT MORNING I HAD WOKEN UP at Dorian's apartment with a hand around my waist, and sunlight on my face.

I had awoken in this same manner almost one year ago, when for my twenty-first birthday, we all dropped acid in Edgerton Park, on a grassy, unnamed hill that thereafter none of us could find again. We danced all night like hand-holding paper figures in a Matisse collage, then crumpled to sleep in the grass. I remember being the first to wake up, finding Madeline's arm draped around my chest and watching, through one half-open eye, the sun threading quickly through the blades of grass, casting an intricate glow over all the earth's edges like an endless spool of white Spanish lace.

It felt exactly like that in Dorian's bedroom as I absently caressed my own fingers over what I assumed to be Madeline's hand. While I was trying to remember last night's dream, I felt a whisper of hair on her skin which I didn't remember being there before.

I turned my head. *Dorian.*

His naked chest was pressed against my back while the rest of him was clothed, both of us tangled up in his luxurious sheets. Madeline was lying along the foot of the bed, her head tipped facedown over the side of the mattress. Dorian's gin-cooled breath flowed from his tiny nostrils onto my cheek like an intoxicating gas. I lifted my hand from his. Once, I would have wished it to remain there forever. Now, he felt too warm, as if under his skin his blood was blazing through his veins at a temperature that burned me. With my own cold fingers, I painstakingly removed his limb from around my body and slid away from him, edging toward the side of the rumpled bed.

In the sudden absence of my body, Dorian extended his arm across the bed—eyes shut, like he was looking for something in his dream—then, finding a pillow, drew it toward his broad, smooth chest, and wrapped himself around it like an infant. He licked his lips, and was suddenly at rest again. The bed creaked as I sat up and stretched my legs toward the floor. I checked for my wallet in my back pocket, then stood up and shuffled through a wreckage of storm-tossed clothes. Despite Dorian's having settled several weeks ago in New York, a rakish pile of suitcases—half-ransacked, a hopeless tangle of socks and spilled sleeves—gave the appearance that he had only yesterday tornadoed off the plane from Paris.

His clothes were all designer—you could tell, even from afar—yet, unlike the piles that formed in the fashion closet at *Régine*, they were layered with soft carelessness. Everything he owned had adopted from him that quality of aristocratic ease, rumpled and unstarched yet still possessing an intrinsic appreciation of its value.

Amid this abundance of *sprezzatura*, the conspicuous dissident was a black leather book, jutting from under the idle arm of a heather-gray cashmere sweater. I pulled it out and traced my fingers over an embossed cover that read *Ford*. Dorian's modeling portfolio. The first page was a torn-out magazine spread: Dorian in a chain-mail sweater, illuminated by dramatic silver light. I traced my fingers over his lips and then his eyes, always seeking some diversion, then over the text in the corner that read, SWEATER—DOLCE & GABBANA. It would have been easy to tell myself that this

Dorian was somehow "different now," that in becoming someone new he had excused himself from our entangled relations, yet Dorian appeared quite innocent of any change at all. There was no malice in his eyes, no superior smirk souring his mouth. I closed the portfolio and felt something fall out of the bottom—a piece of heavy sketch paper, folded up into a thick square. I picked it up from the wooden floor and my heart raced as I unfolded it.

A faint groan, as Madeline lifted her head with an effort and then let it drop. Her hair cascaded once more over the side of the bed, the golden vines of a hanging plant.

Before unfolding the last crease, I knew.

It was me. It was my portrait, which Dorian had started on the first day we met but never finished—only now, here I was in full. My mismatched eyes sprawled huge across my cheeks, radiating color, radiating life. The paper trembled in my hand as his voice reverberated through my memory—"*You know who you remind me of . . . ? The Borghese boy—he has all this food, but he looks so hungry.*" I gulped.

Dorian had taken me to Paris.

I returned the paper to the portfolio, and the portfolio to the suitcase, back under the folds of Dorian's life, and turned wordlessly to leave.

On the way out of Dorian's apartment, I stopped to sit at the piano. Madeline was right. It was a marvelous piano, the biggest piano I'd ever seen, and as I closed the apartment door behind me, I wondered how they'd gotten it through the door, or if they'd opened up the roof and lowered it inside with a crane.

EDMUND MUST HAVE LOVED THE "UNCLASSIFIABLY SUCCULENT" squid at the Spanish-Japanese restaurant I had chosen for his dinner reservation, because every day thereafter I was assigned a new task by him. I signed thank-you notes and looked up Swedish bed-and-breakfast rates; purchased contact lens solution and bid online for rococo furniture (Edmund wanted an "old throne-like chair, something that was sat on by a king, or at *least* a famous duke"). I even "shopped around" after work for lavender-scented mothballs, which consisted of sniffing the selection at various boutiques and sending him my detailed reports.

These were all little things—slightly demoralizing—but it didn't matter. What *did* matter was that eventually the little things would transform into big things, and for the time being, he knew my name, which was more than could be said for George, or even Sabrina, whose name he still inexplicably believed was Susan. After two weeks I was sure that not only did he know my name, but that it was his *favorite* name.

Phone calls from Edmund sounded like this:

"Ethan, I need you to RSVP me to Kate's wedding. Find me a flight to London arriving two days before and departing one day after, and see if Charles can't set up a car service through the countryside."

"Ethan, I need you to schedule a fitting with my tailor. Tell him the last two pants he altered for me were too short, and what does he think, I'm shrinking?"

"Ethan, I need lots of contact solution. Leave the bottles all over the place. My eyes are always dry."

"Ethan, I need you to make me a fruit salad. My housekeepers always forget to pit my cherries, and I can't just keep dismissing them."

"Ethan, I need you to deliver my dry cleaning. Pick up the garment bag this evening from my office and tell Caesar that the McQueen shirt has a grease stain on the collar, and that no, it wasn't me, it was some other fool because I don't eat greasy food."

"Also, Ethan—there are *two* McQueen shirts in that load I just called about, and both look like they have stains, but one of them is distressed on purpose, I'm sure you will be able to tell which."

"Also, Ethan, please—when you take those shirts, tell Caesar I need a full refund for the cashmere sweater he supposedly laundered. Tell him there was a hair on the collar."

Despite the volume of his demanding workload, there was never a cruel or derogatory tone in his delegation of any task—on the contrary, Edmund's exhausted voice had the strain of a person constantly chasing after something with which he could never quite catch up. It was good fortune, not bad, that I credited for my extra workload, although clandestine bathroom breaks became quickly inadequate windows to complete it. While often his more personal errands led me panting around the city on the weekends, office-related tasks required me to stay after-hours at *Régine*.

At the end of the workday, usually seven or eight o'clock, I would follow Sabrina and George out of the fashion closet. Then, before reaching the elevator, I pretended to need a bathroom visit. Sabrina and George would never dream of waiting for me, so I gazed at the bathroom ceiling until I was sure they had disappeared, then swooped back into the fashion closet to finish my work for Edmund.

Quietly entering Edmund's office down the hall, I would tidy up papers or computer files according to his instructions, and often reorient his desk, which a much-consulted feng shui book suggested he was in the habit of repositioning to channel "creativity chi." Because he never actually called me to his office during work hours, I was determined that neither Sabrina nor George should know about it—especially not George. Sabrina already had a post at *Régine*, but George would easily sabotage my efforts to benefit his own ladder-climbing, and if he knew Edmund had taken a liking to me—well, I didn't even want to think of what consequential toxins he could spread to pollute the air.

So that George would never suspect, I began to attack every phone call before the completion of the first ring. Sometimes the hairs on the back of my neck would stiffen a millisecond before the phone rang, and I was answering, "*Régine*," before George had even turned his orange head. If he looked over while I was taking down Edmund's instructions, I'd roll my eyes toward him like it was just another PR person on the line, and when Edmund hung up I would stay on the phone for a few seconds longer than necessary, nodding my head to pander, "Of course, Rachel, we'll get the Valentino to you by this afternoon," or "Have a good day, Simon."

Edmund wasn't just my hero anymore—some far-off figure, a poster on a classroom wall. He was the closest chance I had to realizing the life I wanted, the gatekeeper to my dreams. Edmund was going to save me.

One day, after several weeks of attuning myself to his every need, my neck hairs tingled while I was standing on a ladder hoisting a box of hats: *Edmund*. I could feel him. I prepared myself to scramble down the ladder, but there was no phone call.

The closet door swung open. "Which one of you is Ethan?"

From above, I watched Edmund's half-plucked hairline soar into view like a pale, shiny moon. Arm emerging from under a green capelet, he pointed a bejeweled finger at me—"You're Ethan, right?"

I nodded with petrified shock.

He gestured with a yawn toward George, who appeared as stunned as a person about to get run over by a cab. "Help Ethan, please," Edmund instructed.

George raised his arms, and I let the box slide into his dumbfounded custody, where it bounced against his bulging stomach like a spoon upon bread pudding.

"Come on, boy," Edmund said to me as I stepped off the ladder, careful not to graze George, who was staring at me with a mixture of menace and confusion. Edmund snorted, a deep hog-like snort, and with a swaggering lean wrapped his arm around my shoulder and drew me into a conspiratorial meander away from George.

He opened his mouth, and his saliva made an unsticking sound. "You should know, the next time you make me a fruit salad, the one thing I hate more than cherry pits is cherry *stems*." He halfheartedly waggled a skeletal finger in my face before lowering his voice to a hoarse whisper—"Now listen carefully, because I am trusting you with a *very important* matter. "I'm leaving you the key to my apartment this afternoon," he began, and my heart started to race.

That I should be entrusted with the key to Edmund's home! My stomach leaped into my throat. This was it! After only a few weeks of bland servitude, I would be put to work on something meaningful. I prepared myself to accept the challenge—of selecting clothes, researching story concepts—and felt my own worth brimming as the notes of his overripe cologne swelled in my nostrils.

"See, I keep a collection of diaries," Edmund continued. "Some of them are five, ten years old—just notes, musings—

all my creative output. Over the years, with my schedule, you know—they have reached a state of . . ." The jewels on his fingers glittered like a pinwheel as his hand conjured words with a revolving motion. "Creative . . . disarray . . . so—what I need is somebody to organize them—to just find the ones that come first, and put them all in order . . . Do you think you can do that?"

I nodded fervently as his words settled in my head and I realized that Edmund—a man I barely knew, yet who was interwound so intricately with my dream of success—had extended to me his vote of utmost confidence. If I had any doubt that his request represented the rare and unusual solidarity between us, it evaporated when Edmund *smiled* at me. I looked up to reciprocate, but his teeth were brittle and yellow, the posts of a rotting fence, and to linger over the sight of them ruined the moment—so I looked off to the side of him, away from his ugly teeth and his receding hairline and his sagging everything, and smiled at the air around him.

He patted my back and separated from me, his capelet whooshing over my back. Then he received a phone call, answered "HELLO" like a hearing-impaired person, and torpedoed distractedly away

"What was *that*?" demanded George, as the door shut behind Edmund. George wore a gray blazer today, and we almost matched.

"I—I messed up one of his inspiration boards," I said, trembling with excitement. I was a terrible liar, and pretended to engross myself with an invisible hair on my pants. "He was reprimanding me." I plucked it away and stole an upward glance to see if I had convinced him.

"But how does he even know your name?"

I shrugged, with an expression as dumb as I could muster. George furrowed his pale eyebrows and then, for the first and last time, Sabrina did me a huge favor.

Having been occupied with Clara and the other editors throughout Edmund's visitation, Sabrina called over her cubicle now—"George! Have you heard of Madeline Dupre?"

I froze at the unsettling mention of my best friend's name within the halls of *Régine*.

"No," George replied. "Is she e-mailing us?"

"She's dating Edie Belgraves's son. It's online, I've just—never heard of her."

George turned his head away from me, distracted, while I grabbed the box of hats from him and scurried up the ladder once more.

IT WOULD HAVE BEEN EASY TO WRITE A PLEASANT REAL estate description of Edmund's apartment: *Fabulously located in fashionable West Village, steps from Washington Square Park, NYU, and more. Convenient shopping and charming restaurants nearby. Doorman, gymnasium, and crown molding throughout*. What more?

The white-paneled lobby boasted a Baccarat chandelier and a remarkable echo. The doorman wore impeccably starched white gloves. The whole place smelled strongly of some flower—or rather, not any particular flower, but just "flowers," a variety capable of no offense: Altogether, an airtight impression of generic luxury.

The impression ended abruptly when I turned the key to Edmund's apartment and was simultaneously assaulted by a dark figure and a startling decorating scheme. The black figure lunged. I shielded myself with the door, saw him do the same, and realized the first feature in the foyer of Edmund's apartment was a full-length mirror, as ornate as a window in a Gothic cathedral, hanging on a zebra wall. The reason I could not say zebra *print* was because the room in question wasn't merely painted or wallpapered to look like zebra stripes, but covered from floor to ceiling with actual zebra, like someone had skinned a herd of them and sewn them together with all the stripes running in the same direction. I confirmed this with a shuddering touch—coarse, like horsehair.

I clicked the door behind me and wandered bewilderedly inside, my shoes echoing upon a shiny onyx floor. "Hello?"

Hoping to ward off any more surprises, I knocked against an open doorframe and poked my tousled head into the next room. Moroccan tapestries and Japanese silk wall scrolls. Orchids, calla lilies, birds of paradise. A Renaissance-style ceiling resembling a cloudy sky, complete with painted cherubs and precipitation in the form of a crystal-dripping chandelier. A Victorian camelback sofa, upholstered in purple velvet and covered with tufted leopard-print cushions; a big-screen plasma television and surround sound speakers; Louis XIV-style chairs bordering a claw-foot coffee table; and a waxy gray wall-covering wafting upward from an untraceable breeze.

Puzzled by the gray wall covering, I gave in to my temptation to touch it and thereafter resolved not to place a hand over anything unrelated to my designated responsibilities. It was an elephant skin—a dried-out *elephant skin*—and amid the churning of my stomach I wondered if working at *Régine* make it somehow legal for Edmund to own endangered-animal skins.

Iconic fashion photographs hanging throughout—full-color,

framed in every iteration of gold curlicues—confirmed the apartment did not in fact belong to a taxidermist, and I ventured onward through a dizzying optical illusion of a hallway, its concurrent pink and white stripes painted in a head-splitting hexagonal pattern that was reflected infinitely in another full-length mirror.

The bedroom, in a shocking coral red, was no comfort at all. Magazines around the perimeter were piled to the height of a small person—leaning, crammed—and the floor was a black-and-white checkerboard, with the ceiling covered in a matching damask. Supervising the room was a huge Technicolor Buddha, painted with legs folded and eyes closed as he practiced his meditation during a Warholian acid trip. The one visual relief took the form of an ivory canopy that could be drawn shut over the bed, yet even that was cheetah print on the inside (although thankfully, it appeared, not sewn from actual cheetah skin). I couldn't fathom the underlying design philosophy, but took it as confirmation of Edmund's genius—a glimpse of which his diaries would soon miraculously grant me.

Replete with ornate fluting, his bookshelf was topped with a carving of Medusa, and her eyes bored through me as I poked innocently around for Edmund's diaries. I had expected them to be all together, lined up on a shelf or two, but very few of his books were lined up at all. Instead they were like the magazines on the floor—crammed into haphazard piles, their crevices stuffed with miscellany, everything in danger of spilling out if you removed a single book.

I found the first diary crushed like a bookmark between the pages of a Christian Dior coffee-table publication. Holding in the books above and below, I yanked it out and smiled as I ran my fingers over the yellow satin cover, feeling a thrill at the thought of reading it. I laid it on the bearskin rug at my feet and found a second on a bottom shelf: Tiffany blue, bound in silk with gold-tipped pages, sandwiched between two decades-old copies of *Vogue Italia*.

As I gathered them all up in every size and shape, in shades of coral and mustard and azure blue, I learned that Edmund also collected greeting cards. Tucked into books and diaries and crannies all around I found a dozen cards, always blank on the inside, and paired up with the unused envelopes. *Happiness is a journey, not a destination . . . To the world you may be one person, but to one person you may be the world . . . Life is not about finding yourself, it is about creating yourself.* Some of them were in other languages (*La vie ne vaut d'être vécue sans amour*), and they made me wonder if he bought them on his travels, thinking, "*That would make a nice card for John Galliano,*" then returned home and forgot about them? Or did he buy them for himself, because, well, he just liked feel-good quotes in calligraphic fonts?

I noticed another blue diary on the nightstand. In total, there were four more diaries in its various drawers; one covered by a pile of pills, with no container in sight, and another guarded by a flaccid wind chime, which like Edmund's peaceless Buddha alluded to his vague interest in a New Age aesthetic. For good measure, since the diaries seemed to be everywhere, I decided to check the bathroom—and was unsurprised to find two there, resting in a pearly magazine rack. The bathroom was in fact pearl-themed: It contained a pearl-studded mirror and a bathtub shaped like a giant oyster, presumably so Edmund could pretend to be the pearl in the middle.

I took it as further confirmation of his genius, all these diaries hidden in the corners of his apartment like Easter eggs. When I thought I had almost all of them—surely a few still lurked—I knelt on the bearskin rug with all of them fanned out around me like a parasol, and took a breath.

The first diary. I opened it—winced.

Edmund's handwriting somehow contained greater menace than Charles Manson's scrawl, and it was while trying to discern his near illegible scratches that I came close to thinking he and *Régine* and everybody must all have been playing a huge joke on me.

> *Carla came to the city today she is so fat I can't believe anybody could look so bad in Alaïa we went to dinner—*

It stopped there. I turned the page to see if it continued—that couldn't be all—but it never did, and in fact the next time he had written was twenty pages later, in a different colored ink:

> *Today we went to Indochine for dinner I had the salmon the Times said it was their best dish I sat with Coco Rocha Raquel Zimmerman Edie Campbell FeiFei Sun Daria Strokous Joseph Altuzarra and Georgina St. James Coco Rocha was wearing a Vera Wang chiffon dress and Miu Miu open-toe ankle boots Raquel Zimmerman was wearing a Louis Vuitton plaid cropped jacket and skirt and Marni platform heels Edie Campbell was wearing a Rodarte sweater and sequined skirt with lace overlay and Giuseppe Zanotti boots FeiFei Sun was wearing a Nina Ricci lame jacket Céline tapered pants and Jil Sander boots Daria Strokous was wearing a Marc Jacobs polka-dot jacket Dries Van Noten silk blouse Proenza Schouler macrame skirt and*

Chanel kitten heels Joseph Altuzarra was wearing an Yves Saint Laurent suit and Ferragamo shoes and Georgina St. James is going through a divorce so I don't blame her for wearing head-to-toe Dillard's or something.

That was it. There were no sketches or inspirations, no anecdotes or stories, no reference to his editorial work at all.

I fumbled for another diary from the pile—*Karlie Kloss wore Christian Dior*—then another—*Chanel Balenciaga Versace*—then another, which was empty except for one word in the middle—*open-toe*—just OPEN-TOE in the middle of the page, in the middle of the diary, constituting the entirety of the book's revelations.

I began in anguish to flip through more and more pages, desperate to find something, anything, of value. But there was nothing, just a ramble of designers and famous people; a running tab of names, names, names without any punctuation, except for the end of some long passages where his ink had bled into a kind of mottled period, as though the exercise had exhausted him and he could barely lift his pen to prevent an aneurysmal inkblot.

My bottom lip trembled.

It had been one thing to slowly recognize the bland truth about everyone else at *Régine*—but Edmund too?

Like a slow-moving washing machine, my stomach churned as the truth about him became sickeningly apparent. Even with all the patterns and the colors screaming for attention, the apartment was like the bags under Edmund's eyes: sagging, tired. In the middle of his huge flashy bedroom, his satin-covered, queen-size bed was collapsed in its center like a broken lung, and everywhere the stacks of magazines leaned against each other for relief.

Edmund Benneton wasn't a genius. He was a sham. He was

tired, washed out, relying on twenty-four-karat bells and whistles to sustain his reputation as a "creative" while all along living in sleepless fear of his inevitable undoing. My idol—*Régine*—my dream—it was all a sham.

How far I thought I'd come from poring over *Régine* at my mother's nail salon, dreaming of an escape—only to realize that this was exactly the same.

My arm gravitated onto my lap as the pages flipped over my thumb and the diary finally slipped away from me. I turned and noticed the bear's entire head was still attached to the bearskin rug I was sitting on. It had two glittering glass gemstones for eyes—and suddenly, I couldn't be there anymore. I scrambled in a panic to my feet, excavated a hole on a bookshelf with a swoop of my hand, and shoving, shoving, began to cram the diaries there, patting them in, a worthless row of bleak, colorful spines—pressed the bottom of my hand to my nose—sniffled, with one last, unbelieving glance around me, at Buddha, and Medusa, and cried out.

EVERY DAY THEREAFTER I DESCENDED INTO THE SUBWAY like a buoy being dragged underwater.

"Ladies and gentlemen, we are delayed because of train traffic ahead of us."

One day an old woman with a head scarf spat phlegm into a corner of the train car. She hacked loudly while a wall of people pressed against me, trying to place inches between themselves and her. Someone cleared his throat loudly to remind her that her behavior was inappropriate, but she took it as a sign there was more phlegm in her own and continued to expectorate.

One day two black kids hollered at everybody to "Stand back, stand back, ev'rybody, it's *showtime*." They blasted hip-hop from a handheld radio and started to do handstands before passing around a baseball cap for cash tips. When the train jolted to a stop, one of them accidentally kicked a baby stroller with his Nikes and they escaped onto the platform with dollar bills fluttering behind them.

One day two Asian women got into a fight when one of them bumped a cartful of lettuce heads against the other's cart of onions. But after a minute I wasn't sure if they were mad or if they just knew each other and were talking very loudly in Chinese while pointing in each other's faces.

One day the overhead voice said, "Stand clear of the closing doors, please"—the doors rung *ding-ding!* to close, then bluffing, rung *ding-ding!* to close again—then *ding-ding!* and *ding-ding!* and *ding-ding!* and "Stand clear of the closing doors, please," then *ding-ding!* "Stand clear of the—" *ding-ding!* "Stand clear—" *ding-ding!* and everyone was looking around for whoever was holding the door open *ding-ding! ding-ding! ding-ding!* and it was a lady with an enormous suitcase who clearly did not fit into the subway car *ding-ding!* and I wanted to scream *STAND CLEAR OF THE FUCKING DOOR, PLEASE!* If I wasn't entitled to be happy or successful, wasn't I at least entitled to get home without being stuck in this miserable underground hell with you and your suitcase? *Ding-ding!*

Every day, between all the setbacks, the same woman lent her cheerful but unconvincing voice to the overhead subway speakers—"*Next stop, Fourteenth Street—Next stop, Astor Place—Next stop, Bleecker Street.*" When she said it, it was as if she was teaching the stops to a child with learning difficulties—*FOUR-teenth Street,*

AS-tor Place, BLEE-cker Street—and I wondered if she was proud of herself for stifling the quality of my life, a life that became increasingly more pathetic with every commute. How old was she and how long had her voice been filling the subway trains? Did she live in New York, and if so, did she come onto the subway and tell people, "That's me, that's my voice"?

"Ladies and gentlemen, we are delayed because of train traffic ahead of us."

Maybe she was poor and destitute and wore rags, and when she tried to tell people it was her voice on the loudspeaker they all thought she was another crackpot.

"Ladies and gentlemen, you are getting sadder and more pitiful every second."

Maybe she was just like me, and when she heard her own voice, she thought, *"God, this is so all so exhausting."*

"Ladies and gentlemen, it's never going to go away."

Maybe she was already dead.

"Ladies and gentlemen, and you, Ethan St. James, you're dead too."

It was like this for one, two, three, four, five . . . days? Weeks? I honestly have no idea.

ONCE I ARRIVED AT *RÉGINE*, IT WAS ALWAYS THE SAME.

Somehow it was always me who ended up with the task of finding missing things in our overflowing closet. It was always something dreadfully obscure—either very insignificant (a missing pearl from a Chanel belt), very elusive (a pair of transparent plastic, fingerless Pucci gloves), or very generic (an unlabeled white crewneck Alexander Wang T-shirt, resembling every other unlabeled white crewneck T-shirt we had). Accessories were invariably the worst: Finding a simple top hat from the Giorgio Armani collection involved sifting through about a hundred top hats we had received for a Charlie Chaplin-inspired couture story, looking frantically for the one that most closely resembled our check-in photograph while Sabrina pestered me every minute, "Armani! Armani! Armani!"

Because most of the accessories were unlabeled samples, I had suggested to Sabrina that we begin labeling everything, just writing the name of the designer on a piece of removable masking tape and slapping it somewhere we could easily see later. "You can't just put *ordinary tape* on haute couture," she snapped. I considered proposing to her that we find a tape designed by Valentino.

My so-called "good eye," on which I had so prided myself during my interview with Sabrina, became the bane of my existence, and although most of the missing things turned up after an hour or two of tedious searching, I felt like I was always looking for something I couldn't find.

I knew every morning when I stepped through the closet door, a familiar weight descending over me like a funerary shroud, that during the course of the day Sabrina would bark, George would scoff, Edmund would barge in, and the whole time in the background the fashion editors would gracefully loathe each other while Jane floated around, oblivious to it all.

I could see the truth now about Edmund. Of course the pictures he made were beautiful. He had every imaginable resource at his disposal—the best models and hair and makeup and clothes. He shot only the hottest, of-the-moment girls ("*Call Ford, I need the black girl with the gapped teeth*," he'd say, or "*Who's this? I saw her at Karl's party and now she's shopping with Plum Sykes! Book her for tomorrow's shoot and cancel Natalia.*"). As far as I knew, he had no true inspirations. His "inspiration boards" were just a random sampling of his favorite looks from the current collections, with a few shoes and handbags among them for good measure—everything chosen less for its aesthetic value than for its association with a brand name he liked.

My whole existence now felt like one of his diary entries:

> *Today I photographed in samples from Comme des Garçons Valentino Dries van Noten Fendi Max Mara Gucci Versace Tom Ford Christian Dior Michael Kors Miu Miu Alaïa and Giorgio Armani . . . Meanwhile Sabrina asked George did you see what Dorian Belgraves wore to Karl Lagerfeld's party while I continued looking for Armani and anyway it turned up on Will's desk but it didn't matter anyway because a call came in that Steven Meisel had to postpone the shoot we were prepping so everybody wanted their clothes back and I spent the rest of the day returning everything that had come in which I didn't even have the time to forget was Comme des Garçons Valentino Dries van Noten . . . Sabrina said Dorian Belgraves should do a shoot with his mother Edie . . . Fendi Max Mara Gucci . . . George said that was a brilliant idea . . . Dorian Belgraves Versace Dorian Belgraves Tom Ford Dorian Belgraves Christian Dior Dorian Belgraves Michael Kors Dorian Belgraves Miu Miu Dorian Belgraves Dorian Belgraves Dorian Belgraves*

ON ONE FRIDAY OF AN INDISTINGUISHABLE WEEK AT *RÉGINE*, the editors sent me to pick up a package at the FedEx office.

There were two men waiting at the counter to assist me. The first man's name was Harvey, which I read on a tag on his shirt that said, HELLO, MY NAME IS HARVEY, and below it in smaller letters, PLEASE ASK ME ABOUT OUR MOVING KITS! The other man's name was Bert, and his tag was pretty much the same, except it said, PLEASE ASK ME ABOUT OUR BUY-TWO, GET-ONE DEALS ON SHIPPING TAPE!

Harvey was black, Bert was white, and both had more wrinkles than a prune or a golden raisin. When I handed Harvey the sticky with my tracking number, he said to Bert, "Hey, Bert, you remember how to log off this? I don't want to lose my place," and I noticed that he had been playing solitaire on the computer.

"You just gotta . . ." Bert said, as he slowly stretched his arm out toward Harvey's mouse, in a movement reminiscent of tai chi. He couldn't quite get to it with Harvey in the way, so he said, "Wanna move that way, Harvey?"

And Harvey said, "Sure, Bert," and inched his stool to the side, while trying to remain perched on top of it.

"I'm sorry to rush you," I broke out, "but can you please hurry?"

They blinked at me, like *What's the rush?* and *How fast do you think we can go anyway?*

Hoping to inspire a sense of urgency, I added, "It's for *Régine*."

"What's *Régine*?" they asked together.

I started to take a breath. "It's a fashion magazine," I disclosed. "A very important fashion magazine." Bert's hand hovered over the computer mouse; they had progressed from moving slowly to not moving at all.

"Just—*please!*" I begged with a motion toward Bert's arthritic hand. The screen remained frozen on Harvey's solitaire game.

"A fashion magazine, huh?" Bert prodded. "Do you get to see a lot of women? Like supermodels?"

Harvey looked over and asked me, "That why you got on that nice getup?" referring to my Dior suit from Clara that, being the only understated outfit I owned, now constituted my daily wardrobe. Like a scorekeeper at a ping-pong game, his gape alternated between his computer screen and my suit. My suit won his favor and he altogether gave up any attempt to track my package. "Where could I get a suit like that?" he asked.

Bert seemed interested in the answer as well. Together, they shifted toward me and propped their elbows on the counter, like they expected me to tell them a bedtime story.

"You could go to Bergdorf Goodman," I offered unhelpfully.

"Do you get to see a lot of women?" Bert asked me a second time.

"No."

"You mean you've never worked with Claudia Schiffer?" He turned a little to Harvey. "You know, I asked Claudia Schiffer on a date one time."

"You ain't serious," Harvey scoffed. He warned me, "Don't listen to Bert. He's just old."

"I swear," Bert insisted. "I used to be a busboy at an Italian restaurant—was wipin' up some minestrone soup when she came in. She was with another lady, but I wasn't interested in her. Went right up to Claudia and gave her my phone number on the back of somebody's receipt."

"What you think Claudia Schiffer gonna do with you?" Harvey laughed.

"I was real good-looking then, Harvey! Didn't have a busted leg. I said to Claudia Schiffer, '*Now ma'am, I don't mean to intrude on your dinner, but I gotta tell you, you even prettier in real life than in the magazines.*' She took my number and said '*Thank you*' like a real lady, didn't make me feel bad or nothin'. Never called, though. She was like my fish that swum away. Ever heard that?" he asked me. "Or maybe it's the one that goes, you feed a fish once, you feed him just once, but you feed a fish twice—"

"I—I'm sorry," I said, getting serious, "but I really, really need this package, like—*now*."

Bert squinted, like he wasn't certain what package I was referring to.

"Look," I said, leaning forward, "I'm not technically allowed to tell you this, but you seem like nice guys, so . . . this package I need—" I pointed at the number on my sticky note "—it's actually for *Claudia Schiffer*."

Bert's and Harvey's eyes widened.

"You kiddin'!" Bert said.

"Nope, I'm not, and she really needs it this second, so—"

Bert got to clicking—I could tell he was trying very hard to concentrate—and the next minute he burst, "One thirty-four!"

"One thirty-four?" asked Harvey.

"Claudia's package is in truck one thirty-four! Now what you waiting for? Take the feller out back!"

There must have been a hundred trucks in the lot. Harvey murmured to himself as he scoured the lot for the right one. "Two fiddy-four . . . that ain't it . . . Two fiddy-three . . . that ain't it . . . Two fiddy-two . . . that ain't it . . . we must be in the two-hundreds!" he exclaimed. "Follow me! I know where your truck is!" I followed him through the maze—he was sort of hobbling—and he began once more, "One thirty-nine . . . that ain't it . . . One thirty-eight . . . that ain't it . . ." until at last, "Here it is!" he shouted, with a paralyzed finger in the air, and I breathed an incredible sigh of relief. "Help me up, will ya?"

I held out my hand so he could scramble onto the back,

and he initiated a wrestling match with a large red lever. When after a struggle, which I could tell was intense from the bead of Harvey's sweat that spattered onto my face, it appeared he had emerged victorious, Harvey began to spool up the steel door, then—*SLAM!*—an ungodly crash sent me reeling backward against the hood of another truck.

"*HOLY MOTHER OF JESUS DID YOU SEE THAT?*" yowled Harvey. "That thing almost sliced my fingers clean off!"

"Wait, what?" I cried.

"Looks like the spring in this truck just gave up! Door weighs about a hundred pounds, and without the spring, it just slams shut!"

Bert had joined us limping at our side—poor, confused Bert, who had no hope of understanding my predicament—and, like the spring of their van that had just inexplicably burst, I just . . . burst.

"ARE YOU FUCKING KIDDING ME? DON'T YOU UNDERSTAND THAT MY FUTURE DEPENDS ON THIS PACKAGE? IF YOU THINK I'M GOING TO END UP LIKE YOU, CONTENT WITH MEETING CLAUDIA SCHIFFER AT A RESTAURANT WHILE I CLEAN UP OTHER PEOPLE'S SLOP, THEN YOU ARE FUCKING CRAZY!"

Five minutes later, I was holding a package from Chanel on my lap, and I was in a taxi en route to *Régine*.

chapter eight

Madeline answered the phone just as I was preparing to give up. "Darling!" she exclaimed.

The sounds of a fine restaurant filled my ear: A clatter of dishes and glasses and voices, over the playing of a string quartet.

"I was wondering when you'd finally call me back. Dorian and I are always trying to invite you places, but you never—" She let out a little yelp of surprise, then humming to a companion, marveled, "Mmm, that's delicious."

"Madeline, listen to me, I—"

"I'm sorry, darling," she chewed. "Is everything okay?"

"No," I declared, "Everything is not okay." I lay tangled up in bedsheets with my head upside down off the mattress, a wounded victim in a Goya etching. "I'm going crazy—*Régine*, New York, everything is just driving me crazy." I hastily sat up in bed and locked my arms around my knees. Under its four-foot ceiling, my room felt like a solitary confinement cell as I rocked back and forth, demented. Was this where I was living now? Where was I? What was I doing here?

She held the phone away from her ear and asked her waiter for a lemon wedge. "Darling, can I call you back? They just brought out the entrées and—"

"Madeline, I'm not kidding—if you don't come hold me right now, I swear I'm going to die."

"Why are you being so *dramaaaatic*?"

"I'm not being dramatic! I'm serious . . . I need help," I whimpered, at the precipice of tears.

She made a drowned-out remark to her companion. I heard the scrape of a chair against the floor. Conversations droned rising and falling like mixed radio signals as she traveled through the room, then—"Okay," she said at last, and she must have withdrawn to the bathroom, because a door shut and—silence.

I thought I recognized the echo of a lipstick tube popping open. "Why don't you meditate?" Madeline suggested. "That used to always help you."

"I can't concentrate."

"Just *close* your eyes, I promise."

I covered my eyes with my hand, and squeezing hard, counted, "One . . . two . . ."

"That's better," Madeline said, gently smacking her lips together. "Just take a deep breath . . ."

Three. Four.

". . . picture us luxuriating in the grass, laughing and drinking wine . . ."

Five. Six.

". . . passing around oysters and caviar, while the sun shines and violins play all around . . ."

Seven. Eight.

". . . just breathe, and imagine it all in your head—"

"I don't want it to be in my head!" I blurted. "Why can't things be real?!"

"Ethan, relax!"

"Really though—what do I have to do to make it real?"

"Why don't you just—"

"I *caaaaannn'tttt.*"

"Well there's no use comforting you when you're like this. Remember what you used to always say—the world's just a reflection of our minds, and you can accomplish anything if—"

"I don't believe in that anymore," I wailed at my cheerfully striped sheets.

"Oh, for God's sake, darling, we haven't even been out of college for three months yet."

Madeline's invocation of the pet-like "darling" was suddenly as irritating to me as Dorian's "babe": a frivolous, hollow word, full of indiscriminating intimacy.

"Of course you'd say that. You don't have to work for anything!"

I heard a sharp gasp, and the whip of her lipstick into the bag. "Not that you'd know," she muttered bitterly through clenched teeth, "but I have been working *very* hard on my auditions."

"You don't even *care* about acting."

I heard her fumble with the lock on the bathroom door. "I'm going back to dinner."

"Fine. What is it anyway, a bucket of caviar?"

"Foie gras," she spat, and the door finally swung open, letting all the voices in. "It's Dorian's treat. I'll tell him you send your love."

ALMOST THREE MONTHS AGO, MADELINE HAD BEEN ON AN outdoor stage with eleven others, distinguished by her on-campus political efforts and radiant hair, while my peers sat alongside me in a sea of white lawn chairs, everyone in blue graduation robes and matching mortarboard caps. Behind us our parents craned their necks, eagerly clutching video cameras and signs that read, CONGRATS GRAD! while light fell through the trees like sunbeams through a cathedral dome. If you were the religious type, you could have said that we appeared blessed.

My own parents were in the audience, exhausted from their red-eye the night before, and probably flabbergasted to at last be playing some role in my life. Over the past four years, obligatory summer vacations in Corpus Christi had constituted the main patches of our threadbare relationship, as during the school year I rarely called them, and two times I had escaped a Christmas homecoming by accepting holiday travel invitations with the Dupres instead. The summer after freshman year I had entertained the idea of backpacking by myself through Europe, only to discover the prohibitive reality of transatlantic plane fare, and ruefully accept my inevitable three-month sentence back home. With the fierce singlemindedness that would become the hallmark of every summer thereafter, I worked several jobs and barely saw my parents at all, as I furiously stockpiled funds for my eventual big move. Ambition had disinherited me from them—until I woke up that morning on graduation day to find my mother ironing my ceremonial gown, and almost cried at the tragic realization of what her presence meant.

Now an old man was on the stage, talking for a long time. I didn't know who he was or why he should be there—maybe nobody else did either, and we were all just letting him talk out of politeness—but regardless he sure did *talk*. In fact, he talked like it was the last time he would ever talk to anyone, like he was afraid that when he was done he might just turn over and die, because truly he covered every single topic: Hard work and responsibility, dreams and passion, the "true meaning" of practically every complicated matter, it seemed, including love and friendship. To be honest, I didn't hear anything at all, just gazed at his withered lips on the projector screen, waiting in anguish for him to finish. Every word was a step closer to the end, another brick off the wall that for all of eternity had separated us from our independence, our true purpose in the world. In my mind the wall was crumbling lower and lower with every anecdote and cliché and quote, every invocation of a historical hero and every "*Ralph Waldo Emerson once said*," until beyond the pile of rubble we could finally see a whole cloudless sky and another sun burning brighter than the one behind us. One of us had climbed the remains of the wall in graduation robes, and dropped to the other side—then the rest of us were swarming upward together, climbing and pulling on each other's robes, yelping with delight at discovering the mystery that still awaited on the other side, and when I had almost reached the top—all around, the wall was still flowing downward, I finally got to see. An endless field of rippling gold rye, and everybody spilling into it, rushing toward the new sun . . .

Beside me, Blake laughed at something the old man said. I looked up, watching the passage of a single cloud in the sky. Its slow, dutiful movement away from the sun eliminated the last doubts that we had been singled out in the world for eternal brightness.

Finally, the man paused. Then, maybe because I thought his speech was over—I saw the glimmer of gold beyond him—I listened to his next words, which I repeated to myself every day thereafter.

"You are the best and the brightest," he told us, with more soaring conviction than I had heard in my entire life. "Full of new ideas, and great promise. From this day forward, the entire world will bend to you, like flowers to the light."

I STARTED BY CONTEMPLATING THE ASPIRIN.

Misuse could lead to serious side effects, the bottle promised, *including stomach pains, and in rare cases—death.* Besides that, it didn't offer any clues, like how many one should take to achieve said death, or what constituted a "rare case."

I rattled the bottle; considered the cinematic weight of the moment. If this were some Cannes-worthy drama, I knew exactly where they should pan the camera, what kind of lighting would be just right. I poured the contents onto my palm and began lining up the pills along the edge of the porcelain sink. One, two, three, four . . . ten. Ten pills. I couldn't conceive that ten tiny pills would have any effect beyond giving me a stomachache. With one fluid motion, I scooped them back into my palm like a handful of colorless M&M's. Together they were so small compared to the rest of me—if I decided I was serious, I'd have to get another bottle, at least.

I wondered if, to achieve my intended outcome, I should take them the way someone normally took aspirin? Just pop them in my mouth, two by two, like animals into Noah's Ark, until I was safe from the flood inside my head? Maybe it was a better idea to just eat them: grab a handful, toss them in my mouth at once, and chew them up like a chalk salad.

I tried to think of anybody I knew who had killed themselves. Adults always made it seem like suicide was some kind of epidemic, like kids were doing it all the time, but the only person I sort of knew who had killed himself was Alvin Baker, and the coroners weren't even sure if he had done it on purpose. They had found him in his dorm room in Berkeley Hall, where he'd overdosed, like Marilyn Monroe. The autopsy report was withheld for days and I remember that week hearing terrible rumors that there might have been a murder. It was wrong of us to talk about him while he was dead; nobody really knew him, but of course when something like that happens, it's all, "*He used to shower on our floor*," and "*I had Psych with his roommate*," although you couldn't really blame us all, because, well—how often did anything happen in real life that was like something on TV? The strangest part was how his parents acted—they didn't cry at the wake. But I guess when something terrible like that happens, it's hard to say how anyone should react. Later it went around that Alvin had intentionally overdosed on Ritalin, but ultimately, who knew?

Alvin Baker had been a science major, so I'd never crossed paths with him. I do remember that on the afternoon before his funeral I had been walking home from class when the marching band came out of nowhere into Cross Campus, and started playing songs by The Beatles. They did that kind of thing all the time at Yale—the pep squad, or the Pundits, or whomever, would just get together and make a commotion outside; the point is, it was so common for the marching band to be out on a beautiful autumn day, playing "I Want to Hold Your Hand," that I didn't think twice about it. Nobody was dancing, so I dropped my bag, threw my hands in the air, and did a cartwheel. People could be so infuriating sometimes—here was the marching band playing a great song, and everyone around them just trudging along like some kind of funeral procession. It made me crazy. I danced beside them and made a huge scene.

I felt an arm reach out from the procession. "Hey, Cecily," I said. We'd had a class together the year before—Intro to Evolution, or some requirement—but I didn't know her very well. "Why isn't anybody having fun? This is great!"

"It's for Alvin," she replied. "He died, remember? They're playing his favorite songs."

After that I could barely stand up straight. Moments like that, they sting you like a slap in the face.

Now I was teetering there in the bathroom, thinking about Alvin, when he appeared to me. Except for his picture in the *Yale Daily News*, I had never known what he looked like, but in that moment I saw his face. He wore glasses and a plaid shirt, and he was rolling his eyes, shaking his curly-haired head at me. "*Fuck you*," Alvin Baker said. "*You put those pills back and cut the bullshit.*"

I poured the pills back in the bottle and wiped my hands against my shirt. The pills had gotten soggy in my sweaty palm and left a white residue.

The bathroom heat seemed more excruciating than it had been all summer. I took off all my clothes and sat on the lid of the toilet. My pores filled up with sweat. I thought of Edmund, and grew a little faint.

∽

"I'M LEAVING," GEORGE ANNOUNCED TO ME THE NEXT MORNING, without glancing up from his computer screen.

I yawned, and unbuttoned my suit jacket to take a seat. "Okay. Leaving where?"

"Leaving *Régine*," he said. "Today is my last day."

My chair let out an astonished squeak beneath me. "You're kidding me," I gaped. I was roused to full attention. "That's . . . huge."

"I knew you would be devastated," he said, as he tidied up a stack of papers with his fat fingers. "Just keep the tears to a minimum."

I laughed at him as a wave of unexpected delight rose inside me.

"Here," he said, holding out a densely stuffed manila folder with both hands. "Sabrina doesn't want to be bothered with hiring interns again, so this weekend I got started finding a replacement. These are some résumés we had on file, plus some I got after I placed an ad on the Hoffman-Lynch website last week."

"This is—*amazing*," I said, flabbergasted. "You're not joking, are you?"

"Have I ever 'joked' with you? Take it," he said, and shoved the folder into my hands.

"This is so sudden! What happened? I mean—is everything okay?"

"Okay? Of course it's okay." He gave me a strange look, which transmuted into a knowing laugh. "Oh. You didn't hear? I'm being promoted."

The folder almost fell out of my hands like a brick. "Wait—what?"

"They're hiring me at British *Régine*."

All the glee that had sparkled like a burst of confetti the moment prior now sunk with a whoosh to the carpet. Of course he had been promoted.

"It's in London," George added. "They needed a new assistant there."

"I know where British *Regíne* is," I snapped. A lump formed in my throat as I dropped the folder onto the desk. "You got . . . a real job then?" I asked meekly.

"In two months, I'll be on the masthead there." His chin was resting in his pudgy palm, as he began double-clicking on his files, deleting them one by one to prepare his computer for the next person.

Sabrina was elsewhere in the office, and the fashion closet was dead silent. I stared at my desk for some sign of what I should be feeling, but the only thing there was a diamond-studded Louis Vuitton wristwatch.

Did this mean . . . . *What* did this mean?

George turned and began to say something, but I couldn't hear him over my own thoughts.

How had George gotten a job? If George was as bad as I thought—unoriginal and rude, with brownnosing as his only distinguishing skill, then how—*how?*—had he gotten a job? Before me! At British *Régine*, of all places! That was almost better than working at American *Régine*—he'd get a dream job *and* a whole new life in London, while I . . . well, what about me?

I was wearing Dior, for the love of God! Not to mention that I had gone to Yale, and I had even changed my name, my entire identity, to escape the looming threat of failure—yet how could it be that I might *still* fail, that no matter what I'd done, or what

I did, I could live the rest of my life never becoming the person I so desperately wanted to be?

Did this mean that to make it in the world I had to be—like *George*?

"Did you hear me, Ethan?"

I could only stare at my hands on my lap.

"I'm trying to tell you that you should schedule interviews for new candidates by Wednesday. Jane and Edmund will both be shooting stories next week, so you should train the new intern while the office is quiet."

"I don't understand," I blurted, almost choking on the words. "Why? Why would anybody choose you?"

"Oh, calm down," he said. "You should just be happy you won't see me anymore."

A tear burned in the corner of my eye. George wasn't even rich, or beautiful. At least those reasons I vaguely comprehended, even if they were unfair.

He glimpsed my wounded face, as I tried to swallow the emotion that was welling up in me. "God, you're pathetic," he said.

"It just doesn't make any sense," I said, shaking my head. "Between the two of us, it's me whose been paying my dues, slaving away while you . . ."

He rolled his eyes. "You think that because you've been interning for a few months, you've paid your dues? Some people work for *years* for the job they want."

"Like you?" I scoffed, my misery crystallizing into scorn.

"I know how lucky I am," he said. "But maybe if you weren't such a self-pitying brat, you could *learn* something from me."

My voice escalated: "Learn what? You're *horrible*."

"Lower your voice, if you know what's good for you." He slid a stick of peppermint gum onto his tongue and tossed the foil wrapper into the wastepaper basket. "Remember, I'm the one that's leaving. You'll still have to make it work here, day in and day out, until you've proven you're more than a pitiful slave."

I cemented my teeth together and looked away.

"Now listen to me, Ethan St. James," he chewed. His gum made a sickening smack as he moved it contemptuously from one side of his mouth to the other. He leaned in toward my face while I glared at the *Régine* logo on my screen. The veins in my throat bulged. The smell of artificial mint filled my nostrils. The hair on the side of my head tingled as his mouth hovered by my ear. He opened his lips, and I heard the slow unsticking of saliva as they parted over my earlobe.

"Grow the fuck up. You think I'm so different from you? That I'm here on a free ride, like Sabrina, and everybody else? We're both playing the same game. Except for you—" he leaned back in his chair "—you're just a child. You show up on the first day with all your colors like this is kindergarten, wanting everybody to think you're so special—"

"That's not true," I interjected. My voice was hoarse. "You don't even know me."

"There you go, thinking you're so *unique* all the time, when really what you want is the exact same thing I want—the same thing everybody wants. You don't realize, you're just a clone of everybody here—a less competent clone."

I gritted my teeth and repeated, "You—don't—*know*—me."

He leaned back a little and laughed. "Is that so? I can tell you everything about you in two seconds." He rolled his chair next to mine—*tap!*—and grabbed me by the wrist. I winced as he stretched out my palm and pretended to read it like a fortune-teller. "You want to be the center of attention," he said, as he poked his finger into my flesh. I remained still as he prodded one spot after another on my unflinching hand. "You want to get ahead. You want to be loved. You want to be noticed." Then he traced his finger slowly in a full circle around my palm. "You want to be a beautiful person . . . and be surrounded by beautiful things . . . and have a *beeeaaauuuutiful* life," and to hear him say that word, "beautiful," which in fact *had* ruled my entire life—it suddenly seemed like a terrible, sinister thing, and my fingers curled like the petals of a dying flower. "Don't pretend you're above all that," he said. "Don't pretend, because at the end of the day, you're a person just like the rest of us."

My shoulders fell slack. I gazed at my fingers twitching in George's hand.

He picked up the Louis Vuitton watch resting by my keyboard, and slowly brought it into his own lap. "Remember when I asked you to get that pointless book from the library—how you didn't ask questions?" He unclasped the watch. "You just did it." George began to slide the Louis Vuitton watch onto my wrist. "And after that, the book sat there all day. And the next week, after I made you lug a hundred trunks, while I just sat here arranging gloves, I asked you to take it back to the library. And you still did it. That's why I'm going to London to get paid as a fashion assistant, and you're staying here to work for free, photographing handbag check-ins."

He turned my naked wrist up to shut the clasp—*click!*

"See, what you don't understand is, your degree doesn't matter," he went on. "Your interests don't matter. *You* don't matter. You think anyone cares what you know or what you like or what you *feel*? There are a million nobodies like you—

individuals, whatever. You really think you're the only one? That you're special? We all have lives, you know—'personalities.' Clara and Will, Christine and Sabrina," he rattled, "all of them, and me. But at the end of the day, it's not their names at the top of the magazine. It's not your name or my name—it's *Régine.* And that's how all those people get to be here, because they know that when they're here, they're not Clara or Will or Christine or Sabrina. They're a *grown-up* woman named Régine, and you know what?—Régine might be beautiful on the outside, but on the inside, she wouldn't even care if everybody else in the world died."

I was silent. I thought of Clara and Will and Christine, forced to gather around a plate of cupcakes for Clara's birthday—tense, mistrusting, each of them hiding a knife behind their back in case one of the others moved too quickly. I thought of Clara, dressing me in acceptable neutral shades. "*This is simply the world we live in, my dear,*" she had said.

Outside the fashion closet, I could hear Sabrina buzzing to them, and the copy machine humming, and everybody's cubicle-encased hearts beating in the same mechanical rhythm, slow and calculating. Grown-up. Soulless.

"You think I hate you, and that I actually *like* Sabrina?" he laughed. "You know how she even got that position, right? She's best friends with Ava Burgess's daughter. No fashion experience, no credentials—never worked a day in her life, for a job both of us would kill for. But you know what . . . ? I can't do anything about that, and neither can you." He pointed in the direction of Sabrina's desk. "If you were in Sabrina's chair, it'd be you I would pretend to like—but you're not."

I stared at Sabrina's empty cubicle.

"When I'm gone," George said, "someone else will sit here, and I'd suggest you take advantage of them. Learn your lesson: Be more like Régine." He pointed to the folder full of résumés—all the people who wanted a chance in this place. "These are the candidates I have for you. You can take them or leave them. It makes no difference to me." Then he gestured at the watch he had fastened to my wrist. "It's a nice watch, isn't it?"

My hand was still resting on his lap. I felt the pulse run through his leg, imagined the blood pumping inside of him, and wondered if we were actually the same—just two ambitious young people, who under different circumstances, might even have been friends. I didn't know much about George's story. Perhaps he even had the same dream as me.

I took my hand back and gave a quiet rattle to my wrist. The words *Louis Vuitton* glittered over an ebony face, and I thought about what it would actually mean to own a watch like that—not to just wear it, but to have it in a drawer somewhere, to take it out once in a while and look at it, and know that I had money and power and everything I could ever want. I turned my arm to make the watch sparkle—it was hard, cold—then unclasped it, and laid it back on the table.

"I could never be like Régine," I said, finally.

George returned the watch to its black velvet box. "Too bad."

The closet door swung open.

George closed the box as Sabrina charged past us. "Boys," she said over her shoulder. "There's a Miu Miu glove missing. Black leather—came in with Jane's L.A. trunks last week and they need it back today."

George had kept the glove records the previous week. He opened his mouth—I thought, to inform her—but instead, he lied. "Ethan kept those records last week. He'll find it by the end of the day."

I rolled my eyes. "What time is your flight? Hadn't you better leave right now?"

"Sorry, Ethan. At least," he patted me on the back, "it's only a few more hours."

And remarkably, as promised, it really was.

When the time came for George to go, I was cross-legged on the floor, surrounded by a hundred pairs of black gloves. It could have been that to locate the pair which resembled so many others required my full concentration, but I was almost certain George didn't say a word of farewell to anyone, just took his bag and was gone for good. His parting gift to me was the folder full of people who could replace him, and the résumés were waiting for me around eight, after Sabrina left and all my work was done. By then the glove was found: It had never been missing at all, naturally, but pilfered without any notice by the fashion editors to examine at their desks. Now I could feel George's minty breath lingering over me as I settled back on the carpet to sift through the pile of résumés.

My first prospective intern was Polina Nabokov, who had studied Agriculture at a trade school in Russia and was George's idea of a joke, surely. I started a pile for résumés that constituted a flat-out no, then continued on.

Eric Mendelsonn had misspelled the word "fasshion" in his cover letter. No.

Jenny Kohler was "excited to learn all about the real world of supermodels, like my idol Naomi Campbell." No.

Dorian Belgraves had—

I had to read it twice. *Dorian Belgraves.* The sight of his name slapped me hard across the face like an open palm. No. Absolutely not. I had never mentioned Dorian and my relationship to George, yet that was definitely a joke, to have included in my pile of *Régine* hopefuls the bane of my existence. My body shuddered at the thought of him. If I had any say in the matter, Dorian would *never* step foot inside the fashion closet of *Régine*, not when he had never expressed the slightest interest in being a fashion editor—and especially not to sit in the chair next to me. "*Régine wouldn't even care if everybody else in the world died,*" George had said, and in that moment, I understood.

I folded Dorian's résumé down the middle and started to rip it in half. Like Edmund, who expected every garment or accessory he disapproved of to vanish instantly from view, I never, *ever* wanted to see Dorian's name again. Relishing a visceral satisfaction—*riiiip*—my fingers got halfway down, then inexplicably could go no further. I had every intention to mince his resume to shreds then toss it onto the streets of New York, but my curiosity tugged my hand away: What did Dorian's résumé even look like? I unfolded it cautiously and flattened it against the carpet, the hole in the center flapping like the gaping gill of a shore-washed fish.

His sophomore and junior years resembled my own. There was the *Yale Daily News*, for which we had both contributed weekly arts reviews; Sailing Team, which we thought we'd try, until we unwittingly capsized a two-man boat; Junior Class Council, which we were forced by Madeline to join ("*Don't you want to support all my causes at the monthly meetings?*"). Then there was the gap that had come between us. *Study Abroad*, it read, with transfer credits from La Sorbonne—the line that represented our year apart, and the end of my love for Dorian.

He had never told us he was unhappy at Yale, never said he was applying to go study abroad or even mentioned La Sorbonne. He just left—and when he got there he ignored us, all of our calls and messages. This was before all the newspaper headlines at school, before that one pathetic e-mail, when for a brief but real moment at the beginning of senior year we were afraid something terrible had happened.

It was Madeline who called Dorian's house in Paris. We couldn't guess who would pick up—a maid, maybe—but we certainly hadn't expected it to be his mother. Decades after Edie Belgraves had hit the peak of her beauty and fame, she was still nowhere close to settling down. She was always vacationing—St. Tropez, Cannes, the Hamptons—occasionally modeling, but for the most part basking in the fortune that her face, and her latest husband, had earned her. She was just like Dorian, eternally restless, and less likely to be in her own home than practically anywhere else in the world.

When she answered the phone she was delighted, and not at all distraught over the "something terrible" we had feared. "Why, dearest!" Edie exclaimed. If Dorian's mother liked me, she adored Madeline. Having been raised and discovered in London, she maintained a view of the opposite side of the pond as quaint, and referred to Madeline as Dorian's "sweet American girl."

When Madeline asked her what she had called to know—a very scared, roundabout, "*Where's Dorian*?"—Edie thought it was adorable. "*You really are so good to check in on him! He just arrived at DeGaulle, safe as a pillow.*" Like all the other well-compensated It girls of her set, Edie had taken a lot of drugs in the late eighties, and often said things that didn't make sense, like "safe as a pillow." "You know, why don't you plan a visit? He'll be staying with his father, my ex-husband—it's a great apartment, and everything is better in Paris!"

"Dorian's moved to P-Paris?"

Shortly after that were all the headings in the *Yale Daily News*, then Dorian's one e-mail, and then, Madeline just blamed herself. She thought everything was her fault, that she had somehow driven him away with her grand notions of romance and commitment and devotion, in the spirit of Anna Karenina.

It always went back to a single incident, which she replayed every day like a train roaring down the same tracks, the rails settling deeper into the earth. They had been horseback riding in Montauk, Madeline sitting behind Dorian holding his chest, when she pressed her face into his shoulder and remarked innocently, "Wouldn't you like to do this forever? I mean—for the rest of our lives together?" He gave the reins such a startled jerk that the horse bucked her right off into the grass, and he lost control and the horse went galloping away from her, and every time she told me the story the fall was harder and the horse was wilder and more "fateful," and she would weep for longer at her own foolishness.

I tried to tell her it wasn't her fault—Dorian was just being who he was—but she wouldn't listen because, well, she was just Madeline, and she was just being who *she* was.

After about five minutes smoldering at Dorian's name on his résumé, I realized I had been staring much too long at something that needed to be destroyed. I couldn't rip it anymore, though. There was too much of my own life in it. Finally, I had to just place it to the side—this broken, paper version of Dorian—not in the No pile, or the Yes pile, or even the Maybe pile, but in a distinguished pile on its own.

"I WAS THINKING—" DORIAN CROAKED. HE SWALLOWED, AND against my own skin I felt a shiver run through his body.

It was the end of junior year. Classes were over. Finals week loomed ahead, and beyond it the rumor of summer on the horizon. In two weeks Madeline and I would each have our turn to stand on the porch of our gabled house, surrounded by luggage as a cab pulled up and we waved good-bye to Dorian and another year in college. I would fly to Corpus Christi, to my parents and Spanish television, and Madeline to Washington, DC, to an internship on Capitol Hill. Dorian would also go somewhere—he didn't know yet—wherever rich, aimless people went to escape their rich, aimless lives.

Cool evening fog crept in through the crack of Madeline's open bedroom window. A swirling canopy of marijuana smoke hung over our heads, while more sweet ribbons escaped from a joint mixed with lavender resting nearby on a crystal saucer. Dorian was lying on his back. He stared at the ceiling while Madeline and I lay pressed on either side of him, the three of us naked, our long legs all intertwining.

It had been over a year since our first experience together—that is, my first sexual experience ever—and it hadn't ended there.

In the first weeks, our sexual experimentations were contained by the strict parameters of a general pattern: Dorian and I took turns pleasing and being pleased by Madeline, while between him and me there was no physical contact.

We could only guess at where her liberated sexuality had sprung from; although Madeline was politically open-minded, it had taken her nineteen years of life to find a boy she deemed worthy enough to touch her—and when she did, she found two. She loved us equally, and through our own brands of thrusts and panted utterances, we were able to love her back. Dorian was hard and fast, I was soft and slow, and each of us uniquely capable to reach some deep, essential part of her.

I felt only a passive longing to explore a similar closeness with Dorian. Sex was overwhelming enough with just Madeline, let alone the two of them combined at once, and I figured anyway he was scared, or nervous, or even silently unnerved at the thought of sex with another man.

Our arrangement manifested in this unbalanced expression of affections until one drunken night saw us accidentally aligned in a triangular formation, with my face between Madeline's legs; Madeline's between Dorian's; and Dorian's between mine. I felt his hair fall on my inner thigh; prepared myself to pull away. Then before I could rearrange myself, I felt the slow, tentative pressure of his fingers wrapped around me—then up and down—and then, his lips crossed the threshold that had loomed above us all that time.

After that, the doors of possibility were swung wide open, except for two important doors, which remained firmly shut. The first closed door was penetration between Dorian and me; we experimented with one another, and had sex with Madeline, yet beyond that, we never ventured. The second closed door was more unusual: throughout everything, Dorian and I never kissed. I tried plenty of times, once we'd reached a certain level of comfort, but every moment we came close he would bury his face in my neck, kissing my shoulders or my chest instead.

Now Dorian appeared to be in a trance, his lips barely moving as he murmured, "Do you think—we'll be like this again?"

We had all just had sex, and had hastily wiped up before collapsing in Madeline's bed.

Madeline sat up and propped herself onto one elbow, resting her golden head in her hand. "We still have a few weeks," she said, tracing a circle around his belly button with her other hand. She rubbed her ankle against Dorian's, her toes grazing the hairs on my foot. "Nobody's leaving yet."

"I don't mean about summer. I mean, when we get old." With a glazed look and his hands crossed over his chest, he looked like an embalmed corpse.

"People change so much when they grow up—they get so sad," he said. "Do you think we'll stay the same?"

"Your mother's not sad," said Madeline.

"My mother's not smart enough to be sad," he said, blinking. "Anybody who really thinks at all about life realizes—it just gets worse."

"Then, don't think about it," Madeline said. "Don't think anything at all." She pinched her lips into a small *o* and blew an imaginary eyelash off his face.

Dorian closed his eyes. "I mean, just think about us, all grown up, in offices somewhere . . ."

Now I rolled against him and I tilted my head onto his shoulder. "That will never happen to us," I said. I tucked my fingers between his clasped hands, and gave them a confident jolt. "Listen to me," I said. "That will never, *never* happen to us." My breath pushed the lingering smoke across us.

"Why? It happens to everybody."

"We're not everybody, though," I said. "People who end up

like that aren't even alive like us. They're weak, they're sad. All they can think about is paying their bills. They don't feel things the way that we do." I pressed my cheek against his and said into his ear, "When we leave here, we're going to change the world. We're going to follow our dreams, and—"

"I don't even have dreams."

"Oh, of course you do," Madeline snapped.

I sat up, and for a moment there appeared to be an unprecedented tear hovering in the corner of Dorian's eyelid. I blinked, and the tear disappeared, a raindrop which one moment had been hovering on the tip of a leaf and the next had rolled back toward the stem.

"Where is this depressing nonsense coming from?" Madeline asked. "Kiss me." She nudged him with her nose. Dorian opened his eyes to stare at the ceiling, and she did it again.

The second time he flinched, like a bee had stung him.

"Don't," I whispered to her.

He grasped reflexively at my hand.

Madeline saw his hand wrap around mine. She stiffened. Pressed her lips together. Her face flashed with something new. "Then *you* kiss him," she said to me.

Dorian stopped breathing. Our bodies suddenly were heavy and still, like logs that had been rolled together into a pile. Madeline traced her fingers over Dorian's moonlit stomach again, while my own felt trapped in his clutch. Neither he nor I could move.

"We all love each other here," she continued. Outside a moth flickered against the windowpane. The roof of the neighboring house glowed white in the moonlight, and beyond, a clock tower stood like a sentinel. "Do you love me, Ethan?" she asked.

I nodded slowly.

Madeline leaned over Dorian, her breasts pressing against the back of his hands. "Will you always love me?"

Before I could say yes, I would always love her, Madeline had pressed through the smoke and her lips were upon mine. She kissed me. I swallowed hard at the familiar taste, which was sweeter than a strawberry or a newly picked peach.

She pulled out my hand from Dorian's grasp and rested it on the curve of her swanlike neck. My fingertips spilled across her pulse. I thought of Botticelli, and springtime, and everything teeming vividly with life. My own throat bobbed.

"You'll always love me, right?" she whispered into my mouth. I felt myself nod. My heart pounded in my chest. She unstuck from me and my body followed achingly toward her lips. "Well," she nudged Dorian, "nothing will ever change, boys," she whispered, my saliva shimmering on her bottom lip. "Nothing will ever change." She pushed her knee against his leg, and the mattress groaned. "Go on—kiss one another."

Dorian didn't stir, elbows still locked at his sides. We were both quiet. The heat of embarrassment prickled my cheeks.

"Don't you love each other?" She made our hands into a bundle, surrounding them with her own hands like wrapping paper. "Don't we all—love each other?"

Inches away, Dorian glanced sidelong at me. I felt his stomach tense as he lifted his neck. I closed my eyes, and felt a sudden rush of completeness. *After this moment, I will have known everything good in life.* Madeline's breath, her taste, still lingered like a mask over my own face. My cheek struck his nose—a soft exhalation, a sudden, breathy "oh"—

The kiss was cold and stiff, yet, like a handshake between two adversaries, it softened upon contact. I melted onto him. After all this time—our first kiss. Madeline stroked our hands with her thumb, and unable to control myself, I pushed my tongue into his mouth.

Dorian pulled sharply away. I was torn, a shirt caught on a fencepost.

Turning away from me, he retreated to the pillow, burying his face in it. He breathed in deeply and his whole back swelled. Madeline reached onto the nightstand for the crystal saucer and brought the joint to her lips, handing me a red book of matches. I bent toward her over Dorian's body, and, hands shaking, lit the flame.

BY THE NEXT MORNING ON MY COMMUTE TO *RÉGINE*, I HAD forgotten all about Dorian's résumé. There were more urgent matters vying for my attention: the replenishment of the seat George had vacated, and the potential of his replacement to somehow alleviate the discontentment *Régine* had stirred in me. Contrary to George's advice, I was never going to be the frigid, figurative Régine. To execute his policy of measured professional ruthlessness would require all the effort of a theatrical role: I could think of no undertaking more antithetical to my unrehearsed earnestness than to cast myself in his drama of schemes and subterfuge. Were I somehow to rise to the occasion—if the outlook of such an occasion should be considered an ascent, and not as I suspected, a downward spiral into deeper unhappiness—my first step would have to be enlisting a subordinate as my fellow intern. But wouldn't I rather just have a friend?

On my arrival, unfortunately, the chair in which I hoped to

install a new ally already had a person in it. He turned around as I approached him from behind thinking, *"No—no—this can't be happening,"* expecting the face to belong to George and the first words out of his mouth to be, *"You thought you could get rid of me, did you?"*

Instead it was much worse than I could have ever imagined, yet somehow exactly what I should have predicted. The smile that greeted me was uninhibited—the blast from the heated entryway of a friend's home on a winter day.

"Babe!" he chimed, and in his cheerful greeting I heard my inevitable demise foretold.

I was so stunned to see Dorian there that I froze about ten feet away from his open arms. I took a step back from him.

"What are you doing here?" I balked.

His guileless expression only exacerbated my alarm. "I work here!" he exclaimed, beaming, and to my horror he walked right over and enveloped me in a hug. I stood motionless beneath the blanketlike warmth of his arms over my shoulders, and he continued—in case his meaning had eluded me—"We work together now. I'm the new intern!"

The ground beneath my feet opened up. I plummeted. "But I haven't even interviewed anyone yet," I squeaked. I wasn't sure if I had spoken the words aloud or merely heard them echo in the hopeless chasm of my head.

"Well, Mom sometimes vacations with Jane Delancey, and she mentioned to her they were going to need someone, so—here I am!" He separated from me and grabbed my hand. "Are you surprised?"

"I—yes, I'm definitely surprised, but—"

"Good! I wanted to tell you, but Madeline said it'd make a good surprise. Are you really surprised?"

For the love of God. "Yes, I'm *surprised*," I repeated tersely. "I just—I don't understand."

He shrugged. "I wasn't doing anything else back here except partying, and I was getting tired of making art, so I thought I could try it out, you know, see if I like it."

I gulped. Of course to Dorian my life's ambition would be merely an opportunity to escape boredom.

"I knew you'd be here too, so—now we can be together! Isn't that great!"

I was silent, engulfed by the vastness of my own stupidity—to have blithely thought that because I'd sorted a pile of résumés, and disqualified his, that my actions had any bearing on real life at all . . .

"Dorian, is that you?" came a familiar voice. "Always so handsome!"

Dorian turned sheepishly to Jane—"I didn't know what to wear"—and the kindest thought I could offer about his defense was that at least he had the sense to feel embarrassed. In jeans and a white tee, a particularly undistinguished variation of his usual ensemble, he was more appropriately dressed to watch television on the couch while stirring a bowl of cereal than to start a new job, let alone one at the most prestigious fashion magazine in New York City.

"You look wonderful," Jane said, and I fumed at the unfairness of it—my colorful suits had constituted a violation against *Régine*'s unwritten rules, but any garment touching Dorian's imperial skin was exempt. They embraced and he kissed her cheeks, clasping her influential hands in his.

"I have to let you know—I've never worked in an office before."

"Oh, there's nothing to it," she said. "An office is just a place."

Oh, was it? *"But isn't it a 'corporation'?"* I wanted to interject, just as Clara had said to me, *"where 'we occupy specific roles, with specific ways that we must speak, act, and dress'?"*

Jane rubbed the top of his hand like she was bestowing a benediction on him. "Don't worry. You belong here."

All I wanted was for someone to say the same words to me—"*You belong here, Ethan*"—and yet there was Dorian, less than five minutes at *Régine* and already crowned with the wreath of belonging, an honor for which I had been prepared to work a lifetime.

Jane looked over and smiled at me. "Dorian has told me all about your close friendship. Aren't you glad he's here?"

With my neck trapped in that tight noose, I could barely nod.

"You two are lucky," she said, ushering me closer with a flick of one hand. I had no choice but to let myself be drawn toward them as she said, "Take it from me. A good friendship doesn't come all the time."

I opened my mouth to protest, but no words came out.

"Dorian used to talk about you all the time in St. Tropez—it was you and, what's her name? Margaret?"

"Madeline," I said quietly.

Jane nodded and, smiling, said, "Come here," before pulling Dorian by the hand into her office. "We *must* catch up, I haven't seen you since Cannes." A moment later her door was closed, their laughter emanating from beyond it in a vivid stream.

I collapsed into my chair and closed my eyes. "*Make him go away, make him go away*," I whispered to myself, "*please, make my* best friend *go away*," I groaned. The question was never "*How did Dorian get here?*" but rather, "*Why didn't he get here* sooner?"

With his famous mother—he should have just written her name on a sheet of notebook paper and called it his "résumé"—it was a wonder he hadn't started at *Régine* twenty years ago, crawling around the fashion closet on his hands and knees, teething on Yves Saint Laurent heels.

I peeked now through the glass door at Dorian. Our friendship had been one of my greatest seeds of joy, which I had nurtured into a flower, and eventually displayed with pride on my lapel. Surely now he would charm Edmund, and any favoritism I had cultivated would be choked by Dorian's weed-like presence. I wrung my hands and was looking down when a corner of paper, poking out from underneath my mouse pad, caught my eye. I pulled it out. It was a piece of paper folded in half, with my name written on the outside in permanent marker, in George's unmistakable block letters. I peeled it open.

BE RÉGINE

Dorian swept out of Jane's office. I hid George's note in my pocket when I felt his arms around my neck and his head swooping next to mine. He smiled. "You're so hard to get ahold of now!"

"Late work hours," I said dryly, thumbing the corner of the paper in my pocket. The truth was, after my depression had set in, I had been spending all of my free time in bed.

"Well, no fear—I'm here now!" He unhooked himself from me and said, "Is this my chair?," even though obviously it was. With a comfortable sigh, he sat down and started rearranging the stapler, and the mug full of ballpoint pens.

"You know," I burst, with all the conviction I could muster, "things aren't going to be like they were before."

He selected a blue pen from the mug and tested it out on a sticky note, as if he had never before seen office supplies in his life. "No kidding," he agreed emphatically as he scribbled *Dorian*—a cavalier swish. With a roguish smile, he declared, "Things are going to be so much better now!" My mouth opened a little in shock as he leaned toward me. "You know what this means now that I'm here? We'll leave together every day, and go to all the best parties!"

His sheer brainlessness astounded me. To *think* that *Régine* would be all fun, and that after a day here he'd have enough energy left to party.

Sabrina entered then in her typical fashion—closet door whooshing, just a rush of black—and I never thought I would be so glad to anticipate her yell of, "*Boys!*" and her delegation of the day's intense workload. This moment would be Dorian's rude awakening. Maybe now Sabrina and I could even be friends. She would surely hate Dorian too once she saw the undeserved attention he commanded.

She stopped halfway to her desk. With a smile, she clasped her hands demurely in front of her—no trace of the smoldering girl whose most fervent ambition it was to corroborate with *every* word the superiority of her status—and said, "You're lucky, Dorian. It's a slow day at the office today." She bowed her head, like she was a maid in his service. "Ethan can answer any questions you have, but if you need anything, I'm over here," she offered, pointing to her desk with an inviting finger.

I flinched at the refreshing lack of volume in her voice, the alien, almost *soothing* quality of it—remembering that, of course, Sabrina and Dorian were cut from the same cloth.

The latest issue had wrapped last week, so there was nothing urgent to be done: no garments streaming in for him to inventory, no trunks leaving tomorrow for him to pack. The fashion editors were still developing their ideas for the next issue, and lots of people were on vacation. I looked desperately around for a task to delegate, *anything* to establish Dorian's inferiority.

"Let's organize this wall of hosiery," I said, even though I had organized it myself the week prior. "Can you make sure all the packages are in the right crates?"

In an hour, when he was done with that, I said, "Let's dust all the jewelry cases—they look terrible."

It went on like this all morning. Dorian didn't seem to think I was bullying him, but then again, I wasn't as good at it as George had been. Even when I told Dorian to do something, I sort of asked him, theoretically giving him the option to say no. "Can you take inventory of these scarves?" and "These gloves?" and "These hats?"—ending each of these feeble orders with a word so pathetic I wanted to bang my head against the desk. "*Please?*"

The whole time he kept on talking; his idea of "catching up" with me. He had never talked so much. He talked so much I felt like a piece of luggage at the airport going round and round on the carousel, eluding him whenever he tried to run up and take me. To uphold *Régine*'s policy of institutionalized restraint had never seemed so impossible: I tried with concerted effort to ignore him outright, but was foiled repeatedly by my own nature, responding every time with the fewest words I could manage without feeling like a complete jerk. On several occasions, I was so determined to maintain my uncharacteristic taciturnity that I had to stand up and pretend to use the bathroom. In the end, he probably didn't think I was trying to ignore him at all, just that postgraduate life had instilled in me a bladder problem.

Around lunchtime, Dorian took a break to buy falafels and rice from the Halal cart down the block. To my devastating lack of credit, I couldn't bring myself to yell at him the way that George had to me (*"Don't you know Sabrina* hates *Indian food? You can't just* eat *Indian food,"* he had once said), and in fact, I almost said yes when he asked me if I wanted some.

"Is everything okay?" he finally asked on his return, spooning jasmine rice into his mouth.

I didn't reply.

All of a sudden, in a rare moment of lucidity, he seemed to recognize the tremendous outline of what was wrong between us—the colossal iceberg under the surface. He shuddered "Oh!" with a look of uncharacteristic intensity and, laying aside the Styrofoam tray, gulped and grabbed my shoulder. He looked like a child who had wandered off for miles only to discover that nobody had followed him. "I—" he stammered, a pinch of desperation between his brows. If he didn't say the right thing now—right now—he knew he was going to lose me forever.

I swallowed. This was it. He had caught up to me on the revolving belt and was about to grab me, but I would never let him. *"I am Régine, I am Régine, I am Régine,"* I repeated to myself, straining to remain fixated on a file folder on my computer screen.

"Do you want to go to a few museums this weekend?" he asked. "Your favorite painting—we can go see it."

My favorite painting depicted a redheaded Greek princess named Danaë, sleeping, with her legs curled up against her chest and her long hair trickling around her shoulders like a bough of orange seaweed. It was by Gustav Klimt, and it wasn't even in New York. If Dorian couldn't even remember that much about me, then he was so far away from me he would never, ever catch up. I squinted at him. I should have been devastated, but I had been for a whole year. Now I breathed a sigh of relief. It was true, then. He didn't know me anymore.

"My favorite painting is a Klimt, Dorian," I said, twisting a paper clip between my fingers. "It's in *Vienna*."

"Oh, I know!" he said with an eager shake. He was still holding my shoulder, eyes pleading. "It's on limited exhibition in New York," he explained. "At the Neue Galerie."

I stiffened with surprise, and had to look away.

"We'll go on Saturday," he implored. "Just you and me—I won't even tell Madeline, or she'll be hanging off me the whole time."

In that moment there was so much pressure inside of me to simply say: "*Yes, let's just forget the world, and forget anything ever happened between us—God, I* missed *you.*" But I knew—I knew that the second I caved in to Dorian, it would all be over. This wasn't college. In the real world, we would never be equals, and if I let him, he would easily—unknowingly—crush me and everything I had ever dreamed of, which was everything he already had.

Be Régine, Be Régine, BE RÉGINE!

I forced my eyes back to the screen, my retinas sizzling as I concentrated on a single burning pixel. "Dorian . . ." I made myself say. "I need you to do me a favor." I dragged a blank document pointlessly in and out of a desktop folder labeled *Fashion News*. "Can you get me this volume from the archives library?" Not meeting his eyes, I scribbled down the first combination of months and a year I could think of, a period of no significance whatsoever: *Jan–Mar 1975*.

His confusion over the sudden change of topic transmuted into a slow nod. "Um, okay." He let go of my shoulder and, in a dejected fog, raised a scoop of rice to his mouth.

I pressed the yellow sticky note onto one finger, and held it between him and his next spoonful.

"Right now?" he asked.

I nodded seriously. "Right now."

He put down his Styrofoam tray.

I turned thanklessly back to my screen, and he returned with the volume twenty-five minutes later.

"Do you know where my lunch went?" he asked as he handed it to me.

"I'm sorry, I had to throw it away—Sabrina hates Indian food."

"Really?" he said in a hushed tone that only I could hear. "That's so strange—who doesn't like Indian food?"

He was right—who didn't like Indian food?—but I remained silent, and at the end of the day, I made sure *Jan–Mar 1975* was still unopened, rotting like a hardbound carcass between us.

chapter nine

"You look dashing," Dorian greeted me the next day.

I rolled my eyes and sat down, pretending to be engrossed by my computer—a task made difficult by the fact that my screen was still warming up.

"I missed you and all your suits, babe," he went on.

"Can you not call me that?" I turned to him with a scowl. Today I would spare him no dignity. I had spent most of the previous evening sitting on my mattress in the lotus position, sweating and begging the universe profusely. *"Please make him go away, make him go away . . . just—make something terrible happen to him."* And after that I looked up quotes by Machiavelli on my phone, and tried to recall my one reading of *The Art of War.*

I was proud of myself when the phone rang a moment later, and I got to utter my first real words of the day to him. "Get it," I ordered, as though to a dog.

"Hi, this is Dorian."

I gawked at him open-mouthed and hissed, "'*This is Dorian?*' This is not your private line and they are not trying to call you! You're supposed to answer, '*Régine*'—just one word, simply, professionally—"

For some reason—I think because I had startled him—Dorian reached toward the phone to press a random button, and suddenly, Edmund Benneton's voice came spewing out of the speaker.

"—HEAR ME I AM LOCKED OUT!"

"Edmund!" I replied in a panic, trying to muffle the horrible screech of his voice with a pair of hands over the speaker.

"ETHAN, I AM LOCKED OUT! I FORGOT MY WALLET, AND I'M EXHAUSTED, AND THESE IMBECILES WON'T LET ME IN!" He turned away from the speaker and shouted to the security guard, "DON'T YOU KNOW WHO I AM? YOU ARE GOING TO BE SO SORRY—"

Sabrina was flying toward us, waving her hands. "*Turn that off!*" she shouted.

"IamsosorryEdmundIwilltalktosecurityrightnow," I said to him and hung up the phone.

"Ethan, are you crazy? *What is wrong with you?*" Sabrina glared fiercely at me, towering over the desk with her hand on her waist, her elbow bent at a right angle.

Dorian popped up like a daffodil. "I'm sorry, Sabrina, that was my fault. It was my first time answering the phone."

My eyes flashed over to her, then back to Dorian, then back to Sabrina. I prayed for her to say something like, "Don't let it happen again, Dorian"—"*Please Universe, please Universe, please*"—but I knew . . . Dorian was special. Dorian could do no wrong.

Dorian was friends with Jane. How could Sabrina say anything to *Dorian*? Even if she secretly despised him, all she had to do was *look* at him, and any ill will would melt away like snow on a spring day.

Sabrina's eyes flickered between us. "Ethan—"

I raised my head toward her stern face.

"Show poor Dorian how to take calls," she said, before returning to her desk.

Poor Dorian? No two words had ever been so laughably ill-matched. It wasn't my fault "poor Dorian" had never answered a phone, but I choked back the words and ran downstairs to let Edmund into the building.

When I returned without Edmund—he had gotten fed up, and left to smoke a cigarette—Dorian was utterly wrong to confide in me, with a smirk, "You have to admit, that was pretty funny. I've known Edmund since I was little, and he's the most ridiculous, washed-out—"

I snapped, "Edmund is our boss—not to mention a *genius*," even though I had come a long way from thinking Edmund was any kind of genius at all.

A messenger had just dumped a pile of Dolce & Gabbana garment bags on the carpet, where they waited to be checked in.

"Here, take that camera," I instructed. The camera was closer to me, but I pointed and made him reach for it. My seat was also closer to the garment bags, but I made him reach for those too.

I sat back in my chair and watched him, like a Beverley Hills housewife observing her Adonic pool boy. Despite everything, Dorian was what I would most choose to look at in the world—more so, I hated to admit, than any painting by Klimt, or Monet, or anyone. His back faced me as he dragged the garment bags over, and even though there was nothing extraordinary about this, somehow every movement of Dorian's body was a new fold in a complicated origami.

When he finally looked up, it gave me strange satisfaction to watch the shadows on his face shift like sand dunes, and when he cocked his head, awaiting further instruction, it gave me stranger satisfaction still to say, "Garment bags will now be your responsibility. From now on, any time you see a garment bag enter the closet . . ."

TWO YEARS AGO, DORIAN BOUGHT ME A PAIR OF TWELVE-hundred-dollar women's shoes just to make me laugh and agree to join him at some ridiculous cross-dressing party. Harboring deep reservations over attending events at frat houses, I had joked I would only go with him and Blake to Delta Kappa's annual so-called Drag Ball if I could wear designer high heels—but alas! I had no money! And so I would have to skip the event. Dorian held me at my word and two days later handed me a lavender Bergdorf Goodman bag containing a box of rhinestone-covered Louboutins and a note: *No excuses now!*

Per Blake's instructions, we arrived early on Fraternity Row to "get ready." It was six o'clock on Saturday—an hour marked by the smuggling of cheap liquor into the dorm rooms of underage co-eds intent on exceeding the debauched precedent set the weekend prior. Blake greeted us at the Greek-lettered door in thigh-baring metallic shorts and a pink lace bra, tossing his hairy, muscular arms in the air with a guiltless splash of Pabst Blue Ribbon onto the front steps.

I hugged him and got tangled in his long black synthetic wig. "*Mary Magdalene!*" I cried out with a laugh. The wig was a relic from the previous Halloween, when Blake and I had floated around campus in bedsheet robes informing people that we were "*the two Marys, the Virgin and the Prostitute—but you have to guess which is which.*" In attempting once more to look like a female, he had again succeeded in resembling an overgrown cactus, his muscles bulging under his prickly body hair.

As we entered, the half-caved-in door dragged over the floor and we were promptly greeted by a cloud of Bob Marley and marijuana smoke. Johnny Russell waved from a withering leather loveseat, wearing only a gold bodysuit as he sat with his thick thighs spread in casual confirmation of the many whispered speculations about the size of his endowment. I smiled back, then forced myself to look away while Stephen, the Yale football quarterback, sat similarly wide-legged nearby having lipstick applied to his bearded face by Stan, the defensive linebacker. I only knew this because Blake said, "That's Stephen, the quarterback, and Stan, the defensive linebacker." The sight of it was almost quaint, the linebacker holding his friend's jaw with a blokeish hand, concentrating with furrowed intensity on coloring inside the lines.

It was my first time at a frat house, although that night it was revealed I was inexplicably one of the best among them at beer pong, and thereafter I became a semiregular visitor. Every surface of the place looked sunken in, like the brothers had made a ritual out of smashing everything up. Squashed beer cans poured out of a crumpling trash can in the living room. A littered hallway led to a fridge plastered with magnets from various Yale sports teams, mixed with cheerful alphabet letters spelling, BLESSED BE IMMANUEL KUNT.

Johnny reached up from the loveseat to pass me a bong stained with pink and red lipstick, and after Dorian and I took a hit we left for the bathroom, to get dressed. Coughing, Dorian rattled out a duffel bag full of women's things: stockings and bras and fake nails and a tube of velvet red Chanel lipstick, among various other essentials he had pilfered from Madeline.

Madeline would have murdered Dorian if she'd learned that he had poured her belongings onto a surface crusted with decades of hangover vomit. She would never join us for Drag Ball herself, maintaining as I had that the whole affair was too "boorish"—although really she was probably just afraid to confirm that her boyfriend looked better in stilettos than she did. She was content to let Drag Ball be the one thing we did without her ("*Just you boys*," she'd said, with a nose wrinkle and a dismissive flicker of her hand) while she made an attempt to inspire jealousy by gushing about her dinner plans at Union League Café with "sophisticated" Chelsea Macintosh, whose father was in the Senate but was herself as boring as a piece of paper.

"What great taste in shoes," I exclaimed as I tried on the ostentatious high heels Dorian had gifted me. "You have a knack for women's footwear."

He shoved me from his perch on the edge of the bathtub, and I slid down the door while I laughed at my legs splayed out before me on the blackened bathroom tile. The hilarity of my embellished feet was rivaled only by the straggly brown hairs on my knobby, pale legs—a testament to my Latino origins that I now compared to Dorian's own comparatively hairless skin. The year before I had gotten the idea to wax my legs, hoping to achieve the appearance of smoothness that was Dorian's physical birthright; the attempt had involved a single "Fun & Easy" at-home body wax strip and an anguished yowl heard across the block, resulting in my reluctant acceptance of my body's hirsute condition and a solemn oath to avoid all grooming products involving temperatures above 125 degrees Fahrenheit.

Now I braced myself against the shag-carpeted toilet and rose slowly up, marching back and forth past the splintered mirror. "I don't know what Madeline complains about. I could practically run a marathon in these."

"You can't even run a marathon in sneakers," grunted Dorian, as he tangled himself up in a pair of fishnet tights.

I raised my fists, boxer-style, to my face and pretended to kick him. My ankle wobbled, and Dorian, still sitting, caught me in his arms.

"Would you ever want to be a woman?" he asked suddenly.

He cradled me like a long and lanky child. "It depends. Would you break up with Madeline, and fall madly in love with me?"

Dorian ignored me and gazed at the faint trace of a Yale football logo on the vinyl shower curtain, bleakly overpowered by a crisscross of un-scrubbed splatters. "I think life would be easier as a woman," he mused. "If a woman can't decide on what to do with herself in life, then she just has kids, and everybody thinks she's accomplished enough."

"Only if they're married," I said, encircling his neck with my arms. "It's a full commitment."

"Well then, I guess I'd get married, and become a housewife."

"You would *hate* that!" I declared. "You can barely keep still as it is. Imagine hanging around a big house all day—you'd kill yourself."

"Then I'd have a nanny," he said, "so I could do other things."

"A nanny?" I cried. "Then what would be the point of having kids if you wouldn't even take care of them?"

"Oh, I don't know," he shrugged, "it'd just buy time. I'd have eighteen years at least before I had to make any big decisions again, and nobody would think I was being lazy."

"Don't let Madeline hear you," I said, as I sat up on his lap and clicked my high-heeled toes together. "I'm guessing you wouldn't breastfeed either? Just pass them to the nanny?"

"No—I would breastfeed," Dorian said. He placed a self-conscious hand over his nipple. "Maybe I'd like it—being needed by someone. Don't you think I'd be good at it? Playing board games, and reading picture books, and—"

". . . and cooking, and cleaning, and all those other things that housewives do?" I added. "You would be *terrible* at that."

"Oh, get off!"

"And what about sex?" I added, and yanked at the back of his hair.

"What about it?"

"You'd have to have sex with a man. How else would you be planning to make babies?"

He considered this with a far-off look, then suddenly clutched his stomach. "You're right," he cringed. "I could never let anybody inside of me."

"How about inside here?" I poked him in the belly button.

"Stay away," he warned, and reached for my wrist.

"Why? Maybe you'd like it, if you had some practice," I laughed, jabbing him once, twice, three times in the stomach.

Dorian wrestled me onto his chest from behind and pinned me into a headlock. "How's this for practice?" He bit my ear and pretended to rip it off, while I squirmed and kicked and sent Madeline's lipsticks clattering over the scum-encrusted tile.

IN MY APARTMENT, BELOW MY FOUR-FOOT LOFT BEDROOM, the kitchen light was on.

I flicked it off, not wanting to arouse my roommates' suspicion, although on looking back, it would have appeared less strange for me to be holding a knife in the light (I could have been cutting anything—a pepper, a tomato) than in the dark. Trying to find the knife drawer, I felt around the shadowed countertop and my hand grazed the cutting board and the brittle rind of an orange, which had been left out.

I touched the side of the counter; a cold drawer handle. An uncanny shudder crawled over my neck, as if I expected to reach into the drawer and find a hand there waiting for me. Instead, my fingers fell upon a steak knife. Its predictably serrated edge—one spike after another, its power ruled by order—gave me comfort. The remaining contents of the drawer consisted mostly of ordinary, harmless dinner knives with rounded tips. They were all different sizes and designs, collected over the years from a shifting cast of tenants and never traded out for a new set. I groped around until I found the one I was looking for: the paring knife, small and pointed.

I wrapped my fingers around the plastic handle and just held it inside the drawer, perfectly still for at least a minute. My behavior had no precedent. I had never cut myself as a teenager, and honestly, I had never even thought about it before. I must have been staring at my screen saver, or commanding Dorian to complete a task, when my self-hatred flipped a switch in me, and I remembered that when other people felt miserable, they sometimes cut themselves. The idea had gotten under my skin. I figured that if it made those people feel better, maybe it would make me feel better too. But even now, I wasn't sure I wanted to do it. As far as I could tell, I was just fumbling around in the dark, trying somehow to feel better.

My doubts about life were what made me hate myself the most. I'd never had so much *doubt.* I used to feel so sure of everything—sure that the world would bend to me, like I'd been promised; sure that, as the aphorism dictated, all I had to do in life was "be myself" and wait for the rewards. Trying to "be myself," however, had almost resulted in my disqualification from my own dream, and that other gem—"work hard"—had lately seemed more and more laughable. Once you were through with those tenets, there was little in the way of common wisdom that could be trusted.

If I hadn't been so embarrassed, I would have called Ms. Duncan, my high school English teacher. She had taught me that excellence assures success, and my supposed excellence had gotten me gratefully through college. But what if, in the real world, excellence was replaced in value by money, beauty, social power—all the gifts I didn't have, whose importance I had wrongly believed could be circumvented by the loophole of my own merit?

How had everyone else done it? It was no secret that Jane Delancey had been an ordinary shopgirl at Barneys, back on Seventh Avenue, when she was discovered by Ava Burgess. The newly promoted editrix-in-chief, had been seeking fresh talent for her growing fashion team when she simply took a liking to Jane while buying a veiled hat for her upcoming thirtieth birthday party. It turned out the two had the same birthday—Ava was a year older—

and two weeks later, Jane was filing Ava's papers, two *years* later, Jane was masterminding Ava's photoshoots; and that was it. It was your typical rags-to-riches story, with no plot twists along the way. The rise to the top had been similarly untroubled for Edmund, who had once been a Hoffman-Lynch postal boy. How he went from that to fashion director—well, who knew? But if he and Jane could get there from selling hats and passing out the mail, anyone should be able to do it, especially with an Ivy League degree. After all, wasn't that the purpose of having one—so you could trade it in for a seat at your dream job, with your name in italics on a silk cushion?

I wasn't like Dorian or Madeline, who could retreat into their parents' wealth while they loafed their way through Plans A, B, C, and ever after until they found something that "fulfilled" them and gave them an illusion of independence by the age of thirty. No: I was on borrowed time as my savings disintegrated like a Christmas wreath left up too long. Once upon a time the four thousand dollars that I had saved up in college had seemed so substantial, as though it could support me for a hundred years; now, between rent and food and the other costs of scraping by, the amount in my bank account had dipped into three digits, and was quickly plunging lower and lower. If I didn't make it work somehow—*fast*—then I would be back to Texas where I had started, where it would be like I had never even come close—to anything.

Every day when I woke up I told myself: *Today is going to be the day you make something happen*—but I didn't know how, and nothing ever did happen, except my dread encroaching evermore, like the tide over the deck of a sinking ship.

I stood there breathing heavily while the refrigerator hummed. In one of my roommates' bedrooms, I heard a sitcom on TV. The laugh track sounded like something shattering over and over, a vase that kept on getting broken and put back together again.

I pulled out the knife abruptly from the drawer and held it straight by my side, taking giant, harried steps to the bathroom. With a deep breath, I pressed my back against the door; locked it, and raised the knife to the fluorescent light. Having used it before to open the stitched pockets of my Dior suit, I knew the edge was a little dull. I pressed its tip against my wrist and slowly twisted, trying to draw blood. My skin puckered, like the navel of an orange. I slackened my grip, unsure now if I really wanted to do it. For some reason, I was remembering a movie I had seen in which a class full of Japanese schoolkids had been made to kill each other. They were dying left and right, and every time one of them got stabbed or shot or hacked at with an axe, the blood would come shooting out like a red geyser. My own blood raced now at the thought. I imagined every drop in me like a sperm cell in a Sex Ed video, except instead of swimming happily toward an egg, they were in a panic, trying desperately to escape my knife. I didn't blame them; if I were a drop of blood, I wouldn't want to go geysering all over the place either.

Still holding the knife, I reached into my pocket for my phone, where Madeline's name was in my speed-dial menu. Madeline would know what to do. She hated blood. She hated anything that hurt people—animals too. She always tried to be vegetarian, and would succeed for a few weeks only to be tempted by foie gras or some other "irresistible" favorite.

The screen read MADELINE DUPRE.

The letters of her name were as meaningless as those on a label for canned ham. I couldn't call her, I just—couldn't. What would I say? And what would she say? And she'd be busy anyway.

The phone sort of tumbled out of my hand, clattering to the tile floor at my feet. I was too paralyzed to pick it up. In the back of my head, I thought of something I had heard once, either in real life or on the Internet: *"All you need to do to be happy is to start smiling. Just lift up the corners of your mouth, and that's it, you're happy."* It seemed like as good an idea as any—I mean, what did I have to lose?—but trying just made the corners of my mouth quiver. I closed my eyes. When I opened them, I wasn't smiling but I wasn't frowning either, because I couldn't feel my face at all.

I started thinking about all the sad characters I knew from books. I thought of Esther from the *The Bell Jar*, and how she had dealt with things, but then I couldn't remember if she had gotten better or if she had just killed herself by the end of the book. That made me think of the boy from *Brave New World*, who definitely did kill himself by the end—he hung himself, which was too horrifying a notion to even momentarily entertain—and Romeo and Juliet, and Ophelia, and pretty much everybody in Shakespeare. Now that I really considered it, *everybody* sad in great literature seemed to kill themselves by the end. It was, like, the only thing to do.

To my blood's relief, I put down the knife on the edge of the sink, then I rifled through the medicine cabinet as I had done before. If I truly wanted to kill myself, I could swallow more than just aspirin. Not that I wanted to, but—if I did want to, I could basically eat everything that was in there. Surely, something would have to happen. A person just couldn't mix up all those chemicals in his body and *not* have something happen to him, right?

I began to line up all the bottles, just to *see*—just in case, one day, I went through with it. Just in case I ever wanted to go through with *anything*. The most powerful thing I recognized was Midol. I began pouring out the pills from every bottle—one after the other along the edge of the sink—and then my roommate Veronica knocked on the door.

"Ethan?" she asked. "I'm sorry, do you think I can take a shower? I'm meeting Jonathan for dinner in an hour, and I'm so gross from all this heat."

I didn't answer at first. I just stared at the trail of pills I had made—little droplets the color of bone and oleander and cloudy skies. My favorite ones were the faint purple of a fresh bruise, and they cured indigestion.

"Ethan?"

"Hi," I croaked. I cleared my throat. "Yeah—sure," I said. "Give me—two minutes?"

I poured them all back into the Midol container and stuck it in the cabinet, tossing the empty containers in the trash. Reconsidering, I scooped up all the bottles and returned them to the shelf, empty.

Then I tucked the paring knife in a groove beneath the medicine cabinet and went upstairs to sleep.

THE NEXT DAY DORIAN WAS WEARING A BASIC GRAY T-SHIRT from Alexander Wang.

"What a great shirt," Edmund said to him, as he trotted past in a head-to-toe zebra print ensemble, including black-and-white zigzag pony-hair shoes. Fresh from a vacation in Majorca, he was in fine spirits, having just made a lavish fuss over some "missing" zebra cufflinks.

If before I had feared that Edmund might start to favor

Dorian by giving him assignments, the truth was worse: He started to favor Dorian while still giving me the assignments.

"Ethan, I need you to do some research for me. A very special assignment. I'm sure you will enjoy it. Wish I could do it myself," he briefly entertained, "but you know, there's never any time. I'll need every instance of Spanish influence you can find in the work of Oscar de la Renta between 1950 and 1970. Go through all the archives and make copies of every example there is, even advertisements, and don't leave anything out," he instructed before warning me, "I'll be able to tell if you skipped over any parts."

"Okay," I helplessly agreed. "When do you need this by?"

"Tomorrow morning, first thing please," he said as he tried to grab at something on his tongue—a hair, perhaps, from his own shoe.

I grimaced. Edmund had already assigned me another project for "tomorrow morning, first thing please," involving the arbitrary reorganization of his portable music library to reflect a *chi*-enhancing suggestion in his feng shui book. "Honestly I don't know if all that will be possible before tomorrow," I said. "Jane's trunks are being shipped out tonight, and I've already got your music library before—"

The slamming door cut me off.

"Do you need any help?" Dorian asked, as he sipped a juice box and came up with a poem for the back of his lunch receipt. I smoldered silently at his stupidity. "How far have you gotten with the music library?" he asked. Dorian had always feigned ignorance of flourishing hostilities, believing that with a fumigatory smile they would shrivel like a weed and cease to encroach on his good spirits. This was one thing about him that had infuriated

Madeline, who loved to water any cracks in the ground with her full attention.

"It's fine," I said. I would sooner die of exhaustion in that bleak office than ever accept Dorian's help.

"We only lend out two at a time, sweetheart," the librarian notified me as I stood at the checkout counter buried behind a wall of brick-like archival books. Her white bob peeked over the top: "I suppose I can let you take three, but you'll have to put some of these back."

"It's for Edmund Benneton," I explained.

"Oh, I'm sorry, dear," she said. I couldn't be sure if the apology was for not realizing I worked for Edmund, or because, as someone who worked for Edmund, I just deserved one. She pointed to a glass dish full of candies on the checkout counter, and offered up a wan, conciliatory smile. "Here, have a gumdrop."

With each year broken up into four volumes, twenty years of *Régine* was eighty volumes in total—about two shelves' worth of hardcover books, and a great deal for the librarian to part with. With some reluctance, she let me pile up a rolling cart—and, after helping me and my perilous tower onto the elevator, waved regretfully at me as the doors closed between us.

When Dorian and Sabrina had left the closet for the day ("*Good luck!*" he said. "*Don't touch* anything," she said), I was still combing through 1952. It turned out Oscar de la Renta's repertoire contained more instances of Spanish influence than the King of Spain's bedroom; by the time I was finished with a volume, the sides were fringed with stickies.

At about 1956, the nighttime cleaning lady came around, wearing a mint-green uniform dress with a Peter Pan collar. For someone charged with taking out the trash, she was quite exotic—

tall like an Indian palm tree, with olive skin and grape-colored lips—and I took a momentary break to wonder if at Hoffman-Lynch even janitors had an advantage if they were beautiful. Pushing a cart full of cleaning supplies, she swayed around replacing all the trash bags so that in the morning they could get stuffed again with coffee cups and yesterday's trends. She eventually waved goodbye, like an Arabian princess boarding her jet for the next stop on a world tour, and by 1959 it became clear I wasn't going home that night. To flip through a single year of *Régine*—including features, fashion editorials, and endless advertisements—took about half an hour, if I did it fast. I had no choice but to turn every page. From the impeccable lists he kept in his diaries, I knew Edmund would notice if I had skipped something. If I neglected so much as a single "imperative" moment—a flamenco-inspired swimsuit in July 1964, a matador cape in August—he could easily turn his full attentions to Dorian.

At midnight, the lights flickered off through the entire floor. Thereafter, they'd only come on again if I activated the motion sensor, which required me to stand up and wave my arms like I was directing an airplane to land. Everything was a dark blur between two and eight in the morning, at which point I stapled the paper copies and clicked *Send* on the digital version.

Dorian arrived an hour later to find me snoring over my computer keyboard. "Morning, babe."

I peeked through one eye to find him smiling there beside me and turned my head the other way, praying he was only a bad dream. Surely when I woke up, I would find somebody else there—anybody but him. *Five more minutes, five more minutes*, I thought, but I could feel his eyes on my back and couldn't squeeze mine tight enough to black out the whiteness of his smile in my head.

"You look like you rolled out of bed."

"I wish," I groaned. I started to prop myself up, but was met with resistance from my heavy head. My face rolled back toward the ceiling, and the fluorescent lighting burned through my half-closed lids.

"Wait a second," said Dorian. "You didn't stay here overnight, did you?" He leaned toward me, then reeled back, which I took to mean that I needed a shower. "You know, I can help you with whatever you need. It's not fair for you to do all that work by yourself."

"Yeah," I croaked, "next time we'll have a sleepover by the photocopier." I bobbed up long enough to wordlessly point to the pile of garment bags on the floor and he had enough sense to end the conversation.

If I thought the morning was bad, the rest of the day got only worse. With every hour that passed—slowly, like rain passing through hard layers of scorched earth—my body slumped lower and lower, until finally I decided to stand. I knew that if I sat down I would fall asleep, so for a couple of hours I paced back and forth, waiting for Dorian to do all the work while I saved all my energy to look busy when Sabrina came into view. I disappeared constantly into the kitchenette for coffee, where I prompted frequent throat-clearing from behind me by staring too long at the buttons on the coffeemaker. When I arrived back to the closet, my cup was always empty again, and would tumble out of my fingers into a growing pile in the trash. *Help Hoffman-Lynch Reduce Waste!* the trash can pleaded, and every time I snorted with a demented sense of gratification.

Dorian struggled in earnest to engage me, but, unlike Day One, I now had no trouble ignoring him. I was being spectacularly like the figurative Régine, and I wasn't even trying.

Finally, he said to me, while I was staring at a tortoiseshell button on a Max Mara coat, "I wouldn't take the credit."

I made a grunt-like sound, unintelligible even to myself.

"For helping you," Dorian clarified. "If you need help with Edmund's assignments, I wouldn't steal the credit . . . if that's what you're afraid of."

I blinked at his face. His expression contained the overwhelming comfort of familiarity, and also of truth: Dorian was nothing more and nothing less than me, had nothing more and nothing less than what I wanted for myself. If we were switched I would have done as he had done, and I would do as he did.

I had known this all along. It was the thing that hurt the most.

"Have I changed, Dorian?" I murmured.

He was cross-legged on the floor, surrounded by black lace lingerie. He quietly bent his head, and draped a French lace garter belt on his knee. "No," he lied. "What do you mean?"

"I'm really afraid. I'm afraid I'll never be happy again."

Dorian looked up at me as I crumpled beside him. My knees hit the carpet with a deadening thud. I swayed, and he caught me with the grace of Mary in a Pièta. He didn't say anything. I dug my head into his chest and he put his arms around me, and we remained there, wordless, for five minutes.

"TELL HER I'M NOT HERE!" SABRINA YELLED.

"Sabrina's not here . . . ?" Dorian ventured, with a hopeful glance toward the phone. Like me, he was a terrible liar. I could see him squirm as the person on the other line retorted in the familiar way, something like, "*But I just heard her yell at you.*"

"Is that Jenny from HL Group?" I asked.

He nodded. His green eyes widened, reflecting light from the computer screen.

I rolled my eyes. "Don't worry about her," I assured him. "She's always pestering for their Cavalli clothes back."

"Well, what do I say?" he mouthed, holding the receiver to his chest. "She talks so fast."

"You know what I do?" I confided, "I tell them I'm going to transfer them—"

"To whom?" he whispered urgently, as Jenny from HL Group's voice spiked over the receiver.

"To anybody: Sabrina, Jane, the Queen of England, whomever, then—I just hang up." I took the phone from him and interrupted her. "Hi, Jenny, let me transfer you." *Click!* I pressed the button, and then passed the receiver back to Dorian. "See," I said, straightening my back. "Now don't pick up when she calls back."

Dorian stared at me.

I straightened my shoulders and shot him a defiant look—"What!?" My pose reeked of affectation—this was the "new me," who sat up straight and hung up on Jenny from HL Group.

The next second, the two of us had deflated like balloons and were laughing aloud.

"Hey!" came Sabrina's voice. "What's going on over there?" She sounded like a police officer knocking on the windshield of a couple of teenagers' hot-boxed car, and suddenly, my entire life seemed to have reached such an unprecedented level of ridiculousness that I began to laugh even more.

"*Hey!*"

I reached over to cover Dorian's mouth with my hand, and when that only made us both laugh harder, I realized I had never laughed at *Régine*.

"Do I have to come over there?" Sabrina threatened, and that's what really set me off—that after all my delusions about the grand purpose of my postgraduate life, I was surrounded now by dresses and handbags and high-heeled shoes, and had to answer to a crazy person whose own dreams probably involved e-mail correspondence with the PR girl from Prada. And on top of everything, who should be sitting next to me but Dorian—the bane of my foolish existence? The whole thing was so tragic, so funny, that my hysteria hit fever pitch. I was a broken weather vane, swinging in every direction.

I had no idea why *Dorian* should find this funny, but he was in hysterics too, and that made me laugh even more—to think that together we were the dumbest pair in the world, and combined with Sabrina, the dumbest people in any room, *ever*.

Probably too hesitant to confront Dorian—Jane's favorite—Sabrina never acted on her bluff, and it took about five minutes for me and Dorian to settle down. When we finally did, I realized my hand was still covering Dorian's mouth. I lifted it away from his lips, and my palm glowed with his saliva.

DORIAN HAD BEEN EGGING ME ON SINCE HIS ARRIVAL, PASSing one tennis ball after another into my court, while I just fumed in the center with my arms crossed and let them *tut-tut-tut* toward the unloved corners of the fence.

In a moment distinguished by the completeness of my own stupidity, I finally raked up my racket from the concrete and thwacked the ball back with all my strength.

Ping! "Tell me more about Paris," I demanded.

Ping! "It was beautiful, and dull."

Ping! "That's all?"

Ping! "I missed you and Madeline."

Ping! "Shut up."

Ping! "I did!"

Ping! "You never called, never wrote."

Whoosh! The ball tinkered out of bounds. "I just—I was scared I had made a mistake . . ."

The office was the same place, but now somehow different.

When Sabrina told us to "get the trunks," Dorian and I would leave the closet side by side, like we were heading to recess. When she said, "get lunch—ten minutes—fast!" we scurried out together before she could protest, and although half the time she caught up with us, crying in exasperation, "*Not* both *of you*," her bubbling vitriol would always simmer at the sight of Dorian's privileged face. We pinged back and forth with surprising ease, and soon it felt the way it always had: an electric charge between our rackets. I became determined never to miss a stroke, and began to hit harder. I didn't want to beat him, though—I just wanted him to hit harder back, and to play him for as long as possible.

"It's so hard—all the petticoats," gushed Madeline one night over drinks, after she and I agreed to reconcile. She was showing me and Dorian a picture of her Mary Queen of Scots costume. "You don't realize, but to play such a complex character . . ."

Dorian looked at me as Madeline rested her hands on his knee. There we were again—the three of us, the indomitable trio. Ethan St. James, and Madeline and Dorian in love as ever, yet although he held Madeline closer as she blathered on about grueling undergarments and "women back then," it was me toward whom Dorian flashed a secret, knowing smile—*Ping!*

A few days afterward, a dozen uniformly sized boxes arrived

in the fashion closet around one in the afternoon. A rakishly adhered orange sticker on the side of each read For Immediate Distribution: It was the August issue, the first I had worked on when I arrived three months prior. I ran a blade across the top of the first box and opened the flaps to reveal Scarlett Johansson's prominent pout. I shuffled through the pages, and for the first time I realized how significant a portion of the magazine was made up of advertisements. Previously, the pages of *Régine* had all seemed the same to me; whether they contained advertising or magazine content, it had all been glamour with a "u," every woman and every dress as appealing as the last, as unanimous in their collective beauty as they were in their belonging to the same unreachable world.

Now, flipping past a hundred names that previously had been placeholders for this unreachable world—advertisements for Chanel and Balenciaga and Gucci and Fendi—I stumbled across the August It Girl shoot that I had worked on, and suddenly the world in *Régine* did not seem unreachable at all. In fact, as the It Girl in question was wearing off-white garments and accessories that my own hands had extensively handled—shoes I had crushed into packed trunks, handbags I had tossed into indiscernible piles—I realized for the first time that this world was already much closer than I thought.

Jane swept in just as I was coming across the fashion feature she had styled for that issue—"Darling!" she exclaimed. "Keep me company while I look over all these handbags that just arrived, come, come!"

I turned for one second, excited, then realized of course she was referring to Dorian, whom she was in the habit of pulling to her side for chitchat when she was in the fashion closet for an extended period. I tried hard not to eavesdrop as their voices floated through the racks (" . . . still enjoying *Régine*? . . . I spoke to your mother yesterday . . . we're talking about Mykonos in the next few weeks . . .").

To distract myself from this mildly irritating exchange, I flipped to Jane's editorial, which was titled: "Guinevere: Queen of Rock & Roll." Despite the relative simplicity of her personal style, it turned out that, between Edmund and Jane, she was the true genius. More and more, I was learning that fashion was a language, and that "practicing" it required a mastery of its grammar and vocabulary. Edmund's stories were on the level of *Dick and Jane*—the best models in the best clothes, so what?—while Jane's were, I don't know, the Brothers Grimm or something, imaginative, drawing from a rich history of storytelling, with every model a character in a fantastical, fully articulated world. I would give anything to—

"—come on set this weekend?"

I perked up suddenly, like a bloodhound detecting a hot scent.

"This weekend?" Dorian replied.

"Yes!" Jane insisted. "You must come see the shoot!—it'll be divine!"

Versace-clad Guinevere slipped right off my knee as the rest of their conversation faded away. Dorian basically said yes, he'd go. Jane basically said wonderful, she was so proud of him, and oh, look at this Dolce clutch, wasn't it just delightful?

Now I shattered my tennis racket against the concrete. Dorian, however, scarcely noticed me upon his return, and in fact he seemed to have forgotten altogether about our match: he slunk over to the pool on the other side of the chain-link fence and collapsed grandly into a cushioned seersucker chaise, running his fingers through his sun-kissed hair. Producing a martini out of nowhere, he began to sip as though he had just finished a tiresome task—a spot of polo or a lap in his private pool—while his whole body was caressed by the reflections of the water. I slammed the tennis court gate and stormed off over the lawn, while he called out in a casual tone, over his bronzed shoulder:

"Are you going to the shoot this weekend?"

"No," I said, and began to disfigure a paper clip.

He held out his drink toward me—in real life it was just ginger ale, and scarcely a generous offering considering he could never finish a whole can by himself. The crooked straw fell cock-eyed like a little umbrella. "But don't you want to get experience?" he asked me.

I took a measured breath. "Of course I do, but Jane doesn't want me to come." I tossed the mangled clip into a corner and picked up the magazine that had fallen by my feet.

He took a slurp and tilted his head, as if trying to remember the capital of somewhere, or calculate an arithmetic problem, then said, "Sure she does. She just didn't think of it."

I shook my head. "She's never asked me to come on set. It's fine—I don't care."

"Of course you care. Don't you want to go?"

"I mean, yes, I'd *like* to go, but—"

Dorian strode back to Jane's side before I could say another word. I heard her say, "What is it, dear?" He leaned toward her and whispered something, then

"Oh my goodness, is that all? Of course he can!" she said. Jane raised her voice and called out to me, "Yes, yes, of course you can, Ethan!" She stood on her tippy-toes and waved her little hand at me over the racks.

I unsurely raised my own hand in response, then Dorian was by my side.

"Does that mean . . . ?" I began dumbfoundedly.

"She says you can come to the shoot this weekend."

I yelped and I threw my arms around him. "Babe—you're the best!"

Dorian shrugged, poking through the box of magazines while I clenched the back of his T-shirt in excitement. "You could've asked her too," he said.

"What do you mean?" I asked over his back, my chin resting on his shoulder as my hands loosened.

"I mean, you work ten feet away from her. You shouldn't be so scared of everything."

I pulled away.

If consideration for the feelings of others was a line he straddled, Dorian suddenly took a gigantic leap across it onto the far side. "You used to be so free," he said.

My jaw dropped, and the relief that soared through me—after all my bitterness, Dorian had at last proven his enduring sweetness—it just burst, like a hot air balloon that one moment was being elevated by a blue flame, then the next moment had gone sputtering down to the ground into a searing heap.

Of course, it was no big deal for *him*. Did he really think that, without the advantages of wealth, beauty, and supermodel parentage, the ten feet between me and the creative director of *Régine* was any less than a chasm of a thousand miles?

"Are you okay?" he asked. This was perceptive, for him.

"I'm stepping out," I said. "Tell Sabrina that Clara sent me on a coffee run." I rose toward the door without so much as my wallet or phone, and left Dorian dumbfounded behind me.

"Hey, wait a minute—" he started. The side of his chair

cracked against the desktop as he trailed after me through the closet doors. "I didn't mean to make you mad, I just—"

I pretended not to hear him as I marched with the leaden austerity of a soldier toward the foyer doors. It was the first time I'd traveled the halls of *Régine* like I truly belonged there, indifferent to everything but my own singular passage.

"Ethan, I'm sorry, I don't want to upset you," he said. I witnessed the rare appearance of several heads sticking out of cubicles in Editorial to frown at us.

The glass doors reflected us both with polished indifference as Dorian reached for my arm.

"I can't have this conversation with you right now," I said. I opened the door, somehow expecting him to stay on the other side of it—but of course, he followed me into the elevator lobby.

"I'm sorry, I just—I thought you'd want to go to the shoot, and—"

The veins in my neck bulged as I spun around, and spat, "*I do want to go!*"

He leaned back a little. "So if you want to go, what's the problem?"

I slammed the Down button on the elevator. "Nothing, Dorian—you don't get it."

"Yeah, I guess I don't."

"Nothing is *fair*, Dorian!" I half-shouted. "This isn't how it's supposed to go! I'm supposed to show up,"—I slapped my hand into my palm—"and work hard,"—*slap!*—"then things are supposed to *happen* for me!"—*slap!*—"When is *my life* going to start? It's like—nobody cares one bit about me, and then *you* show up, and—" I threw my hands up "—you don't even care about this job! You don't care about—anything!—but you still get *every*thing!"

"Well . . . Jane just knows me, so you shouldn't take it personally that she asked me—"

"It's not about Jane! It's not even about you, it's just—" I pressed my palms to my temples and walked away.

"I don't know what you want from me. I was just trying to help."

"I don't *need* your help."

"Well," Dorian shrugged, "it looks like you kind of do."

I spun around—"Just *shut up!*" If anybody could hear me through the glass, I didn't care. "Don't you get it? I can't just waltz into her office and say, 'Hey Jane, I love your work, want to take me on set with you?'"

"Why not?" he asked.

The elevator arrived.

"Can you just—leave?" I pointed in the other direction. "Sabrina is going to—"

He clip-clopped into the elevator after me while I crossed my arms against my chest and glared at the small television. At Hoffman-Lynch, they had been embedded in all the elevators to inform everyone of the company's newest programs and awards and million-dollar acquisitions.

"Did you know Hoffman-Lynch Publications recently won number one—?"

I was grateful for someone else stepping in the elevator with us, a tight-lipped woman I had never seen before. As I had come to expect at *Régine*, she didn't acknowledge our presence—although the pinch around her lips softened considerably at the sight of Dorian.

I thought her presence had finally silenced Dorian, but he prodded, "Where are you going anyway?"

The elevator doors closed. "I don't know," I snapped.

"You don't know where you're going?"

"*No.*"

He laughed. "Well, I guess, now that we're already out of the office—let's go get falafels."

I gaped at him openly. "Are you *playing* with me right now?"

The woman in the corner glared, the lines around her mouth hardening once more, like a lattice crust on an apple pie. I leaned toward her to glare back. "*What are you looking at?*" I demanded.

With a suddenly fearful glance, she turned to her phone while I devoted myself to mentally destroying her outfit—stupid black blouse! stupid black skirt! stupid black heels! How dare *she* disapprove of *me*, while she stood there in her sickening *Régine* uniform—unoriginal and colorless, probably purchased at too high a price tag for the sake of blending seamlessly into this *ugly* place, this bulwark of adulthood and dullness and routine—*How dare she?*

The elevator arrived at the ground floor with a *ping!* and the woman escaped before the doors had separated all the way.

"So are we getting off? Seriously, I'm kind of hungry." He took one step over the threshold of the elevator and looked back at me. "If you don't want to, then I'll just go. I can bring you a grape soda."

He knew I liked grape soda.

A small crowd of people peered expectantly into the elevator—holding sushi containers and organic juices and low-calorie snacks—eyebrows raised, as if I was wasting their precious time. Stupid faces. Stupid clothes. They were all so *stupid*.

Dorian pulled me out by the hand while they poured in like ants filling a colony. "They're all so stupid, aren't they?" he said, echoing the voice inside my own head.

I snorted, and let out a slightly hysterical laugh.

"What? It's true," he said.

I walked over to my proverbial racket, which in the wake of my tantrum lay sad and splintering on the tennis court; picked it up; and with a whoosh, returned the ball into the hopeful air.

Ping! I said, "You're going to be the end of me, you know."

Ping! "I know."

I LIFTED MY BAG ONTO MY CHEST, RIFLING FOR THE ADDRESS that I had nearly committed to memory the night before. It was six and there was an early morning chill, the sun lingering sleepily behind the cover of a hundred skyscrapers, a teenager beneath an impenetrable fortress of parent-hindering bedsheets.

"The fashion team is the first to arrive and the last to leave," Jane had said to me and Dorian. "There may be glamour in the pictures, but never in the call time." She had warned us both not to sleep in, although more useful advice would have been about getting any sleep at all. Like a piece of wood, I had lain petrified all night with my eyes open, afraid that if I fell into a slumber it would be too deep, and then when I opened my eyes it would be noon, and I would be late for the shoot and Jane would never ask me to come on set again and I would get cast out from *Régine* before I ever got to the good part. In between periods of anxious bed-rumpling I'd mapped out the journey from my apartment to the photoshoot location not once or twice but five times, each time recalculating the time to get there so that I was sure to give myself enough leeway. Now it seemed that, despite all this, I was at the wrong address.

Jane had said it was a theater, but this didn't look like any theater I'd ever seen. There was no marquee, no ticket booth, not even a sign—just a stronghold of plywood boards hedging the entire structure like brambles around Sleeping Beauty's castle. My fingers combed through a jumble of pens and crumbled receipts at the bottom of my bag until finally I found the address on a little note that had got stuck in the pages of *The Stranger*, which I had been trying to read in short bursts on the subway with limited progress.

The paper said, *5 Beekman.* I stared up at the boarded wall, where a continuous grid of fading wheat-pasted posters bubbled up like decaying snakeskin. Above guerilla advertisements for coconut water juice boxes and Lana del Rey's *Born to Die* album, a spray-painted scrawl alleged that I was, in fact, standing at 5 Beekman. I turned around. The street was quiet and gray, teeming along the edges with the rosy blush of an impending sunrise. Two boys were unloading a white van. They were lanky and tall—scruffy, wearing band Ts and skinny jeans—and after they slammed the back door of the van, they approached carrying large nylon bags and wheeling a hefty black trunk between them.

"Are you here for the *Régine* shoot?" I asked.

"This way," they said, pointing to a plywood board that, like several others, was guarded by Lana Del Rey. She offered only jaded disinterest as the board swung open on a hinge, and when I followed the boys, the one in a Nirvana shirt said, "The actual front door's been closed for like, fifty years."

We entered a hallway illuminated by a dangling, flickering light. Having plunged through a tarnished ornamental wreath in the ceiling, it twirled in the middle of the hall from an exposed cable, encased in a brass cage that cast its prism-like shadow against a concrete wall. Gravity had decreed a similar fate for a musty damask wall-covering lying puddled below.

Ahead of me the boys creaked open a door. My heart stopped.

Blood velvet flowed as far as the eye could see—an endless ripple of plush red chairs. On either side, three gilded balconies were tiered like sand dunes, overlooking a shrouded stage. A tech crew was busy rigging a constellation of steel bars before the stage, like an empyrean jungle gym.

The first one gestured to the scaffolding. "Is the model going to be sitting up there?"

"They want to shoot her from above," the other replied.

I caught my breath, clasping my hand over my mouth. Like an old-time movie projection, a reel flickered across my mind: a woman gliding across the stage like a billow of burning gossamer. Not two hours later, she was real, and her name was Belinda.

Belinda had red hair. She had freckles on her face and arms. She was six-feet-two-inches tall, and wore a size 9 1/2 shoe, according to the list of measurements in the black *FORD*-embossed portfolio she carried in her yellow Chloé handbag. Incidentally, she was also the current face of a half-dozen major fashion campaigns, including Valentino and Lanvin, and except for one occasion at the airport when I asked Joan Didion for the hour, Belinda was the first famous person I had ever really talked to. She was also seventeen years old.

Dorian, of course, knew Belinda from Paris—although at first he didn't recognize her slender neck.

She was sitting in a tufted red velvet chair, one of eight spaced at even intervals along the counter of a wooden vanity, surrounded by rusted, dust-caked mirrors—the remains of an antiquated dressing room, repurposed now by *Regine*'s Hair and Makeup artists. On one side of Belinda, Hair had laid out his blow-dryer, straightener, texturizing shears, thinning shears, clippers, squirt bottle, big brushes, small brushes, combs, hair razors; on the other, Makeup had arranged her eyeshadow, foundation, powder, concealer, mascara, eyeliner, brushes as bushy as a mustache and as thin as a single whisker, and miniature bottles of pigments in every shade, coral red and tangerine, Tiffany blue and alabaster white.

Hair was rick-racking bobby pins into Belinda's red mane while Makeup reclined against the counter, using the underside of her wrist to test a color palette that the next moment was knocked to the ground by Belinda's arm. Her transgressive limb dangled over the back of the chair as she turned around.

"Belgraves?" she exclaimed in a husky British accent.

Dorian lit up in surprise as she hopped down and tossed her arms around him, cell phone clutched in one hand. "Why do you get to waltz in so bloody late?"

"I'm not modeling today," he said over their embrace. "I'm not modeling anymore at all. I'm an intern."

"An intern?" She frowned. She stepped back and clenched his shoulders with an expression of mild concern. "What does that mean?"

"Ask him," he pointed at me. "He's an intern too."

"Is he joking?" She turned to me. "Are you his agent?"

I shook my head, and she squinted back at Dorian: "You always were so *strange*."

Makeup nudged Belinda to return to the Hair and Makeup chair.

"Are you still doing those little drawings?" she asked. Her floral chiffon miniskirt swayed as she pressed her knobby knee into the tufted chair. "He makes these wonderful little drawings," she explained to Makeup, who was waiting for Belinda to make her face available once more. "They'll be worth a fortune someday. Still," she turned back to Dorian, "I think you're crazy."

"Please," urged Makeup, "we have a lot of work to do."

"Well, look at that face though!" Belinda faultlessly protested. "Don't you think he's crazy to give up modeling?"

Makeup indulged her with a hasty nod as Belinda slid back into the rusted chair with a creak. She crossed her legs into a lotus position and fanned out her skirt, wiggling her toes in her moccasin slippers. "How am I ever going to find a boyfriend when they're all crazy?" She finally settled in with a toss of her hair, pulling a copy of *Esquire* across the edge of the counter into her lap. She pointed to the cover, and informed us, "I'm shopping for boyfriends."

Hair took another strand and began to weave it through a bobby pin like a complicated fishing fly.

"You ended things with Brandon, then?" Dorian asked, leaning against the back of the adjacent chair.

I stood beside him as Belinda laughed, revealing a gapped tooth which reminded me of Madeline. "Of course not. We're madly in love." She shuffled through the magazine while Makeup lifted her chin. "I'm only seventeen though, and life ends at twenty-one. At least that's what my agent says, and my mom too—only she thinks it's thirty. I'm just thinking ahead, in case I have a midlife crisis and break up with him."

Makeup had managed at last to touch her brush to Belinda's face when the model spun around. "Does anybody have any gum?"

An exasperated breath from Makeup; she crossed her arms and waited for Dorian to pull a Wrigley's peppermint package out of his pocket.

Belinda folded a piece into her mouth and flipped to the main fashion editorial, where Sean O'Pry was standing in a full suit on an unlikely precipice in the forest, seducing the camera with eyes that required a sizable paycheck just to open in the morning. "What's your opinion of Sean O'Pry?" she asked.

Dorian peered over her shoulder and began to play with a bobby pin from the counter. "I thought you dated him already."

"I thought so too once, after I read it in a magazine," she recalled. "Do you ever think so too, about you, after you read it in a magazine?" Belinda looked up to rehearse a look of deep contemplation in the mirror, then to the detriment of Makeup's already much-strained patience, puckered her lips and tried out several angles of her chin. "We did live in the apartments though, for a short while."

I'd heard of model apartments, where agencies set up their promising young talents who were trying to make it in the industry. The idea always reminded me of a sleep-away summer camp, where instead of just one attractive counselor (every camp had at least one counselor who everyone crushed over, and tried to corner in a canoe on some pond), they were *all* attractive counselors. Instead of summer days spent diving into lakes and telling ghost stories, they roamed New York City with a portfolio of their own photographs, attending auditions, casting calls, and later on, all the best parties, before crashing home to a tent they shared with the future face of Maybelline—which was staked on a hill across from the future faces of Gucci and Armani—while each of them wondered if they would "make it," or if they would get sent back after the summer to Brazil or Poland or whatever perfect provincial gene pool they called home.

"How is your girlfriend doing?" she asked Dorian. "The civilian?" She looked up in the direction of Makeup's slanted brush and explained in a hushed voice, "His girlfriend's not a model."

I was shocked to hear that Dorian had told anyone in Paris about Madeline.

"She's an actress now," Dorian said. "Or well, she wants to be an actress."

Belinda smiled, genuinely touched. "Wonderful! So she'll know what it's like. It's good to be with someone who knows what it's like." She didn't explain what "it" was, exactly, but shut the magazine as Jane walked into the dressing room. Belinda pointed with a solemn shake of her head to the handsomely etched face on the back cover. "My biggest disappointment in life," she said with a vivid sigh, and a curl of her slippered toes. "A total dream, until finally we hooked up, and I found out he had a spot on his—oh!" she exclaimed, at the sudden appearance of Jane's reflection in the mirror.

"Go on." Jane grinned, placing her hands on Belinda's shoulders. "I'm dying to hear about your life's greatest disappointment."

"It was just—" Belinda blushed. "You know how some people have a mole somewhere? Well, he did, only he had it on his—you know." She pointed between Dorian's legs and made a little wiggling motion with her finger. "The size of a nickel."

chapter ten

Jane let the dress fall gently around Belinda's body, while Dorian held the model's Boudiccan red hair: helmet-sleek on top, then frizzy from the ears down, with an arrow-like part through the center. The back of the dress was designed to plunge to Belinda's lower spine, while the front was embellished from top-to-floor-length bottom with copper beads. The metal droplets chorused over the floor like a whispering cascade of holy water. Divine transformation.

Where, moments ago, there had been an ordinary seventeen-year-old girl—beautiful perhaps, but ultimately mortal, with her half-chewed fingernails and roughed-up knees—there now stood among us an angel.

All around her hovered a reverential silence, as even the garment racks seemed to lean toward her in anticipation of a heavenly utterance. Sabrina hung beside me, her shoulder almost touching mine, both of us poised in suspense like two un-rung bells. It was the closest she and I had come to harmony.

"Ethan," I heard.

For some reason, I was nervous, shaking a little. I just—couldn't believe it was real, that Belinda had become what I had always dreamed about, the woman in the magazine. She was Jane's vision: the apparition of an actress who fell asleep at curtain call and, one hundred years later, woke up, brittle and rusted in a dilapidated theater. But now she was my vision too, and that of every other person whose mind drifted away while poring over the pages of a fashion editorial, all of us carrying into our dreams these beauties who never moved, never breathed, yet somehow glowed with the promise of another world, tiptoeing on the thread of spider's silk that separated the real and the imagined.

"Ethan, darling," Jane repeated. She reached out toward me as she lifted the hem of Belinda's dress from the floor. "Can you pass me my apron?"

The apron dangled off the garment rack. It was faded and fraying, with a lint roller in one pocket and a plastic box of safety pins in the other, fringed by black rubber clamps. I strung it over Jane's head, and she removed a small clamp, which she used to clip the waistline of Belinda's dress.

She stood back, withdrew a crinkled hair from Belinda's moistened lips; a palm on the seraph's naked spine, she asked, "Ready, love?"

Belinda nodded without a word. Even she felt the hallowed magnitude of her own presence. She stumbled, then reaching for Jane's shoulder, admitted with a whisper, "The dress is heavy."

Extending her arm for support, Jane lifted the clinking

train, and side by side they inched toward the stage door. Hair and Makeup followed closely behind, flanked by photo assistants like altar boys, so that together we formed a procession down the bloodred aisle.

As Jane positioned Belinda on the stage, the photographer fired a test flash: a beep, and the theater was awash with white light.

"Tyler, can you turn up the fill light?" the photographer asked, and one of the altar boys twiddled with a light behind Belinda's head.

A computer screen by the photographer's side displayed the images his camera captured. Eventually, after Belinda had flowed through a stream of poses, there would appear on the screen the unedited image that millions of eyes around the world would see, an image that might trickle into their subconscious, and in some small, untraceable way, affect the course of human culture.

Belinda waved at us with an uncomfortable look. Jane was stooped over the photographer's chair, and didn't notice.

"What is it?" I called over the aisles.

She pointed pleadingly with a copper nail toward her face, like she was at the dinner table and had accidentally bitten into something she was allergic to. I traveled down the aisle to her, the crunch of dead insects underfoot.

"Mm—my gum," Belinda moaned. "I forgot to spit out my gum."

"Is that all?" I held out my hand like a cup.

"You're sure?"

I insisted with a nod. Aiming to preserve her lipstick, she pinched the wad between her teeth and pushed it out with her tongue.

"Oh," she gushed with relief, and licked the inside of her mouth.

"We're ready," the photographer said, and a flash filled the theater once more.

I exited his frame, and paused at the end of the aisle; stared at the gum in my hand—putrid pink, like a masticated balloon. I looked up at Belinda. *Flash!* Down at my hand. *Flash!* This was it. *Flash!* My dream was so close, I could feel it in my very *hands*. I looked toward the crew. The light was flashing over and over now, a shatter of lightning over Belinda's head.

Nobody was watching me.

I popped Belinda's gum into my own mouth. It was still sweet, and I laughed to myself.

AFTER THE SHOOT, WE RETURNED TO *RÉGINE* TO UNLOAD THE trunks.

"Go home," Jane said. "It's Sunday night. You can do all that tomorrow."

Dorian wiped an imaginary layer of sweat off his forehead with the back of his hand. "Wait up for me," he said to me, sprinting to the bathroom as Jane disappeared with a smile into her office.

I sat in my chair and stretched my legs out, lightly rotating side to side as I stared at the ceiling. I could hear Jane typing—punching her keyboard slowly, one letter at a time, like she was playing whack-a-mole with a single finger. The only other noise was the mouselike squeak of my chair.

Faintly, from all the way down the hall outside, Jane's voice called out, "Dorian? . . . Ethan?"

I stopped turning, passed all the racks, left the fashion closet, and approached Jane's door. "Hi," I said, resting a hand against the metal doorframe.

With one hand she stretched her white ceramic mug out toward me, and with the other she covered her mouth, yawning. "Can you please make me a tea, darling? I'm falling asleep, but I want to finish this proposal." She pinched her fingers together in front of her face and shut one eye—"A little bit of honey."

I stepped out with her mug into the quiet hallway, and the overhead lights flickered on to illuminate my path to the kitchenette. The office was serene, humming, and it filled me with a strange sense of peace to imagine all the chairs tucked into desks on the other side of the cubicle walls, like children in their beds. When I returned to Jane's office I rapped lightly on the door and entered, steadying the mug as I remembered our first encounter in the women's bathroom.

"I'll take it," Jane said, reaching out. The surface of her fingers reminded me of wrinkled tomato skins.

I had never been in Jane's office. Like a museum, the walls brimmed with pictures. Neighbors included a kabuki princess and Jacqueline Kennedy; a Botticellian saint and Isabella Blow, all coexisting, in clean simple frames, on a wall of global inspirations. As I was leaning over her desk, I thought to myself that this was the most alone I had ever been with Jane, and noticed behind her one of my favorite Impressionist paintings: a bonneted woman in a blue frock, peering up from a book while her daughter gazed through a gate into a cloud of smoke.

Absentmindedly, kind of to myself, I murmured, "I love Manet."

"Hmm?" She cupped the mug with both hands through the handle and brought it to her lips.

"Oh, sorry—I just, I love that Manet painting," I said.

She glanced over her shoulder to remind herself what was hanging there. "Oh, yes. Everybody thinks it's Monet."

"Really? They're so completely different."

"Most people don't have a very good eye, I'm afraid," she said. "They see blotches and they think, 'Impressionism! Must be Monet!,' like every painter was the same." She shrugged and took a sip.

"My favorite's Manet," I confided. "Of the Impressionists, at least."

Her screen saver flickered to life, illuminating a face etched with soft lines, and I caught myself. "Actually, I'm sorry, I know you're working. I don't mean to distract you."

She brushed one hand dismissively through the air. "Don't be silly! You think I wouldn't rather talk to you about Manet than stare at a screen that can't talk back? I hate computers. I'm waiting for the day they all crash, so I can practice my cursive again."

I laughed out loud—it was exactly the kind of thing that Madeline would say.

"How old are you? You've probably never even heard of cursive writing," she sighed. "I take it you like art then? Manet's one of my favorites too, by the way."

She peered at me, and it was the first time I'd seen her eyes so close: blue, but unlike mine—my right eye, at least, which swirled like water, constantly searching—hers seemed calm, like air.

I laughed in spite of myself. "Like art? It's why I'm at *Régine* at all."

She took off her glasses and folded them like dragonfly wings in her hand. "Of course you like art! I remember you on your first day—in your bright, wonderful suit." She smiled, and the wrinkles around her mouth spread like pond ripples.

"That was inappropriate." I blushed, remembering my conversation with Clara. "I didn't mean to offend anybody, I just—didn't know."

"You didn't offend anybody," she shook her head. "Not me, at least. I saw you and my heart jumped up. I thought to myself—at last! Some color! Somebody with life in them! I know what they told you—about rank, and rules, and to be fair—it's true. But is it right? No. The world can't make progress without risk."

Across the room, a rocking bamboo fountain on the windowsill went *kerplunk!* The stone basin filled with water, as elsewhere in the room an invisible clock ticktocked closer and closer to nightfall.

"Ethan—" She toyed with the corner of a paper on her desk. "Would you be interested in helping me prep my next shoot? Brainstorm ideas, pull inspiration references—art, fashion—all of that?"

"I—" My heart leaped into my throat.

Kerplunk! went the fountain.

"Yes." I swallowed, nodding vigorously. "Yes, that would be—that would be amazing."

She smiled. "I'm glad. Go on then," she said, motioning to her work. "We'll talk soon."

Kerplunk!

I rushed toward the door. "Thank you," I whispered, hands prayerfully clasped against my chest. I closed her door behind me, and stumbled into the fluorescent glow of the hallway. Reentering the fashion closet I whispered, "Dorian!" but he was still in the bathroom.

Jane's words cycled over and over in my head as I paced the room—could it be that the creative director of *Régine* had just invited me to work on her next project? I passed the shelves and the garment racks and the desks, unable to contain my excitement. This was it! Jane's proposal represented the beginning of a new chapter at *Régine*.

I wanted to shout, "*I made it! I'm making it—it's happening!*" I wanted to shout it to Dorian and Madeline. I wanted to shout it to George, and to Edmund; to Clara, who had choked up when she told me success was possible for an outsider, and to Sabrina, who had compared me to a piece of yarn, unsuitable to fit into the needle of my improbable dream. I wanted to shout it to Ms. Duncan, who had believed in me, and apologize for doubting her. I wanted to shout it to all the people in my life, everyone I had ever met. The crowd of faces multiplied in my mind's eye—a ballroom full of teachers and friends, advocates and adversaries alike—when suddenly a spotlight shone over two faces. I wanted to shout it to my mom and dad.

I scrambled for the phone in my book bag, and dialed the same digits that, almost twenty years ago, I had practiced on a worksheet in kindergarten. There had been lines for practicing my address and phone number, with space for a drawing of my house.

"If anything ever happens," Mrs. Sanchez had said, as she handed out the assignment, with her hair braid like a thick black rope against the back of her paisley dress, "it's important to always be able to reach Mommy and Daddy." And the next day my worksheet was all filled in, with a drawing of a gray rectangle labeled "mY HoUs," and a couple of fruits in the front yard.

Now my father picked up, no doubt resembling more than ever the hairy coconut that I had labeled "dAdY."

"*¿Oigo?*" he grunted.

I heard the familiar sounds in the background—the same rush of water over my mother's hands in the kitchen sink; the same anchorwoman on the news, whose coiffure I was sure had remained unaltered through decades of local tragedy, all the stolen purses and dramatic pet rescues and sound bites including some Spanish variation of "*I've never seen anything like it!*"

A smile broke out over my face. I opened my mouth, but no words came out. My father also didn't speak, engrossed, surely, by some captivating screen graphic on the news. ". . . *ahora les paso a Bárbara, en vivo en el parque, donde se informa de un árbol podrido que se ha caído a las ocho de esta mañana* . . ."

"Reynaldo," my mother urged in the background, "who is it?"

My father remembered me and sputtered, "*¿Quién habla?*"

Silence hung in the thousands of miles between us, between me and my library books and flypaper ribbon and black beans for dinner; "*¡Oye, cabrón!*" and the click-clack of Lola's nails on the laminate tile; wandering the sidewalks at dusk, dreaming of something more, something bigger. I had done it. I had escaped.

Dorian's hand dug into my hair from behind. "Who are you talking to?" he asked, grabbing his jacket from the back of his chair. "Let's go!"

I hesitated to find words for Reynaldo San Jamar, father of Elián San Jamar, who would become me, Ethan St. James, until—

"*Estoy tan contento, papá,*" I said at last, and hung up.

OUR FOOTSTEPS ECHOED AS DORIAN AND I CROSSED THE empty Hoffman-Lynch lobby.

"Let's go to a party!" I shouted. My sudden burst reverberated through the vast hall—" . . . *arty . . . arty . . . arty*," tumbling back toward us like a pitter-patter of invisible ping-pong balls strewn over the black marble.

"Now?" he asked incredulously. "Aren't you tired?"

"Oh, come on!" I laughed, with a persuasive hand over his shoulder. "The one time I want to go with you to a party and you're tired?"

"I'm not saying *I'm* tired," he backtracked, "I'm just—"

"Then come on!" I squeezed my arms around his waist from behind and dove us into the revolving doors. Silence like a vacuum, before—*thwack!*—a million feet clip-clopping endlessly everywhere, and alarms blaring in the distance. "Please, Dorian! I feel—at the top of the world tonight! Like everything is going to be okay!"

"Everything was always going to be okay."

I latched onto his arm, intoxicated by recklessness. "*Please, please, please!* Take me to the best party in Manhattan tonight!"

He pretended to slump to the ground with exhaustion, but agreed at last with a winsome sigh. A streetlamp cast a glow over our faces as I pulled him toward the curb, and ten minutes later a cab had whisked us to the Meatpacking District, and dropped us off in front of a hotel called The Standard.

Dorian paid the cabdriver—a fifty, but who was keeping track?—while diamond headlights soared down the West Side Highway beyond. I hopped out. The moonlight dribbled on the cobblestones, glistening like lemon juice on a road paved with oysters.

"Come on," he said, placing his hand on my back as we approached a line of at least fifty people. They were bobbing faintly, switching from one foot to the other as they checked their phones to pass the time, and I remembered—Dorian didn't wait anywhere.

The doorman was a black twentysomething in a tailored cherry-red suit. He was holding an idle clipboard against his body, inviting the whole front of the line to watch as he inspected his nails in the dim light.

"Hey, Ivan." Dorian tapped him from behind. "I'm going in."

"Oh, hey, Belgraves," he greeted with a cool nod. "Go on. Some of your girls are here."

"Kaija?"

"She's pounding them back." Ivan made a chugging motion with his hand.

Dorian smiled. "See you later." It was as unceremonious as if he was greeting his own roommate.

Ivan looked at me as Dorian wordlessly took my hand, drawing me beside him. Ivan flipped foggily through the pages of his so-called guest list in his clipboard; with a flick of his wrist toward the bouncer, he said, "They're good," not marking anything off. Dorian squeezed Ivan's shoulder and pulled me inside. The bouncer didn't ask us for ID, and the last thing I heard was Ivan telling someone else, "Sorry, there's a list tonight, you're welcome to stand in line though."

We stepped into a dark elevator with a security guard in one corner, and I grinned with a hysterical brand of joy as Dorian said, "Top floor."

"Are you always on the list?" I asked.

"You're cute." Dorian smiled. "There is no list. Ivan just holds a clipboard, and lets in people he knows or who are wearing high-end designers."

I laughed, and Dorian let go of my hand to check his phone.

"We'll meet up with Kaija inside," he said. "You remember her, right? From my birthday?"

Between the highlights of that sparkling night—Dorian passed out in my arms, and Madeline vomiting onto our cab door in the rain—Dorian's friend Kaija had been a forgettable afterthought. Still, I answered with a half-attentive nod while trying to foist a smile on the hulking security guard. When he only stared at the wall ahead, I smiled wider, uncontrollably, until a neon pattern on the ceiling distracted me.

The doors closed. As the elevator soared up, a slow, rain-like hum surrounded us. The steel walls trembled like a boiling kettle—then, reaching a whistling crescendo, shook like we had whooshed into a hurricane. The elevator paused, overwhelmed by thunderous bass, then the doors slid open like floodgates to let a tsunami of pounding music crash over us.

Like an aquarium, a wall of floor-to-ceiling windows reflected an endless black ripple of human silhouettes, the tops of heads undulating like cresting waves. Dorian's eyes sparkled. It was so clear, even in the sheer darkness, that the room was filled with people like him—beautiful people, important people. A wonderful thought splashed over me: maybe now, I could be like these people too. Gently, Dorian slid his hand under my arm, and we plunged in.

Voices bubbled up past our ears. Like divers entering a school of fish, we passed through a sea of shimmering faces, everyone illuminated by distant city lights through the windows.

I gasped at a famous face, pausing to look back. "Is that—?"

Dorian glanced over and nodded, nudging me back into motion. "We can say hi later if you want," he promised. At the bar, he approached a white spine in a dress with a see-through chiffon back. "Hey, babe," he whispered into a diamond-studded ear.

The spine jerked, a martini sloshing over the shiny bracelet on an oleander wrist. With sweeping annoyance the girl exclaimed, "Jesus, Dorian!"

She looked like a movie starlet—not a modern one, who made scenes for paparazzi and starred in franchise trilogies—but one out of golden-era Hollywood, whose sultry gaze belonged in black and white. Her starlit face glowed with a Metro-Goldwyn-Mayer luster, fanlike lashes brushed with black mascara. She stooped down a bit in her heels to let Dorian kiss her cheek, carefully holding one hand up toward an exotic red turban that, like a satin python, had coiled itself around her raven-haired head.

"The situation's dire," she dully informed him. "It's ten o'clock, and I'm not seeing things that aren't supposed to be there." Her voice was low and hoarse, like she had begun smoking Pall Mall cigarettes in the womb.

"Calm down, it's a Sunday for God's sake," Dorian said. He pulled me to his side. "Plum, this is my best friend from Yale I told you about—Ethan."

"Hello, friend from *Yaaale*." She held out a hand like she was playing at being an aristocrat—and announced, wiggling her elegant fingers, "I'm Plum Bonavich." She draped her arm around my shoulders and, enveloping me in sweet perfume, whispered loud enough for Dorian to hear, "Now that we're acquainted, I really must ask—do you know any *Yale* men in need of a wife?"

I laughed, and Dorian said, "Don't listen to her—she already has a full roster of male benefactors." He poked at the girl beside Plum, who was busy dripping the last of her martini into her throat. "Hello to you too," he said.

With a fine swoop, the girl clinked the glass onto the marble bar and shuddered, "These drinks just never last a girl."

"Kaija, you remember Ethan, right?" Dorian asked her. She turned, and of course, I recognized her not from his party but, like so many of his other friends, from a dozen magazines. In a loose-fitting white silk shirt and no bra, her small, pointed nipples attracted the most light in the whole room. Her skin was coconut brown, her teased hair like a palm tree's fronds in the dark.

I thought her hand was moving toward mine to shake, but instead she buried it into Dorian's hair. "What's going on here?" she said. "You gave up on modeling, and now you gave up on combing your hair?"

Plum turned to provide her opinion. "That's what's wrong with the world these days. Nobody checks their hair anymore."

Dorian swatted Kaija away. "Just so you both know, I've been *working* all day."

"So? Other people have to look at your hair, you know. It's not enough to be *beeeautiful.*" She squeezed Dorian's cheek and shook it like a dog with a toy.

"It's not even artfully disheveled," Plum added.

"You try to walk into a club with us looking like that, and we'll just leave you on the street, and throw martinis at you from the window—and anyway," said Kaija, poking Dorian in the chest, "you want to talk work—guess who had to laugh for ten hours straight?"

"One of those *fun* photo shoots?" Dorian guessed.

"Mario was photographing, of course." She rolled her eyes. "'*Just have fun, girls! Have fun!*' he says over and over. Puts you in the worst mood—you get bunions from trying to tap-dance for him."

"Don't blame Mario for your big feet," said Plum.

"I don't have 'big' feet," Kaija snapped, pantomiming a quote-unquote with her parrotlike fingers. "I'm almost seven feet tall, for God's sake, of course I have slightly *bigger* feet."

"What are you, a ten?"

"An eleven," Kaija waved dismissively. "Anyway these *Bazaar* people should know by now. They bring the tiniest shoes—they think we're all Chinese or something."

"You're so stupid," said Plum. "That was in ancient China."

Kaija shrugged, raising her hand over the bar. "I don't need a comeback when you're wearing that hat."

"For the last time, it's a headwrap, and it's custom-made," she said, pointing to the red satin coil on her head. "It was four thousand dollars."

"You should put a price sticker on it," I suggested.

Plum considered this, teasing herself with the twirl of an olive-ornamented toothpick before her heavily lashed eyes. Evidently discovering an insight on the surface of the olive, she slid the toothpick into her mouth and closed her eyes with momentary relish. "You're right," she said with the shrug of a vaulted eyebrow. "Everything should have a price tag." She tossed the toothpick into her martini and clinked it down against the bar. "It would make life much more honest."

"I think you'll be honest enough in two seconds when that martini hits you," said Dorian. "Didn't your therapist ask you to watch your partying habits?"

"Partying? Who's partying?" With an upraised hand toward the bartender, she pushed herself in front of Kaija and clanked her diamond-braceleted wrist. "Champagne?" she asked us, before turning back to the bar: "Four glasses of Veuve Clicquot, please."

We had been in possession of our champagne flutes for five seconds before Plum pressed Dorian, "Well, don't just stand there while all the bubbles die out!"

"What's the matter, Dorian?" Kaija asked. "Don't you like champagne anymore?"

"Relax, both of you," said Dorian. "What are you getting so excited about?"

Plum's palm fell open, as though divulging to him a matter of common sense. "What is there to get excited about, if not champagne?"

"It's the fourth state of matter," said Kaija.

"After solids, liquids, and cocaine," added Plum, who then remembered—"Oh!" She reached into her clutch—it looked like Valentino—and pulled out an amber bottle of prescription pills. "These aren't bad either." She jangled the contents in Kaija's face and popped the top off with a polished, merlot-colored nail. "Here," she said. Kaija stuck out her hand to catch a tiny orchid-pink droplet in her palm. Plum gave one to Dorian and held my wrist as she shook the bottle. "You can take two, since you're new," she smiled.

"What are these?" I asked.

She shrugged and said, "I don't know," before tossing one between her scarlet lips and chasing it with champagne.

"Don't forget about work tomorrow," Dorian warned.

"Shut up. Do you even know me?" I scoffed. "Or have you already forgotten what a couple of reckless youths we are?"

"Of course I know you—which is why I'm saying—"

Exulting in Dorian's reservations—it felt amazing to be irresponsible!—I nudged the pills onto my tongue and swallowed them down with a stream of bubbles, not feeling a thing. "Cheers!" I held up an empty glass, and the girls clinked.

Over the next ten minutes our group did a magnificent—albeit effortless—job of attracting new members. First were two girls, definitely models; both blonde, and in the dark nearly identical in black leather jackets from the same Alexander Wang collection. One of them pushed Kaija trying to get the bartender's attention, and when Kaija turned to make a fuss ("*Can't you see I'm standing here?*"), it turned out they were all signed with IMG agency, and immediately became friends ("*Oh my God, if I have to shoot for* Bazaar *again I'll kill myself.*"). After that, we were joined by a stylist I recognized from a cover story in *WWD*. At about five feet, he overcompensated with pink hair and a dozen forceful anecdotes about the celebrities he had worked with (regarding his cover shoot with Nicki Minaj for *Elle* that month: "She kept wanting her boobs to show, and I was like, 'Bitch, cover yourself, this is Christian Dior!' "). The designer of an emerging label came up to thank Plum for wearing her dress to a CFDA event the week before, and finally a swarm of male models started trying to pair themselves off with the girls.

All along Dorian introduced me to passing faces as his best friend. I grasped at a lot of hands, and pecked a lot of cheeks, buoyed above the crowd by my continuous incredulity until one of the male models seemed to express an interest in Dorian. Possessing within the too-small circumference of his head the most extreme qualities of the male ideal, the model seemed to me an exaggerated package: inflamed lips and flowing chestnut-brown hair, thick brows and emerald eyes slanted exotically in a face as tan and square as a cardboard box.

"Who are you with?" he asked Dorian, referring either to his modeling agency, or whether he was single.

"Nobody," Dorian said casually, then clarified, "I'm not a model."

I was sure he hoped the model would express surprise that despite his own model-worthy looks, he had chosen some nobler path. But the cardboard box just said, "You could get signed—you have a good face," which I guess was his idea of a come-on. Dorian changed the subject with some charming comment about the cityscape through the window ("It's very Van Gogh, no?") and as I watched the box struggle to form a response, I was reminded why I shouldn't be so hard on Dorian. Beautiful people were never required by society to be smart, and for being one, Dorian was practically a genius.

I had started to lose track of their enlightened conversation when I got distracted by a queasy feeling and had to close my eyes. I felt my heart strike against my chest like a drumstick—*kaboom, kaboom, kaboom*—and I heard Plum count, "One—two—three—four," and when I opened my eyes she was staring at her fingers, concentrating very hard. "Four," she repeated. "This is her fourth divorce." She blinked hard, then I blinked hard, then somehow we were no longer by the bar but passing into the next room, onto a dance floor full of lights and bobbing heads. Next to my ear, someone said, "I never accept a drink unless it's spiked," and somebody else said, "Tequila brings back memories of not having memories," and then I think Kaija said to no one in particular, "If all of us liked each other, we would have nothing to talk about," but I didn't see her lips move so I wasn't sure it was her, and after that I lost track of who was saying what and whether any of it was even being said to me, and all the voices became a blur.

"*. . . have so much trouble typing with my fake nails . . . if it feels comfortable, then you shouldn't wear it . . . why fat people think black will make them skinny? . . . everyone is texting me . . . I need to go to the bathroom, there's the hottest guy over there . . . don't you hate it when* *your roommate's sweater doesn't fit? . . . out of lobster at Indochine, I was forced to get the filet mignon . . .*"

The next time I looked around, a swimming pool had been unveiled in the middle of the room, while a burlesque queen was dancing on an adjacent platform. In a black bustier and fishnet stockings, she resembled a French courtesan at a funeral, her white-blonde hair held up in a towering bouffant by a spider-web of ornate black pins. Slowly unfastening her corset, she let it slide to her feet, and stalked back and forth in her high heels like a black-cat shadow on Halloween, before, suddenly—she leaped over the pool.

Catching hold of an upholstered leather swing I hadn't seen, she went swooshing through the air like a nude pendulum, heels gleaming behind her. Her white fingers rippling over the water, she perfumed the air with the scent of chlorine; then swinging back and forth, back and forth, she began to splash.

"Come on! Come on!" Dorian's voice rushed past me, as if I was zooming by on a roller coaster. The whole room was like that—one minute loud, as the roller coaster plummeted toward the populated ground, then *whoosh!* I went shooting into the silent sky and it all died away.

I saw Dorian jam my suit jacket between the couch and the window—"Nobody will take it," he said, even though I had scarcely felt him undress me to begin with. He began to un-button my shirt—fast, like we were running out of time. I let my head drop back and my jaw fall slack. A laugh escaped my throat. Dorian wrestled the shirt away, and the coolness of the air-conditioned room fell upon my chest. I felt a yank around my sleeves—evidently the buttons on my sleeves had stumped him—then another set of fingers was pressing down my bottom lip.

"Open up," Kaija cooed into my ear, nudging the cold edge of a glass against my teeth. Champagne filled my mouth—I choked a little, laughing blindly, then let the bubbles spill down my throat while Dorian gave one last tug and stumbled away with my shirt. When I lifted my head, he had tied it around his head like a turban—"Look, Plum, I look like you."

Bubbles trickled like sweet acid rain down the corners of my smiling mouth, dripping down my neck, filling my clavicle like an overflowing stream.

Dorian giggled into my face. "Are you happy?" he asked. He wrapped his arm around my neck and pressed our foreheads together, and I remembered thinking the first time I'd seen him after his return from Paris—across the nightclub, with a martini against my lips—that Dorian Belgraves was so far . . . that after he had left, he would always be so *far*.

Now he was all I could see. Everything about him was as I had remembered it: his lips, his strong hands, that incredible feeling of being somehow connected to him.

By this point, his shirt was off too. He glistened with champagne, froth running down the middle of his chest. We were both stripped down to our boxer briefs, and for the briefest second I wondered where my pants were, and my shoes, and how any of them had gone away. Dorian pulled me to the pool's edge. We sat with our legs in the water for a minute, maybe ten. The temperature was cool: I was reminded of bygone summers, licking popsicles and standing in front of the open refrigerator door. Then I was inside. We were inside.

It was only a few of us in the beginning—me and Dorian and Kaija, while Plum complained about having nowhere dry enough to put her expensive clothes. More heads popped up around us like grapes. In the dark the sofa adjacent to the pool began to look like a cutting board, with discarded clothes piling up like fruit rinds—and in no time the pool was brimming with everyone from the pink-haired stylist to Plum, who had given up resisting and was gliding around in her cornucopian headpiece and a waterlogged white lace slip.

The topless burlesque dancer drifted with nymphean serenity in front of me. Behind her, a shout was heard from the sofa, as a pair of arms flailed over the water: the pool's first casualty. He teetered—the surface of the pool surged as a swarm of bodies escaped from underneath his lunging shadow—then *splash!*, the air sparkled, and a rain-like pitter-patter descended over the crowd. Too late, the dancer shielded her painted face with a forearm. An upward surge of bubbles at the site of the collision produced a drenched head and a shout about "my fucking Gucci shirt, man!" Not a minute later, another shout rang out, and the perilous pile of clothes on the sofa tumbled inevitably into the water. The expensive mass bobbed on the surface, then began to sink as the garments unstuck amid the pressure of the pulsating jets.

A stranger's face appeared before me. Too much champagne, combined with the mystery of their long, clinging hair, made their gender unclear: he or she came nearer, just two glassy eyes and a pair of searching lips. Bodies all around—the pool was too popular. In all the commotion, I had tried to keep my glasses dry, but now pressed them against my face and escaped with a deep breath in the only direction I could think of: downward.

Water lopped over my head. My hair floated. Sudden quiet, except for bubbles pouring apocalyptically out of holes in the wall. All around I saw stammering feet and clothing grazing like catfish along the murky bottom.

When I came back up for air I realized I was still holding my champagne flute. I pushed my hair out of my face and took a breath, gazing through the empty glass. I guided it bobbing along the surface, like a crystal buoy, then pulled it under by the stem; filled it with water; and dumped it out again.

It was a game Dorian might have liked too.

Dorian. Expecting to find him right behind me, I swirled around, only to find people I didn't know at all. I tried to remember when I'd last seen him, but the only memory I had was of the male model with the square face, and this made me sad. I began phasing in and out of consciousness. The contents of my stomach bucked in the water. I felt like throwing up. The lights in the pool had started flashing now, and every time they came on I found myself peering up at a new face, each one dripping and cool and different from the last. As I drifted it was like a slideshow—the faces flashing one after the other, just darkness *BEAUTIFUL FACE* darkness *BEAUTIFUL FACE* darkness *BEAUTIFUL FACE* darkness *BEAUTIFUL FACE* darkness . . .

All the voices faded in and out, like before. Behind my ear I heard . . . *just drink more, it'll make the pain go away* . . . then a *creak!* as the roller coaster of my own wavering cognition took off again, and I was up and down, and up and down again—soaring through the sky, and swooping down past all the never-ending voices . . . *there are two kinds of girls, those that know they're fucked and* . . . *whooshhhhhhhhh* silence in the sky, just birds chirping and . . . *so I look over and he's practically face-raping her, with his* . . . clouds drifting coolly by, while the sun beams, and the . . . *best part about it is I can talk shit to her, about her, at her* . . . air is so perfect and still, and the people below look like . . . *they've been chasing their liquor with wine, it's disgusting, like* . . . little ants, tittering over a peaceful hill, and . . . *won't you go with me to the bathroom . . . ?*

The mention of the bathroom jolted me. I'd had a lot to drink.

I emerged from the water into a haze of bodies and manufactured fog—shivering, bumping into shadows.

Sticky floor. My shoes—where are my shoes? Actually, where are my—*wow*. Naked. I'm basically naked and everyone can see. Calm down, naked is all right—you're young and reckless and bohemian, remember? Yes, but—is that broken glass? No, just ice. Is that Marc Jacobs? Is that Sofia Coppola? Is that George? I wonder what George is doing now. I hope George hates his life. I hate George. I shouldn't hate anyone, but I do—I hate him, I hate him, I definitely broken glass. That's what I get for hating George. I don't hate George, I don't hate George—what am I doing right now? Dorian. Where is Dorian? I like Dorian. I love Dorian. Of *course* I love Dorian. And he loves me too, except he's probably with that model, that cardboard-box model. I'm going to find Dorian. I'm going to find him and—Bathroom. Excuse me, where's the bathroom? Hey—!

"Hey, where's the bathroom?"

"That's the line right there."

My stomach made a full revolution inside me. I gazed at the floor and began to sway, my feet stumbling in front of me. "Excuse me," I murmured at the floor. I pushed to the front of the line—some guy said, "Hey!" I knocked him out of the way and swung the door open. "Sorry," I said, shouldering away somebody who was washing their hands. Seizing the mirror, I vomited all over the sink.

"COME ON," DORIAN PRODDED.

I yawned, and swatted at him.

"Come on, you big baby, let's go."

"What's happening?" I moaned.

"What's happening is I'm trying to take off your shirt," he said, in an exasperated tone that made it clear he had been trying to do this for quite some time. I opened my eyes; found myself faceup on the mattress in my apartment, with Dorian's legs straddled on either side of me.

"Oh," I said seriously, as it dawned on me: Dorian wanted to have sex. A bucket of cold water fell through my body. I was suddenly quite awake. "I—" I thought briefly of Madeline, but I tipped her over in my head like a vase off a ledge. "Well, all right," I said, and decided not to ask any questions. I couldn't remember how we'd gotten to that point—had we kissed already? Had we done anything else? I struggled to lift myself, and my head swayed around in a circle.

"Finally," he said. His face was illuminated by my bedside lamp, while behind him the four-foot loft ceiling was pressed directly above his head.

His warm hands under my shirt incited a rushed floundering of my limbs.

"Just—hold still," he said, as I tried to squirm from under the wet fabric.

"Do I look okay?" I asked, self-conscious.

"What?" He tilted his head. "You look fine. Who cares?"

"I just—are you sure you wouldn't rather—I don't know, take a shower before?"

He rolled his eyes. "Oh, stop it—"

"What?"

"Do you think I'm trying to *undress* you?"

"Well, isn't that what's happening?"

"Yeah, but—not like that." He laughed and rolled his eyes again. "You're all wet," he said, shaking a clean white shirt in my face. "I'm just trying to change your shirt."

A mist of disappointment sizzled over me. I frowned. "Oh." I slumped back on the mattress and limply crossed my hands over my wet chest.

He laughed outright again.

"Go ahead, laugh at me then," I said. "I'm going to sleep."

"Oh babe, don't be like that—it's okay—I just—"

"No, get off if you're going to just laugh at me," I said, pushing his thighs from around my body.

"I'm not laughing at you—I just—come on, let me change your shirt!" He tried to look serious, but now that he'd started laughing, he couldn't stop. "Okay, fine, I'm not laughing, I'm not laughing. Sit up."

"No." I pouted.

"Sit up, you big baby," he nudged. "You're going to get sick tonight and then I'm going to have to do everything at work."

"Don't you want to sleep with me?" I moaned.

He laughed. "Well, yeah, and that's exactly what I plan to do, sleep *next* to you, as soon as I get you out of this shirt, now come *ooonnnnn*, babe, I'm exhausted."

I rolled my eyes and barked, "Go away," and tried to tug my sheets from under his blokeish knees.

"All right, babe, seriously, I'm not laughing—you think I don't know you? Remember that water-gun fight we had on the Davenport lawn?—you woke up in a puddle on Madeline's floor and were sick for two weeks, now—"

"Yes, that was over a year ago, before you left us," I retorted, and gave the blanket a yank.

"Come on, that has nothing to do with anything. Why would you bring that up now?"

"Why shouldn't I? You never do," I mumbled. "You just pretend like it never happened, like—"

A knock against the doorframe. "What's going on?" came a familiar voice.

I turned my face to see Madeline standing on the loft ladder, blinking for the first time at my room. "Gosh, your apartment is small," she said, and poked her golden head in.

"What are you—?" I began.

"Dorian said you were sick," Madeline explained, and crawled inside. She smiled and reached into a plastic bag she had brought. "Here—I got you some Pellegrino, and some saltine crackers—and your favorite!" She held up a glass bottle of grape soda, and then swooped in. "Hi," she said, and kissed Dorian hello. With a hand on his back, she knelt beside me, and ran her fingers through my damp hair.

I frowned, and escaped her touch with a grimace.

"What's wrong?" she asked. "Aren't you happy to see me?"

"Don't take it personally," Dorian muttered. "He's being . . ."

I flipped over and dug my head into the pillow with a muffled shout. "Just—give me my blanket!"

Dorian lifted his knee and threw the blanket in a heap on my head. "Take the fucking blanket then. Fine. Do you want me to leave?"

"Stop it," Madeline intervened. "That's not necessary." She wrapped her hands around his forearm and held him there in place.

I remained silent, and covered my head.

Dorian tore his arm away from Madeline's grasp and gave me a prod. "I *said*, do you want me to leave?" he demanded.

A clicking sound, as Madeline opened her mouth to protest—then silence, and the hum of the fridge below us.

"No," I said. "I never wanted you to leave."

Dorian swallowed. "Get up and let me change your shirt, please."

Shifting, I pushed the blankets away and sat up.

"Thank you," he said, and started to unpeel me. As the shirt came up I covered my skinny chest with one arm, with an embarrassed glance at Madeline, who had calmly arranged the crackers and bottled drinks by the lamp and was now folding up the plastic bag beneath her arm.

I took a deep breath. Dorian's breath smelled like champagne, mixed with gin and tonic. He took my wet shirt and draped it over the corner of the mattress, and I watched his muscles ripple as—

I sneezed.

"See?" He pointed. "I knew it. I knew you were going to get sick."

I sneezed again. Madeline reached into her purse, and handed me a tissue.

"What did I tell you?" Dorian went on, "you always—"

I tossed the crumpled tissue in his obnoxious face. "Shut up."

"Lift your arms."

I felt the cool, clean cotton drift over me.

"There," he sighed. "That only took twenty minutes."

Madeline came around from behind me and kissed my neck, her perfume enveloping me. "My boys, my sweet boys," she smiled. She wrapped her arm around my waist and felt for my hand, while her other hand extended to Dorian. "Just like it used to be."

"That boy—the male model," I said, rubbing my eye. "You didn't really like him, did you?"

"Don't listen to him," Dorian explained to Madeline. "He's just—"

"I know." Taking her hands back, she tilted her head and removed the backing from her pearl earring.

"Don't pretend you don't remember," I whined. "That model. The male model. His face was like—a square, a horrible, ugly square." I looked at my hands on my lap as Dorian began to lay me down. "I mean, I guess it's fine if you like that sort of thing, but—"

Cradling my head in his hand, he lowered me onto the pillow, his face suspended over mine like a chandelier. "Just get to bed, babe."

I implored him one last time, "Are you sure you don't want to at least kiss me? Because if you wanted to, I promise I—"

"I'm sure."

"How about your shirt?" I asked, reaching out to unbutton it. "You're all wet, and—you know." It hung down like a piece of cotton chainmail, reeking of chlorine. I got one button, two buttons, and was starting to see down his incredible chest when he pinned my hand back against the mattress.

"Hold on now," he said. The wet shirt shuddered. "I can do it myself. Just—you get to bed."

"Well," Madeline laughed, "I guess this is what I get for missing a night out with the boys." She laid down her earrings onto the base of the lamp with a soft clink, and stripped off her silk blouse.

I was tugging at Dorian's shirt now, trying to tear it off him, like in the movies.

He took my other hand and pinned it to the mattress too, so that his slick, half-dressed body was suspended above me, wet shirt swinging. I floundered a little to free myself, then relaxed and blinked up at him.

"Listen to me, babe—you are extremely drunk," he said.

"You're going to wake up tomorrow, and everything's going to be all right. You have to trust me. There's water right there if you need some, and we'll be here the whole time, okay?"

I licked my lips and gazed up at his mouth.

"*Okay?*" He shook me by both wrists with his hands. The mattress creak-creaked, and a diamond of sweat, or maybe pool water, fell from his hair onto my forehead. I flinched at the drop of cold, shuddering as it dripped into my eye.

"Sorry," he said, wiping it off with his thumb.

Before he could protest, I thrust my face up to his unsuspecting mouth and kissed him.

I held it as long as I dared—*one Mississippi, two Mississippi*, eyes shut, hanging from his lips like a child from a monkey bar. He breathed on my face and I pulled back, a slow string of saliva forming like a glistening clothesline between us, before—*pop!* just like a soap bubble—it disappeared, and all that was left was a shiny bead on Dorian's bottom lip.

The whole thing was fast—like stealing another kid's ice-cream cone, and running off.

Dorian blinked a couple of times, stunned. He opened his mouth, as though conflicted between a breath and an utterance, but before he could decide I slipped out from under his grasp. I turned over, covered myself with my blanket, and giggled.

I could hear him shift his weight, trying to think of something.

"That's your fault," he said to Madeline finally. "You're the one who always encouraged—"

"Oh, stop it," she snapped. "Who cares?"

I peeked out from under the covers as he glowered at her meaningfully. Madeline rolled her eyes and slipped out of her skirt, which crumbled into a pleated jacquard mound. "Don't be so childish," she told Dorian. She adjusted her burgundy lace bra, then sliding into bed in front of me, turned her head to kiss my cheek.

"Hold me," she said. I was in a haze, the taste of Dorian's lips filling me like ether.

Madeline pressed her back against me, and I dangled my arm around her tiny waist. She smiled through a satisfied sigh as she curled up her legs, squeezing my hand against her cool, naked stomach. "Come on now," she whined at Dorian, "turn off the light and get in."

He clicked off the lamp and slumped into the mattress beside me. The heavy breathing began. I felt his eyes upon my back. For a minute he was still. Then he sighed and wrapped himself around me from behind—the three of us woven together once more, like a rope—while in the dark Madeline murmured over and over, "Nothing has changed, nothing has changed . . ."

chapter eleven

The next morning we awoke in a pool of intermingled sweat, the sun cooking our ripe flesh through the tin ceiling above our heads.

Madeline woke up first. She crawled on her knees and nudged Dorian and me. "You have work soon," she reminded us.

Dorian was still holding me. I heard his lips smack together in my ear.

"I'm going to shower," Madeline whispered. She leaned over my body to kiss him, and her hair fell over my face as their lips touched. I felt her slide toward the edge of the mattress, then heard the ladder creak as she descended.

Dorian peeled himself away from me like a piece of plastic wrap and sat up, bumping his head.

I stirred. The sudden absence of his warm, damp body felt

so uncomfortable that I groaned, and pressing the sheets against me, sat up slowly beside him. Sweat ran down our arms. Beneath our overlapping bodies on the sheets we had left a seeping blotch, a damp, faintly lilac bruise, as if we had been three sweating slices of grapefruit set upon a napkin overnight.

A vaguely succulent smell hung in the air, chlorine mixing with the nectar from our pores. It dripped like condensation into memories of yesterday's reality: champagne, pool water, and my saliva on Dorian's lips.

"Messages from Mom," Dorian said next to me. "That's how I know it was a fun night."

I turned my head up, still lost in a trance—perplexed to see him there at all, instead of faded away like a dream.

"She hates it when I'm photographed drinking," he continued, holding his phone between his hands on his lap. "For her it's okay, because models are paid to be incoherent. But she thinks if I try to get a real job, people will think all I do is drink champagne for a living."

"Well, that's sort of true, isn't it?" I yawned.

"Shut up." He went yawning after me, and gave my shoulder a push.

Thirsty, I licked my lips a little. "What are you talking about anyway?"

He handed me the phone. His mother had sent him a halfhearted, "Not again, Dorian," with a link to *New York* magazine's website, and a slideshow of the previous night's party.

"Are you in here?" I asked, scrolling through.

Of course he was. With the exception of the empty glass against his lips, Dorian looked like a figure on the ceiling of the Sistine Chapel, floating in the pool with his angelic consorts

Kaija and Plum, his luminous white arm around some black mass draped against his shoulder like a wet fur cloak. I began to scroll away, then realized, in a sudden flash of recognition—it was me. I was the cloak.

I laughed out loud. I didn't remember having my picture taken at all, yet there I was, with my dopey, drunken grin shining out from under my waterlogged hair.

I had been photographed at a party, I realized—just like some kind of socialite. Did it mean, perhaps, that I was really on my way to becoming . . . somebody?

"What's it say?" Dorian asked me.

I was so enlivened to think that someone had photographed me at all that I hadn't scrolled down to read the caption.

"It's just our names. *Kaija Goodman, Plum Bonavich, Dorian Belgraves* . . . oh . . ." I trailed off, choking a little on my own saliva. ". . . *Guest*," I finished.

That was me . . . *Guest*, like an extra in the bottom of a film credit roll: *Girl at Diner 1 . . . Girl at Diner 2 . . . Man Walking Dog . . . Guest.*

"They didn't know my name," I said.

"You're lucky then, aren't you? Otherwise your mom might be complaining to you too."

I handed Dorian back his phone.

"Don't worry, there'll be other parties," he said, sensing my dejection. I felt his hand touch my head. The gesture reminded me of going to church as a young boy, when the pastor cupped his hand over me and said in Spanish, "May the Lord bless you and keep you." That was always my favorite part of the mass, because afterward my head tingled and I liked to think that it was the Holy Spirit flowing through me.

He ran his fingers lightly through my hair, his touch feeling like a *hundred* Holy Sprits flowing through me. I looked up from my lap and into one of those moments in life marked by utmost clarity. From the depths of Dorian's expansive eyes, I saw the truth flowing: Aside from Madeline, Dorian was the best love I had—the best love I'd ever had, and ever would. A love so perfect, it even *looked* perfect.

"Dorian, I—" I started. I placed my hands on his knee, and I leaned toward him. His legs were folded underneath him, the sheets clinging to his thighs. I wanted to kiss him, but my heart began to beat too hard in my chest. I was seized with panic, and looked sharply away. I couldn't do it.

His hand slowed down in my hair. I gulped down at the sheets and felt a wave of disappointment, of sadness toward myself, as I realized that if once I had been fearless and carefree, the best and the brightest, my time had passed. I was dark now—empty. I was everything I didn't want to be. Terrified, I clutched his knees and gasped. He was looking at me, eyes shining. As I met his gaze the panic rose in me once more—the thought of failing, doing something wrong. The old Ethan would have kissed Dorian—he didn't need to be drunk, would have swooped in stone-sober and done it, but this Ethan . . . My heartbeat spiked, to think that I could be so different now.

Dorian's hand stopped. He opened his mouth to say something, and I knew the moment was passing. It would pass and I would regret it for my whole life, and become one of those people who carried their regrets like an empty shell—one of those people I said I'd never become. A shriveled compromise, an *adult*.

I was paralyzed at the thought of facing him, the thought of moving or doing anything at all, and yet if I didn't, I knew I would be lost forever. The thought scared me so much, I forced myself to look at him and think, *I'm still me, I'm still me!* My blood began to trickle outward from the center of my quavering chest. *This is what it feels like to have emotion!—to be moved!—to be alive!—This is what it feels like to be young!* My heart pumped faster and faster until blood was throbbing through my veins. I was enflamed, all my youth screaming, "*Do it! Do it!*" a kid rushing through a field, wild and free, and I knew—I knew I had to kiss him, so I leaned forward and—

Dorian emitted a small gasp, like a child going underwater. I felt a light pressure against my chest, but it was already done.

The second our mouths touched, I was seventeen again, and any question of my dying youth silenced by a loud roar of adrenaline, a primordial desire to sear our flesh together.

I pushed forward, heaving and hungry.

Suddenly—*crack!*—I think I heard it before I felt it, just the single deft collision of two hard, unyielding things. My arms flew. I went reeling backward in one smooth arc, a complete reversal of my own forward momentum.

I was stunned, like a fried cable.

Dorian's Botticelli mouth was open—awestruck, apologetic. He glanced between me and his open palm, which was stiffly shaking. I flinched: his palm was the first clue.

After an agonizing one . . . two . . . three . . . four . . . the second clue revealed itself; rivulets of blood pouring down my face. I couldn't feel the source. I reached up—my nose, I realized. Suddenly I flashed back to several months ago: Dorian standing before me for the first time since graduation, shards of bitten martini glass on my tongue, blood escaping from my mouth. The whole front of me had been warm then, as it was now.

Mentally processing in that slow, stilted way of his, Dorian twitched, unsure of what to do. He cocked his neck like a bird. His mouth was still open, and for the first time I saw no light at all in his eyes, just sadness as he finally understood what he had done to me—not just now, but all along.

He rushed to jump across the widening hole between us, with "I—I'm so sorry—" He reached forward. There was a protruding vein in his neck that I had never seen before, a wire keeping him upright.

I winced. Gobs of crimson fell between us. My own embarrassment made my blood course faster. "I thought—" I began, but it was no use. When I looked down, the blood had dripped onto my arm and it was easy to imagine the paring knife flashing in my other hand as the life seeped out of my crooked, outstretched wrist.

I finally felt the first stab of pain. I cried out, and patted around for something to stop the bleeding. Dorian let out a childlike moan, and joined me. Together we seemed to be searching for a lost thing—a phone in a nightclub, or a piece of cutlery that had fallen under the table. He moved the bottle of water, and picked up a sock, as if he had forgotten our purpose and was simply tidying up. Then he seemed to remember, and in desperation he clenched my bedsheets. I was gasping, the blood was in my mouth—it might have taken him a minute, or less, or longer—but he yanked, and offered up the striped sheet toward my nose. I pressed it against my entire face, to staunch the bleeding and my own shame. The blood didn't soak the sheet, but coursed down its folds like peppermint streaks.

Madeline appeared then at the top of the ladder. She held a towel around her waist, mouth open as her golden hair dripped water between her naked breasts.

Dorian looked at her, then back at me. To me he said, "I don't—love you—like that—but I do love you—" his voice full of effort, yet still hollow. As if to prove his point, he lumbered forward—to put his arm around me, or make things better somehow—and I heard a sickening crunch. My glasses were pressed beneath his knee, the rims crushed into the bed. When he lifted himself slowly away, the eyes were two empty holes and the glass sparkled like diamonds on the naked mattress.

SABRINA WAS SHAKING HER HANDS IN THE AIR LIKE A GODS-cursing aborigine. "Is this some joke I'm not aware of? You are *both* half an hour late, without so much as an e-mail to let me know? Ethan? Dorian?"

We glanced at one another. Dorian's shirt had my blood on it, but if Sabrina noticed anything strange between us—the spilled blood, a gulf of quiet sadness—she responded only with a wild, wordless sputter.

Dorian and I had been silent all the way to work. I'm not sure why we didn't just take a cab—it was the obvious thing to do, but we had both been too stunned to think of it as we fumbled around trying to make sense of things, while Madeline just got in the way.

I'd had to leave my glasses on the sheets, the clear shards dangling from the tortoiseshell rims like the bashed-in teeth of a disfigured grin.

It wasn't unlike the time Dorian had drawn a picture of me, when he asked me to remove my glasses, and left me in a blur; this time though—unexplainably—I felt more comfortable in my half-blind state. Dorian led me down the stairs to the subway, the whole time holding my hand firmly, determined to prove something to me—that even if he didn't care for me *that* way, he still cared. After two failed attempts, he put his whole hand over mine and swiped my MetroCard for me. When our hands touched there was a fizzle, like a drop of water onto an incandescent bulb.

Even though she wasn't going with us, Madeline followed us grimly to the platform. "Are you okay?" she whispered, as the train that would take me and Dorian away whooshed in. She pressed her forehead against mine, and held my face between both hands. "I'll see you later." The train doors opened. Bodies swarmed around us, and Madeline stepped away.

When the doors closed and the train departed, I saw her staring at the platform floor, her hand pressed against her mouth like she had just realized a terrible thing was about to happen.

There was a single open seat on the train. Dorian tried to get me settled there, but I shook my head. I felt close to him, yet completely emasculated. He must have felt similarly, but in reverse, because as the subway filled with people he drew me closer with a protective arm around my frail back. I ached to lay my head on his chest, but refrained in a singular assertion of personal dignity—and the six inches between us quivered with visceral anxiety.

I closed my eyes. The doors whirred open and people clambered in, continuing despite me or Dorian or Madeline to live their lives. They crowded closer and closer at each stop until finally, at Union Square, their pressure was too great, and the distance between me and Dorian was forced to close. We pressed together. I melted onto him, resting my cheek on his shoulder, feeling the relief of a liberated cramp.

He stared over me at the tunnels rushing outside the window, while I glanced around the subway car without my glasses. With everything out of focus—all the balding heads, and cell-phone-illuminated pores, and pleather straps peeling off shapeless fake Louis Vuitton bags—it was like a Goya painting. The masses shifting their world-weary weight, their helpless heads lurching as the train dragged them haltingly to hell. The hands were the most sublime part—grasping, outstretched, clinging hopelessly to the train's cold metal poles, everybody looking like they were about to plummet into the Inferno.

Only one lady reading a book, her palm pressed elegantly against an overhead bar, fingers fanned out like she was drying them at the nail salon, retained any dignity whatsoever, and I thanked her quietly on behalf of human civilization.

ANYWAY, SABRINA DIDN'T NOTICE ANYTHING BETWEEN ME and Dorian. I wanted to warn her that I wouldn't be able to see today before she had me trying blurrily to discern Prada from Pucci, but there was no time, and she didn't seem to care, exploding, "Just—get to your desk! Everybody needs their samples back—I've already done Prada, Dior, and Oscar—I need you to pull Kors and Vuitton right away—like, in the next five minutes—then check the e-mails I forwarded to you for the rest."

Dorian and I moved together in the direction of our desks. We bumped each other as we crossed toward our respective seats, and he stiffened, glancing at the carpet, uttering his first word to me since the train—a tremulous, "Sorry."

"Not you, Ethan." Sabrina held out her hand to stop me. "Clara needs to speak with you." She scissored with a stocking-clad *snip-snip-snip* toward the editors' cubicle and I followed her out of the closet like a miscreant being led to the principal's office. "He's right here, Clara," Sabrina announced, and with a cutting swish of her skirt left my side.

"*Eeeeethaann.*" Clara swiveled her chair around to face me. "Hello, my darling. Please follow me." She rose, nudged her hand politely against my arm, and hastily wafted down the hallway like a sweet-smelling smoke ring.

My stomach flopped. No doubt Clara was obligated to reprimand me on my tardiness. My mind stumbled through an obstacle course of pleas: *Today had been the first time! It was only for thirty minutes!* and even—*Dorian was late too!* We arrived at a door I had never entered before, and when Clara opened it I realized we were inside the conference room.

The conference room was where all the important people had their meetings. It was where they sat around discussing how many issues reached how many people, and how many of those people were female or divorced or college-educated, and whether they got their issues on the newsstand or by subscription, and, in the end, how could they get more people to buy it? It was where they discussed how to redo florals once again for spring and whether Gwyneth's baby would make her too fat to do a February spread, and I was perplexed that Clara would bring me here to tell me that I shouldn't be late again.

No sooner had the door closed than she expounded, in an uncharacteristically dull voice, "Someone has sued the Hoffman-Lynch Corporation."

Her silk skirt glimmered as she tucked it hastily beneath her to sit, while I felt blindly for a chair of my own.

"Do you know what that means, Ethan?" she asked sharply.

The bristle in her voice made me miss the seat. "I'm sorry, I just—" I began to explain about my glasses.

"That means Hoffman-Lynch is being charged with violating labor laws—misrepresenting their internship program to take advantage of young people—people who want a chance at the fashion industry."

I tried to process this, but my only takeaway was relief that Clara's displeasure had been provoked by something other than me.

"It's a *Bazaar* intern," she scathed. "Some state-schooled brat—she says she was treated like a slave or something just because, I don't know, they had her making copies while she had a stomachache," she flapped her hand around like a dying brown bird "—I mean, please, what does anybody expect when they sign up for these things? Summer camp? Of course it's hard, but you've never felt *exploited*, have you?"

Having under Edmund's workload personified the dictionary definition of "exploited," I struggled to conjure up any level of support for this outright fallacy.

With a sigh, she remembered herself and straightened up, patting away some imaginary wrinkle on her skirt. "The bottom line for you is . . ."

I blinked at her blurry face.

". . . they're taking away all our interns."

My neck cracked. "Taking . . . away . . . ?"

"For legal reasons," she explained, "Hoffman-Lynch is dismissing all unpaid interns." She paused, then added, "Effective immediately."

In a moment when I should have felt shock, passive acceptance descended over me like a Caravaggioesque fog. It was like the ending of a movie I had seen many times before, which every time I hoped would turn out different, but never did: in it I was boarding the Texas-bound red-eye flight that would take me away from my happy ending; crossing from the Jetway onto the plane with my eyes lowered in shame and my potential folded up in my suitcase, silently praying for the plane to crash and deliver me from my misery.

As the terror of my inevitable homecoming stirred in the deepest part of me, I blurted—"Who will assist Edmund?"—clinging to some nonexistent tatter of hope. "Edmund—he can't do anything himself! I mean—what I mean is, he's a genius, so . . . won't he still need someone to assist him?"

The plane was rumbling to a start beneath my feet, when to my amazement, Clara nodded. "You're right," she said. "That's why we're bringing some interns on board as staff—as assistants."

I grabbed my chair with both hands. Through the blurriness I thought I saw a strange look on her face—a *smile*? It must have been a smile . . . and it dawned on me. I wasn't going to Texas at all. I was going to work for Edmund, the foremost authority of my dream world. I leaped out of my third-class airplane seat and screamed, "*Get me off of here!*" and all of a sudden I was swearing my loyalty to Edmund again. If, as the emperor, he wanted to strut naked throughout the town, then who was I to stop him? The whole time I would point and say, "*Look at those marvelous new clothes! The hat! The collar! How divine!*"—no matter that the fantasy was a lie, and the townspeople wretched and stupid, and Edmund not marvelous at all but just a naked old man whose clown-like shortcomings everybody was afraid to point out.

Clara wasn't firing me . . . she was *hiring* me. I shook my head in wide-eyed disbelief, as she bowed her head, a blonde curl tumbling delicately into her face. "Did you hear me, Ethan?" she asked.

"N—no," I trembled, leaning toward her. "I'm sorry, I—I didn't actually. I didn't hear anything." I wiped my sweaty palms against my pants and smiled a little, one nostril wheezing while the other crackled with dried blood. I wanted to hug Clara, but if I moved I would start screaming out—"*I knew it! I knew it all along!*"—so I gulped, and folded my clammy hands over one knee, over the pants that Clara, and *Régine,* had generously bestowed upon me several months ago, trying to project the dignified look that would befit a young man of my new status—an employee of Hoffman-Lynch, the best magazine publisher in the world, where I'd be paid to walk the halls that for years had seen some of the greatest visionaries in the industry rise to prominence and bask in the glory of *Régine*'s spotlight . . . and now it was my turn. *My turn.* "I'm sorry," I told Clara, "I really don't mean to be so quiet, I'm just—it's such big news. What's next? How do I start?"

"Well, like I said, I'm sorry to be the one to tell you this. I've told you before that I have the utmost respect for your personal style, and I still think you have a hopeful future. It's going to be tough finding a job in magazines, but maybe, you know, you'll find a great position in PR, and of course, I'd personally be happy to write you any recommendations you need."

"PR . . . ?" I trailed off. "Wait, what are you talking about?"

"Or anything you'd like, I don't know. People who leave *Régine* find jobs in PR without much trouble, and I mean, you went to Yale, so . . ."

I closed my eyes and shook my head. "I—don't—understand. Aren't you hiring me to be Edmund's new assistant? I thought that's what you just said? That there'll be no more unpaid interns and he needs an assistant—a real one, like on the masthead . . . with a salary," I croaked.

"Well, yes, it's a paid position, with a salary, and line on the masthead, but . . . I'm sorry, Ethan, really, but it's just that we're . . ." Clara paused, then started over. "*Régine* is hiring *Sabrina* to be Edmund's new assistant."

My jaw dropped. "Wait, *what*?" I could think of nothing worse than Sabrina profiting from a misfortune with my name on it. "But Sabrina is *already* an assistant. What will happen to . . . " I was shaking—horrified—couldn't go on.

"There will be two—Edmund will have an assistant, and Jane will have her own as well. Jane has thought for some time now that Sabrina's personality does not fit her editorial vision. She is looking for somebody more creative, with a background in art."

I let this settle over me, as relieved as if I was standing in a parched field and it had started to rain.

Maybe I was supposed to end up with *Jane*, not Edmund! As Jane's assistant, I would work every day with someone who shared my appreciation for beauty, true beauty—my heart's purpose and the real reason for my desire to work at *Régine*.

"Can I apply to be Jane's assistant?" I almost whispered. "Who can I talk to?" I thought of how Jane had described me last night: "*Somebody with life in them!*" I was perfect for her. We were perfect for each other. This journey couldn't end here. It *wouldn't* end here.

Clara took a deep breath.

Even half-blind, I could tell something was wrong. She started fiddling uncomfortably with her skirt, and she must have felt a twinge of guilt, or pity, or something—because she couldn't look me in the eye. Instead her eyes focused on the door, while my own clung to her lips. I saw a mirage of hope shimmer over them, then—

"I'm afraid that position is already taken." She swallowed. "*Régine* is hiring Dorian to be Jane's new assistant."

She reached forward and placed her hand on my shoulder. "I'm sorry, Ethan," she said. Then with a helpless shrug, she stood up, and left me there alone.

TOMORROW MARKED THE START OF JUNIOR YEAR. MADELINE and Dorian were sprawled on the sagging Victorian sofa in our living room while I sat on the floor—all of us exchanging stories from our summer vacations apart, waiting for the ecstasy to take effect.

It was a sunny summer day—one of those by which we would measure all other summer days: blood flowing with sweat through our veins as we gazed at each other through heavy-lidded eyes, intoxicated by ourselves.

Dorian hung his arm around my neck. As in every place where our limbs crossed—Madeline's hand on my shoulder, Dorian's leg on her knees—a pool of slick sweat was beginning to drip between us. Moist, mismatched pillows moaned beneath our weight, while a futile breeze blew through the open bay window. A glass saucer glistened beside my feet, having moments earlier passed between our sweating fingers. We had all reached in—the pills were robin's egg blue—and swallowed together on a count of "One—two—three—forever young."

I had only swallowed one tab, even though we'd each bought

two. I always planned to "hold on" to a second pill, to take when the first was wearing off. I also always changed my mind.

No matter how many times I'd done ecstasy, I always worried that the effects just wouldn't hit me. That maybe this time, this batch—fifteen dollars a pill, and "explosive," according to Ted Hamilton, who had been selling to us from his dorm since freshman year—would have the same effect as a daily multivitamin. I was terrified that, like Blake and his lager-blooded Pi Phi brothers, who required entire kegs to feel merely "buzzed," I would one day have taken too many drugs, and would never be able to get high again—the precursor to the more serious fear I would eventually feel at *Régine*, that I'd reached the highest level of joy that was permitted in a single life, and God, or the President, or whoever kept track of these things, would say to me, "*Now, now, you've had enough*" and I would never feel happy again.

Now I slipped the second pill in the oyster-like crevice between my gum and my bottom lip where, thanks to my prestigious education, I knew it would dissolve into my bloodstream fast. Madeline was telling us about her summer vacation in Nice. I gazed beyond her at a poster of Frida Kahlo on the far wall, crowded by eighteenth-century botanical drawings of flowers. Names like *Trillium grandiflorum* curled all around her braided head in the heat.

". . . and I guess I just believed him . . ." Madeline was saying. "Anyway, it turned out fine, because I'd never seen a green motorcycle before, and . . ." She blinked, forgetting what else. "Will you give me a back massage?" she asked me.

The sun in her blue eyes, she unstuck herself from the couch to join me on the floor. I edged backward to make room for her, while a drop of sweat fell from the tip of her nose. She sat between my legs; hung her head forward, sweeping her dampened gold hair to one side, and I lowered my hands upon her spine.

Above us, Dorian strummed a guitar, his latest hobby. He began to sing. I whistled through parched lips, and Madeline patted her own knee to the lumbering beat.

Rock me mamma like the wind and the rain,

Rock me mamma like a southbound train . . .

One minute I was massaging Madeline through a sweat-soaked silk blouse, and the next my fingers were pressed against her milky skin, the blouse strewn inexplicably to the side. Her lace bra was loose around her midsection, straps hanging to the side of her body. She cupped her hands over her breasts as I rubbed my thumbs in circles over her skin, smoothing away the imprint of her bra strap. She had a few freckles on her shoulder, stars in a white sky.

"Can I massage your face?" I asked.

She wordlessly rolled her golden head back over my shoulder. With her eyes closed to the ceiling, she relaxed her hands over her breasts and the sun fell through her slackened fingers.

I pressed my thumbs, lubricated by her perfume-like sweat, over her brow bone, and became aware of her skull beneath my fingers—her eye sockets and sloping cheekbones, the hinge where her mouth opened and closed. I contemplated which was more extraordinary: that strange, complex bone, or her skin, which draped perfectly over it like a veil.

"How magnificent you are," I said, and rubbed my cheek against hers.

A laugh escaped her lips as she reached back with one hand and touched my head, her fingers weaving in and out through my hair.

I heard a hollow smack of saliva as Madeline's deep breath swelled in my ear: "I think—it's happening, darling."

I let her words wash over me like a cool wave. It was happening. I lifted my head and announced, "We're rolling." When nobody moved, I repeated a little louder, "We're rolling," as my body tensed up and then relaxed. A waterfall of excitement rushed through me. Madeline squeezed my knee and leaned forward to let her bra fall finally away. With the side of her forearm draped over her naked chest, she reached for her silk blouse.

I couldn't control my body. Indian-style, I crossed my legs. I rubbed my palms together. I rocked forward and back, forward and back. Madeline and Dorian were so still, they could have been sleeping. I swallowed. When I couldn't take it—my legs were cramping up, I needed to move—I reached for the sofa's velvet arm and pulled myself up. My hands waved fresh air into the room from the window. It always happened like this, rolling on ecstasy—you took a pill or two, waited for something to happen, then—*bam!*—it was happening, and you were inside it, and pretty soon you were on your feet shouting, "*Guys! Let's go on an adventure!*"

Eyes flickering, Dorian stretched both hands toward me from the sofa. I pulled him into my arms. He fell onto my chest and wrapped his arm around my waist, then the three of us strung together and stumbled out into the late afternoon. Dorian led us with his guitar. Madeline hopped onto his back. We waved to Jack Dockendorf, and Cathleen Kwon, and Master Phillips from Pierson College. We waved to a man on the Skull & Bones stoop, and we waved to Oliver Munn.

"How was your summer?" Oliver asked.

"You smell divine," Madeline replied. "Here's a song about the freckle on your lip."

And we made one up.

Except for Ted Hamilton, who gave us a knowing look and said, "I told you! What'd I tell you?" nobody asked us if we were high. We were simply how they knew us to be.

Soon the sun began to set, and we turned pink around the edges. Dorian was still carrying Madeline, and when we got to the center of Cross Campus the sprinklers had turned the grass spongy and wet.

Wanting a turn on Dorian's back, I tugged on Madeline's leg. "You're hogging him," I said. Then I pulled too hard and the three of us tumbled onto the grass and didn't get up again.

The rest of the night we just stayed there. Friends were summoned through phone calls and wild gestures across the lawn, and by around eight o'clock the whole courtyard was alive, all of us laughing and playing guitar and massaging each other's backs. We glowed in the light from the vaulted windows. Someone brought a bubble machine. A security guard named Maureen popped a floating sud on her nightly patrol and said, "Isn't that nice?" while everyone passed around a thermos filled with iced Earl Grey someone had brought, and dipped their fingers into a pomegranate.

A FEW HOURS LATER, WE WERE ALONE AGAIN IN OUR UNbreakable trinity.

Dorian saddled up to me and wrapped his white arms around my neck. "Your turn," he said. "You've been touching everyone else all night." I laughed and said okay and laid back with my head on his knee, face toward the night sky, legs extended on the wet grass.

A few feet away, Madeline also lay down and recited from memory a line by William Blake: "The heavens laugh with you in your jubilee . . . my heart is at your festival . . . my head hath its coronal. . . . The fullness of your bliss, I feel—I feel it all . . . "

Dorian took off my glasses and placed them beside me. I blinked and looked up at him. His blurry hands descended upon my forehead, and above them I could vaguely make out his hair, blending with the dark sky. His fingers pressed into my skin. My blood rushed to fill every imprint they left, and soon my whole face was warm, tingling like a vibrating guitar string. He put his thumbs over my eyelids and gently stroked in an outward motion. He moved so slowly I thought he might have been distracted by something else.

"Isn't it amazing," he whispered, "that two people can be so close—that one would let the other touch the most sacred part of them?"

I asked him what he meant.

"Your eyes," he said. "They're the most important thing to you, and so vulnerable—yet I'm touching them, and you trust me completely."

He caressed my lashes, and I didn't flinch.

"Do you remember how we met?" he asked.

I smiled at the memory of him with his sketchbook, asking to draw my portrait. "Of course—you made me take off my glasses. I was so nervous."

"You shouldn't have been. You know I'd never hurt you, right?"

I yawned, eyes closed under his fingers. "You're so beautiful, Dorian . . ."

He leaned over, and I felt a lock of his hair tumble over my face. "No," he said, his cool breath on my cheek, "you are." I heard the saliva bob in his throat. "You are so, so beautiful."

I tried to open my eyes, but he cupped them with his hands, one on each eye.

"Don't look," he said. "Just keep them closed, and say that you will always love me."

I smiled and grabbed his wrist—tried to pull his hand away.

"Please," he insisted. "It's important to me."

I ran my fingers up the length of his wrist. "Of course I love you, silly."

"You always will?"

"Yes."

"No matter what happens?"

"What's going to happen?"

"Nothing," he promised. "Nothing's going to happen."

IT REALLY WASN'T DORIAN'S FAULT. IT WASN'T ANYBODY'S fault, but it definitely wasn't Dorian's. I knew Dorian hadn't come into *Régine* to ruin my life—he was too pure, too good. He was too much like me. I didn't even blame anyone for choosing him over me: this was just the world we lived in. I knew that when they told him he got the job, his first reaction would be joy, unbridled joy—he wouldn't think about salary or being on the masthead. He'd think, *Wow, my first job! Everyone will be so proud! And I'll get to see Jane every day—and Ethan! Wait—what will happen to Ethan?* I knew how bad he would feel, I just *knew*, and I couldn't bear to see the look on his face, so—I just stood up and left.

I remembered the assistant who'd also just stood up and left, abandoning her expensive python bag on her desk. Maybe she too had left to tumble off a roof, and maybe in fact, she eventually did.

"WELCOME, MR. ST. JAMES!" HORACE, EDMUND'S DOORMAN bellowed. "You're all wet . . ."

Edmund's roof was black with hardened tar. Rainfall never seemed so much like suicide—every raindrop jumping off a cloud, with a long plummet to the earth.

I knew my life wasn't bad—not if you looked at it from a certain angle, if you thought the important things in life were food and a roof. If you thought about things that way, then sure, I was a fool and selfish, because other people had much worse lives than I did.

It wasn't really about that, though. It wasn't about *Régine*, either.

"*What are you so scared of?*" Dorian had asked me once, and I think that's what it was about; although, right then, I wasn't scared of all the normal things. I wasn't scared of what would happen if I tumbled a hundred stories, the rain kissing my back. I wasn't scared of hitting anything on the way down—a satellite or an open window or a gargoyle—or crashing through a windshield, all the glass twinkling around me. I wasn't even scared of the most likely thing: hitting the concrete, a surface so hard that the entire city had been built upon it.

I didn't know why, but I wasn't scared of those things.

What I was scared of—at least, what I *think* I was scared of—was everything else. I was scared of growing up. I was scared of compromising. I was scared of never living up to the dream I'd had; scared that everything good had ended already, and that I could never get it back. That no song would ever be as good as Pachelbel's "Canon in D," no book as good as *The Age of Innocence*, no taste as good as oysters with Madeline, and nothing at all as good as being high with her and Dorian. Everybody always said first loves are the hardest to get over. My first loves were flowers, and Yale, and the fantastic vision of my future life—what more? I could jump or not—life was already over.

Maybe not life. But the best parts of life—the dream—it was all over.

It had ended several months ago, when Clara had explained to me that, due to the unwritten rules of the world, I must trade my turquoise suit for gray; except what she had really been saying, which only now I understood, was, "*You have been inducted, by no choice of your own, into this world, and to live in it you must sacrifice your joy.*"

The "world," of course, wasn't *Régine*. The world was simply adult life, and there was no escaping it.

I didn't believe that anyone at *Régine*, or anywhere, chose unhappiness; they didn't choose to be cruel or unkind, or to lose their enthusiasm for life. Neither did I truly believe that anyone I'd met that summer was actually a bad person—not George, or Edmund, or even Sabrina. Like everyone else, they had simply signed a contract. They had spaces to fill and boxes to check, and a dotted line to sign every night when they went to bed.

Everyone did—except I didn't want to. If I agreed to stay in this world, I knew I'd be fighting forever—all the rules, all the nonsense, a system that long before my birth had already been built to contain me. It was a system I had no control over, so much bigger than me or any dream I had.

And even if, like in Madeline's political dream, we lived to see the system fall—as if it was a concrete structure that had been built around us that we could physically demolish—there was still the biggest system of all, which was *time.* We could never escape time. Time made us age, and age made us fearful, and in order to feel safe, we built up the very concrete structure that imprisoned us.

I could change my name, and my clothes, and the way I behaved, yet under time's dark shadow, I would never see the light.

On top of this, I knew that love between me and Madeline and Dorian would die. It had already begun to die, and without it, I wasn't sure what I would do. How I could possibly live knowing that the people I loved would no longer love me, knowing that life would wedge itself between us? The blindness of youth obliterated for us the differences that adults saw—money, and beauty, and power. Now we were beginning to see too, and soon we would never be the same again.

If I went back home, most likely I'd end up doing nine to five in an office somewhere, with none of my dreams coming to fruition and all of my best years just memories. Sure, there'd be some good things—the laughs I got at the annual company party, the friendly secretary named Pamela, her desk covered with pictures of her labradoodle dressed in bonnets and crocheted mittens. I'd keep sticky tabs full of watercooler jokes on my computer, and I'd meet a lover through a friend of a friend—someone with okay hair, and an okay sense of humor—and we'd have okay sex with the lights off. Maybe I'd go on a few trips, and get married, and who knew? Who cared?

Maybe, compared to death, a mediocre life was somehow "better," but something told me it just—wasn't for me. None of it was. I'd heard of people who'd had near-death experiences—a car hit them or something, and later, when they could neither walk nor speak except through a respirator, while everyone was thanking God for saving them, they were rasping through the respirator, "*I just knew it wasn't my time. I could feel, it wasn't my time to go*," like everybody had a "time." For me, it was the exact opposite.

I thought it must be my time to go.

I hadn't talked to God since Lola had died, when I had realized that if I didn't leave Corpus Christi, I would end up just like her. Back then, I had crawled into bed, hands clasped, and prayed, "*Please God, save me from this place.*" Now I bowed my head to the rain, and thought the exact same thing. *Please God, save me from this place—this world.* I thought it as loud as possible, hoping he could hear me above the New York City traffic.

I wondered if anyone in New York would even notice someone falling from the sky. Most likely they would be running to a meeting, or taking a cigarette break, picking up coffee or dry cleaning or an Alexander McQueen package from FedEx, and they would never notice. I'd get run over by ongoing traffic and cause a couple of taxi drivers to wonder, "*What was that bump?*" while rain pounded on the windshield and I got flattened into nothing. Edmund probably wouldn't know I'd even been to his apartment until a few months later when he was firing Rosita, and she asked in Spanish, "*Is that why I never saw him again, the boy with the glasses? Did you fire him too?*"

Maybe some people would know instinctually when I died, like a shudder would go through them or something—at least my mom and dad, and Madeline, and Dorian—and years later they would tell the story to someone. My parents to each other, and Madeline to her kids, and Dorian to his own assistant, who worked for him at a big magazine. A story about how I came into their lives and left, bookended by, "*He was a beautiful person—he tried to do beautiful things.*"

And it occurred to me that, after all these years of chasing after it, I didn't even know what it meant—"beautiful." I came to the city for as much as I could get, but maybe I just had no idea. I mean, girls in magazines were beautiful, right? That's what I had always thought, along with operas and sunsets, and certain rinds of fruit when they curled up, but right now—right now I wondered if I'd ever seen a beautiful thing at all.

I opened my eyes and the blurry ground rose up to meet me. I saw the whole ugly city swarming with people like life-sucking bacteria, except now, with the worst of it behind me, it didn't seem so bad—as though by unfocusing a microscope I had revealed something unexpected.

I took a breath. Maybe it just wasn't the right time yet. Maybe I should wait another day or two—to fall when the weather was better, when I could turn around and plummet backward with my eyes to the sky and the sun shining on my face. Edmund's roof would always be here waiting. I could come up here as many times as I needed—every day even, until I was ready . . .

And what? Prolong it all?

I looked up, and rain rushed into my eyes.

It had to be now.

Except the sky seemed so much closer now than it had ever been before. Five minutes. *I'll do it*, I told myself. Just let me stay alive for five more minutes, to look at the sky.

Pushing my hair back against my skull, I lowered myself into a sitting position over the ledge. My feet dangled, I laid back on my elbows and tilted my head up. I gazed at the clouds; let the water pour into my eyes and wash away my vision.

With a tiny shrug of my body, I relaxed, and fell to rest.

about the author

R. J. Hernández is a writer living in New York City. He was raised in Miami by Cuban-American parents and graduated from Yale University in 2011. This is his first novel.